To Kill the President

the

President

SAM BOURNE

HarperCollins*Publishers*

HarperCollins*Publishers* Ltd
1 London Bridge Street,
London SE1 9GF

www.harpercollins.co.uk

First published by HarperCollins*Publishers* 2017

8

A catalogue record for this book is available from the British Library

ISBN: 978-0-00-741372-0 (PB B-format)
ISBN: 978-0-00-741373-7 (PB A-format)
ISBN: 978-0-00-741374-4 (TPB)

This novel is entirely a work of fiction.
The names, characters and incidents portrayed in it are
the work of the author's imagination. Any resemblance to
actual persons, living or dead, events or localities is
entirely coincidental.

Set in Meridien by Palimpsest Book Production Ltd, Falkirk, Stirlingshire

Printed and bound by CPI Group (UK) Ltd, Croydon, CR0 4YY

MIX
Paper from
responsible sources
FSC C007454

For my sister Dani:
funny, warm and always good company.
A devoted mother to her boys, her determination
knows no limits. This is for her, with a brother's love.

1

Alexandria, Virginia, Monday, 3.20am

It began the night the President sought to bring about the end of the world.

The first Robert Kassian knew of it was when his phone started vibrating on the nightstand. He woke with a start, his heart thumping. It took him a second to understand where the sound was coming from: he wondered if he had dreamed it. He reached for the nightstand, fumbling to make the vibrations stop. The task was urgent: his wife was a light sleeper who, once stirred, stayed awake.

Only then did he realize this was no alarm, but an incoming call. He took in the next two facts at once: it was 3.20am and the call was from the White House switchboard.

'Mr Kassian?'

'Yes,' he whispered, peeling the duvet back and moving towards the bathroom, the phone jammed against his ear. He had barely opened his eyes.

'Please hold for the Situation Room.'

So it was happening. The three am call Washington folks always talked about. He'd only been Chief of Staff for four months and this was the first call of its kind. Sure, there had been late-night crises – plenty of those – and urgent meetings just after dawn. The pace had been relentless and round the clock since the inauguration in January. In the last week, that had only intensified. But a bona fide emergency in the middle of the night? This was the first.

A couple of clicks and he was put through. Instantly he could hear a commotion; there was a banging sound. A voice came on. A woman, young and nervous.

'Mr Kassian. This is Lieutenant Mary Rajak. We have a situation, sir. I think you need to get down here right away.'

Now he could hear shouting. He wondered if this woman had been taken hostage. Maybe the White House was under siege. He blinked hard, his brain now revving.

'What kind of situation?'

Kassian was sure he heard the woman dip her voice. 'It involves the President.'

Jesus Christ. Had the President been taken hostage? How would anyone . . . 'What's happened?'

'Please, sir. Just come.'

'I'm on my way. But can you—' He stopped himself. He could hear someone shouting. A man. It sounded as if his voice was coming from the next room.

'Hold on, sir.' He guessed she was putting her hand over the receiver. 'Yes, I'm speaking to Mr Kassian right now. He's on his way.'

In the second that followed, he could hear it clearly. It was unmistakable. There couldn't be a soul on the planet who didn't recognize it. Over the last two years, that voice had been heard every day, once at least, whether on the news or in a video that went viral, sometimes mocking an opponent or taunting a heckler at a rally, sometimes being impersonated by a TV comic or a precocious kid in a school playground. But no one had heard the voice like this, bellowing with rage – real, not confected. *Get out of my way. I'm your Commander in fucking Chief and this is an order.*

As he listened, Kassian grabbed a shirt and reached for the first suit his hand could find. 'What the hell is going on there, lieutenant?'

'It's difficult to explain on the phone, sir.'

'This is a secure line.'

'I don't think we have much time, sir.' Her voice was trembling.

'In a nutshell, lieutenant.'

She spoke quietly, as if fearful of being overheard. 'North Korea, sir. The President wants to order a nuclear strike.'

'Jesus fuck.'

'Yes, sir.'

'Has something happened? Is there an imminent attack on the United States?'

'No, sir.'

'So, what the—'

'A statement, sir. From Pyongyang.'

'A what?'

'Please, sir. This is very urgent.'

'A statement? You mean, this is because they *said* some-thing?'

'That's right, sir.'

'OK. OK. What's he doing now?'

'He's demanding to be put through to the Pentagon War Room, sir.'

Kassian felt his stomach lurch. He'd had upwards of sixty handover meetings, briefings from every branch of the US government before the inauguration, cramming his head with more information than he had learned in all his previous fifty years. But only one session had struck the fear of God into him. It came when he, the soon-to-be President and the Defense Secretary were instructed in the procedure for launching a nuclear strike.

It was so simple, it was terrifying. The President had merely to call the War Room at the Department of Defense, state the secret codes that confirmed he was indeed the President and give the order. That was it. No process, no meetings, no discussion. And no one with any authority to say no. That was the whole point. The system had stayed that way since Truman, enabling the Commander in Chief to act within seconds of an all-out attack on the country.

But no one planned for this situation. Or this Commander in Chief.

'What shall I do, sir?' The woman sounded like she was quaking.

Kassian was now downstairs. His movements had stirred the security detail who guarded his house. The lead officer was standing, close to the front door. Kassian made a driving gesture with his right hand. They headed to the car.

'Has he got the codes? Did the military aide give him the codes?'

'He tried not to, sir. He delayed as long as he could.'

'But he's got them?'

'The President put his hands around his neck and threatened to strangle him.'

'OK. OK.' Kassian looked out of the window, watching a sleeping Alexandria speed by. Even at this pace, he could make out the lawn signs that had sprouted all over this town and – in certain places – across the country. *Not My President.*

'Have you called Jim? Secretary Bruton. Have you called him?'

'He's being spoken to now, sir.'

'OK. In the meantime, you need to tell the President the procedure for such a decision requires the presence of Secretary Bruton and myself. There is a sequence we need to follow.'

'But, that's not—'

'Just tell him.'

'Shall I put you on the phone to him, sir?'

Kassian weighed it up. Instinct told him it would not work. The President would not take it, not from him. Military officers – neutral, anonymous – stood a better chance: there was a possibility he would hear their words as the response of a system, a machine, with no inherent hostility to him, no feelings either way. So far that had proved the best way to stop him.

'No, I'll talk to him when I get there.'

'But you may not get here in time.'

Kassian remembered what the President's daughter had said about her father in a TV interview during the campaign. 'You never say "No." You say, "Yes, but maybe not right now."' The interviewer had laughed, joking that it was kind of like dealing with a toddler. The daughter had laughed back, saying, 'Whatever works, right?'

'All right. Tell him, you've spoken to us. We support him and want to be with him on this one. And the best way to ensure this decision goes well for him is if he waits for me and Secretary Bruton.'

There was a banging sound. It could have been a fist pounding the desk or a door being slammed, Kassian could not be sure. He hoped it was the latter. Maybe the President had stormed out of the Situation Room in frustration, his will thwarted. Perhaps he would just go to bed or watch TV. The man hardly ever slept.

But then the officer spoke again. 'He's been put through,

sir. He's talking to the War Room at the Pentagon right now.'

Kassian felt a heave in his guts. Good God, what was this man about to do?

He killed the call and moved to make another, dialling Jim Bruton's cell. It was hard to press the buttons; his hands were trembling. And as he put the phone to his ear, all he could think of were the words from that briefing, perhaps three days before the President was sworn in. *At your command, sir, will be thousands of weapons, each one ten or twenty times more lethal than the bomb dropped on Hiroshima . . . Retaliation by the enemy will be automatic, swift and devastating. The combination of an initial US strike and the enemy's counter-strike will lead to the deaths of hundreds of millions of people within a matter of hours . . . Yes, sir, we have gamed that out: our most conservative scenario projects a global catastrophe that would end civilization itself, sir . . . On your command, eight hundred and fifty missile warheads will take flight within no more than fifteen minutes . . . No, sir. Once the order is given, there can be no stopping, no recall and no turning back.*

Busy signal. He tried again. And then again. Until at last he heard that trademark, Louisiana drawl, the one voice in Washington he truly trusted, the voice he'd heard in countless moments of mortal danger – though none as terrifying as this.

'Bob, is that you?'

'Jim, thank God. Listen, you have to get hold of the War Room right now, before he does. You have to tell them—'

'I already did. I told them they have to stall.'

'How?'

'They're telling him there's a malfunction in satellite comms. They can't reach the subs.'

'He'll never believe that.'

'What else have we got? He's mad as a snake, raging and squawking.' Bruton's voice dropped. 'He's going to fucking kill us all, Bob. You do realize that? He says he wants Option B.'

'Which one is that?' Kassian remembered – how could he forget – the 'black book', carried by the President's personal military aide, the aide who was with him at all times, setting out the menu of options, the different target lists. He just couldn't remember which one was B.

'North Korea *and* China.'

'Mother of God.'

'And he's going to do it in the next sixty seconds. Just as soon as that poor bastard in the War Room runs out of excuses.'

'You have to tell him it's an illegal order.'

'What's that?'

'Call the War Room. Tell them they are *required* to disobey an illegal order.'

'But that's bullshit. You know he has total and absolute authority. He can do whatever the fuck he wants. I can't stop him, Joint Chiefs can't stop him, Congress can't stop him. This is *his* show. One hundred per cent.'

'Yes, but they only have to obey an order that is constitutional.'

'Meaning?'

'Meaning, the Commander in Chief must believe that he is defending the country against an actual or imminent attack.'

'Well, maybe he does believe that.'

'It's a war of *words*, Jim. Five days of *words*. No reasonable person could say we're under threat of *an attack*.'

'But that's the point. He's not a—'

'Well, tell your men that is the test they must apply. In

7

fact they don't need to make any decision. You're telling them. This is an illegal order.'

'It doesn't work like that. He's the Commander in Chief, he's—'

'We don't have time for a fucking debate, Jim. Tell them. It's that or we're all dead.'

He hung up. And, as his car turned into Pennsylvania Avenue, Bob Kassian closed his eyes and, for the first time since he was a child, he prayed.

2

The White House, Monday, 8.45am
'What in fuck's name is that?'

Maggie Costello was in the outer office, where her boss's PA and two others sat. She had only just spotted that on a back wall, just behind the secretary's head, alongside the portraits of previous holders of this grand office – the White House Counsel – was a calendar. Not the usual one found in Washington government buildings, showing spectacular landscapes of the great American outdoors, but the kind you'd see in a car repair shop. The image for this month, May, depicted a woman on all fours, facing the camera, wearing nothing but tiny bikini bottoms, her mouth gaping open, her tongue visible.

The PA, a black woman in her fifties, gave a resigned shrug.

'Seriously, Eleanor, who put that up there?'

The PA scowled at Maggie, a look that said, *Don't get me into trouble.*

Maggie leaned forward, letting her voice drop to a whisper. 'I won't tell anyone.'

Eleanor looked over her shoulder and said, 'Mr McNamara's orders. He's put them up all over the West Wing. He said it was about time this place got in touch with the working people of America. About time it looked like a regular American workplace.'

'You're not even joking, are you?'

The woman shook her head.

Maggie leaned across, stretching over Eleanor's shoulder and, in one move, ripped the calendar clean off. Then, she tore through the thick, glossy paper once, twice, and headed towards the trash. Habit made her look for the green bin for paper.

'No more recycling, Maggie. He's got rid of that too. "It's not called the Green Faggot House. It's called the White House."'

'That's what he said?'

'Uh-huh.'

Maggie dumped the remnants of the swimsuit calendar in the sole trash can and marched into her office, slamming the door behind her.

She would have complained to her nominal boss, the man who carried the title of Counsel, but he was an absentee holder of the post, a pal of the President who served as his personal bankruptcy lawyer and been rewarded with a White House sinecure. Maggie had met him only once, at a cocktail party to celebrate his appointment; he hadn't been seen at the White House since.

She reached for her phone and sent a text message to Richard.

What the hell are we doing here?

In the old days, there would have been scores of women, at all levels, who would have done what she had just done, or backed her up. But now, in this department, it was just her and Eleanor. The rest were all men, almost all of them white. And that pattern held across the White House.

A few seconds later, he replied. Am in with Commerce folks. Talk later tonight?

She shoved the phone across the desk, letting it collide with the picture she kept of herself with the previous President – a tiny gesture of rebellion in this new era. Right now, she felt like cursing that man. It was – partly – his fault she was still here.

'Listen, Maggie,' he had said. 'I know how you feel about my successor—', but she didn't let him finish.

'You see, even that, I can't stomach. *My successor*. How can you say that, like this is normal? This is not normal. He's a liar and a cheat and a bigot and should be nowhere near this place.'

The outgoing President had indulged her, the way he always did. 'Maggie, you're a woman of great passion. It's why you've served this administration – and me – so well. But the people have spoken. He'll be my President – and he should be yours.'

'But no one's telling you to stay and bloody work here.'

'I'm not sure I'm the right demographic,' he smiled.

'Exactly. That's another thing. It's all white men. Hundreds of them. Every appointment he's made. It's like there are millions and millions of people he doesn't even see.'

'So, if you stay, you can even up the score a little. Woman, native Dubliner. That's two boxes you check, right there.'

'But—'

'This isn't just about him, Maggie. Just like it was never about me. It's about the country. You need to make sure the train stays on the tracks.'

'Sure, so that he can ram it into the buffers. Besides,

what would I even do for him? Former UN aid worker, former peace negotiator, *woman* – I'm not exactly his cup of tea, am I?'

'You could do for him the same thing you did for me. Troubleshooter in chief. The woman who knows how to get to the bottom of any crisis and solve it.'

'But that requires *trust*.'

'I know, Maggie.'

'You trusted me and I trusted you. Totally.'

'I know and I cherish that. But you'll find a way. You always do.'

Maggie looked at the photograph, marvelling at the naiveté of her earlier self. Even a year ago she would never have believed this was possible. Mind you, nor would anyone else.

And then she felt it, that familiar stab of guilt and with it the attendant nausea. It seemed to rise from a specific place, a site of revulsion deep in her guts. If only she hadn't . . .

In an attempt to push that dread thought out of her mind, she thumbed out another message to Richard.

How early can you leave tonight?
Let's eat at my place. Really need—

But before she had finished, her office door flung open. She heard him before she saw him. 'Are you decent?'

Crawford 'Mac' McNamara, senior counsellor to the President. If Maggie and all the other non-partisans who had stayed on were dedicated to keeping the train on the tracks, McNamara was the man who decided the destination. Even Bob Kassian, the nominal Chief of Staff, was a mere bureaucrat compared to McNamara. In the White House solar system, only one star burned more brightly.

Of course, Maggie was several moons below him – even under the previous president, her official title never reflected her true status – which under the old Washington rules meant a man of his rank would never deign to say so much as two words to her, let alone make the journey to come see her in *her* office. But McNamara was the self-styled outlaw, the sorcerer who had shredded the Washington rulebook to get his man elected President. Protocol could go hang. Memos were for dweebs, minuted meetings were for assholes. Instead he patrolled the West Wing each day, strolling into whichever office he wanted to whenever he wanted to. The Oval was no exception. McNamara saw the President first thing in the morning and last thing at night; he was the all-powerful voice in his ear.

Nor was this the first time he had made the journey to see Maggie. 'Isn't it obvious?' Richard had said, when they discussed it over Chinese takeout the other night. 'You're the most attractive woman in the office and he's . . . intrigued. I'd be flattered.'

Maggie's reply had been concise: *Ugh*. And now here he was again, middle-aged but wearing cargo-style shorts, with square, capacious pockets, and a Linkin Park T-shirt. He wore socks, but no shoes. His head was almost completely bald.

'You seen the paper today, Costello?' He threw over a copy of the *Washington Post*, landing it just in front of her. It was folded open on a story about a new poll, confirming the country was 'more divided than at any time since the civil war'.

'Why are you showing me this, Mr McNamara?'

'Ooh, did someone just let my father in the building? *Mister* McNamara? Who's that? It's *Mac*, Maggie. *Mac.* Thought all you liberals dug that informality thing in the workplace.' He made a mincing gesture and raised the pitch of his voice. 'Oh, we're all *equal*. Treat me *equally*.'

She reminded herself of what she and Richard had agreed. That perhaps they could mitigate the effects of this presidency, even in a small way, by being here, on the inside. They had a duty to make a difference, if they could. She took that vow again now. 'How can I help you, Mister . . . Mac.'

'Look at the paper, Maggie.'

'"First states roll out registry of Muslim citizens. Arizona, Texas, pilot new scheme."'

'Not that story. The one I've marked, next to it. Look where we are with eighteen to twenty-four-year-olds.'

'Twenty-three per cent approve, seventy-four per cent disapprove, three per cent don't know.'

'Exactly. Twenty-two last month, now up to twenty-three. The young are coming round to us, Maggie. I can *feel* it.' And with that he threw his head back and burst into song, his own version of a David Bowie classic.

'*Alllllllt-Right, we are the young Americans!*' As he repeated the line, he did a slow turn, his eyes closed, head nodding – a middle-aged rocker on stage in a nostalgia tour.

Maggie said nothing.

'OK, you got me. That's not why I came in here.'

'If it's about that calendar, there's no way that's going back up.'

'I noticed the lovely Miss May was missing in action. Are you to blame for that? Are we still doing that, the student protest thing?'

'Under the legal definition of sexual harassment, just putting that on the wall counts as creating a hostile environment.'

He smiled and shook his head. 'None of you get it, do

you? Not even a little bit. Don't you realize that's why the folks elected the big guy last November? I mean, sure it helped that his opponent had endangered national security by using an unsecured phone.'

Maggie rolled her eyes.

'But the main reason was *precisely* this kind of bullshit. Because folks were sick to their hind legs of prissy little missies spouting horseshit like "hostile environment".' He made the quotation marks with his fingers, delivering the two-word phrase in a high-pitched voice now accompanied by an effeminate swing of the hips. 'People are sick of being told that being a normal, red-blooded white man is a federal crime.'

'I'm sure you didn't come here to re-fight the election campaign, Mac.'

'No, but as it happens, it's all relevant.' McNamara helped himself to a chair, sat back in it and put his shoeless, socked feet on her desk. Maggie all but recoiled.

'Here's the thing,' he said. 'I need you to make something go away.'

Maggie raised her eyebrows.

'It came up in the campaign and it's coming up again now.'

Maggie still said nothing. She saw no reason to make this any easier for him.

Eventually, he lowered his voice. 'I think you Washington insiders call them "bimbo eruptions".'

Maggie paused. 'Do you mean the President has been having extra-marital affairs?'

'No!' Mac smiled. 'Not *affairs*. Nothing that you'd call an affair.'

'Oh, you mean sexual assault. Grabbing random women.'

'I mean *accusations* of that.'

15

'More accusers coming forward? People from the past, alleging that—'

'Partly that.'

'Oh, so not just the past? The *present*. Here? In this place? Jesus, Mac, they impeached the last man who did that.'

'Oh, I'm not worried about *that*. The House leadership are rimming our asshole. The tongue's in deep.'

Maggie did her best to show no expression. She knew he wanted a reaction out of her and she was damned if she was going to give it to him. He went on: 'None of them will dare move on this. Remember, he's bigger in their districts than they are. But it's a distraction. I need you to make it go away.'

'Sounds like a matter for his personal lawyer.'

'No. He's the President now. An attack on him is an attack on the Presidency.'

'That's not quite—'

'Besides, you're the right person for this.' He began to get up. Before Maggie had a chance to ask what he meant, he leered, 'You've got the right equipment.'

He closed the door after him, allowing Maggie to sink her head into her hands. She needed to see Richard.

They'd only been dating a couple of months, but given how many of her old friends had left the White House, he had become the default confidant. Three years younger than her and absurdly handsome – one of those Washington men who, no matter how early their first meeting, had already managed a run – he was far from her usual type. Appointed during the transition, he had nevertheless shared her doubts about the wisdom of serving the new administration. Along with the former president, Richard Parris had been a big influence on her decision to keep at it. 'Maggie, we're powerless on the outside. Imagine how

16

guilty we'd both feel if we saw something horrible happen and we could have done something – anything – to stop it.'

At first Richard didn't quite understand why that argument resonated with her so deeply. There was a reason, but she tried to hold it back from Richard the way she held it back from everyone else. Eventually, in bed one night, she gave in and told him. Just thinking about that now brought it back: a guilt so present it was almost physical, bobbing to the surface like a cork. She pushed it back down, a psychological manoeuvre she made at least a dozen times a day.

She headed down the stairs now to find him, to suggest they take a walk. She needed to unload. She began rehearsing the speech she'd make. *We're not softening the blow, Richard. We're* legitimizing *it. We're nothing more than a fig leaf for them. I did not come to Washington to help an abuser of women get away with it. That is not the reason—*

But her train of thought was interrupted. She had just turned the corner when she saw a group emerging from the Oval Office. Richard was among them – odd, for someone at his level – but he didn't notice her. Instead he was busy smiling and laughing with the only woman in the group, whose hair alone made her instantly recognizable. Thick and lustrous, it shone with wealth. There was no mistaking her.

Now Richard was showing the woman his phone, bringing a warm smile and a reciprocal gesture, as she showed him hers. Their faces – young and gorgeous, as they appeared to Maggie – seemed to be glowing in the electronic light. It was clear. Her boyfriend was flirting with the President's daughter.

3

New York, Monday, 9.20am

Having zero charisma had its advantages, Bob Kassian reflected. Seated in business class on the shuttle to New York, a single Secret Service agent at his side, few people had bothered him. A couple of travellers had flashed him the thumbs-up. A reporter from Fox had tried to engage him in conversation at the gate, but Kassian had given such short, monosyllabic answers – delivered in his barely audible, low hush – that the woman had soon backed off. As for the rest, he reckoned they had simply not recognized him. He didn't do the Sunday talkshows, he made few speeches. And that was just fine.

Especially this morning. He would have struggled to pose for selfies, grinning broadly with the fanboys in their correctly coloured baseball caps. How they revered his boss. If only they knew what he knew, if only they had seen what he had seen just a few hours ago. (A grim thought surfaced: perhaps it would make no difference. Nothing seemed to shift their devotion to this man.)

For the thousandth time he wondered if he had done

the right thing. A backroom operative, he had never been a committed partisan. He had fallen in with this crowd simply because those were his friends and contacts. He had established a reputation as a man who could run things – big things – smoothly. After the army, everyone told him skills like his could make him a fortune. They were right. He went to New York, to one of the big financial houses, and was paid unimaginable sums. But he missed what he had loved most about the army: purpose. Politics seemed like a decent second-best.

As for this job? He knew what prompted the offer: he would be presented as the responsible adult on the team, his calm, technocratic presence a token of reassurance to a nervous party establishment. It sounded old-fashioned but he felt it was his patriotic duty to say yes. If he hadn't, one of the crazies surely would have. And, from the inside, he could perhaps act as a restraining influence, holding back a President who would otherwise be listening to the swivel-eyed extremists led by Crawford McNamara who clearly had the ear of the Commander in Chief.

Now in the back of the car ferrying him to Manhattan, he closed his eyes, grateful to be cocooned, however briefly.

Somehow, they had survived. The sun had come up, the sky had not fallen in. Civilization had not ended. For that he could not congratulate either himself or his closest ally, Jim Bruton. It wasn't their intervention that had stopped the President giving the order.

The truth was, he had been about to do it. The President had been put through to the colonel in the Pentagon War Room, who had, following procedure, issued the challenge code: Echo Bravo, or whatever it was. The President had responded, giving the codes that confirmed his identity: say,

Delta Zulu. And then he had told the war room his decision, explaining that he had chosen from the menu of strike options and selected Option B.

At that point – and kudos to him for the effort – the colonel had suggested that the President might want to consider going a la carte for this highly unusual situation. Highly unusual in that the United States was not under attack, the only scenario for which anybody had been trained or prepared. Nice try on the colonel's part: ordering a special 'dish' would have taken hours or days. It would have bought Kassian and the others what they needed: time. But the President was adamant. Option B. Now.

Apparently, there was a stillness in the room then. Even the President briefly stopped raging. The colonel turned to the team in the War Room and gave the signal. They set about formatting the 'emergency action message' that would unleash the forces reflecting the President's choice – the bombs that would have destroyed the world. That task would have taken about a minute.

But after about fifteen seconds, a young intelligence analyst told the colonel to wait. He had seen a report of a new statement from Pyongyang, apparently backing down on the earlier one that had so offended the President. It had just come in.

The line connecting the Pentagon and the White House was still open and the colonel spoke. 'Mr President, we have reason to believe the North Koreans have backed down.'

'What's that?'

'Sir, they have fully capitulated. An abject apology.'

'Are you sure?'

'That is our information, sir, yes.'

'OK.'

There were twenty seconds left till the action message went live.

'Does that mean you wish to abort the order, sir?'

'What did the North Koreans say exactly?'

'Sir, we have ten seconds to decide. Should I abort the order?'

'Fuck them.'

'Sir?'

'All right, all right. Abort.'

And that's how they had averted Armageddon. One sharp-eyed desk officer may well have saved the world. Quick-witted and creative, more than sharp-eyed, as it turned out. Jim Bruton arrived at the Pentagon minutes afterwards, where the colonel on duty discreetly let him know him that the supposedly abject statement from North Korea, fortuitously released just seconds before the trigger was about to be squeezed, was more a work of wishful thinking than reality. The analyst had correctly read the situation, understanding that his immediate commanding officer and the Defense Secretary were desperately looking for an excuse to delay, and he had provided them with what they needed. In the process, he had left Bruton with a new headache – he now needed to generate a text that looked plausibly like a full apology from Pyongyang – but, given the stakes, that could be forgiven. Jim had immediately recommended the officer and the entire duty team in the War Room for a Defense Superior Service Medal.

Kassian had now reached the Waldorf Astoria hotel. Without looking either left or right, he made straight for the elevators, letting his Secret Service agent clear a path, press the button and select the floor. Avoiding eye contact with hotel guests, he caught himself in the mirror. He retained a full head of hair, but it seemed to be greying by the day. Back in January, it was all dark. He was still tall, still lean. His wife insisted he remained handsome: 'Real handsome, not Washington handsome,' was how she put it. But what he saw in his eyes was something else: a look of alarm and worry that was becoming permanent. The face staring back at him seemed haunted.

They stepped out on the fifth floor and went to the suite whose number he had been given. They were let in by a warm, rounded blonde woman in her mid-forties who introduced herself as the Swedish ambassador to the United Nations. She struck him as unexpectedly maternal.

There was an awkward moment or two as Kassian's agent checked for security, including – especially – for bugs. Then the agent was introduced to his counterpart, who did the same. Only when both were satisfied, and had nodded in the direction of the Swedish host, did she give the signal that, a second later, meant a door – presumably to one of the bedrooms – was opened. Through which stepped out a man Kassian recognized as the Ambassador to the United Nations of the People's Republic of China.

Kassian, still standing, offered his hand, which the Chinese diplomat took firmly. Kassian knew the man was just a year older than he was: fifty-one. He wore a plain blue suit, an off-white shirt and oversized, 1970s-style glasses. No retro chic was intended. They were just old.

Their host gestured for them both to sit down in the living area – two couches, armchair, coffee table – at the centre of the suite. In an accent that suggested an expensive education in England, she spoke first.

'Gentlemen, as you know, we were asked to make a space available for you to talk in a way that would remain completely unrecorded and confidential. It was Mr Kassian's suggestion that you meet here, rather than in Washington, where he suspected discretion would be harder to achieve, especially perhaps for him.' She smiled. 'He was also aware, with all due respect to the Republic's ambassador in Washington, that you, Mr Lei, are widely reputed to be even closer and, dare I say, more influential with your government in Beijing.'

She paused and continued. 'I should stress that Sweden has no selfish interest of our own in whatever issue has brought you both here. But you will both be aware of Sweden's great and historic interest in advancing the cause of peace in the world. If there is anything that can be done to avoid war, then my country will give whatever we can.

'I repeat that what is said in this room will remain confidential. No word of it shall be spoken by us. We will deny this meeting ever took place. No one knows any of us are here. This room is booked in the name of an anonymous Swedish businessman. As it happens, there are quite a few of those.' That did as was intended, and brought smiles from both men. 'Mr Kassian, it was you who suggested we meet. Why don't you begin?'

'Thank you, ambassador. And thank you, sir, for coming to meet me here today and at such short notice. You know, I hope, that I would not have asked our mutual friend,' he nodded towards the Swede, 'to bring us together unless I regarded it as of the gravest importance.'

Zheng Lei looked at him impassively.

Kassian glanced down at his own hands, wondering if they might start trembling again. 'I don't know how much, if anything, you know of what happened last night in the White House.' No response from the man opposite. 'But I'm going to be extremely frank. I can see no other way.'

23

He cleared his throat. He had thought about what he would say – on the plane, in the car – but that had not prepared him for the sensation of actually saying it.

'In the early hours of this morning, my country came within ten seconds – less than ten seconds, in fact – of launching an all-out nuclear assault on the Democratic People's Republic of Korea and,' he heard a dryness enter his throat, 'the People's Republic of China.'

The Swedish ambassador gasped at that. An involuntary, and entirely genuine, sound. Her hand now covered her mouth. Kassian went on.

'The President had given the order. The War Room at the Pentagon was in the process of encrypting and communicating that order to nuclear commanders around the world, including firing crews based on land, in our underground launch facilities, as well as those on submarines and onboard our bombers in the sky. Only an ingenious and brave intervention from one of our military officers, at the very last moment, caused the order to be aborted.'

The Chinese ambassador kept his gaze on the coffee table positioned between them. Kassian decided to read that as a reaction of sorts: perhaps this man was fearful of looking him in the eye, lest he give himself away. Kassian spoke again.

'What prompted the attack was the statement issued by the DPRK late last night our time. It appeared to taunt the President. If I may quote.' Kassian reached into his breast pocket, and unfolded a single piece of paper. '"The Workers' Party knows it confronts in Washington a paper tiger, a coward and a small man. We will demonstrate our strength – for we know our enemy's weakness."'

Still Zheng said nothing. Kassian went on.

'Ordinarily, under previous administrations perhaps, such

statements might be dismissed as rhetoric.' He thought he saw the tiniest hint of a nod from the ambassador. It encouraged him.

'But these are not ordinary times. For one thing, the DPRK has repeatedly signalled its intention to build a nuclear weapon capable of reaching the west coast of the United States. Capable of hitting Los Angeles. Our intelligence suggests that the DPRK is either at, or close to, that stage.

'However there is a more – how should I put this? – *pressing* way in which these are not ordinary times. The leader of my country is not a politician. And he is not a military man. He hears statements like these' – he held up the sheet of paper – 'the way a young man might hear them in a bar.' He hadn't planned to say this; he wondered if he had made a mistake. 'He hears them as a provocation. He believes he is being dared to prove the North Koreans wrong.'

At that, Zheng sat up, readying himself to speak. Kassian did not know if that meant he had succeeded or failed.

'Mr Kassian, are you a student of history?' His English was impeccable.

'Excuse me?'

'Your résumé says you studied the liberal arts at Princeton. But it doesn't tell me if you studied history.'

'Some.'

'I see. Well, I am a student of history. My specialism is the history of this country, in fact. Especially the last century. I took great interest in the Presidency of Richard Nixon. I wrote my master's thesis on Mr Nixon's relations with Asia.'

'I see.'

'Do you know why I bring this up now?'

'I sense you're about to tell me.'

'Because Mr Nixon was very careful to have his closest aides – Dr Kissinger especially – travel the world warning everyone that their boss was a madman.' At this he smiled. "Crazy! Unhinged!" Nixon was not offended. He encouraged it. He wanted America's enemies to be frightened. "America has all these bombs – and Nixon is crazy enough to use them!"'

'And you think that's what I am doing now?'

'History does not repeat itself, Mr Kassian. But it does sometimes rhyme.'

The American found himself looking to the Swedish ambassador, by way of an appeal. She nodded, but only to encourage him to reply. She was not about to take sides.

'Mr Lei. I have taken quite a risk by coming here this morning. My President does not know I am here. I would be fired if he knew. I can assure you I am not doing his bidding.'

'Then why are you here?'

'I'm here because I am scared.' The words surprised Kassian as much as the other two, perhaps more. 'I don't think you understand what I'm telling you. Your neighbour was within seven or eight seconds of being wiped off the map this morning and your country within seconds of being hit by a nuclear bombardment. Every last one of North Korea's people would have been killed, along with millions of your own countrymen. Children. Families. Perhaps even your own family.' Kassian thought he saw a shadow pass across Zheng's face. 'This is not a tactic. This is not a game. This is deadly fucking serious.'

'Mr Kassian—'

'No. Listen to me. I'm warning you because I think – no, I *know* – that this could end in catastrophe. For the entire planet. He's ready to do it. He *did* do it. He gave the order.'

'So why didn't it happen?'

'We found a way to stop him.'

'How?'

Mr Kassian stole a sheepish look in the Swede's direction. Without meaning to, he heard his voice dip. 'We told him the DPRK had apologized for the statement.'

'I see.'

'It was the only way.'

'So now you need my country to use its leverage over the Democratic People's Republic to persuade them to make good on the lie you told to stop your "crazy" President blowing up the world?'

'That's about the size of it, yes. And the North Koreans need to do it soon. They also need somehow to backdate it, so it appears they issued the statement at around 3.45am Eastern Standard Time.'

Kassian hesitated before making that last request. Partly because he feared it might be asking too much, but also because he had wondered if it was even necessary. These days, you could probably get away with falsifying a timestamp: in this era when everyone was ready to shout 'fake news' about anything, who would know or care? Not the President, who paid no attention to detail and who barely read the papers put in front of him.

But Kassian knew that wouldn't hold. Crawford McNamara, for one, immersed himself in the minutiae and was assiduous in his reading of documents. As a master purveyor of fake news, he rarely allowed himself to be a consumer of it.

'That won't be easy, Mr Kassian. The North Korean people are a very proud nation. They take pride in their defiance

27

of the American tyrant. They will not fall to their knees.'

'No one is asking them to fall to their knees, Mr Zheng. Just a form of words that gets us through to—'

'You seem to forget something, Mr Kassian.'

'What's that?'

'That North Korea and the United States now have something in common. Both these nations are led by very unpredictable men – with very thin skins.'

Kassian nodded. He knew it was bad diplomatic form to appear to be agreeing with criticism of one's own leader, but he couldn't help himself. Besides, it seemed to bear fruit. Zheng spoke again.

'Nevertheless, I appreciate the approach you have made to me. I will see what can be done.'

Kassian hoped he hid his relief. 'I am grateful, Mr Zheng. But I'm afraid I need to ask even more of you.'

The ambassador said nothing.

'The reality is that so long as the DPRK is led by this man, his presence will provoke the President I serve. You might say that is unjust or disproportionate. Even that it is irrational. There are some who might well agree with you. But that is the fact of the matter. So long as North Korea is led by its current ruler, a great danger exists. The risk is mainly to the DPRK, of course, but China is mortally threatened too. He could have chosen to hit just North Korea last night. But his orders were to strike at China too. So long as that regime remains in place, your country is in grave danger. The whole world is in grave danger.'

'You are asking the People's Republic to topple the ruler of the DPRK? Seriously? This is the request you would have me discuss with my government?'

Kassian signalled that this was indeed his request.

Zheng smiled and said, 'Now I know for sure that you

28

are on this mission alone. Your State Department would never have let you come here saying such nonsense! This is craziness, Mr Kassian. Complete craziness.

'Of course we would not do that. If we topple the regime in North Korea, the country would collapse in an hour and by nightfall it would be entirely ruled from Seoul. My government has not forgotten what happened to Germany in 1989. The Berlin Wall came down and, a day or two later, Germany was one country again, ruled by the west. A united Korea would be wonderful for America, but not so good for China. Like you say in the United States, "We have seen this movie before: we know how it ends!"'

'So you won't help, even though I have been honest with you and told you I believe there is a risk of all-out nuclear war on your territory and in your backyard?'

Zheng shook his head. 'I cannot give you what you want.' He cleared his throat. 'Remember, Beijing is not so different from Washington. Maybe it's not so visible. There's not so much publicity. But we have arguments too. Factions who compete for power. If my president were to do what you ask, there would be much opposition from some very powerful people. It would be a great risk for him. So I cannot give you what you ask.'

'I'm very sorry to hear that.'

'But I can give you something else.'

'What's that?'

'Time.'

'I don't follow.'

The Chinese diplomat took off his glasses, rubbed his eyes and put the spectacles back on. 'You said I have some influence in the governing circle in my country and, with some modesty, perhaps you are right. So here's what I can promise you. We will give you five days to resolve the problem you have with your President. For these five days, the People's Republic of China will,' he paused, looking for the right word, '*restrain* the hand of our friends in the north of Korea. But once these five days are passed, we can offer no guarantee. Then, if the young leader in Pyongyang is provoked once more, it will be his right to respond with great force.

'You and I agree that that would be a disaster for all of us. But this is how it must be. I repeat: you have five days, Mr Kassian. I hope for all our sakes you use them wisely.'

4

Maggie was home at seven pm. Unheard of, at least under
the previous president. Back then, Maggie regarded eighteen-
hour days as the norm. That felt a long time ago.

Ideally, she wanted to flop into bed, pull the duvet over
her head and not come out for a week. Pathetic, she knew,
to have her priorities so out of whack. So right, she said
to herself, when your main problem was that the free
world was led by a bigoted sociopath – let alone one you
worked for – that was somehow bearable. But seeing your
boyfriend smile at another woman, suddenly *that* is too
much? What kind of person are you, Maggie Costello?

This was not a new question. She was used to inter-
rogating herself this way and almost always in these
circumstances. 'Boyfriend trouble', as Eleanor at work put
it, making Maggie feel fifteen years old. 'Heartache' had
been her mother's preferred term.

The consensus among her friends – and family – was that
Maggie was a bad picker, that she chose men who were
either absurdly unsuitable or transparently unavailable.

31

There had certainly been several in that first category. She thought fleetingly of Edward, her first Washington boyfriend and a certifiable control freak. How funny: they had lived together, yet now she hardly thought of him.

There were a few in the second category too: relationships doomed from the start. She thought back to her much younger self, working for an NGO in the Congo, part of a team charged with brokering a ceasefire. She had become involved with a leader of one of the armed factions, hopelessly compromising her status as a mediator. That mistake had cost her dear. The affair had been charged and intense, of course, but it was obvious now – and surely obvious then – that it could never have worked.

But then she thought of Uri, the man she had met in Jerusalem, who had followed her here. Nothing unsuitable about him. He was gorgeous, clever, loving. And he had been available too. He had wanted to settle down, to have a family. It had been Maggie who had been unavailable, too restless to fix on one place or one person. It had been Maggie who had said no. Just bad timing with that one, she told herself.

She had made it to the bed when the phone rang. Shit. She had told Richard to meet her back here for Chinese. What if that was him? She didn't want to see him, but she was pleased he wanted to come. Or maybe not. She had no idea.

She looked down at her phone. Not Richard. But her sister.

'Hi, Liz.'

There was a pause and then, 'Oh, Maggie.'

'What? What is it? Has something happened to the kids? Are they OK?'

'Yes,' her sister sniffed. 'They're fine. It's not them.'

Truth be told, Maggie was not yet used to having her sister phone like this. Not used to her being in the same timezone. But Liz's husband had been offered a job in Atlanta two years ago and so they'd left Dublin. 'Now that Ma's gone,' Liz had said, 'it makes sense, don't you think?' Maggie had agreed of course, but she wasn't convinced. Having the Atlantic Ocean between her and her closest relatives had worked pretty well until now: why mess with a winning formula?

'So what is it? Is it you? Are you ill?'

'No. Nothing like that. Do you remember I told you about that girl in my class?'

'Which one?' Maggie had moved to the kitchen, where she was opening and closing cupboard doors, looking for a serviceable bottle of whisky. She didn't want any of that hipster shite Richard claimed to like.

'Mia.'

'The one who was raped?'

'Yes. Really lovely girl. Quiet, but smart. Thoughtful.'

'What happened?'

'Well, she got pregnant.'

'Christ.'

'Yes. And she wanted an abortion. She thought about it. She had counselling. And she was, like, "There is no way I can have this baby."'

'Course.'

'But guess what? Thanks to the Supreme fucking Court, there is no way within six hundred miles of here that she could get an abortion.'

'Oh no.' Maggie found a bottle of Laphroaig behind the tins of peeled tomatoes, several of them with pre 9/11 use-by dates. She poured herself a glass.

'No exceptions, remember? Not even for rape or incest. Maybe for "life of the mother". She's been getting counselling,

33

seeing doctors, trying to establish that her life is in danger.'

'You're kidding.'

'No, I'm not.'

'And she just can't find two doctors who will agree to say it, to say her life is in danger.'

'Why? How difficult can—'

'I was pleading with the principal, saying we have to do something. I went to the police. No one would listen. And Mia's saying, "I can feel this thing growing inside me. Because of *him*. I can't bear it, Miss Costello. I can't bear it."'

Maggie felt the dread rising. She knocked back the glass. And poured herself another. 'Go on.'

'I made a plan. I thought, I'm going to raise the money and put her on a plane to Canada. Or maybe Cuba or something. But I'll get her out of here and we'll do it. I was going to see her parents tonight, to arrange it.'

'What happened?'

At that, her younger sister let out the most awful howl. And then there was an explosion of snot and tears. Maggie knew. But she waited for her sister to say the words.

'This morning. She wasn't in school.' More sobbing. 'And I was worried. I had this feeling, you know?'

'Yes.'

'And then this afternoon . . .' Liz was struggling to get the words out. 'This afternoon, after school, Mia's sister went home. And she's only twelve, this girl. She gets home. And she finds . . . she finds . . .'

Maggie waited in dread for the inevitable.

'. . . her hanging there. Her own sister.'

And there it was. Maggie felt her gut contract. 'Oh, Liz, I'm so sorry. That's so terrible.'

'I can't believe it, Mags. It's so cruel.'

'It is.'

'I mean what is *wrong* with this country? It's so fucked up.' Liz blew her nose and regrouped. 'Because of a decision by one vote on the Supreme fucking Court, a beautiful, bright, kind girl is dead. *Dead*.'

Maggie knew what was coming.

'And how did that one vote get there? Eh, Maggie? How did it get there?'

'I know.'

'It got there because this President put it there, didn't he, appointing that medieval bastard to be a Supreme Court judge. That's how.'

'Liz—'

'I cannot believe you work for that evil man, Maggie. I just cannot believe it.'

'It's not as simple—'

'My own sister! My own, high-and-mighty, save-the-world, help-the poor, end-all-the-wars sister, Saint fucking Maggie Costello is actually working for this man. *Serving* this evil man.'

'It's not like I—'

'I don't want to hear it, Maggie. Mia is dead and you're helping the man who killed her. End of.'

And with that the line went dead. Maggie, who had been standing throughout, slumped into a chair. Not for the first time she reflected that the bitterest arguments come when you know you're wrong and your opponent's right. And, right on cue, the hard knot of guilt tightened inside her – becoming harder than Liz could possibly have imagined.

Before it had time to break the surface, there was a buzz from downstairs. *Richard.*

Until Liz called, Maggie had told herself she wanted to be alone. Now, though, the idea of a diversion appealed.

And, without admitting it to herself, she welcomed the opportunity to balance the scales: she knew Richard would insist that what she was doing was no crime, that there was right on her side too. She did not believe it, not really. But it would be good to hear it.

She answered the door and, to her own surprise, Maggie did not let him speak, kissing him long and deep instead. He was taller than she was, with a head of thick, dark hair, cut in a retro style that meant he could have passed for a 1940s movie star. He'd recently shaved off the beard, which Maggie regretted – she thought it made him look French and intellectual – as an act of deference to the new regime. Richard said he'd heard the President regarded men with facial hair as 'unreliable'.

He responded to her kiss, dropping his bag to the floor. He pushed her backwards, towards the bedroom. Taking the lead, she unbuckled his belt and pulled off his clothes, enjoying the sight and touch and taste of his skin. She wanted to devour as much of him as she could take. Her need was hungry. And urgent.

They didn't really start talking till long after nine, arranged on the sofa, both of them wearing a loose combination of underwear, sweatpants and pyjamas, with assorted cartons of Chinese takeout on the table in front of them. It was raining softly outside, the TV was on. It felt cosy.

Maggie told him about her phone call with Liz. He nodded sympathetically while she was telling the story, then held her when she reached the end. For a while they stayed like that, in silence.

After a while, they traded the odd nugget of workplace gossip. He'd heard there'd been some tantrum in the middle of the night: the speculation in the office was that the

President and the First Lady had had another screaming match. She was hardly ever around; the staff called her 'the invisible woman'. But that didn't stop her and the President having the most vicious fight on the phone. According to Richard, last night's had reached a whole new level. 'It was full-on nuclear,' he said.

Maggie listened, but her heart was not fully in it. Professional duty meant she had to hold back. She could not discuss the material she had glimpsed that day, supplied to her by Crawford McNamara's assistant. What he had called 'bimbo eruptions' amounted to a pattern of behaviour by the President that would have had lesser men disciplined for sexual harassment or charged with sexual assault. A cleaner in the Residence had complained to her manager that the President had manoeuvred her into a guest bathroom and groped her between the legs. The manager had spelled out to the cleaner – no doubt at length and in detail – the seriousness of such a charge and the dire consequences if her allegation turned out to be false. Unsurprisingly, the woman had declined to take the matter any further.

Physically less intrusive, but actually more shocking, was the very discreet note that had been sent by the Dutch embassy and passed on to the White House via the State Department. It said the government of the Netherlands would not be making any formal complaint at this stage, but it wished it to be noted that the ambassador believed the President had kissed her inappropriately at a recent diplomatic reception, causing her humiliation and distress. It said that several witnesses had been present who would be willing to verify her version of events, so that it would be 'wise to accept her complaint in good grace and to ensure nothing like it happened again'.

Maggie had been astonished by the sheer cheek of it. She

37

could imagine the reaction of her old mentor, Stuart Goldstein. *The chutzpah of the man is beyond belief,* he'd have said. To do such a thing not just with a domestic servant, whose word he could brutally dismiss – such were the realities of Washington's society – but with a foreign ambassador, and with people watching!

What made this worse was that even if this incident were to be made public, there was no guarantee it would inflict that much damage on him, still less destroy his presidency. Revelations about his conduct just as damning had emerged during the campaign. People like Maggie had made the mistake then of thinking they would be terminal to his candidacy. They had proved to be nothing of the sort. So why would this be any different? She suspected the Dutch knew as much, and that was one reason why they had kept their objection muted.

So she held back, listening to Richard's chatter, chipping in now and then, the two of them talking about nothing, tiptoeing around both of the big subjects on Maggie's mind.

Eventually, as relaxed as she could manage it, Maggie said, 'Did I see you come out of the Oval today? Big step up.'

'It's true. Second best thing to happen to me today.' He stroked her thigh, held her gaze. She felt her face grow hot. Had she misinterpreted what she had seen? It wouldn't be the first time.

'How come?'

'Frank's not around. They needed someone from Commerce liaison to sit in.'

'To sit in on what?'

'Come on, Mags. Ground rules, remember. Chinese wall. Even here.'

Maggie picked at a stray noodle on her plate. 'You mean,

you discussed something that may be of interest to the White House legal office? Should I be alerting the ethics team?'

'Maggie!'

And then, as relaxed and as offhand as she could, 'I saw the daughter was also there.'

'Yeah, she sort of dropped by.'

'Oh, was she not there for the whole meeting?'

'You know, I can't remember, honestly.' Maggie watched Richard's throat, always a giveaway.

He swallowed.

'Well, she was either there at the start or she wasn't.'

'Is this an interview? Should you be reading me my rights?'

'Sorry.' Maggie got up to get water from the kitchen. She shouted from there, her tone striving for nonchalance. 'So what's she like then?'

'Who?'

'You know who. You seemed kind of friendly.'

'Well, it's like everyone says. She's very charming.'

'Très charmante.'

'Exactly.'

Maggie resumed her place on the couch. She wanted to ask what the two of them had been looking at on their phones, but restrained herself. She didn't want to sound like a stalker. 'Attractive, too.'

He smiled, leaned over and began tickling Maggie's sides. Then he kissed her. 'Maggie Costello, I do believe you're jealous.'

'Of course I'm not,' Maggie laughed. 'Nothing of the sort. The very idea . . .'

'You sure?' he said, reaching for the remote.

'I'm sure. If only because the last thing in the world I'd want is to have that man as my father.'

'Are we back on that again?'

'Did I tell you what McNamara asked me to do today?'

'Hold on.' Richard had tuned to CNN. Above a 'Breaking News' caption was a live shot of protesters in Florida, clashing with men in uniform. He turned up the volume.

. . . escalated in the last hour or so. As you know, Kelly, officers of the new United States Deportation Force have been deployed across the state, part of the first phase of rounding up undocumented migrants. The USDF have come here in very big numbers and they're armed. But as you can see, they're meeting stiff resistance. Locals here in Miami have formed a human chain, insisting that they will not let the USDF pass. But you can see around me, Kelly, the officers are wielding nightsticks and they're – hold on, whoa – they're beating two men right in front of me. Press! We're press! I'm sorry, Kelly, I don't know if you can still hear me. Dave, our cameraman, is down. I'm just gonna keep . . . We're press! CNN! . . . The USDF men are charging into this crowd now. They seem to be smashing the heads of anyone and everyone in their way. People are screaming and running and trying to get away. There are children here, Kelly . . .

Richard turned the TV off.

They were silent for a while until Maggie said, '"I cannot believe you work for that evil man." That's what Liz said.'

'Look,' Richard replied. 'We've been over this. We can either be like everyone else in this country, sitting on the sofa, watching the news and doing nothing. Or we can stay where we are right now. On the inside. Where we can make a difference.'

She had clung to that line, parroting it to herself for months. She felt it more keenly than anyone could possibly know. She of all people needed it to be true. How else was she to make amends?

'But what difference are we actually making, Richard? I mean, look.'

She grabbed the remote and turned the TV back on. It looked like a full-blown riot. A few of the protesters had started burning tyres. In the corner of the screen, she could see a USDF officer clubbing a man who lay unmoving on the ground.

Maggie stood up. 'This is not right, Richard. Something's going to crack, very soon. I can feel it.'

5

The Watergate Building, Washington, DC, Monday, 7.25pm
'Here. Scotch, water, no ice. Let's talk on the balcony.'

Robert Kassian let Jim Bruton steer him through the living room and outside. Bruton closed the door behind them, tight shut. 'You can't be too careful.'

It was a warm, May evening – in that precious interim between the bone-chilling Washington winter and the stifling, damp summer. He'd been here over ten years, but still Kassian didn't care for this city. He dreamed often of moving back home to Cleveland or perhaps, who knows, California. But if the place was bearable at all, it was in springtime.

He looked at the glass dwarfed by Bruton's hand, then down at his own. Physically, they were an odd match. They always had been. Bruton was a bear of a man. He'd played college football and, while the muscle tone had gone, the size had not. He was always the broadest, tallest man in the room. Kassian was perhaps an inch shorter than him, no more. But he was thinner and, he knew, with a fraction of his friend's presence. Bruton spoke often and in a voice that demanded attention. Few would ever have guessed at their shared past.

Bruton spoke first. 'So, tell me about New York.'

Kassian sipped from his glass and took in the view of the Potomac. The lights of the city were winking. 'Not good, Jim. Not good at all.'

'Did Zheng even understand what you were telling him?'

'He understood. I'm not sure he believed me, but he understood.'

'Will he get us the statement, from the North Koreans?'

'I think so. Later tonight, he said.'

'Has the President brought it up?'

'At the briefing this morning, he mentioned it. The CIA briefer looked blank. I jumped in. I said we were still working on a translation.'

Bruton shook his head. 'This is horrible.'

'The good news is, there's been nothing more out of Pyongyang. I think Beijing have told them to zip it.'

'For five days.'

'Exactly. Five days.'

'And then?'

'Then North Korea would have every justification, given what happened this morning, to launch a pre-emptive attack on the United States. And China can't promise they won't stop them.'

There was a moment of silence. They both looked towards the Kennedy Center, illuminated and shining. Inside, doubt-less hundreds of well-dressed, well-paid members of the capital's elite were blissfully unaware of how close they had come just sixteen hours earlier to being incinerated.

Bruton spoke first. 'Even if Pyongyang come to Jesus, play nice, it still could happen again. With them or with someone else.'

'Of course it could.'

'And next time we might not get so lucky.'

'The War Room couldn't pull the same stunt twice.'

The two men paused again. Kassian would think often of the moment that followed. Were they awed by the thought they were about to utter, by the weight of it? Or were they hesitating, wondering which one of them was going to say it out loud first?

In the end, it was Kassian. 'The current situation is unsustainable.'

Bruton nodded.

Kassian went on. 'At any moment, a civilization-ending decision could be made.'

'And there's not a blind thing we could do to stop it. We're impotent.'

'On this, his power is absolute. He's the nuclear monarch.'

Bruton raised his eyebrows.

'That's the term of art apparently, you know in "the national security community". Can you believe that? No one even hides it.'

'So he has no obligation to discuss anything with us?'

'Not with us, not with Congress. Nobody. He can take this step at any time, for any reason. And we now know he's ready to take it.'

Bruton knocked back his whisky. 'Do you remember the oath we took, right at the start?'

'I do.'

And suddenly, there on the balcony of the Watergate, the White House Chief of Staff and the US Secretary of Defense both raised their right hands and, in the dark, declared, 'I do solemnly swear that I will support and defend the Constitution of the United States against all enemies, foreign and domestic; that I will bear true faith and allegiance to the same; and that I will obey the orders of the President of the United States and the orders of the officers appointed over me, according to regulations and the Uniform Code of Military Justice. So help me God.'

Kassian drained his whisky glass. 'Our oath is to defend the Constitution. It's this republic we have to save. *Against all enemies.*'

'Yeah, but now you're cherrypicking.' *Cherr-pickin'.* 'What about "obeying the orders of the President of the United States"? That's in there too.'

'Like I said this morning, we are only required to obey those orders which are lawful. An unprovoked nuclear strike that will destroy America and most of the human race cannot be lawful.'

Bruton knew where they were heading. They both did. 'It is our constitutional duty then.'

'Yes, Jim, I believe it is. I believe we are honour-bound, by virtue of the oath we swore, to do all we can to remove the President.'

6

Robert Kassian considered asking the Secret Service man to knock on the man's door, but feared that might backfire. The mere sight of an agent on a suburban street (and no matter how much they bragged to the contrary, they always looked obvious) would attract too much attention, might scare their man off.

But neither could they simply turn up themselves, unannounced. That too would get attention. Even if he was not recognizable, Jim Bruton was. Within a few minutes, somebody would have tweeted a photo with the caption: *Guess who just turned up in this neighbourhood. What *are* they up to?*

The obvious solution was to call ahead. But every call on their phones was logged. Same was true of the driver's. It was not worth the risk.

So they simply pulled up in Kassian's official car – which was fractionally the less visible of the two – and asked the driver to go knock on the door and inform Dr Jeffrey Frankel that the White House Chief of Staff was waiting outside on an urgent matter and ask if he would be so kind as to allow him to come in.

To Kassian's relief, the doctor and his wife were alone. No house full of teenagers, no Washington dinner party: that, he hoped, would reduce the likelihood of a leak. Dr Frankel said nothing in the hallway, though when he saw that there were two of them – that the Defense Secretary was here too – he furrowed his brow. He waved them into his study, which looked out onto the street.

'Excuse me,' Kassian said, closing the curtains without asking the doctor's permission. 'Just to ensure a little more privacy.'

Dr Frankel's face creased in irritation. He looked older than the sixty-four years registered in the White House personnel database. His face was lined, even wizened. What hair he had was white and wiry, framing a birdlike face.

Kassian looked around. There were pictures on display on every available surface: Frankel and wife on vacation in Florida; Frankel and daughters deep-sea fishing; Frankel raising a glass at a bar mitzvah; relaxed and smiling with adult children and a horde of grandchildren, at what appeared to be a Thanksgiving dinner.

Of the fact that Frankel was physician to the President of the United States, and that he had ministered to several other key Washington players, there was no sign. Kassian had seen enough private studies in this town to know this was unusual. The lack of an 'ego wall' made Frankel a rare creature. Everyone said they cherished family above all, but this man seemed to mean it.

'Dr Frankel,' he began at last. 'It's very good of you to see us at home and at such short notice.'

'All right.' Translation: *Don't waste my time with pleasantries.* Kassian remembered that one of the very few groups of people who had as high an opinion of themselves as politicians were doctors. They were very seldom overawed.

Now Bruton spoke. 'Doctor, we wouldn't be here unless we had one helluva big problem.'

'I'm sure. But why is your problem my problem, Mr Bruton?'

'Because we need your help.'

Kassian tried to make amends by adding swiftly, 'We need your *judgement.*'

'Enough with the riddles. Tell me what's going on.'

Bruton led, as always. He proceeded to describe what had happened during the night. He dropped in the odd military term, always useful when trying to strong-arm a civilian, but otherwise kept it straight. At the end, the Defense Secretary looked over at Kassian. His eyes said: *Close the deal.*

Kassian swallowed, then said, 'Dr Frankel. The United States constitution allows for this situation. The Twenty-fifth Amendment says—'

'I know what it says. I'm the Chief Physician at the White House. Of course I know what it says.'

'So now you know why we're here.'

'Have you spoken to the Vice President and the other cabinet secretaries? The amendment is very clear that any declaration that the President is unfit "to discharge the powers and duties of his office" has to come from the Vice President and a majority of the heads of those departments of the federal government. They're the ones you should be talking to.'

Kassian shot a look at Bruton. The Vice President was all but an unknown quantity, to them and to the rest of Washington. A former mayor plucked from obscurity by the President, he had cannily allowed himself to become a blank screen on which every faction could project their fantasies.

The op-ed pages, along with a cluster of House liberals, imagined him to be the moderate on a white charger who would ride to the republic's rescue. Meanwhile the party's ideologically pure wing nurtured the hope that he was a conservative true believer, just waiting for the right moment to emerge. Neither camp had much to go on besides its own wishful thinking.

'Sir, with all due respect,' said Kassian. 'I think those individuals' first response would be to ask for an expert medical opinion.'

'That's what I'd ask for,' Bruton said, before adding, 'So this ball is going to come bouncing back to you, one way or another.'

'Especially,' Kassian said by way of reinforcement, 'because you weren't his personal physician, before January. You're seen as fair. Impartial.'

Frankel hauled himself out of his chair and walked the short distance to the door. Bruton shot a look at Kassian: *Is he about to walk out? Is he about to call the President?*

But it appeared the doctor just wanted to pace around the room. He stopped to look at one of the photographs, showing what Kassian guessed was a son's graduation.

'I will respect the confidence of this meeting,' Frankel said finally. 'I respect your offices, just as I respect the office of the presidency. And I also believe you've come to me in good faith. The events you describe are indeed alarming.'

Bruton let out a noisy sigh. 'Well, that's good to hear. People said you were a good man and—'

'But this is not straightforward.'

'We understand.'

'I also swore an oath. You understand that, hmm? I'm a doctor. I can't make up a diagnosis, no matter how expedient – politically expedient – it might be. The minute I do that, I stop being a doctor. I become one of you.'

'Dr Frankel, when did you last examine the President?'
Kassian hoped to prevent Bruton coming in too hard.

'I see him once a week. I saw him on Tuesday.'

'Tuesday? So before the current . . .' Kassian hesitated
before lighting on the appropriate word, '. . . *situation* with
North Korea. And how would you describe his health?'

'He's not young. He's overweight. He has some diabetes,
which he manages with—'

'What about his *mental* health, Dr Frankel? How would
you describe his state of mind?'

At this, the doctor paused. Then he paced a little more,
before returning to his chair. 'Look, he's not like you and
me. He's . . . unpredictable. He's volatile. He can have strong
. . . moods.'

Bruton jumped on that. 'And what if those mood swings
made him unable to—'

The doctor overrode him. 'But to declare that a *pathology*,
that's something quite different. To declare that that makes
him unable—'

Kassian tried to find a way through. 'We've seen the
evidence of it, Dr Frankel. We've seen how his violent
temper, his mood, has led him to act directly at odds with
his oath to protect and defend the United States.'

'Are you sure you haven't seen him merely discharge the
powers and duties of his office in a way that you – and I
perhaps – do not like? That does not make him *unable* to
discharge those duties. There is a difference.'

'For Christ's sake, doctor.' Bruton was now on his feet.
'This is not medical school. This is not debate camp. This is
not a drill. You've got to see that there's more at stake here.'

'I do see that.'

'This is a life and death situation. But not just one or two
lives. This is about the life of the whole fucking human race.'

'I understand. More, perhaps than you realize. But you must see that I cannot make my decision on that basis.' He looked down at his fingers. 'You don't need to tell me how high the stakes are. This cannot be a political judgement. If it is, it's worthless. It has to be a medical one. They're not the same thing.'

'So what would—'

'I've seen some signs of what you describe. It is undeniable that there are signs of . . . erratic behaviour. But the same could be said of many men, especially of his age.'

'But we're not talking about "many men",' said Bruton, his patience thinning and his voice rising. 'We're talking about the President of the United States, the man with his finger on the trigger of an arsenal that could destroy the entire goddamn world!'

The doctor ignored Bruton. His gaze remained fixed on his fingers. To Kassian, he seemed like a man locked in his own thoughts, wrestling with the dilemma. Now he spoke, but less to them than to himself.

'The medical question is: what symptoms would have to be present for this to constitute an inability to fulfil his duties? Would we need to establish mental impairment? Is a tendency to ignore evidence, or to act rashly, sufficient? Or must there be clear proof of an unwillingness, or inability, to think through the consequences of one's actions? How high, or low, does the bar need to be set?'

'Dr Frankel?'

The doctor looked up, to meet Kassian's gaze. 'I cannot make this decision straight away. I must examine the patient, run a full battery of tests. I would, ordinarily, wish to consult with colleagues to—'

'That definitely cannot happen.' Bruton, his voice raised. 'Complete confidentiality is, as you know, of paramount importance,' said Kassian, pausing to let his words sink in. When he was satisfied, he said: 'Besides, there isn't time. What happened last night could happen again.'

'At the very least, I need to consult my files at length—'

'On him?' Bruton said, barely keeping the lid on. 'I hear there *aren't* any medical records. It was an issue in the campaign, remember? Press thought he hadn't let any doctor come near him in years.'

'What the rumour mill says is not relevant to me. I need to have another look through my notes and weigh the question that you've put to me. This is not a decision to be taken lightly. It takes time.'

Bruton seemed poised to throw a punch. Kassian cut in: 'That's fine, doctor. The Secretary and I will wait for you in the hallway.'

'No. I need several hours at—'

'If we had more time, we'd give it to you. We'll wait for you in the hallway.'

And so they waited, the pair of them, Kassian sitting, Bruton pacing and occasionally the other way around. Once, Mrs Frankel appeared – a kindly woman of the same vintage as her husband – who asked if either of them would like something to drink, perhaps some homemade lemonade on this warm evening. Kassian was thirsty, but he didn't say yes. Somehow he sensed that a patina of normality would only make this situation even more enervating, for him at least.

Finally, perhaps forty minutes later, the doctor emerged from his study. He looked at both men, moving his gaze from one to the other, until finally, and with no expression either of them could discern, he said: 'Come inside. Let me give you my answer.'

7

Chevy Chase, Maryland, Tuesday, 6.05am

At just after six, the sun already bright, the call came. The doctor answered it, barely dipping his voice. Unlike him, his wife was a heavy sleeper. There was no risk she would wake.

'Yes. I understand. I'll be there right away. No, no, you did the right thing. If he's asleep now that's very good. Certainly no need to wake him up. What? We can assess that when I get there. I won't be long.'

He dressed quickly, working through the possible scenarios in his own mind. Nothing in what he had heard alarmed him. But this was a relatively new administration; the staff at the Residence were still getting to know their new charge. They did not yet know what was ordinary, which made it harder to work out what was extraordinary.

As he brushed his teeth, Jeffrey Frankel reflected again on his meeting the previous evening with Robert Kassian and General Bruton. Nothing like that had ever happened before. Indeed, he doubted if he had ever exchanged more than two words with either man's predecessors.

He wondered if he had given them the right answer. He had spent most of the night wrestling with that question.

He reached for his briefcase, by the front door, as always; grabbed his keys, on the hook by the front door, as always, and stepped outside.

Washington was always so beautiful at this time of year: the clear blue skies, the trees in bloom, the sun not yet chokingly hot. He looked up and down the street: one jogger had just rounded the corner, out of view, leaving not a soul in sight.

Frankel walked the six yards to his car, clicked the doors open and settled into the driver's seat. Only when he checked the rearview mirror did he see that there were two men sitting in the back. He jolted, as if ten thousand volts had been put through him, and let out a little yelp.

Instantly a gloved hand was placed flat over his mouth, the fingers forming a ridge that simultaneously blocked his nostrils. He could smell the latex. 'Don't scream. Don't say anything. Just drive.' It was the older of the two men who spoke: short, muscled, unsmiling. 'My assistant here is holding a gun which is aimed directly at your back. He will shoot you if you do anything stupid. Do you understand?'

The doctor could hardly breathe. He began to think about his heart and his blood pressure. He stayed frozen.

'Do you understand me, Dr Frankel?'

'Yes,' he said, though the sound was muffled and unintelligible.

'Good. Now just drive to the end of this street, turn right and park up. Then I'll take my hand away from your mouth.' The younger man, with long hair, remained silent. Only the older, broader man spoke. 'That's it. Just past this hydrant. OK, here. Just park here.' The man did as he had

54

promised and took away his hand. Frankel panted, gulping down air.

The men let him do that for a second or two. Then they ordered him to shift himself into the passenger seat. He had to adjust it to make room for his legs: it was set for his wife. Then, calmly, the older of the two men got out of the car and re-entered, this time taking the driving seat, which he too adjusted.

'We're going on a little trip,' he said. 'The first thing I'm going to need you to do is give my friend your phone. Can you do that?'

Frankel dug into his pocket and handed his phone to the long-haired man sitting behind him. Frankel always associated the back seat with his children and grandchildren. He thought of them now and wondered if he would ever see them again.

'Don't worry. You'll get it back. We just need a little privacy right now. OK?'

'Yes.'

'Are you comfortable? You OK?'

'Yes.'

'Good. This won't take long. We'll be there in ten minutes. No traffic at this time of day.' The man smiled, a move that made Frankel queasy.

This was obviously connected to the meeting last night. He was being punished, though for what he could not precisely say. If only he had never opened the door to Kassian and Bruton. If only he had refused to have the conversation. If only he had invoked patient–doctor confidentiality from the start, insisting that there was nothing further to discuss. If only he had left the White House in January, with everyone else. If only he had never joined.

If only he had remained in private practice, seeing coughing toddlers and aching seniors in Chevy Chase. If only he could see his children again . . .

'Some music, doctor?' The driver began to fiddle with the radio.

'No, I don't want any music. I want you to tell me what's going on.' Instantly he felt some pressure in the back of the seat. He did not need to be told that the younger man had pressed the barrel of the gun closer towards him.

The car was now heading east on Military Road. There had never been so little traffic. Each time a stop light appeared, Frankel would pray that it would turn red. And as they crossed 31st it seemed destined to go his way. Surely it couldn't stay green so long. But somehow it did.

The car barely slowed down. Only once did it draw so close to another vehicle that Frankel could see the face of the driver. He didn't dare tap on the glass of his window – he thought that would count as the something 'stupid' that was punishable by a bullet in the back. But he did try to stare sufficiently hard that he might win the driver's attention. If he could only make her turn around, he would mouth the word 'Help!' But she never turned her head.

Eventually they had reached Rock Creek Park and the driver brought the vehicle to a halt.

'OK,' he said, his voice light as he turned off the engine, even cheery. 'Here's our stop.'

It was then that Frankel felt the anxiety distil into panic and undiluted adrenalin. He was not a man given to rages; he shouted rarely, but now he heard himself. 'I will not get out of this car until you tell me who you are and what is going on here! Who are you?'

The older man swivelled to look at him. 'I'm sorry, doctor,

but we can't tell you that. Believe me, this will work out much better for you if you just do what we say. OK?'

'No. It's not OK. I insist you tell me who you are this instant. Otherwise I am staying put. You'll have to shoot me if you don't like it.' He folded his arms, in a gesture of stubborn defiance he might have learned from his three-year-old grandson.

At that, the older man gave a nod to the younger one who got out of the car, closed the rear door and instantly opened the one by Frankel. At the same time, the other man got out too, closing his door and coming round so that the two of them – both packed with muscle – were looming over him, while he remained seated and inside. Now the younger man leaned in and in a single motion unbuckled Frankel and pulled him out, tugging him by the lapels of his jacket.

Then, in a movement that must have looked comic – a parody of the MGM dance routines his mother loved – the two men each took one of Frankel's arms, threaded it through their own and marched forward, lifting Frankel clean off the ground. He heard the electronic sound of his Honda being locked and sensed the keys being returned to his pocket, and felt ridiculous, lifted so effortlessly by these two men. He could tell it involved no strain for them at all.

They advanced swiftly into the park, along its winding paths, their pace barely slowed by the soft, damp terrain. Eventually they turned off into a kind of dip, where the petals of that spring's blossom had fallen and were turning into mulch. It was a gorgeous spot, lit only by the odd fragment of morning sunlight.

'All right, here we are,' the older man said, as he slowed down and lowered Frankel to the ground. 'Gun, please.'

The junior reached into his jacket and produced a weapon which a second or two later the doctor recognized as his own. His wife's Colt .25, a small automatic pistol, nickel-plated for a more 'attractive' look, right down to the nickel coin embedded into the butt. That was the word she had used when she bought it: 'attractive'. He had pleaded with her not to bring it into the house; he wanted nothing to do with it. Yet here it was. How on earth had these men got hold of it?

'OK, so here's how this is going to work, Dr Frankel. You're going to do exactly what we say and make this clean and simple. If you don't, if you make this messy, then you're going to die anyway – but, after you're dead, maybe in a few days' time, we'll go back and kill your wife and maybe one of your grandkids. Say Joey. Or maybe Olivia. She's cute. Except, with them, we'll make it last longer and be more painful. OK? Are we good?'

'What? What are you saying?'

'We're saying you're going to help us this morning, by taking this gun and putting it under your chin and pulling the trigger. Don't worry, we'll help. But it needs to be your prints, I'm afraid.'

Frankel felt his bowels straining. He was so confused, but he believed what these psychopathic men were telling him: that they would not hesitate to kill his family. They wanted this to look like suicide and he had no option but to co-operate.

And yet, such is the survival instinct, his body rebelled against the decision he had half-made. He began to wriggle, to resist. But the younger man simply tightened his grip as easily as if turning the screw on a vice. The doctor remained fixed in place, on this patch of earth, as he felt the older man open up his fingers and put the gun into his hand.

He wondered about accepting the weapon and using it against them, but there was no scope for that. They had him by the wrist; they had full control of the angle. And now, as easily as if they were manipulating a mannequin, or a child's doll, they retracted his arm until he could feel the cold metal of the barrel on the soft skin under his chin.

Now he felt the latex fingers tugging at his own index finger, curling it around the trigger. He heard some shuffling as the two men got into position, ensuring they were out of the bullet's path. And, aware of how feeble this was, how uselessly impotent he was, he felt his finger curl a notch tighter, a notch tighter, a notch tighter until he could feel no more.

8

She woke to a text message, her phone giving a perky little chime that did not even slightly reflect her mood. Maggie looked over at the other pillow to realize Richard had already left: his morning run, no doubt.

She reached for the device, aware in that small movement that she was mildly hungover. The memory of it came back to her now. She had started early yesterday evening, knocking back the Laphroaig on the phone to her sister who had told her that awful story. And then her sister's words resurfaced. *I cannot believe you work for that evil man, Maggie.*

She used the Touch ID on her phone, pressing the pad of her index finger onto the circle at the bottom, which duly unlocked the device, and squinted to read the message. It was from Crawford McNamara:

Need to see you urgently.

One thing Maggie had noticed about this man. His written communications were entirely free of the sexist banter, faux flirtation and borderline racism that made up his speech. In his emails and text messages, there was no gleeful breaking of the supposed taboos of political correctness. Smart operator that he was, he was careful to leave no trail that could indict him on page A1 of the *Washington Post*. He would not bequeath an incriminating email cache for WikiLeaks or anyone else to publish during the re-election campaign which, she had no doubt, he was already planning.

Maggie hunted around for some clean clothes, and was poised to revive a shirt from the laundry basket, when she found one still wrapped in dry cleaners' cellophane. She didn't like it, but it would do.

With no more than half a cup of coffee inside her, as well as the low throb of last night's whisky, she was in front of McNamara twenty minutes later.

'So here's the deal,' he said, before she'd even sat down. Once she had, he stood up, so that he could pace the room, circling around her, forcing her to twist her neck to maintain eye contact. She noticed a framed quotation behind his desk, rendered in the style of a New England sampler. 'It is better to live one day as a lion than a hundred years as a sheep.' The line was unattributed, but she knew the source. Benito bloody Mussolini.

'A runner – not your boyfriend, someone else – was out in Rock Creek Park this morning.'

'OK.'

'And she's listening to the Gabfest or NPR or some other liberal shit in her state-of-the-art earbuds, when, guess what, she trips over a pair of legs. Turns out it's a corpse.'

'Right.'

'She calls the park police, because she's a good citizen, and they identify the body and you'll never believe who it is.'

Maggie waited for the reveal, then realized McNamara

was waiting for her. She briefly closed her eyes. 'You seriously want me to guess?'

'I thought it might be fun. Never mind.' Now he sat himself on her side of the desk, so that his knees, exposed and hairy in his cargo shorts, were just a few inches away from Maggie's face. He was wearing cologne, a fairly expensive one.

'The dead man is none other than Dr Jeffrey Frankel, of these parts.'

'The White House doctor? Jesus.'

'The very same. Seems he blew his brains out early this morning.'

'Christ. Why would he do that?'

'I don't know. And nor do you. And nor does anyone else. Not yet anyway. But I tell you what I do know.'

'What's that?'

'That as soon as this death is announced, and I mean within ten seconds, maybe five, there will be two hundred different crackheads saying it was murder. Within ten minutes, there'll be fully fleshed-out theories assigning guilt, motive and culprit. And by tonight, maybe tomorrow morning at the latest, every asshole in America will be linking to some five-thousand-word blog titled, "The Unanswered Questions about the Death of Dr Jeffrey Frankel".'

'And you know this because you—'

'—because I am the *king* of this world. That's right, Costello.' He stood again. 'I was once the master and lord supremo of this dominion. These people are my people. The lonely virgins living in their moms' basements who never read a conspiracy theory they didn't believe, and who never saw a corpse within twenty-five miles of the Beltway that died of natural causes – they are,' and here McNamara raised his arms aloft, in the manner of a TV evangelist, to mimic a Southern preacher's accent, *'my people.'*

'They'll be all over this.'

'They will *love* it. This is gonna give Bill O'Reilly orgasms for the next six months. I know because it'd have done the same for me and my old comrades back in the day.'

'Not that long ago.'

'Yep.' He adopted a baritone, as if doing a movie voice-over. '"The road from the wilder shores of the patriotic right to the White House proved shorter than any of them ever expected." But I know you don't hold that against me. I know you're going to do your solemn duty.'

'Which is what?'

'You're going to conduct the independent investigation by the White House Counsel's office set up by the President to look into this tragic occurrence.'

'Me?'

'Yes, you. Your reputation travels before you, Miss Costello. That's why I asked you to deal with those bimbo eruptions.' He saw Maggie wince, but ignored it. 'Which, incidentally, you can drop now. I'll give that particular hospital pass to someone else. Look, I know you dug the previous folks out of some serious shit. Bottom line is, you're a troubleshooter and we have here some major league trouble that needs shooting. Besides.'

'Besides, what?'

'People inside and outside know that you're not one of us. In fact, I know you *hate* us. But that's just a bonus. The thing is, you're obviously not a loyalist. You're not a partisan hack, everyone knows that.' He gave her a knowing wink, which made her queasy. 'Starting assumption of the wing-nuts – I'm sorry, the *concerned citizens* – will be that this is a cover-up. But why would the respected Maggie Costello –

loyal servant of the other team – engage in a cover-up to help this President?'

Maggie felt the old guilt rising, accompanied by its ever-present companion: a biliousness as complete as if she were on the deck of a heaving boat. 'She wouldn't. Because I wouldn't. And I won't.'

'Exactly.' McNamara did a kind of vertical clap, letting his hands slap against each other in a chopping motion. 'That's my girl! You be as independent and rigorous as you want. Do whatever it takes. Those conspiracy theories will get started in the next hour or two. Your job is to—'

'To get to the truth.'

'I was going to say, your job is to shut them down. To deny them the oxygen on which they feed. How you do it is up to you. But I know this phenomenon. I've seen it a million times. Your mission is to strangle it at birth. Don't let me down.'

9

'Jim, a moment of your time?'

They were filing out of the Oval Office, after yet another meeting of principals to discuss the stand-off with North Korea. The President had been subdued, Bob Kassian thought. He'd watched him idly twisting a pen between his fingers and turning at intervals to glance at the TV set, now permanently turned to a hostile cable TV network ('It gets his juices flowing,' McNamara had explained, before adding a leering reference to the First Lady.) The TV was muted, but subtitles gave a rough, if delayed, sense of the on-air conversation. Kassian was at the wrong angle but what he could see displeased him.

. . . painted himself into a corner. I agree with Mark and John. At this point, anything short of a military response will look as if the President's wimped out. You can't issue red lines and not enforce them . . .

Not for the first time, Kassian found himself cursing the media. Perhaps they didn't realize how closely the President paid attention to them, to television especially. For them it might be no more than time-filling hot air, but it had an effect. The President took each of their remarks as a challenge. No, it was more basic than that. As a *dare*. When they said he was being weak, he'd lash out just to show that he was strong. Fine, when it was only the campaign. Fine, when lashing out merely meant bad-mouthing some senator or congressman who had bruised his ego. But the stakes were higher now.

Indeed, Kassian had made some discreet inquiries of the senior butler in the Residence. It turned out that shortly after one am yesterday, the President had asked to see playbacks of the Sunday talkshows that had aired the previous day. Several pundits had demanded a show of US 'resoluteness' in the face of Pyongyang's provocations. It struck Kassian as highly plausible that it was these goads to action from a few talking heads on NBC and CBS, rather than the specific wording of a statement from the DPRK Workers' Party, that had pushed the Commander in Chief to the threshold of all-out nuclear war.

The meeting in the Oval Office had been devoted entirely to the North Korea question, pitting hawks against doves. As so often, those who had seen armed combat with their own eyes were most cautious. Those whose familiarity with war extended to owning the director's cut of *Saving Private Ryan* were more gung-ho. It was yet another fact of DC life that Kassian could not stand.

At one point, the discussion had moved onto the 'paper tiger' statement put out by Pyongyang, the one that had pushed the President into his late-night meltdown. Kassian felt his back muscles tense. He caught Jim Bruton's eye for the briefest of moments. They both braced themselves for the inevitable response from the President: *Oh, yeah but they apologized to me over that*. At which point, the others would look puzzled and demand to see the text and things would get very awkward.

But, thank God, he was not paying attention. His eye was fixed on the TV, chiefly, Kassian suspected, on the straight blonde hair and shiny, waxed legs of the Fox morning anchor, seated on the couch between two middle-aged white men.

A new worry replaced the first. What if the President asked why the media were not trumpeting the humiliating climbdown he had forced the North Koreans to make? But that was the one upside of working for a man with an apparently extreme case of attention-deficit disorder, a man who seemed to struggle to focus on one subject for more than a few seconds: played right, it was not hard to get him to move on.

Now as they filed out, agreeing only to meet again in twenty-four hours' time if not sooner, Kassian steered the Defense Secretary as subtly as he could down a corridor and out into the covered walkway, the colonnade that looked out onto the Rose Garden.

Only once he was sure they were neither overlooked nor overheard did Kassian allow his demeanour to change. The two men had already spoken once by phone earlier that morning, so now they could pick up where they left off.

'You've heard about Frankel?' Bruton began. 'The state his body was in?'

'I heard,' Kassian replied.

'I mean, Jesus Christ, Bob. We were there just a few hours before. It's so obvious.'

'Listen, Jim. I hear McNamara is hoping to have a new physician in place by tomorrow morning. Perhaps even tonight.'

'Jeez, that's quick.'

'Like he doesn't want to leave anything to chance.'

'Shouldn't that be you? Choosing the White House doctor: that's up to the Chief of Staff, no?'

'Of course it *should* be.' Kassian looked over his shoulder. He could see two reporters, heading towards the briefing room. (Had Frankel's death been announced already?) 'But guess who got involved over breakfast this morning?'

'You're kidding. Daughter? Son-in-law? Don't tell me. Both?'

'I don't know. Maybe. But however early I get in here, McNamara's already on it. He meets the boss in the Residence every morning. Cup of coffee, shooting the breeze. Taking the temperature from the daughter—'

'And the son-in-law.'

'The whole imperial court. Czar, Czarina—'

'He's a regular Rasputin.'

'Anyway,' sighed Kassian. 'He's ahead of me on this one. Now he gets to do what they all wanted to do on day one.'

'Appoint the family physician?'

'Yep. The loyal retainer.'

'That guy who signed off the bullshit statement during the campaign?' Bruton allowed himself a smile. 'It's a wonder that jackass wasn't struck off years ago.'

'Well, his position is safe now,' said Kassian. 'And we can forget him signing off any "inability" medical letter.'

'That's why they want him there. He'll have one job.'

They stood and faced outwards together. Kassian wondered if they were too visible. 'Frankel was right about one thing,' he said.

'What's that?'

'There's nothing in the Twenty-fifth about an expert opinion. Nothing about a doctor's certificate.'

'So?'

'It makes things even harder. For us, I mean.' Kassian reached into his breast pocket and pulled out a thin booklet, no bigger than a wallet. 'Since this is the document we swore to defend, I thought I ought to look at it. I read it again this morning.' He started flicking through the pages. He came to one towards the end. 'Here we go,' he said.

'Key bit is Section Four.' He read out loud. '"Whenever the Vice President and a majority of either the principal officers of the executive departments, yadda yadda, transmit . . . their written declaration that the President is unable to discharge the powers and duties of his office, the Vice President shall immediately assume the powers and duties of the office as Acting President."'

'So we'd have to have the Veep and a majority of the cabinet,' said Bruton. 'Not *or. And*. Fuck. We'd have to have both.' He twisted the sole of his cowboy boot into the ground, just like he did when stubbing out a cigarette butt on the road to Baghdad. His frustration was visible.

Kassian said, 'My hunch is there's no way we can bring the VP on board with this. He couldn't do it.'

'Folks would say he was out for himself.'

'He'd be dead to the base if he backed a stunt like this. Forever. And he's smart. "The assassin never inherits the crown."'

Kassian put the document back in his pocket. 'So what if the cabinet came together – without him – and wrote the statement? Presented it to the Veep as a *fait accompli*. Nothing to do with him, he can't be blamed. He just has to go along with it.'

Bruton shook his head. 'Fine in theory. And he gets what's going on. Or at least he should, a man like him. But the others? Look at them, Bob. I sit around the table with those guys. They're nodding dogs. So long as they're getting their beef and gravy, they'll salute. Have you seen even one of them voice misgivings about anything?'

'Tom is anxious, I know that.'

'The Ag Sec? You think the President is going to be removed from office because he's lost the Department of Agriculture?'

'Barbara is also unhappy. Health and Human Services is a significant department.'

'Yeah, but Barbara's husband is a tranny, Bob.'

'Excuse me?'

'"Transitioning to become a woman."'

Kassian exhaled. 'I did not know that.'

'McNamara's been holding onto it for weeks. Leverage.' Bruton opened his eyes wide, as if to say: *We're not in Kansas any more, Toto.*

'We did the right thing with the doctor, but it's not helped us,' Kassian said, mindful that they both ought to get back to their offices before people – McNamara – started getting suspicious. 'We can't get the VP. We can't get the cabinet. We don't have any of the tools in place to trigger the Twenty-fifth and we have no prospect of getting them.'

Bruton sighed. 'We're back to impeachment.'

'We've been over this, Jim. "Treason, bribery, or other high crimes and misdemeanours".'

'But what's a freakin' higher crime or misdemeanour than ordering the end of the freakin' world? Jesus.'

'Look, you don't have to persuade *me*. It's Capitol Hill we'd have to persuade. And they're in lockstep with him. They're *terrified* of crossing him. They wouldn't believe us anyway. There's no way we could provide the proof – not unless we want to make public what happened yesterday. Which could trigger a nuclear war all by itself.'

'So you're telling me we're all out of options,' Bruton said.

'I think so, yes.'

There was a silence between them, filled by what they both knew but did not want to say. In truth, it had hovered over them since that first phone call in the small hours of yesterday morning. They both knew it.

Eventually Kassian, so used to letting Bruton lead, spoke first. 'The Twenty-fifth Amendment is closed to us. So is impeachment. Not for reasons that anyone could defend, not because of public servants taking a different view of what's best for the safety of the country, but because of politicians thinking of what's best for their careers.'

Bruton nodded, willing Kassian to speak for both of them – and to say it.

'And yet it remains true that this man poses a clear and present danger to the republic, to the Constitution and to the safety of the world.'

That was enough for Bruton. As if that were his cue, he stood taller and straightened his jacket. He fixed the Chief of Staff in the eye. Kassian wondered if the Defense Secretary was about to salute.

Instead Jim Bruton said in a voice at once quiet, but firm, 'I'm satisfied we've exhausted all other means. As patriots, who've sworn an oath to defend this nation against all enemies, foreign and domestic, I believe we have only one option left to us. I believe it is our duty to kill the President.'

10

Maggie had thought of heading first to the Park Police who were handling the investigation into the death of Dr Jeffrey Frankel, but instinct told her that could wait. She hailed a cab instead for E Street, South West: the Office of the Chief Medical Examiner.

En route, she noticed a huge mural on the side of a building. It depicted the President with fangs and devil's horns and, in huge letters alongside it, the words, *Not In Our Name*.

Once she'd arrived, she flashed her White House credential and asked to see the most senior person present. She was swiftly introduced to a woman, Dr Amy Fong, who led Maggie into an office, closed the door and asked if she was there to identify the body.

Maggie had to think quickly. She had assumed a family member would already have done that. If they hadn't, they certainly should. Surely it wasn't right for her, who barely knew Frankel, to perform such a final, even intimate act.

But she also intuited what giving the wrong answer might mean. If she said no, then why was she there? Why would this office give her any information or access? If, on the other hand, she said yes then, crucially, they would surely have to show her the body. 'That's right,' she said.

They walked down one corridor, through a set of double doors, then another and finally into an examination suite. As they walked, Dr Fong explained that the identification would have to be done very quickly. 'I'm afraid we're under extreme time pressure. The family are hoping to have the funeral today. Jewish thing, I think.'

And there, on a thick counter, lay the white, inert body of a man in his sixties. She only allowed herself a glance above the neck: enough to see that while much of the face was left, the back of the head seemed to have been reduced to a bloody pulp.

Not for the first time, she reflected on the strange unreality of a dead body. It seemed to her like a waxwork or a movie prop, a fake. It was as if, once the breath of life was gone, a human body belonged to another realm altogether. Or perhaps that's just what she needed to tell herself.

Now the woman and the doctor doing the examination, who had, Maggie noticed, blood on his overalls and on his latex gloves, conferred briefly. The man then picked up a clipboard and pen, turned to Maggie, asked her to confirm her name, date of birth and address – which she gave as the White House – before asking her 'to identify the deceased'.

Now there was no hiding. Maggie had to come round to the doctor's side of the counter and look properly at the face of the dead man.

She had seen corpses before. A lifetime ago, during that mediation effort in Congo, she had been led to the site of a massacre: the leader of one of the parties to the talks refused to continue unless Maggie, as chair of the negotiations, had seen with her own eyes 'what our enemies are doing to us'.

On that occasion, though, she had not had to focus as intently – or closely – on one person, as she did now.

As she had already glimpsed, the face was still mostly intact. But the skull was a mess, a congealed tangle of blood, brain and bone. The contrast between the front and back – between a face that still promised a person, capable of a smile or a glance, and a mess of gore that would make you wince if you saw it in a butcher's shop – stopped Maggie short. It filled her with a queasy thought: that the distance between the human and the animal is much shorter than we like to think.

And then she noticed something else. Two little indentations on the bridge of the dead man's nose, the traces left by a lifetime of wearing glasses. And in a second she was back in Ireland: a child, sitting on her grandfather's lap, fascinated by those same marks on his face, grooves indented by time that suggested the old man belonged with the rocks and cliffs, as ancient as geology.

What had this doctor on the slab, perhaps the same age her grandfather had been when she was little, gone through that had led him to put a gun to his throat and pull the trigger? What had made him that desperate?

And then, unbidden, came a different image. She saw the seventeen-year-old girl Liz had told her about last night. Mia. She imagined her hanging in her room, and all because she could not see a way out of a pregnancy that had been inflicted on her. A child herself with a child in her belly, she had been found by another child, her twelve-year-old sister.

Involuntarily, Maggie closed her eyes. So much pain in the world. It seemed to be brimming over. As if the world had more sorrow than it could contain. And, there was no denying it, the man she worked for, the man she served, was adding to it. Each day, with his laws, his deportation squads, his insults, his bile and venom, he was adding to this overflowing volume of anguish. And there was Liz's voice again, as loud as ever. *I cannot believe you work for that evil man.*

'Are you all right, Miss Costello?'

She opened her eyes, only realizing at that moment how long she had kept them closed.

'Are you feeling a little faint? Would you like a glass of water?'

'I'm OK.'

'It happens a lot here.' It was Fong, passing her a paper cup filled with ice cold water.

Maggie drank it down, then forced herself to give a smile. Then she answered the question the male doctor had asked her. 'This is Dr Jeffrey Frankel, White House physician.'

'Have you known the deceased for more than three years?'

'Yes.'

'And how is he known to you?'

The present tense made her pause. 'We both work at the same place.'

'And there is no doubt in your mind that this is Dr Jeffrey Frankel?'

'No doubt at all.'

'All right.' And with that he reached for the sheet which lay at the bottom of the counter and pulled it upwards, covering Frankel's shoulder and then his face. As far as he was concerned, Maggie's work here was done. He gave a slight nod towards his colleague, as if to suggest Maggie should now leave.

'Excuse me,' Maggie said. 'Can I just ask: on the basis of what you've seen, is there anything to suggest this was not suicide?'

The woman spoke before her colleague could reply. 'We'll be issuing a full report in the regular way. Once the examination is fully complete.'

'I appreciate that,' Maggie said. 'It's just I've been sent here by the White House. I will be expected to deliver a full report.' Registering the woman's unmoved expression, Maggie added: 'To the President. He will want to know what happened to his personal physician.'

The two officials looked at each other. Sensing an opening, Maggie pressed her case. 'I will stress that what I am relaying are unofficial, interim findings, awaiting confirmation.' And then: 'I will put nothing in writing until we have had your official report.'

That seemed to be the reassurance the woman was waiting for. In Washington, DC, the world capital of ass-covering, fear of the written record was the spectre that loomed largest.

'All right, Ms Costello. You can ask my colleague one or two questions. But there are no guarantees he can answer.'

'Of course. Doctor, have you seen anything that would make you doubt that what happened here was an act of suicide?'

'Nothing so far.'

'In terms of ballistics, residue or burn marks on the hands, position of the entry and exit wounds, all—'

'All of that. It all points to suicide.'

'He just put a gun in his mouth, pulled the trigger?'

'In or just by his mouth. Seems that way, yes. I'm afraid so.'

'And you've seen the police report presumably?'

The doctor looked over at his boss, who gave him a nod.

'Yes.' He raised his clipboard again. 'And one of the officers was here with me. Just before you came.'

'And what he saw—'

'She.'

'—she saw fits with a finding of suicide?'

'Yep. The deceased was found with a gun in his right hand. Full match on the prints.'

'Everything in the right position? Gun held the right way?'

'Yes.'

'The angle matching the wounds?'

'Like I said. Yes.'

'No anomalies or discrepancies at all?'

'None.'

'Open and shut case? I can tell the Pres . . . my bosses that this is a tragic but straightforward case of suicide.'

'That's it, yes.'

'OK,' Maggie said, collecting herself as if to leave. 'Thank you.'

Maggie was nearly at the door before she turned and said, 'You know what: belt and braces. I can predict exactly what my boss is going to ask me. There will be photographs from the crime scene. Could you just let me take a quick pass through those?' There was a pause Maggie didn't like. 'So I can tell the White House how incredibly helpful the Office of the Chief Medical Examiner has been?'

'I already explained that we have very little time, Miss Costello. And, besides, this is police evidence. I really—'

'I understand. Just the pictures of how Dr Frankel was found. He and the President had known each other a long time. They were close.'

The woman didn't even attempt to hide her reluctance, sighing as she tilted her head to suggest her colleague lead

77

Maggie to the computer which was perched on a high table, close to the examination counter. He pulled up a stool on wheels and, with Maggie and Fong watching over his shoulder, he clicked several times until he had opened a folder of photographs. From the time stamps, Maggie could see they were taken at 7.12am today.

There were dozens. 'Can we just scoot through them?' Maggie said, trying to keep it light.

The first few showed Frankel lying in a shaded part of the park, perhaps six yards off the joggers' track, among shrubs and underbrush. A swathe of trampled twigs and grasses was visible from the track to where the corpse lay.

The pictures got closer now, focusing on the body. Frankel appeared to be wearing trousers and a sports jacket, with a shirt and no tie. Nicely polished leather loafers. Classic Washington, smart-casual attire. He had his glasses on.

Maggie touched the doctor's shoulder. 'The glasses. Was he wearing—'

'Yes,' he said. 'When the body was brought here, the glasses were there. We removed them, along with his other personal effects.'

'OK.'

He carried on scrolling through. The police had photographed the dead man from every angle. They had also taken pictures of the ground nearby. Maggie saw several images of tree bark spattered with what she guessed was blood, bone and brain material.

Something in the image she was looking at jarred, something she couldn't quite put her finger on.

Finally, there were a dozen photos of a car: a Honda Civic, parked near Rock Creek. Frankel's car: shown from all angles, both inside and out. She scrutinized it, trying to think herself into the shoes of a conspiracy theorist, trying to notice what they would notice. The exterior was unre-markable, no dents or scratches that she could see. The car looked worn and well-used, unflashy for a man who'd have had a decent income, but otherwise wholly ordinary. The interior was neat: she saw a couple of CDs in the slot near the handbrake, a bottle of de-icer held in the passenger door. She looked and looked, but that seemed to be that.

Indeed, it was only after she had said her goodbyes, thanking Dr Fong and her colleague, and had hailed a cab and was sitting in the back, staring out of the window, returning to the White House that a thought struck her. Her eyes had skated over this one detail, but she had not absorbed its meaning – until now.

11

The White House, Tuesday, 6.16pm

Ordinarily, Bob Kassian dreaded occasions like these. He would do his best to arrive late and leave early which, in his role as Chief of Staff, was not just possible but expected. Of course he was too busy to spend more than a few precious minutes at a reception, hobnobbing with diplomats and selected 'business leaders'. (In the previous era, a party like this would also have included a few journalists and academics, specialists in the relevant region, but McNamara had decreed that he'd had 'enough of experts' and so that custom had been terminated. Kassian disagreed but said nothing: pick your battles.) If anything, it would look suspiciously low energy and low status if the Chief of Staff were present there too long. Official Washington would be disappointed.

But tonight was different. Not the event itself: a reception in the East Room for the King of Saudi Arabia was as unappetizing as any other. But it provided a perfect opportunity to talk, discreetly and unheard, with the Secretary of Defense. If they had met in Kassian's office in the White

House, it would have looked too deliberate: a meeting, rather than a chat. Even more so if Kassian had made a special journey to the Pentagon. But grabbing a few moments to talk at a cocktail party? That was perfectly natural. Especially during a nuclear crisis, when discussion between the key players was around the clock. If someone spotted the two of them in earnest conversation, the most damaging interpretation would be that they were cementing an alliance that excluded the National Security Advisor: in other words a standard Washington turf war. No one would imagine they were plotting the assassination of the President of the United States. Hiding in plain sight: a tactic that had always served them both so well.

They now picked up where they had left off earlier that day. Once they had made the core decision, establishing the objective, they had moved swiftly to method. They talked first about what he, Kassian, referred to as 'direct' options.

Was there a way the two of them could kill the President themselves? The advantages were obvious. They would not be reliant on the discretion, or resolve, of anyone but each other. They could move fast, at a moment solely of their choosing. But could it be done?

Could they get themselves alone in a room with him, perhaps with a syringe containing a drug that might simulate a heart attack? Where would they source such a drug, without arousing suspicion? Once administered, would it leave a trace?

They were sure they could find answers to those questions. But as they went through the various scenarios, they found themselves running into the same brick walls. There was the simple fact that the President was almost never alone. On the contrary, he was the most closely defended human being on the planet. The Secret Service employed

6,750 people for the sole task of keeping him safe. There were agents in the Residence, agents in the office, agents wherever he travelled. Even if he were to demand a private, one-to-one chat with either his Chief of Staff or his Defense Secretary there was always a chance someone could join them at any moment. The one person who might have had a reason to be alone with the President, to demand complete privacy, with the time and space to do what needed to be done, was his personal physician. But that man was dead.

Even if they had found a way around that particular obstacle, and neither Kassian nor Bruton could easily see it, they'd run into the other, more serious hurdle: the fact that any one of the 'direct' options would make them immediate suspects. Had, say, Jim emerged from a private meeting in the Oval Office, only for the President to be found dead a few minutes later, he would be the first one accused. Yes, they might be able to engineer a delay to serve as an alibi, but if the death were eventually exposed as murder rather than the result of natural causes – and any post-mortem would be extremely thorough – then the automatic assumption would be that this had been an inside job. It might not be either one of them who was identified as the killer, but there would be no doubting that the President had been murdered by someone with proximity to power.

Neither needed to spell out what was obvious to the pair of them: that the personal consequences were not the issue here. Their fear was not that one or both of them might face justice and be made to pay for the crime of a presidential assassination. That was not why they needed to avoid any culpability.

'If the finger pointed at you, Jim, can you even imagine it?' Kassian had said. 'The Secretary of Defense? It would be a military coup.'

Plenty of people, he argued, including many millions who couldn't stand the President, would nevertheless be appalled at the brutality of such an act and its apparent contempt for democracy and the Constitution. Given the divisions that had been exposed in the election, and the loathing this President had aroused since, they both believed such an outcome could split the country in two. You could imagine it: the newspapers, the cities and coasts, much of the intelligence community in one camp; the rural counties, law enforcement and the border agencies in the other. Each side with its own political party, its own sympathetic TV networks, its own colours: a civil war of red versus blue.

America, they agreed, had always had the potential to do that again; the most lethal conflict the country had ever fought was against itself. An act of murder by the head of the US military would be the spark to relight the fire.

This was why it could not be either one of them who wielded the knife directly. That they would have the physical courage to do it, and damn the consequences – even if that meant risking their own life and liberty – neither doubted. The focus of their conversation in this crowded room, as they waited for the desert king to enter, was not saving their own skins, but saving the republic.

A man in a very expensive suit and with a head of thick, dark hair was hovering, waiting to introduce himself. Bruton turned and offered a handshake. 'Good to see you,' he said: the default Washington formulation, delicately insuring yourself against the possibility you had met before. Only a DC rookie ever made the mistake of saying, 'Nice to meet you.'

The man turned out to be the Ambassador of Egypt, delighted to get a few moments with the Secretary of Defense. He mentioned something about an upcoming visit of his president and Bruton agreed that he would be delighted to meet to discuss further co-operation between their two countries, remembering to add, just in time, that of course he would consult with colleagues too. No need to piss off State.

The ambassador offered a graceful bow of the head and withdrew. They were bound to get interrupted again. They didn't have much time.

'So if not us, who?' Bruton said by way of resumption. Then, without waiting for an answer, he offered one of his own. 'You know, Bob, we're not alone on this. There are senior people who feel the same way we do: at Langley, throughout the military, hell, even in the Secret Service. I could put together a group in a heartbeat, no doubt in my mind. Good men, all of them.'

'I know you could, Jim. But it's just too risky.'

'Not if we pick the right people.'

'It just takes one, Jim.' He said the words through closed lips, lowering the volume yet further. 'One person who agrees with us that the man is out of control but thinks this is a step too far. Who reckons our plan would, you know, violate the Constitution.'

'All right, so they don't join.'

'And then what? They won't just shake your hand, say, "Sorry, Jim, can't be with you on this one" and wish you the best of luck. They'll feel duty bound to tell the President. How could they do anything else?'

'All right.'

'It will only take one to feel that way. Just one.' Kassian paused. 'You gotta remember, Jim, none of them went through what we went through yesterday.'

There was a silence between them as they imagined trying to explain it to someone else, to convey what they had witnessed: an American President who was ready – more than ready, *determined* – to give the order that might well have destroyed all human life, or at least made life on earth not worth living.

'So it's just us,' Bruton said finally. 'Not for the first time.'

'And yet it can't be just us,' said Kassian. 'That's our problem. For the country's sake, it needs to look like it has nothing to do with us. It has to be a public act, by some random outsider.'

'Lee Harvey Oswald.'

'John Wilkes Booth.'

Bruton nodded. 'That's some circle we have to square.'

'Yes, Jim, it is. And we have next to no time to square it.'

12

Chevy Chase, Maryland, Tuesday, 6.45pm

Maggie had witnessed this ritual more than once, but the intensity of it struck her with as much power now as if it were the first time.

The front door was open, a crowd of people spilling out onto the stoop. Maggie had to force her way through, just as she'd done once in Jerusalem and – she recalled with melancholy – not so many years ago, here in Washington, DC. No one stopped her, no one asked who she was. This was a house of mourning and anyone who turned up was assumed to be grieving the dead.

She pushed her way into the main living room, which was even more packed than the hallway. She could have been on a commuter train; she could barely move her arms. She counted at least a dozen White House colleagues, including several men whose faces were rendered unfamiliar by the addition of skull-caps.

A man she took to be a rabbi stood at the front, leading the room in Hebrew prayers. Some spiritedly joined in the ancient tunes, some mumbled along, others stood in respectful silence. All stood as if under a heavy cloak of grief. Several wore expressions that were desperate.

She scanned the room. The full range of ages. Plenty who were obviously Dr Frankel's contemporaries: men she guessed were fellow medics, as well as some she'd have marked down as lawyers or accountants. But there were also scores of people her own age too: friends of the Frankel children, no doubt.

On two of the walls, there were mirrors covered by sheets. It came back to her. That too was a Jewish custom. She remembered it being explained to her in Jerusalem: no scope for vanity or attention to the self when all focus must be on the dead.

But on every other available inch of wall-space, and on the shelves jostling with books and ornaments – including an eight-branched candelabrum, a silver goblet and a pair of antique candlesticks – were family photographs. Dozens of them. Pictures of kids on beaches, now and thirty years ago; graduation photos; black-and-white portraits of turn-of-the-century Americans, their heads held high in that immigrant pose of aspiring formality.

On the shelf nearest her, something caught Maggie's eye. Printed on white card, in a stylish typeface, was an invitation.

Jeffrey and Helen Frankel along with Philip and Miriam Stern invite you to the wedding of their children, Sheryl and Mark . . .

No name was printed in the space just below. Maggie squinted to make out the date. A summer wedding, just six weeks from now.

It was only circumstantial, nothing you'd present in a

court of law. But it felt obvious that Jeffrey Frankel was a committed family man, surrounded by people he loved and who loved him, with plans for the immediate future. Maggie had known a couple of people with suicidal depression. But that's not what she was seeing here.

Now the rabbi was speaking in English. 'As for man, his days are as grass. As a flower of the field, so he flourishes . . .'

There was more Hebrew, a eulogy from one of the dead man's teenage grandchildren, a precociously well-spoken girl whose lower lip began to wobble as she reached the final paragraph of her written speech, and finally an instruction from the rabbi for guests to form a line so that they could give their good wishes to the bereaved. This was the ritual Maggie remembered. Indeed, it was what she was here for.

She was about to take her place in the queue, when a former White House colleague appeared at her side, bending down to kiss her on the cheek, simultaneously squeezing her shoulder: a gesture of mourners' solidarity. It was Ben Jackson, formerly of the NSC; he'd been pretty junior when she was on the foreign policy team, even though they were around the same age, but he'd worked his way up in the last administration, leaving weeks after the new President was elected.

'I didn't see you at the funeral,' he began but before she'd had a chance to reply, he said, 'What an awful business. How's it been there?' He didn't need to say what he meant by 'there'.

'Actually, I've barely been in the office today. But people will be taking this pretty badly, I'm sure.'

'And what about you, Maggie? How's it been for you these last few months?'

She did her best not to bristle, though she suspected her

shoulders had tightened. Had she heard smugness in that inquiry? Or at the very least an implied judgement? *I cannot believe you work for that evil man.*

'Well,' she smiled. 'It's different. You can certainly say that.'

'Heroic of you to stay on, I gotta say. A few of us were together the other night and we were saying, "OK, could not do that myself, but hey: relieved one of the good guys is there, fighting the good fight."'

Maggie smiled weakly, unsettled by the notion of a 'few of us', out in Washington, talking about her. 'Well, I do what I can.'

'Though what the hell is he playing at with the North Koreans? It's like every time he sees a hornets' nest, he just has to jab it with a stick.' He illustrated his point, by helpfully jabbing the air with an imaginary stick. 'And that stuff he said about black people not being the same as "real Americans" 'cause they never *chose* to come here, I mean, does he even listen to the words that come out of his mouth?'

Maggie's head began to dip. It wasn't his fault. Her friends talked the same way to her whenever they had the chance. So did Liz, obviously. And the woman who cut her hair. Pretty well everyone but Richard. She couldn't disagree with them on the specifics. They were right. What the President said at his rallies, or on TV or online was – eight times out of ten – either appalling or a lie. Or both. She could not defend it.

It was obvious to anyone looking in from the outside. She could not possibly stay. But what none of them understood was why she could not possibly leave.

She stopped listening. But while her head was down, she was struck by Ben Jackson's shoes. Absolutely nothing interesting about them at all: standard-issue, Washington-man black brogues. Except what set them apart in a town where high-achieving men always wore ironed shirts and polished footwear was that they were splattered with mud.

Jackson was still talking, making a point about the President's business interests, but she interrupted. 'You were at the funeral, right?'

'What? Yes.'

'Just now? You came here from there?'

'Yes.'

'And that's how your shoes got muddy?'

'What?' He looked down. 'Oh yes. Really wet out there. And you have to go right by the graveside, and shovel in the earth. No offence, but it's actually kind of medieval, the whole . . .'

But Maggie wasn't listening. She was remembering. She was seeing again the photograph they had shown her at the Chief Medical Examiner's office.

Maybe when other people looked at photographs of a man whose brains had been blown out, they couldn't help but look straight to the head. But Maggie had kept her examination of Frankel's head as brief as she could get away with. When Fong and her colleague had displayed the photographs of the body, Maggie had found her eye drawn in the other direction – at the dead man's feet.

Something about them had struck her as odd at the time, but she had not been able to put her finger on it. Until now.

Last night had been wet: spring rain, gentle – even romantic when she and Richard had heard it against the windows – but on and off for hours. The pictures from Rock Creek confirmed that those showers had not been confined to Dupont Circle: inches away from Frankel's body the pathways had grown muddy, the hard ground softened. And yet his shoes carried not a trace of dirt. They were as pristine as if they'd touched nothing more than the carpet of the West Wing. He would have had to have walked very gingerly through the park to keep them in that condition and, even then, he would have picked up at least a spot or two. But why would a man take such care if he were about to end his life?

Now she tied that together with the other oddity she'd spotted among the last photographs the pathologist had shown her: the images of the interior of the car. Frankel was a tall man. Maggie had known that much just seeing him around the White House. The document she had glimpsed at the Chief Medical Examiner's office described him as six foot one. And yet the photograph of the car showed the driver's seat brought forward, close to the steering wheel. That was how Liz's car always looked. Whenever Maggie visited her in Atlanta and borrowed the keys, she would always have to slide the seat back to make room for her legs, which were much longer than her sister's. There was no way Frankel could have driven his own car with the seat in that position.

No, Maggie was certain. Someone else had driven Frankel to Rock Creek Park. And the doctor had not walked to the place where his body was found. Maggie imagined him carried, perhaps unconscious, over the shoulder by one man or else lifted by a couple of men, clean off the ground. One of them, wearing gloves, must have put the gun in Frankel's mouth or under his chin and forced his finger on the trigger. But who would have done that? And why?

And what about the police? The Medical Examiner's office must have seen what she had seen. They *had* to have done. Surely they'd passed both anomalies on to the police or, if they hadn't, they must have assumed that the police themselves had spotted them. They were obvious, weren't they?

They would have been grounds enough to have demanded a more detailed autopsy at the very least, to run a few extra tests.

But that couldn't have happened and now it could never happen. Frankel had been buried a few hours ago, swiftly, in accordance with Jewish custom. The family must have demanded it. Though why did the Chief Medical Examiner agree to it, when there were clearly unanswered questions that stood in the way of a straightforward ruling of suicide?

Ben Jackson had lost interest. Spotting someone else, he gave Maggie another peck on the cheek and insisted they should have lunch. She nodded goodbye and looked ahead in the shuffling queue, still moving in only the fractions of inches. Behind her she could hear a couple, perhaps in their thirties.

'. . . and Laura were so close. Do you remember the speech he gave at her wedding? And the way her mom was begging him to sit down, because he'd gone on too long?'

'He was so proud.'

'I'm not sure how she'll get over this.'

'And what about Sheryl? This won't be—'

But the rest was lost as they were swallowed up in the big hug of another friend.

Maggie looked ahead and felt that sensation which came to her less often these days, but could still leave a sting. No matter how many years she had lived in this country, she did not have roots here the way these people had roots; she could not fill a roomful of friends and relatives like this. In Dublin, yes. But not here. This place would never be home.

By now, it was nearly her turn. She had made her way to the front of the room, where five people were sitting on five low chairs. She guessed that three were Dr Frankel's adult children – including the two daughters, Laura and Sheryl – one was his wife and the older man must have been a brother. This too she remembered: these were the people deemed to be the official mourners, the immediate family.

The man in front of her worked his way across the group, shaking hands with the others before lingering to talk to the Frankel son. He leaned in for an awkward hug with his bereaved friend, who remained seated.

Now Maggie stepped forward, introducing herself to the son, daughters and brother, explaining that she worked at the White House with their father and that she was sorry for their loss. When she reached the wife, she shook her hand and said, 'Mrs Frankel, I am so sorry. This must be so hard.'

The woman nodded, but said nothing.

Maggie tried again. 'None of us can understand it. Not at all. It seems so . . . out of character.'

Helen Frankel clasped Maggie's hands and said, 'Of course it's out of character! Jeffrey would never do such a thing. Never!'

'But the police say the gun was his.'

'Mine actually. He didn't want it in the house. He never picked it up. It was me,' she sniffed. Maggie saw her eyes were rimmed red.

'It was you?'

'Yes, me. Who said we should have a gun. To keep us safe.' She shook her head, furious with herself. She was still holding onto Maggie's hand. 'Such a terrible mistake. Terrible.'

Then, pushing to confirm what she already knew, Maggie nodded and said, 'And with Sheryl's wedding coming up too.'

At that the woman squeezed Maggie's hand harder. 'This

is it, you see. It makes no sense. You know Jeffrey. He *lived* for his family. He would not have missed his baby daughter's wedding. Not in a million years.'

'He had everything to live for.'

'He wanted to see Sheryl have children. He loved being a grandfather, you know that.'

'It makes no sense.'

'He loved life! This was a man who loved life.'

Maggie could sense the couple behind her, edging closer. They'd finished their conversations with the other mourners and were now giving her the tacit, but unmistakable signal to wrap things up and let someone else have their turn. It was time to make her move.

Looking directly into the widow's raw eyes, she said, 'What I'm trying to understand is whether anything happened at all, maybe something out of the ordinary, that could have, you know, distressed him.'

At that moment, the woman glanced over Maggie's shoulder, acknowledging the presence of the couple behind her. Maggie feared the moment had been punctured, the spell broken. She tried to lock Helen's gaze back onto hers. 'Do you remember anything, Mrs Frankel? Anything that happened to Jeffrey in the last few days that might have distressed your husband?'

She looked down. 'He seemed happy. He was talking about a vacation in Europe, after the wedding. We'd never been to Rome. Not together, I went once, before we were married but—'

'Could something have happened at work, perhaps?'

'He didn't really talk about that. He didn't bring his work home.'

'Maybe something with the President? Had the President

perhaps . . .' Maggie stopped herself. She could see a thought had passed across the woman's eyes, like a plane across the sky.

'The only thing I can think of.'

'Yes.'

'Talking of bringing work home—'

Maggie nodded.

'—was last night. That was unusual, I suppose.'

Maggie stayed silent, aware that she was taking a risk: the couple behind her might step into the lull and seize Mrs Frankel's attention for themselves. But instinct told her she needed to keep quiet.

'Jeffrey doesn't often get visited at home. But Mr Kassian and General Bruton came here last night. They went into Jeffrey's study with him.'

'The Defense Secretary? And the Chief of Staff? Here? Last night?'

'I offered them lemonade.'

'Do you know why they were here?'

'They didn't want any. Even though it's homemade. And it was such a warm night.'

'Do you know what they wanted, Mrs Frankel? It could be important.'

But she was already looking away, extending her arms to hug the woman who'd been waiting so long. Maggie heard a muffled, 'We're so sorry, Helen.' She squeezed her way back through the throng, raising her eyebrows in recognition as she saw more colleagues, most of them former rather than current. But she was in no mood to linger. She needed to be outside, to be able to breathe. She needed to be far away from here, and absorb what she had just been told – and what it meant.

There was now no doubt in her mind that Dr Jeffrey Frankel, physician to the President, had been murdered. Much harder to face was the fact that his widow had, inadvertently, pointed the finger of suspicion at two of the most senior figures in the United States government.

13

The Willard Hotel, Washington, DC, Tuesday, 6.53pm
'And no checking your phone.'

Robert Kassian said nothing. He was checking his phone.
'Bob!'

His wife couldn't see him, but she knew. She was in the bathroom, getting ready for tonight's reception: his second of the evening. He had bidden Jim Bruton goodbye, slipped out of the East Room and come straight here.

As he perched on the end of the bed, waiting for her, he wondered: was the use of this suite a perk of Pamela being a board member, or had it been granted as a gesture towards his needs, as White House Chief of Staff? If the latter, it was considerate. Privacy, space to meet his wife and make the transition from the working day to the evening: it was helpful. Unless – and the thought appalled him – someone in his office had *demanded* it, treating this tiny not-for-profit as if it were one of the mega-charities the White House was used to. He thought about thumbing out a quick email to his assistant, but thought better of it. What if Pamela poked her head around the bathroom door and caught him in the act?

She was in there adjusting her dress, perfecting her make-up, he didn't know which. He'd been in there once, to make a judgement on jewellery – earrings or bracelet or both? – and she had seemed almost ready then. But that meant nothing. It was perfectly possible that a choice of necklace had triggered a rethink of the entire ensemble, dress included.

Ordinarily, he quite enjoyed this ritual. He still liked seeing his wife in her underwear. He took pleasure in the seriousness of it. And he liked this occasion especially: the annual dinner of the Coalition for Shelter, raising funds for the homeless of DC. It was a noble cause and, best of all, thanks to his wife's seat on the board, he was there purely as a spouse.

Sure, people would be lining up to speak to him all night, just as they had, mainly in vain, at the White House event earlier. He got that: Washington society was all about prox-imity to power. He occupied too coveted a perch in the DC jungle to be ignorable. But at least they'd have to disguise it a bit. This evening was not about him, but his wife. He could follow his usual preference, and recede into the background, and this time people would give him credit for modesty, admiring him as a supportive partner and enlightened man.

But the stipulation that he stay off the phone? That was ridiculous. Ordinarily, maybe. But these were not ordinary times. He would have to be glued to it, in case the President decided to unload the entire US nuclear arsenal on North Korea and China or to stage some other horror show, as yet unimagined. But he didn't say that. Of course he didn't. Pamela was the one person to whom Robert Kassian could never say no.

He looked out of the window, down 14th Street. They were near enough to the White House that there were protesters on almost every corner. Almost directly below was a mixed group, black and white, but overwhelmingly young, with the usual collection of banners: 'Not My President', 'We're Better Than This', 'Not In Our Name' and one that had started appearing recently, 'We're All God's Children'. There were klaxons and chants, but up here it was hard for Kassian to hear the words they were using. He could guess though.

Eventually Pamela emerged and soon they were heading towards the Pierce Room on the lower ground floor. Kassian deliberately walked behind his wife, letting her greet people first when anyone approached for a handshake. She looked luminous; he was proud of her. When she was safely rapt in conversation with a key funder, he allowed himself a glance at his phone. Twitter was full of the Frankel death. The body was barely in the ground and the bush telegraph was already crackling.

What I'd like @WhiteHouse to explain is the delay between the time of death and the first announcement. Did you guys need time to get your story straight?

This wasn't some random nut. Or rather it was a random nut, but one with an audience. Kassian clicked to discover that the man asking this question had 1.2 million followers.

What did @WhiteHouse doc Geoffrey Frankel know and when did he know it.

That came from the account of someone who billed himself as a 'conservative talkshow host' and 'Fox News contributor'. He'd probably been on once, but still his misspelled and unpunctuated question had got 1400 retweets.

Reinforcement came from the left, from a site that specialized in intelligence leaks:

MSM say it's absurd to say Frankel silenced because he held info that cd undermine the Presidency. Not absurd at all: Plenty of precedents

Among liberals and mainstream journalists the tone was different. Some linked to earnest articles about suicide among older men. Others lamented the easy availability of guns, which could 'turn a bad mood into a catastrophe'.

Others rushed for the moral high ground. One female commentator came out early with:

Can we please let the Frankel family grieve in peace?

While an official in the former administration tweeted:

I knew Jeffrey Frankel. A good, loyal American. Is it too much to ask that we hold off on the speculation for 24 hours?

And an MSNBC anchor tried to send the same message with a smile:

Radical suggestion. When a human being, a person with family and loved ones, is found dead, can we all shut the fuck up? *sheesh*

But of course it was no good. No one could get enough of the Frankel death. The right assumed the left had got rid of him because he knew too much about the previous president, though what possible threat that could pose now they didn't explain. The left believed the right had killed him because he was poised to embarrass the current President by revealing some devastating secret. And still others, striking a sophisticated pose, suggested the White House was at war, with factions both supportive of and hostile to the President and that the latter camp had killed the doctor as part of this internal civil war. In making this argument, they usually named McNamara as head of the loyalist faction, but were all over the place when it came to the dissenters. A couple mentioned the Secretary of Health and Human Services, but that was it. One mentioned Bruton; nobody mentioned him.

It was time for dinner. He was seated next to Helene Kitson, the formidable chief executive of the Coalition for Shelter. He knew and liked her, but he could see from the start this was not going to be easy. An African-American in her late thirties, it would be a statistical miracle if she were not a firm supporter of the other party, even under normal circumstances. But these were not normal circumstances. And tonight she had a face like thunder. Still she managed to squeeze out an opening pleasantry.

'Mr Kassian, we are so grateful for you joining us tonight.'

'Glad to be here, Helene. And please: it's Bob.'

'Bob.'

He began cutting into his pyramid of smoked salmon, even as he braced himself. 'So what's on your mind, Helene?'

'Can I be completely candid?'

'I think you're going to be,' he smiled.

'I fear this city is going to explode.'

He stopped eating and put his silverware down. 'Really?'

'Yes, really. This is a racially diverse city, but it's a racially divided city too.'

'That's been true a long time, Helene.' He regretted that: it sounded condescending. 'What I mean is: go on.'

'What happened last week in Phoenix. White young men running through Latino neighbourhoods, pounding on doors, smashing shop windows, dragging out anyone they suspected of being an undocumented migrant—'

'The governor of the state has restored calm there now.'

'Sure, after twenty-four hours of what was basically a pogrom.'

'Those were terrible scenes, no doubt about it. But you can't really blame the—'

'I'm not talking about blame, Mr Kassian.'

'Bob.'

'I'm not *interested* in blame, Bob. I'm interested in *prevention*. And what I'm trying to say is, there's no reason that couldn't happen here.'

'In DC?'

'Sure. People think it's just a black–white thing here, but it's not. There's nearly a million Latinos in the DC metro area.'

'A million?'

'Yep. If you count the people who come here to work. A million.'

'And some of them are illegal?'

'Some will be undocumented, of course. That's not the point. It's people *thinking* they're undocumented that's the problem.'

'And going out to find them.'

'Just the whole idea of a deportation force has legitimized this kind of behaviour. You must see that, Bob. The moment your President started—'

'*Our* President. He's your President too.'

'The moment he set up that deportation force, he essentially said these people are an enemy within. They're a legitimate target.'

'Well, obviously I can't agree with that,' Bob said, finishing the starter on his plate. It was a formulation he was using often these days. Perhaps no one noticed the wiggle room it contained – provided by that 'can't' – but he did. Maybe it would have taken a lawyer to tease it out, but he knew he was not quite telling Helene Kitson that he *didn't* agree with her – just that he could not. It carried enough of a hint that he might well want to agree with her, if only his job allowed him to. Whether she heard it that way was a different matter.

'And you know what's incredible?' Kassian noticed she had barely touched her food. 'No one will dare write about this stuff.'

'In this city? Are you sure?' Kassian was smiling. 'People are not usually shy about voicing trenchant opinions around here.'

'Oh, that *used* to be true, I grant you. But, Bob, don't tell me you don't see it. This place is changing. It's *already* changed.'

'Changed? In what way?' He caught Pamela's eye, across the table. His wife could see that Helene was in her stride. She mouthed a single word: 'Sorry.'

'The press! They're so tame. Ever since he did that thing with the IRS. They're all scared he's going to come after them the same way.'

'Oh, I think that will come as news to my colleagues in the President's press team,' he said, offering a world-weary smile. But he knew she was right. In his first month in office the President had unleashed the Internal Revenue Service against the owner of one of the country's biggest newspaper groups, to pursue 'irregularities' in the parent company's tax affairs. When his opponents said this was a blatant attempt to gag a critical press, his defenders fanned out across cable TV to say it was no such thing: the President was just making sure that 'the richest people in America paid their fair share of tax'. Naturally, that produced a howling gale of mockery from the late-night comedians, who pointed out there was more evidence that Elvis was alive than there was that the President had ever paid a cent in income tax.

The more serious objection arose from the words of the

President himself. During the election campaign he had explicitly warned the owner of that newspaper, the one that kept needling him, that, if he won, he would use the full machinery of the federal government to come after him. At the time, people wrote it off as bluster. They assumed he was joking, talking like Tony Soprano, striking a street-fighting pose. But this, Kassian reflected, had proved to be one of those times, and there were many, when it was wise to take the President at his word: both seriously and literally.

Perhaps Kitson had seen Pamela's little mouthed apology, because now, as she sat back in her chair, allowing the waiter to remove her plate, she said, 'I'm sorry I'm giving you a hard time. You've shown us the good grace of coming to our annual dinner and here I am, beating up on you. My mother would not approve.' She smiled a wide, conciliatory smile which Kassian did his best to reciprocate.

'So tell me,' he said. 'How are things with the shelter? Are you getting what you need?'

'Well, events like this help. The time and generosity of people like Pamela.'

'I'm glad.'

'But of course, the need is great.' She paused. 'I don't want to beat up on you again.'

'It's OK.'

'Well, poverty is not going down, put it that way. People are really struggling. Including people who used to have a safety net.'

He gestured for her to explain.

'Veterans.'

'But that's always been an issue, hasn't it?' Kassian said, swiftly attaching the word 'sadly' to the end of his sentence.

'That's true. And most of them have got the VA. I'm talking about a specific kind of veteran.'

Kassian furrowed his brow.

'Latinos.'

'Ah.'

'They don't always want to go to the VA.'

'Because Veterans Affairs would demand—'

'Papers. Some of these men are undocumented.'

'But if they wore the nation's uniform, if they served—'

'Sometimes it's not about them. It's about their families. Maybe they themselves would be OK, because they served. But they've got a brother or a wife or a sister or a mom. These new rules—'

'The executive order?'

'They're harsh, Bob. And they're being implemented harshly. So you've got a veteran who a year ago would have gone straight to the VA for help. Maybe he doesn't want to be on anyone's radar right now. Doesn't want that knock on the door at his mom's house.'

'I had no idea.'

'We don't talk about it much. The comms team say it's too "contested".'

They both smiled at that. And then she apologized once more. 'See, I'm doing it again. The voice of doom! It's no good. If our board knew I was talking this way . . . I'm meant to be *inspiring* you.'

'No, no, you are inspiring me. Really.'

She patted him gratefully on the forearm and turned to talk to the man on her other side. And as the wheels in Kassian's mind started turning, he reflected on the meaning of the word *inspiration*. If it meant sparking an idea, then Helene Kitson, Chief Executive of the Coalition for Shelter, had done just that.

14

As Maggie scrolled through the tweets under the hashtag #FrankelDeath, she saw that, though it grieved her to admit it, McNamara had been right. Every wacko conspiracy theorist and crank was all over this one.

The White House doctor had been murdered by the previous occupant of the White House. He had been murdered on the orders of the *next* occupant of the White House (who apparently had already been selected and was currently serving as the minority leader in the Senate). Alternatively, he had been murdered by Russian intelligence, to demonstrate their reach. He had been murdered by a North Korean death squad, to serve as a warning to the bellicose US President. He had been murdered by the drug companies, because he had been urging the President to move on excessive charges for prescription drugs. The former Imperial Wizard of the Ku Klux Klan thought everyone was missing the obvious point:

Frankel was a Jew. The Rothschild banking elites killed

one of their own to put us off the scent. But it won't work! #WhiteRising

Tweets, Facebook posts, blogs – the world was full of experts on a death that had happened just a few hours ago and about which information was almost non-existent. People like Maggie, those she liked and followed on social media, were united in harrumphing their disapproval. Clearly, they sighed, Dr Frankel had been a troubled man driven to taking the ultimate action. How sick was our culture that people could not just accept that as the sorrowful truth that it was?

Ordinarily, Maggie would have placed herself in their camp. And yet, based not on her prejudice but simply everything she had seen and discovered today, she had to conclude that – just as a stopped clock is right twice a day – this time the conspiracists had stumbled across the truth.

Not the garbage about North Korea or the minority leader, admittedly, but the kernel of truth without which these theories could not even take root. They believed the suicide claim was a lie, and on that basic point they were right.

But where they came unstuck was motive. Why would anyone want to bump off the White House *doctor*? No one could have been further from the political action than him. He was scrupulously non-partisan, serving not just the previous president but the one before that. Maggie had checked his personnel file, supplied to her courtesy of Crawford McNamara. There was no history to speak of, no complaints lodged against him, no claims of indiscretion. Even if someone worried that he knew too much, they would have had no grounds to suspect he would ever leak. As far as she could see, he never had.

The key, Maggie felt, must lie with that meeting Frankel had had last night, with Bruton and Kassian. It was too much of a coincidence that, hours after a home visit from two of the most powerful men in the White House – and therefore the world – the doctor had ended up dead.

But what business would those two men have had with Frankel? He was way below them in the Washington food chain, in a city where such things mattered. For them to visit him at home was especially puzzling. Even if they had needed to see him, why wouldn't Kassian – as Chief of Staff – simply summon him to his office? Let's say Kassian was worried about the President's health; perhaps he had seen some alarming test results. He might well want a discreet word. But what would any of this have to do with the Secretary of Defense?

It struck her that she didn't know much about either man, not really. Their appointments had come when she was at the denial stage, barely paying attention to the news. She had spent most of those days during the transition either attempting to tie up loose ends for the outgoing president, listening to him as he tried to persuade her to stay for the good of the country, or wanting to curl up under the duvet, vowing not to emerge until four years had passed and this nightmare might be over. That was when she was not cursing the candidate who had lost, or else hating herself for . . . everything.

The result was that she had not read the long profiles of Bob Kassian, or tuned into the Senate confirmation hearings for Jim Bruton. The new President had nominated them, and as far as Maggie was concerned, that was indictment enough.

So now she dug into her laptop to see what she could see. Kassian first. Long-time party operative, brief spells in the corporate world, but otherwise a devoted servant and backroom player: his DC career had begun with stints serving as a legislative assistant and then legislative director to the senior senator from Ohio (who, Maggie noted, had been one of those slow to endorse the President during the primaries). Kassian had moved over to run party headquarters ahead of the last election cycle. They'd lost, but no one had blamed him. On the contrary, a New Yorker profile said he was widely credited with staunching the bleeding. 'With Kassian, a certain catastrophe became a mere defeat.'

He was solid and, truth be told, a little vanilla. He had never run for office himself, though there was, inevitably, some talk of him returning to his home state to seek the governor's mansion once he was done at the White House. But he had never faced the relentless scrutiny of a campaign, a process which tended to flush out the full life story.

The only point of genuine interest she could see, usually dispensed with in a paragraph or two, was that Kassian was a veteran. He had served in the army, 75th Ranger Regiment, after college, including a stint in Iraq during Desert Storm. There were plenty of boilerplate quotes – 'It was a privilege to serve my nation . . .' or 'Those of us who have worn the nation's uniform . . .' – but no detail. She wondered if, given his skill set and later career, he had in fact only ever been a bureaucrat in khaki, confined to a desk in HQ. She had come across plenty like that in her time: the only weapon they'd fired in anger was a computer keyboard.

The Secretary of Defense was much more of a known quantity. A Sunday talkshow favourite, General Bruton had been a key commander in the second Gulf War – though plenty suspected it was his record as a TV pundit rather than on the battlefield that had attracted the President's attention. (As a rule, the President tended to appoint only those who were TV regulars: he did little to dispel the impression that his chief insight on the world, even now that he sat in the Oval Office, came not from intelligence briefings or his advisers or books or the expert opinion of the think tanks, or even from the quality press, but from talking heads sounding off in thirty-second soundbites on television.)

Bruton too had had a brief spell in the boardroom and that gave Maggie an idea. She went back to the tab she'd left open with the fullest profile of Kassian, in the *Wall Street Journal*. She scanned her way through it till she reached the stint he'd had on the board of two companies before returning to politics. One was a pharmaceutical giant, the other a health insurer – both interests of his former boss in the Senate. Was this – medicine – the link to Frankel?

Now she toggled to the equivalent article on Bruton. His corporate experience was more extensive; he'd been involved as a director or board member of several firms. Predictably, they were defence industry contractors, one a supplier of high-end GPS equipment, another related to 'logistics', while a third was one of those 'Strategic Risk Assessment' outfits that always struck Maggie as highly dubious – inhabiting the twilight between government intelligence and the profit-seekers of private industry. She was not naïve; she knew these two worlds were linked by a revolving door and that most of these companies were staffed by ex-military and ex-CIA men. But it never smelled right.

She sat back and rubbed her eyes. She had hoped this area would yield the overlap between Kassian and Bruton that might somehow explain that late-night visit to Frankel and everything that followed. But she couldn't see the connection.

A buzz at the door. She checked her watch. It was late, later than Richard usually came over. Despite the hour, despite how tired she was, despite the absorption in the task, she felt that familiar tingle of anticipation. She repressed her desire. She needed to focus.

He came in, slung his bag on the couch and flopped into a chair. 'I am telling you, that place was *batshit crazy* today.'

'Over Frankel?'

'Like no one could talk about anything else. And all this weird shit going on around his office.'

Maggie passed him a glass of whisky, which he rejected. Without thinking, Maggie sipped at it herself. 'What kind of weird shit?'

'People going in and out; secretaries, clerks.'

'You saw this?'

'And they're coming out with boxes. Removing files, I guess.'

'Removing files?'

'They said they were following police instructions, to seal the office. But I didn't see any police.'

'So did they seal the office?'

'They said that's what they were doing. And I suppose eventually they locked it. But there can't have been much left in there by the time they'd finished.'

'Jesus.'

'I know. You're working on this, right?'

'Yes.'

'McNamara put you on it.'

She didn't reply. She was thinking.

He got up, shifted to the kitchen area and poured himself a glass of sparkling mineral water.

Maggie called out, trying to ask a question that didn't sound as if she was asking. Richard was a stickler; there was a strong risk he would use the words 'Chinese wall' again. As casually as she could, she said, 'So who told the secretaries to empty out Frankel's stuff?'

'I heard it was Kassian. Apparently he ordered it done first thing this morning. Soon as they found out.'

First thing this morning. Had Kassian known about this even earlier than Crawford McNamara? And if so, how? Maggie made a mental note to construct an exact timeline. If Kassian had somehow been aware of Frankel's death before any official word had reached the White House, that would raise an immediate and obvious suspicion.

'Anyway, what about you, Mags? What kind of day did you have?'

She began to tell him about the scene in the Frankel house, the intensity of the grief, the closeness of family and friends, how none of it pointed to suicide as far as she could see. He nodded along, saying that that was what people had been saying at work too. That Frankel was old school, a bit stiff, but solid. No one had ever suspected any kind of mental illness. Some had taken that to prove you never could tell, that people could hide even the darkest secrets. But most thought it made the whole thing a bit . . . suspect.

By now, they were next to each other on the couch and, maybe it was the whisky, or perhaps just the presence of him so close, but she finally lost the battle she'd been fighting since she'd heard the buzz at the door. She wanted him. The intensity of it almost surprised her. She had only to place her lips on his, and she felt herself devoured by desire.

Later, while he slept, she stared at the ceiling, going over each point again and again. She had told Richard about Helen Frankel's mention of a conversation between her husband and Kassian and Bruton, and he had not dismissed it but taken it seriously. She was encouraged. She was sure that the answer lay, somehow, with those two men.

The obvious thing to do was to go steaming into Kassian's

112

office first thing in the morning and demand an explanation for that late-night house call to Dr Frankel. But rushing in before she'd accumulated the evidence and thought through all the implications: no, she had made that mistake before, with huge and dreadful consequences. As the familiar nausea resurfaced, she vowed that she would not make that mistake again.

Now, in the dark, she reached for her phone, picking up where she'd left off on the laptop. Richard's naked chest, rising and falling with each breath, was lit by the glow.

She looked again at that profile of Bruton. A thought was forming.

Like every article on the Defense Secretary, it devoted most of its attention to his service during the Iraqi invasion of 2003. That was where he had made his reputation. But of course, Maggie now thought, his military career had not begun then. Given his age, he would have seen action long before.

She scrolled through that piece and others, but all were maddeningly vague. She decided to go around another way. Using just one hand, she typed in *Jim Bruton Desert Storm*.

As she'd expected, confirmation came swiftly. He had been a veteran of that war. But on his precise role, there was next to nothing. They'd both been there, Kassian and Bruton. But on what they'd done or where they'd been, details were strikingly scarce. These were public figures, people whose past lives were usually compelled to be open books. But, for both men, this chapter was, it seemed, deliberately opaque.

Maggie didn't understand it. She didn't know why or what possible connection it could have to Frankel's death. But something told her that she needed to know about this past. She would have to uncover what she guessed was a secret from long ago, shared by two men now at the very centre of American power.

15

'At ease, soldier.'

'Yes, sir.'

Jim Bruton waited for the click that meant the door of this, his inner office, was closed, before embracing the man in front of him. This was not the usual male bear-hug, fleeting and rote. It was sustained, a second or two longer than was required. The warmth between them was real.

'How long's it been, sergeant? Three years? Four?'

'It's been six years and seven months, sir. We last saw each other at Fort Bragg. I was working as a trainer and you came to—'

'Give the commencement address. Of course. You got a good memory, sergeant.'

They both paused. Jim reflected on the strangeness of this situation, two men calling each other 'sergeant' and 'sir', because that was what they'd always done and to change it now would be awkward. What would he call him? Sergeant Garcia? Julian? Nothing sounded quite right.

He took in the man opposite him. Bruton was glad to see

that he seemed to be in very good shape. Aged forty-five, his hair silvered now and cropped short, he carried no hint of the paunch that Washington life had bequeathed on Bruton (though somehow, he had noticed, not on Kassian). Difficult to tell through civilian clothing, but Garcia appeared lean, his muscles taut. Out on the street, he could have passed for a former athlete, maybe a professional coach. But his eyes were dimmed by a weariness that Bruton recognized. He had once had it himself. Maybe he still did.

'Well, as you can see, life comes at you pretty fast,' Bruton said, gesturing at his office. He suspected his old comrade was uncomfortable being here. Bruton was used to that. The Pentagon was an intimidating place for people not used to it. That was part of the point: power projection was the business this department was in. That was especially true of the inner sanctum, the Secretary's office. There were plenty of Pentagon veterans who never made it here.

It was all but designed to intimidate. Naturally, it occupied the most prestigious spot in the vast complex, on the third floor of the outermost of the Pentagon's five 'rings', directly above the grand portico entrance, facing the river. It was huge too, with three different meeting areas in the one room, including a circular table, big enough for four, on one side of the desk and a rectangular one, suitable for ten, on the other. On the walls, there were the requisite flags and portraits of previous holders of the office, of course, but also a long, horizontal digital display, showing the time of day in Washington, London, Baghdad, Kabul, Islamabad, Seoul and Moscow. (It struck Bruton as pretentious, but he'd never got around to having it removed.) The carpet was a shade of deep, presidential blue. But there any similarity with the Oval Office ended: this room was much bigger.

Still, none of this was the true source of what Bruton guessed was Garcia's discomfort. Even if the office had been small and understated, his guest would surely have been shifting in his seat. The problem, Bruton supposed, was that this was a man who had spent most of his adult life in the field, operating in the shadows, living off his wits. Even if he had retired a couple of years ago, suddenly being summoned to head office, having to behave like an employee of a big organization, must have felt wrong. The organization might be the Department of Defense, but to Julian Garcia it must still have felt civilian and therefore alien. Even being so close to an American city might have been unsettling: a career in active intelligence, on the ground rather than behind a desk, meant he was more used to the backstreets of Kabul or the desert wastelands of Iraq. People talked of corporate time-servers becoming institutionalized. They talked far less often about men like Garcia, who had become de-institutionalized. And yet it was a real phenomenon. Bruton knew that, because it had so nearly happened to him.

'What are you up to these days, sergeant?'

'Oh, the usual thing for men like me, sir. Security consultant. Saudi. The Emirates.'

'I'd heard something like that. We were lucky you were in the country. Such short notice.'

'Visiting my sister, sir. Family stuff.'

'Yes. I know about that. And I'm sorry.'

'But you know that wherever I'd been, sir – wherever it was in the world – I'd have come here. You only had to say the word.'

'That's good to hear, sergeant.'

'It's the truth. Twice you saved my life, sir, and those two times are only the ones I know about.'

'Well, we looked out for each other. All of us. That's what we did.'

'It's what we *do*, sir. Always.'

Bruton let out a sigh of unmistakable relief. That 'always' was especially welcome. 'I suppose you want to know why I've asked you here.' He signalled for the two of them to sit at the smaller table.

'I read from your file that, even at the end of your service, you were regarded as the best marksman in the United States military. Do you know your final set of scores?'

'They don't tell us, sir. Only if we make the grade.'

'That's right, isn't it? I remember that now.' He was speaking to himself as much as to his guest. 'Well, *I* know your scores. You closed out on a thirty-nine point nine-six average. Out of a possible forty.'

Garcia gave a tiny nod.

Bruton went on. 'You were an exceptional soldier, Garcia. From the very top of the top drawer. You have first-rate computer skills and have counter-intelligence experience in the field. I've read your file very closely.' He looked up. Garcia absorbed the praise but did not swell from it. Bruton could see that he was waiting for instructions.

The Defense Secretary leaned forward. 'Tell me something, Sergeant Garcia. You left the service nearly two years ago. It would be natural if you'd relaxed a little, if—'

'I'm still active, sir. I'm still fit. I've had to be. For my new . . . clients.' Bruton registered the hesitation over that last word.

'Well, that's good. Because I need you to undertake a mission that will require great sharpness. It's of such importance and such secrecy that you will take orders from me and me alone. No one else knows about it or can know about it. If word of this mission were ever to leak, I would deny it and would have to take drastic steps to sustain that denial. That might even mean drastic steps against you, sergeant.'

'I understand, sir,' Garcia said.

'I need you to take out a high-value target.'

Garcia neither nodded nor shook his head. He was waiting.

'This target will be well defended. Extremely well defended. And you will have to take him out in a public place. What's more, it will not be enough that you're not caught. There can be no trail of evidence or suspicion that in any way, because of our connection, implicates me. You'll soon see why. If that means you have to involve another person, then you can do it, but under the same conditions. It would have to be someone we would both trust with our lives. Do you understand what I have told you so far?'

'Yes, sir.'

'I should also warn you that you have nothing like the amount of time you need, not even close. This mission has to be complete within the next three days. You will have to start work as soon as you leave this office. Are you still with me?'

'Yes, sir.'

'Good. I wish I could say there was something in this for you. But there isn't. I can't even pay you. I can give you a few thousand dollars in cash, for the very basic costs. Some logistical help and back-up. But that's it.'

'I don't need payment, sir.'

Bruton felt moved by this man's loyalty and – though it would have sounded corny to say it out loud – his sense of duty.

'I have not yet told you the target for this operation.'

'No, sir.'

'I need to say something before I do that. I need to tell you that I am still the man who you knew on that battlefield, when you and I were side by side, up to our necks in blood and shit and piss. I am still the man who was proud to lead you and so many other good men, including the ones who never came back. I was ready to give my life to this country then and I am still. You need to know that none of that has changed. Not for me and, I suspect, not for you either.'

'That's right, sir.'

'In the order I'm about to give you, I act as a patriot, a man who has sworn to defend this republic. And when you accept that order, I hope you will see that you too will be acting as a patriot, serving this nation that we both love.'

'I understand, sir.'

'Good. I'm glad we understand each other. Because, Sergeant Garcia, your target is the President of the United States.'

There was a pause, as Garcia dipped his head, taking in what he'd heard. Something in his expression told Bruton that this instruction had not come as a complete surprise. Perhaps Garcia had intuited it even before he walked through the door, maybe even before he came to Washington this morning. He was no fool; he could read the newspapers, same as anyone else.

So he registered not shock, but rather the weight of the mission that had just been placed on his shoulders. And then, in a gesture that might have surprised them both, Julian Garcia got to his feet and, there, in his civilian clothes, he pulled his right hand towards his brow and delivered a crisp salute in the direction of the Secretary of Defense. Staring straight ahead, he said simply, 'Yes, sir.'

16

Landmannalaugar, Iceland, 7.40am, three weeks earlier
The long days suited him. Sunrise at four am, sunset at
eleven pm: he loved this time of year, the sense of endless
day. Each year it was the same story. Birkir Arnason would
stagger through the interminable, nocturnal winter and
would decide by early January, when the sun would show
its face for only four or five hours, that that was it, no more.
It was time to leave this strange little island and head to,
what the hell, California: he'd had plenty of offers.

But then spring would come and with it the evenings of
light and the mornings where it felt like no hardship to
spring out of bed at five am because the sun was there to
greet you. And his country ready to be unwrapped, after
months hidden under layers of snow, and to be revealed as
clean and perfect.

The best thing, he always said, about having founded a
start-up was not the money, but the autonomy that the
money made possible. Not yet thirty, he was the boss of a
company with two hundred employees working at headquarters in Reykjavik and several hundred more around the

world and with a share price that meant he was sitting on tens, maybe hundreds, of millions of dollars, should he ever choose to sell. But what was best was this: the fact that on a weekday morning in May, he could decide that he didn't want to go to the office today, that he wanted instead to jump into his super-Jeep with its absurdly wide tyres and ludicrously high chassis, and drive to the highlands, through waist-deep pools and along roads strewn with rocks the size of fists. All it took was one email. No one asked where they could reach him. (Most of them could take a guess.) No one asked when he would be back. No one judged him. He was the boss and he was free.

So now, as he walked, he closed his eyes and breathed in the pristine air. He barely needed to look around. He knew that on his right were hillsides that had turned a very particular shade of green, the colour of oxidized copper. He knew that he only had to swivel left to look over the field of rocks that resembled a deranged sculpture garden, each formation a troll cast in dark grey lava. He'd been here so often he could single out his favourite characters – the lawyer, leaning forward to make his point; the nun; the mother with her child – all frozen forever.

Now he headed up a sharp slope, the gradient just steep enough to be rewarding. He let his mind wander onto work. Had he been right to stand so firm? The deal on the table would have made him crazy rich. He would never have to work another day in his life. He could walk here every day, and spend the winters in Malibu or Sydney or wherever the hell he wanted. For a suite of games and apps, it was ridiculous money. His partners were surely right: they were young, they would think of other ideas. This was not their last shot.

But that was not his prime concern. His worry was not what his business meant to him, but what it meant to the buyer. It was not the same thing. For him, this was a company that had begun as an enthusiasm, a game he and his friends wanted to play: they'd invented it because they liked it. And now it had spread across the world, delighting kids in every language. What's more, and he didn't want to be pompous about it, but it was teaching them a thing or two, too. Each time they got a wrong answer they'd see the right one. It was only an app, but it stood for facts. Even for truth. It meant something.

He was not convinced the bidders quite saw it that way. For them, it was a toehold in a market they'd not yet conquered. It was a way to develop brand loyalty among kids, winning their devotion early, turning them into lifelong customers. (The research showed remarkable longevity for consumer habits developed in childhood.) For that reason, whatever the bidders' promises, he knew that the app's current name, the name he and his partners had chosen (it had come to them over a plate of chips on Vitastigur Street when they were first-year students), would be ditched, eventually. It would be replaced by that single word. It had to be. Why else were they prepared to pay out several billion dollars for a few games?

His buddies were desperate for him to say yes. As he reached the brow of the hill, looking at the snow that still capped the mountains across the valley, he succumbed again to guilt: with his controlling stake in the business and his decisive vote, he was the one standing between them and a life-changing fortune. They wanted to get on with their lives. He was denying them a future. And yet he knew they respected his judgement. When he told them to trust him, that they could make more magic together, they believed him. But now, under this vast blue sky, that only made him feel guiltier.

He looked downward, at the hikers' hut that marked the start and end of the trail. Almost no one here this early in the morning. Just that fellow solo walker, dressed all in black, who he'd spotted two hundred yards or so behind: a kindred spirit perhaps. He walked on.

As he threaded his way down the path, he marvelled for the thousandth time at the gashes in the ground from which steam rose, sometimes in thin, curling wisps, sometimes in full, locomotive clouds. The sense that the ground beneath his feet was a mere lid on this bubbling, roiling cauldron below had thrilled him as a child and it did still. Who knew what seismic brew was cooking down there? This whole lava field had formed so recently, they could put a date on it. He had learned it at school: 1477. Imagine that, the earth taking shape before your eyes. Beneath your feet.

He wheeled around. He'd heard a crunching sound and he expected to see someone coming up behind him, a walker who'd made brisk progress. But there was no one there.

Which meant Birkir Arnason was wholly unprepared for the blow that came. He suddenly felt himself shoved around his midriff, in the manner of a rugby tackle. Two strong arms had encircled his waist, while a shoulder was on his hip, pushing him backward. Still on his feet, he was now bulldozed fifteen yards off the path.

Until this moment, sheer surprise had prevented him fighting back. Only now did he let his fists fly, randomly lashing out at the black-clad figure whose grip on him did not loosen. He could not see his face. He still maintained the rugby tackle posture, so that his head was down. All Birkir could do was thump the man on the back. But it did no good.

He could feel that he was now on softer, boggier ground.

The air was becoming harder to breathe. It was harder to see too: he was enveloped in mist. He could sense the terrain was turning wet – and hot.

And now a thought hit him with full force, as hard as the attack a few seconds ago. He understood.

The realization made him push back, the adrenalin converting itself into new strength. With great exertion, he got his hands around the neck of his assailant and began to squeeze.

But it did not last long. The man simply released his grip on Birkir's waist, transferring his energy to his arms, which he used to force Birkir's hands off his throat. But that gave the prey a chance to escape the predator. Birkir began to run. He stumbled at first, but soon he was back on the trail.

Now he could get some momentum. He felt himself pick up speed. He was heading downhill. If only he could reach the hut, someone—

But then he felt himself fall forward, his face thudding into the ground. Only once he was down did he realize that the man had caught him by the ankle.

Birkir somehow wriggled away and got to his feet. But no more than a second or two later, the man in black, himself breathless, piled into him from behind, gripping him as he steamrollered him along the path, then off it. Once again, Birkir could sense the mist and the heat.

Then, with one shove into his back, he was down on the ground. His attacker pulled him for a yard or two by his ankles, heedless of the stones and plants that were cutting and tearing into Birkir's flesh. Horizontal like this, he was powerless. His head was pounding from the fall. The man was too strong for him. He knew what was coming.

Now he could smell it, the sulphurous reek of a hot

geothermal pool. Even at this moment, his brain was functioning well enough to determine that this man had chosen his spot well, striking just where the pools were at their most dangerous, reaching temperatures far beyond boiling point.

Birkir struggled, he shook, he tried to break free, but somehow he knew it was futile. He could barely see the man who was about to do this to him: his face was clouded in hot steam.

Was that his own voice begging for mercy? He could hardly tell. He was wondering only if he was about to be pushed into the seething waters head first, which would surely have the advantage of depriving him of all consciousness, or if he was about to feel his flesh burning. His brain flooded with the fear of being scalded alive.

In the last seconds, he wondered if anyone would ever know what happened to him, if any trace of his body or clothes would remain. Or would every last piece of him be dissolved in these waters?

He tried to draw a final measure of comfort from that thought: that he was about to be devoured and ingested by a landscape he had loved.

17

The White House, Wednesday, 9.23am
Walking the corridors, Maggie was trying to pick up what Richard had described, the sense of an office in the grip of rumour and speculation. The trouble was, so many of her usual ports of call were no longer here. Her most reliable sources of office gossip had, naturally, left with the transition. There were still too many faces she hardly knew. More importantly, there was no way of knowing if they were friend or foe.

The obvious starting point would be Eleanor, but she wasn't around. Maggie was just pulling up a legal pad, getting ready to organize her thoughts on one of its long, yellow pages when truly the last person she wanted to see – the man she was not ready to see – appeared. McNamara.

He announced his arrival with his usual trick, putting his head around the door first, knocking on it second. The appearance of courtesy, but giving her no chance to say no.

'If it isn't Margaret Costello, ace investigator.'

'Hello, Mac.'

'I'm not saying this, OK? Because if I did, I would be

creating a "hostile environment"' – the air quotes again – 'so these are words I am *not* saying. Are we clear? But – off the record – Richard is one lucky motherfucker. Those pants: ow! Smokin'!'

'Completely inappropriate.'

'Remember: I did not say those words. Not one of them.'

'One of these days, Mr McNamara, I am going to put my phone down on this desk, record the way you talk to female staffers and sue you for everything you've got.'

'I'm ahead of you, Ms Costello.' He emphasized the hard 's' on Ms, so it made a buzzing sound: *Mzzz*. 'I have the nerds working on that already. Now: to business. How's the Mysterious Case of the Suicidal Doctor?'

Maggie could feel her flesh crawl. The idea that she was helping this man appalled her. But now, she told herself, she had her own reason to do this work. Fuck McNamara. She wanted to find out what had happened to Frankel for her own sake: a crime had been committed which she could not ignore. Doing this work would enable her to get to the truth, regardless of whether that helped McNamara or not.

'Well, I know what you wanted from me on this.'

'Shutdown.'

'But I'm afraid it's not quite as simple as we'd hoped.'

Only now did McNamara sit down, pulling up a chair and putting his feet on her desk. Given that he was wearing shorts, Maggie believed there was a clear risk she might see what she very much did not want to see. She kept her gaze locked onto his eyes.

'What's happened?'

'I'm afraid I don't think suicide makes sense.'

'Shit.' He bit the top of his thumbnail. 'Why not?'

Instinct made Maggie keep back what she'd seen at the

Medical Examiner's office. 'The way his family spoke about him.'

'You've met the family?'

'Last night.'

'You were at the *shiva*?'

'Yes.'

'Rather you than me.'

'What's that? What did you say?'

'Never mind. What d'you find out?'

She shook her head and decided to stay focused. Remember, she told herself, it's in your interest to keep this channel open. 'You know, everything to live for. Daughter's wedding coming up. Devoted grandfather. Contented guy.'

McNamara was back to chewing his nail. 'No history of mental illness? Depression?'

'Not that anyone talked about. The opposite. Solid, stable man.'

'Or maybe they're covering up for him? Ashamed that the old man was cuckoo?'

'No. I don't think so.'

'So let's say you're right.' McNamara crossed his legs at the ankles, prompting Maggie to look at the floor. He was so close she could see the individual hairs on his calves. She could smell him, a thin layer of expensive cologne covering the sweat and what she imagined was the rotting stink beneath. 'Who on earth would want the White House doctor dead? Who would even care about that guy?'

'Well, you for one. If you thought he knew something about the President that would be embarrassing. Or damaging.'

'Now, now. Don't tell me you're reading all that shit online?'

'I've looked at some of it. Haven't you?'

'Never drink your own piss, Maggie. Oldest lesson in the book.'

Now she hesitated, wondering how much she should reveal of Kassian and Bruton's late-night visit to Dr Frankel. Her instinctive answer would be: nothing. Her level of trust in McNamara was zero.

But, realistically, what were the chances McNamara didn't already know what she knew? Also zero. She would be giving nothing away. But by seeing his reaction, she might gain something. She might also get some cash in the bank with McNamara, persuade him that she was, if not an ally, then at least useful to him. The more information she gave him, the more he might give her. That was how this town worked: information was the reserve currency.

And yet she held back. Just for now, she told herself. She could change her mind soon. But for the moment, this would remain her own private knowledge. What she had was valuable. It was worth holding onto.

Eleanor did not need warming up, chiefly because they had been friends from the first day Maggie arrived in this place. Back then, they were both new and, they eventually confessed to each other, both felt like imposters. Maggie was Irish, a former aid worker who'd cut her teeth as a peace negotiator, always more comfortable in the field than navigating the swamps of Washington. Eleanor was African-American, twenty years older than Maggie and had been middle-aged even then, a woman whose children had already grown. Her résumé consisted of decades working as secretary to the then-new president in his home state. For her, Washington was as distant as Versailles and half as appealing. She and Maggie had clicked instantly.

'Coffee?' Maggie said. Eleanor needed no further

persuasion. They headed out of the office together, crossing through Lafayette Square and heading for the Au Bon Pain on 17th and H: a regular route of theirs.

The first few hundred yards were taken up by Eleanor detailing all the serial office atrocities Crawford McNamara had performed. Other things being equal, she would of course have left the White House after the election. She felt as out of place in the new set-up as Maggie did. But, as she put it, she was at an age 'when you don't just walk into another job'. The former president had offered her a role, running his post-White House life. But after eight years in Washington her kids had put down roots and found jobs of their own. She couldn't just 'up and leave'.

Now she was having to shout over the protesters, whose 'Not My President' demo had become a permanent fixture, almost a vigil, outside the White House.

'The thing is, something like this doesn't happen every day, Maggie. It's happening every *hour*.'

'It's impossible to keep up.'

'Like, before there might be an "incident", or what have you, every six months. And they'd often be quite subtle, you know what I mean?'

'Like Shapiro and the coffee?'

'Exactly! Irritating or whatever. Maybe a little old-fashioned. But not like—'

'Outright naked misogyny.'

'No! This is something else.'

'Completely different category. And you know what, this whole *administration* is like that. They're doing ten things a day that, in normal times, even just one would be a proper scandal.'

Eleanor shook her head and said, 'I still like the way you say "proper", Maggie.'

As they ordered their coffee, Maggie asked Eleanor what gossip she'd picked up – meaning from the West Wing secretaries and PAs, who always knew everything.

Predictably, next to no one believed that Frankel had killed himself. Didn't fit the man; made no sense. Which was useful to hear, though Maggie was careful to say nothing of her own findings.

And then Maggie asked what proved to be a crucial question.

'Have you heard about anything out of the ordinary over the last few days – I mean, apart from *everything*, obviously—' They both smiled in mutual acknowledgement of how their once supremely efficient, scandal-free workplace had become a madhouse. 'Anything which might, I don't know, have been stressful for Dr Frankel?'

'Well, you heard about Sunday night, right?'

'Some big domestic with the missus?'

'What?'

'Didn't he have a bust-up with the First Lady?'

'Oh, maybe that's what it was.'

'No, go on,' said Maggie. 'What were you going to say?'

'Well, maybe it's wrong. You know what people are like, they often talk such horseshit.'

'All right, but humour me. What did you hear?'

'Just that he flew into a complete rage in the middle of the night. Summoning aides, waking everyone, storming into the Sit Room.'

'The Sit Room?'

'That's what I heard.'

'And do you know what it was about?'

'Just that he was swearing and shouting. The staff in the Residence were terrified, apparently.'

'Or what might have sparked it?'

'You know Martinez? The butler?'

'Wasn't he sacked?'

'He's leaving in the summer. Anyway, he says the boss was watching the Sunday talkshows. You know, he records them?'

'So something to do with that?'

'Maybe. I mean who the hell knows with this guy?'

On the way back, Maggie listened to Eleanor complain some more about McNamara, and then talk about her son, before settling on the perennial topic of her daughter's useless boyfriend. Eventually that prompted the older woman to give her a raised eyebrow which, Maggie knew, was an inquiry as to how things were going with Richard. Maggie considered confessing her worries about the flirting she thought she had spotted with the First Daughter, but thought better of it. It would only sound ridiculous. Besides, Maggie had always picked up from Eleanor a vague sense of disapproval when it came to Richard. Nothing you could put your finger on, but enough that Maggie didn't want to feed her any ammunition.

They said goodbye in the corridor. Then Maggie made straight for the Situation Room.

The duty officer was unfamiliar, but she was undeterred. She asked if they could speak in a side room. She could see that he was on secondment from the CIA, which she decided to view as an advantage. He would be used to internal investigations by the Agency's office of the Inspector General and so she simply said that he should see her as doing the equivalent job for the White House.

She asked him what had happened on Sunday night.

He looked her straight in the eye and said that he had not been briefed on that.

'On what?'

'On what happened on Sunday night.'

'But you know something happened?'

'Like I say, ma'am, I was not on duty and I have not been briefed on that incident.'

'So there was an incident?'

'I've not been briefed, ma'am.'

They went round and round like that until Maggie, exasperated, asked to see the duty log for that evening. He stalled on that too, saying that would require the permission of the Watch Commander.

'All right,' she sighed. 'I would like to see the roster of Watch Teams for the last two weeks.' Pre-empting any resistance, she added, 'And under Executive Order 13490, Ethics Commitments by Executive Branch Personnel, Section Seven, the provision relating to Assent to Enforcement, I have the authority to demand immediate sight of those documents. Which is what I am doing. Right now.' She smiled sweetly.

He attempted to say that it would take some time to produce a hard copy. She gave that short shrift, saying that he could save them both some time by sitting down in front of a computer and logging into the roster. She would hover over his shoulder.

His reluctance was obvious, but he did what he was told, scrolling through the calendar until he reached the overnight shift that took in the early hours of Monday morning. As she expected, there were five names: three duty officers, a communications assistant and an intelligence analyst. She scribbled all five names down, but she knew that for her purposes it was the comms officer she wanted.

'Mary Rajak,' Maggie repeated. 'And how can I reach Ms Rajak?'

'I'm afraid Lieutenant Rajak is on leave, ma'am.' Maggie was sure she saw a hint of a smile.

'Leave? For how long?'

'Indefinite, ma'am.'

'I don't understand.'

'Lieutenant Rajak is on sick leave, Ms Costello. She's been signed off for stress.'

18

East Falls Church, Virginia, Wednesday, 12.44pm
Julian Garcia would have dropped everything, wherever he was on the face of the earth, to answer a call from Jim Bruton, the man he would think of forever as his commanding officer. As it turned out, he had not had to make too great a journey.

When he got the call – *number withheld*, it had said on his phone – from the Defense Secretary the previous night, he had been visiting his sister in Philadelphia. After what they had both been through, it wasn't right to let her suffer alone. Even though it had been so many years since they had lived under the same roof, even though her husband and children were strangers to him, he found it helped a little. Just to be with someone whose memories overlapped with his.

Besides, he had another reason to make the short journey south towards Washington.

He had heard about Jorge Hernandez's situation perhaps six weeks ago. The men of the unit, they had their own ways to stay in touch. They couldn't use Facebook or email, obviously. But they had their ways. 'Jungle drums,' Jorge called it.

So when Bruton's call came, Jorge came straight to mind. Garcia had planned it immediately: he would go to the Pentagon and come here directly afterwards. He knew it was an indulgence; he had no time for such a detour. Bruton had given him a month-long mission to complete in three days. But, as he had told the Defense Secretary, they were part of a group that looked out for each other. Always.

Hernandez's home was modest, a bungalow on Roosevelt Street, with a small car outside. Tidy, designed to attract no attention. Garcia recognized it: in the places he had lived – 'homes' would be overstating it – he had created much the same look.

As soon as Hernandez opened the door, Garcia could see the situation was as bleak as he'd heard. His comrade was stooped, the skin around his neck loose, his face a sallow shade somewhere between grey and yellow.

Jorge managed a smile. 'Welcome to the horror show,' he said.

He ushered Garcia into a living room, sparsely furnished – a couple of fake leather chairs and a big TV playing cable news – then disappeared into a kitchen and came back holding two beers. 'It's early, I know.'

They clinked bottles and Hernandez spoke first, jabbing at his own chest. 'It's in here. My gullet. The *oesophagus*, the doctors call it. Bottom line: I can't eat much and I'm gonna die soon.'

Garcia chugged back the beer. 'That's what I heard.'

A long pause and then Hernandez said, 'I'm glad you came. It's good to say goodbye.'

Garcia didn't argue with him. 'Even a cat got only nine lives.'

They both smiled. Then Garcia spoke again. 'I mean, how many times did you cheat that motherfucker?'

'Which motherfucker's that?'

'The angel of death. Five times? Six?'

Hernandez liked the question. He counted on his hands. 'Basra, twice. Tora Bora, twice. Tikrit, once. Pakistan, once.'

'When you eyeballed OBL?'

'I wasn't even counting that one. Seven.'

'At least.'

Another pause, another swig of beer. 'Can you get around at least?'

'That's the hell of it. I look like shit, but I can function. I can walk, I can drive. You'd meet me and think, "All right. He might have a year or two."'

'But?'

'It's probably a few weeks. Anyway, one thing I can tell you. The only thing worse than dying is talking about it so goddamn much. So: what brings you to sunny Virginia?'

'I can't talk about it.'

'Ah, that's exciting. I wish I had something I couldn't talk about. I mean it. *A mission*. That would be good. Instead of sitting here all day, watching that asshole.' He gestured towards the TV, where – muted – the President was holding forth to a gaggle of reporters in the Oval Office. The subtitles said he was denouncing immigrants. Not just undocumented ones but all of them. *'We're a big country, but not that big,'* the President was saying. *'Now if you look at the last election, and if you counted only the people whose grandparents were born here . . .'*

Jorge Hernandez smiled a bitter smile. 'I guess neither of us would make that cut-off.'

'Nope.'

'Can you believe that? Good enough to kill and be killed

for this country, but our President says we don't deserve to vote.' Hernandez began to cough.

'Take it easy, brother,' Garcia said, leaning forward to take the bottle of beer from his friend's hand.

'I'm good, I'm good.' Jorge brushed off some foam – part beer, part saliva – that had landed on his thighs. 'But I wish I could do something. I don't have anyone here.'

'What about your nephew? The one you were always writing to?'

'Antonio? I got him through college. Texas A&M. He was at grad school. That kid's some kind of genius, Julian.'

Garcia could feel a 'but' coming.

'But after my brother was gone, the wife, she never liked me. She wouldn't let me speak to the boy no more. Six years, no contact.'

'That's rough, man.'

'But two weeks ago they deported him. Put the boy – he's got, like, a PhD or something – they put him on a bus, dumped him in Mexico.'

'But your family's not—'

'—even from Mexico. That's right. But to that guy,' he gestured at the mute President on the TV screen, 'we're all the same.'

He coughed some more and then spoke again. 'You don't need me to tell you that. I heard about your mom.'

Garcia nodded.

'So don't tell me anything, obviously. But this job you've got to do. Is it high-risk?'

'Yes.'

'Your life in danger?'

'If I do it properly, yes.'

'What does that mean?'

'It sounds strange, but it means that right now I think

138

the only way to secure all the objectives of the mission is if someone gets caught. If I go free, if I walk away, that could risk everything. They need someone to blame, so they can say "Case closed."'

'And when you say "caught" – I don't know who the enemy is – but if you get caught, what does that mean? Do these people take prisoners? Or are you going to end up getting your head chopped off on YouTube?'

'Not that.'

'But maybe dead?'

'Maybe.'

'And you would do that? You would do that for him?' He didn't even look at the TV screen this time.

'I wouldn't do it for him, no.'

They were quiet together. Garcia could hear the clock ticking in his old friend's kitchen.

Finally, Hernandez spoke once more. 'Why did you come here today?'

'I came here to say goodbye, Jorge.'

'And a dying man gets to have a last request, don't he?'

'Yes. Yes, you do.'

'Tell me, is there anyone you trust in the world more than me?'

'No one.'

'Good. So listen to what I have to say.'

19

It turned out that Mary Rajak lived with another woman, also working for the Defense Intelligence Agency. She was young enough for that to mean they were simply room-mates, or they could have been a couple. There was no way to know for sure; the file was silent on that issue.

Parked just down the street, but with a clear line of sight to the front door of the small, timber-clad house the two women shared on Leighton Avenue, Maggie glanced once more at the printout she had obtained (with Eleanor's help). It was a personnel file and therefore yielded little: born and raised in rural Nebraska, stellar college career, straight to the DIA, highly rated as an analyst. Maggie didn't need a file to tell her that. It was obvious. Only the best and brightest were loaned to the White House.

Maggie had been here twenty minutes, trying to work out a gameplan. She had wondered about sending a text but found it impossible to strike the right tone. Every formulation she tried sounded like a trap or a hoax. *Hi Mary, you don't know me but I'm a colleague of yours at the White House . . .*

The car radio was on. Checking the time, Maggie turned it up.

This is NPR News in Washington. The United States has appealed for calm in its ongoing nuclear stand-off with North Korea. Speaking following a meeting with his French counterpart at the Pentagon this morning, Defense Secretary Jim Bruton said he hoped the North Koreans were choosing to 'pause and reflect' rather than allowing the situation to deteriorate further.

Diplomatic sources in Pyongyang, however, reportedly believe that any pause is likely to be short-lived, and that plans for further nuclear testing remain active . . .

Maggie listened closely as the clip of Bruton played. He sounded firm, even unbending. But he was not reckless; he was not bellicose. Given the President he served, Maggie found his voice unexpectedly reassuring.

My message to Pyongyang is clear. This is a dispute we can resolve calmly and that is our intention. But let there be no misunderstanding. The United States will always defend itself, through overwhelming force if necessary.

Maggie wondered who the real audience for that remark was. Obviously the DPRK. But she suspected there was some internal positioning going on too: there always was. Instinct made her wonder if the reference to 'overwhelming force' was there to placate the hawkish faction in the White House, perhaps even the man at the top.

Now the radio was on to a second story, outrage over a tweet the President had sent in the middle of the night, relating to a sixteen-year-old singer who had just won a TV talent contest. Maggie could hear the embarrassment in the voice of the female reporter who had to repeat the tweet verbatim: *That skirt far too short for a teenager on primetime. Still, if she wants to perform a private show for me @WhiteHouse, the answer is yes!* Women's groups had condemned the

President. His allies said he had clearly intended to be humorous and complimentary to the young woman, who had told Fox News she was 'thrilled' by the President's remarks.

Next came an item about Silicon Valley mourning the tragic death of Icelandic tech pioneer Birkir Arnason – missing for a few weeks, police had now concluded that he had stumbled and fallen into a geothermal pool on a hike in his native country – but Maggie was not listening. She was thinking about Bruton and the North Korean situation. Not so long ago, she'd have been involved in a crisis like this. The previous president would have wanted to hear her views, especially on negotiation strategy. That was her background, after all: peace mediation. She could imagine what she'd be saying, if she were in the room. *We have to give them a way to climb down the tree. We need to allow them not to lose face . . .*

But that was a lifetime ago. She was not in the room now. She was here, with a job to do.

Much as she dreaded the prospect, Maggie realized there was only one way to do it. She would have to knock on Mary Rajak's door, cold.

She knew the woman was inside. She could see her car parked on the street, its plates helpfully detailed in the personnel file. So Maggie ventured up the path and knocked. Somehow a knock, rather than the bell, seemed less intrusive. There was no response.

Maggie tried again. Still nothing. Then she tried the bell. Nothing. She turned around and looked at the front lawn. Overgrown.

Maggie pulled back the screen door, moved close until her mouth was almost touching the pane of glass and spoke.

'Mary, you're not in any trouble, I promise. My name's

Maggie, I work in the Counsel's office at the White House – and I'm on your side. I just need to talk.' She paused, before saying again, for good measure, 'I promise you, you're not in trouble.'

Still nothing.

Maggie didn't leave, but decided to take a calculated risk. Actually, 'calculated' was flattering herself. It was based on nothing more than a hunch. She knocked on the glass door. 'Just so you know, Mary: I've been working at the White House for a few years. I was not appointed by this President.' She paused to let that sink in. 'I came to work for the previous one.'

Now there was movement, a shadow which she took to be Mary. Maggie guessed she'd been sitting on the stairs, out of view, listening.

A few seconds later, she was there, on the other side of the glass. Wearing grey sweatpants and a loose T-shirt, she looked pale, drawn, her hair pulled back into a serviceable ponytail. Her eyes seemed to be sunk into hollows. She did not smile but said in a quiet voice, 'Can I see some ID?'

The door opened a crack, allowing Maggie to squeeze her White House pass through, holding it up long enough for Mary Rajak to read it properly. Instinct made her take a pace back; she wanted to give this woman space.

At last the door opened fully. Rajak said nothing. She simply turned around and started walking towards the kitchen. Maggie followed. They sat at a small table. Mary didn't offer her anything to drink. Maggie took that not as rudeness, but as confirmation that this woman was in an awful state.

'Mary, I'm glad you let me in. Thank you.'

She said nothing. Maggie thought of the personnel file, including its beaming photo. That Mary Rajak was dynamic,

143

confident. The woman in front of her – hunched, listless – could have been a different person.

Maggie tried again. 'I see you were on duty on Sunday night. The overnight shift.'

A small nod.

'And you've not been back since. I'm guessing something happened that night. Something bad.'

Now Rajak met Maggie's eye. Her expression was accusing but, more than that, it was . . . wounded. Maggie understood that expression, very deeply.

'You felt let down. Am I right, Mary?' Another pause. 'Who let you down?'

Now Rajak spoke. In a quiet voice, she said: 'If I talk to you, what happens to me?'

'Nothing happens to you unless you want it to happen. What you tell me is in the strictest confidence. I will do nothing with it, unless and until you decide you want me to do something.'

'And so you won't tell anyone we talked?'

'Not unless you tell me to.' Maggie smiled. 'Look, Mary. I know something happened that night and I need to build up a picture of what it was. I don't need to say who told me. That's how this works. White House staff are allowed to talk to me and I'm allowed to keep what they say confidential.'

Rajak stood up, went to the refrigerator, brought out a bottle of 7-UP and a couple of glasses and put them on the table. Suddenly, Maggie was struck by how young this woman was. Without even meaning to, Maggie put her hand on hers. 'You take your time.'

Rajak proceeded to describe what had been a turbulent, terrifying hour. The President had suddenly appeared in the Situation Room shortly after three am, ranting and raving about North Korea and Option B and 'teaching those motherfuckers a lesson'. Trailing after him was his military aide, clutching the briefcase that contained the black book and the nuclear codes. The nuclear football. 'I've never seen a man look so frightened in my entire life,' Mary said.

The President had been flushed and irate and instantly demanded to be put through to the Pentagon War Room. It all happened so fast, the duty team could barely take in what was going on. 'We had been monitoring events all night, as always. There'd been no attack on the United States, no missile launch, no test, no report of any incoming threat. We didn't understand it.'

Maggie could barely believe what she was hearing. She attempted to control the expression on her face, to look unfazed. She had learned that people in Mary Rajak's situation found it much easier if they could persuade themselves that they were merely confirming information that was already known. Signal that they were in fact making a stunning revelation and they could get spooked – and clam up. But while she could at least try to arrange her features, she had no control over her pallor – and Maggie could feel the blood draining from her face. She suspected she had gone ghostly white.

Rajak went on. 'The senior officer was trying to get the President to calm down. "Please explain exactly what you want us to do, sir", that kind of thing. He just wanted him to take a breath. But it was no good. "What the fuck has it got to do with you?" he said.'

Maggie nodded.

'He just wanted to be put through to the War Room. We all knew what that meant. I mean, he had the football right there.'

'The aide was holding it?'

'Yes, he's got the briefcase and I can see his hands are trembling.'

'So what did you do?' Maggie could guess the answer.

'It's strange. Even without talking about it, without even needing to say it, we all kind of understood that we had to buy ourselves some time. The duty officer turned to us, and just with his eyes – he sort of opened them wide, like this – he was telling us, you know, "Do something, anything, to stall."'

Maggie knew what was coming. 'And you're the comms officer. So you start making calls.'

'Yes. I called the Defense Secretary.'

'Is that what you're trained to do?'

'No. That's just it. The rules say that if the President wants to order a nuclear strike, then he can do it. Just like that. Doesn't need to consult anyone.'

'So why did you call the Defense Secretary?'

'Don't you get it? We were *desperate*. This guy was going to blow up the whole fucking planet.'

Only then did Maggie notice the ends of Rajak's fingers: they were red raw, the skin picked around the nails, down to the quick. 'Of course. I completely understand. Calling General Bruton was smart. Did he help?'

'I don't know what he did. I just wanted them to get down there.'

'Them?'

'Him and Mr Kassian.'

So that was it, thought Maggie. 'Did either of them manage to speak to the President?'

At that, Maggie noticed, Rajak seemed to bristle, her back stiffening. She got up, taking her glass to the sink and began to wash it.

'Mary?'

146

She said nothing. She just stood there, her back to Maggie.

'Did something else happen, Mary?'

Maggie got to her feet, walked over to Rajak and placed a hand on her shoulder. 'It's OK,' she said. 'You don't have to tell me.'

Slowly, Rajak turned around until she was facing Maggie. Her eyes were glittering. She reached for a tissue and blew her nose. 'Actually, that's what I thought you were here for. I thought you'd heard. Or maybe there was a recording or something, though I don't think they have it there, I'm not sure.'

This poor woman sounded so confused. Maggie gestured toward the table. 'Why don't you tell me in your own words?'

'I'd got Secretary Bruton on the line. I told the President. I said he could pick up the call in one of the conference rooms. And he said, "Why don't you show me where that is?" So I go out and he's behind me, and he asks me to fog the windows. You know that's—'

'Yes, I know.' It was a feature in the small breakout rooms that were part of the Situation Room complex: at the flick of a switch, you could render the windows opaque, allowing the President to talk to a foreign counterpart or one of his generals in complete privacy.

'So I do what he says and I lean over to the phone, to put Secretary Bruton through, and before I can get to it, the President reaches for my hand and grabs my wrist. I thought he was just stopping me from putting the call through.'

Maggie nodded. She hoped her eyes were transmitting all the sympathy and empathy she was feeling. She was thinking not only of the woman in front of her but also of Liz, her sister, and Liz's seventeen-year-old student, Mia, the young, frightened girl who had taken her own life. And of the cleaner in the White House Residence. And all the countless others.

Mary blew her nose again. 'And then he . . . he—'

'It's OK, Mary.'

'He lunged at me. Not with his face, with his hand. He just grabbed me. *There*. And hard too, he squeezed hard.' She looked at the floor. 'He said something to me too.'

Maggie paused and waited until she was sure that Mary wanted to be asked. 'What did he say, Mary?'

'He said, "Don't say anything. Don't think anything. I don't need any of you to think. I'm the brains round here. You're just . . ."' Mary dipped her head. Without even seeing her face, Maggie knew she was blushing: she could feel the heat radiating from Mary's face. Her shame seemed to throb.

'You're just what, Mary?'

'He said, "You're just . . . cunt. That's what you are."'

'And he said this as he grabbed you there?'

'It was so *angry*, you know what I mean? Like it had nothing to do with sex at all. Just like that part of me was an object that he wanted to press hard in his hands, as if he was getting all this frustration out.'

'I understand – and I'm so sorry. What happened then?'

'He stormed back into the main room and I don't know what happened after that. I just sat in that conference room trembling. I couldn't go back in. Not right away. I stayed in that room – and then I vomited into the trash.'

Maggie gave Rajak's hand a squeeze. 'You're very brave to have told me about this, Mary. I'm guessing you've told no one else.'

'I didn't want to.' She looked at Maggie, her eyes rimmed in red. 'I was worried it might compromise national security. Maybe information like that could be used against the United States?'

Maggie wanted to hug this woman, just a few years younger than her, but so full of idealism and innocence. Wanting to see the best in her country, wanting even to see the best in a President who had abused her trust – who had abused her.

She stayed there a while longer, holding Mary Rajak's hand, repeating several times the obvious, but necessary, truth – that this was not her fault – and urging her to see that she had done everything right. Her decision to call Kassian and Bruton may well have averted a global catastrophe.

'You know what I like to think?' Rajak sniffed, just before Maggie left. 'Well, we were trying to buy time, weren't we? So maybe, even though it was so horrible, maybe those few seconds in that side room made a difference.'

At the front door, Maggie gave the woman her cellphone number then walked back to her car, imagining those crazed few minutes just three nights ago. She imagined the calls to Kassian and Bruton, scrambling those men awake in the dead of night. She imagined the conversations each of them had had with Rajak – and then with each other. Now she began to see how the next few hours had unfolded, until Dr Jeffrey Frankel lay dead with his brains among the twigs and stones and mud of Rock Creek Park.

And once she could picture that, she could see what was coming next.

20

At school his teacher had told him that he lied so well he could be a writer one day. He had laughed at her, loudly, so that the other boys would hear him. He wanted them to know that, like them, he considered the idea too soft – 'too gay' were the exact words – even to entertain. He was Julian Garcia, the strongest kid on the block. He was going to be a soldier.

He thought of her now, that teacher – Miss Green was her name – and here, silent and alone, decided to give her some credit. She had seen something in him and she wasn't wrong. He did lie well. And he did like making up stories. But he had been right too. He had grown up to be a soldier.

He had become a sergeant in the Rangers, engaged in covert operations. At first, most of his work had relied on his physical strength, the fitness he had developed once he was recruited away from the Rangers to train at Fort Bragg with the 1st Special Forces Operational Detachment-Delta: Delta Force. The selection process alone had involved a timed eighteen-mile 'ruck-march' through the night, carrying thirty-five pounds in his rucksack. Once that was done, it was forty miles – again, timed – with a forty-five-pound rucksack on his back and across rough, steep terrain. Eventually, he was clearing distances of a hundred miles or more, learning to ignore the weight on his back even as it cut deep welts in his shoulders, and navigating himself across vast distances with no equipment – no phones back then – except his weapon. A compass was a rare luxury.

In time, he had developed a specialism. He did well in the language classes, taking Arabic and Russian, but was especially adept with a computer keyboard. From the earliest days of the internet, he knew his way around its byways and backstreets. He had done a couple of secondments with Cyber Command, deepening his understanding of counter-intelligence. As the technology had developed, so had he: through a combination of encryption and imagination he steadily became expert in crisscrossing the online world in disguise, sometimes trailing a false identity behind him, but always leaving no trace of his own.

It was the perfect preparation for the task he now faced. But as he immersed himself deeper in it, he understood that technical prowess would only take him so far. This was about more than algorithms and hacking skills. This was a project of the imagination. He was in the process of inventing a fictional character, just as Miss Green had had them do in class in one of those assignments he had to pretend he did not enjoy. Except this character would live not on a page in his exercise book, but in the real world. He was creating a man.

He looked around at the other people here, in the middle of the afternoon. The usual crowd for a public library: a group of schoolchildren, supervised by three or four teachers, all female. An older man, typing with one finger, alternating his gaze between keyboard and screen with each stroke, a pen and paper at his side. Another methodically studying that day's newspaper, reading each page in turn, as if it were a book. One more asleep in his chair, his snoring just quiet enough that no one had the heart to shake him awake. Needless to say, this being Anacostia, almost all of them, youngest to oldest, were black. He looked around, to check if he was the only Latino man here. If he was, and if someone remembered that, it was no disaster.

He dug into his pocket and pulled out a new USB stick, a flash drive with plenty of memory. He found the slot on the machine, a fairly wheezy old PC, and pushed the stick in.

Next he went on the PC's internet browser and typed in five letters. T-A-I-L-S. There was a string of entries, but he clicked on the second one. Up came a page, so basic it might have been set up as a school project. In purple and white, with just one logo and no photos or video, it described itself as 'the amnesiac incognito live system' and promised 'Privacy for anyone anywhere'. Garcia clicked on 'Install' and waited for the software to download onto the USB stick.

Once it had, he removed the stick and reached into his shoulder bag for his laptop. It was a basic machine bought an hour ago with the cash he'd been given – though he had taken care to scuff it up a bit, for appearances' sake. He popped in the USB drive and fired up the computer, booting it from Tails rather than the laptop's own operating system. That way, he would be able to wander around the internet with total anonymity, leaving no trace on this or any other machine. If he wanted to send a message, it would be encrypted. He now had a one-way on-ramp online: he would have access to everyone, but they would have no access to him.

He gazed at the blank screen, an artist's empty canvas. He began with that primary layer of modern identity, a Facebook profile. He left the photograph blank; he would take care of that later. For now, it was the words that mattered.

In Spanish he wrote:

Jorge Hernandez. Patriot, Militant, Fighter!

He liked the exclamation mark. Now he wondered about italics.

Jorge Hernandez. Patriot, Militant, Fighter!

That looked better. Perhaps capital letters on the word *FIGHTER!* Yes, that was good.

He hesitated, a twinge of guilt passing through him once more. He knew his old friend was about to die, that Hernandez believed he only had a few more weeks at most, but here Garcia was killing him a second time – destroying his good name. They had talked about that, Jorge and him, at length. But Hernandez had been adamant.

He'd always been a smart man but, if anything, illness seemed to have sharpened him. With a few, well-aimed questions – and the honest answers Garcia had given in reply – he had worked out the mission Garcia had been given. The sudden summons to Washington, DC, coupled with the fact that their former commanding officer now served as the Secretary of Defense, could not be explained away that easily. 'That man has the entire American army at his command,' Hernandez had smiled. 'Why the fuck would he call for a washed-up old *spic* like you?'

Julian tried to resist, to say that Jorge had no reason to get drawn into this. 'Live out your final days in peace.'

'That's exactly what I don't want to do. Just sitting here, wasting away, watching the TV and eating babyfood I can't taste. I'm a soldier. Only thing I was ever good at.'

As for the mission itself, he needed little persuasion. For one thing, he felt the same debt of loyalty to Jim Bruton that Garcia did – that they all did. 'I'd have been in a box long ago if it hadn't been for that man.' But the target made sense to him too. As Hernandez put it: 'All the family I have in the world is my nephew. And that asshole kicked him out of the country.'

Garcia had explained what was at stake: that this process would mean the destruction of Jorge's reputation. 'After you're dead, a lot of people will hate you.'

'But I won't care. I'll be dead.'

Garcia warned him: this would trash the Hernandez name.

'Listen, my friend. My mother is dead. I have no wife and no sons and no daughters.'

'There's still your nephew.'

'Something tells me the boy will understand.'

In the end, Garcia had surrendered to his old comrade's determination. The man would not back down. 'I'm dying, Julian. If you let me do this with you, you'll be giving me a lifeline. You'll be letting me believe my life actually means something.'

'It could be very messy, Jorge. The way this—'

'Don't say any more. This is what I want. It is my last request.'

So Garcia had nodded. They had shaken hands and then hugged, sealing their agreement.

And now he was here, in front of this computer. The immediate requirement was to assemble the posts which, with a few keystrokes, he could dupe the machine into thinking Jorge Hernandez had made not today but over the last two years. This would be time-consuming but not dull. He had sought out a half dozen individuals on Facebook who, he had decided, shared this new Hernandez's politics.

He looked at the articles or videos they had posted and, when the fit was right, he had Hernandez post them too.

The choices made themselves. Condemnations of the President's rhetoric against immigration from eighteen months ago; condemnations of his action against undocumented migrants since taking office. Videos from Univision, op-eds from the *Miami Herald* and *La Opinion*, and memes and GIFs galore. He took particular liking to a GIF of the then candidate eating a taco, which he had Hernandez mock directly.

You wanna know where you can shove that taco, asshole?

Most of the articles or posts he shared without comment, but occasionally he appended a little note of his own. For those, he thought back to the handful of letters and emails Jorge had showed him, to give Garcia a sense of the way he wrote. (Naturally, and helpfully, Hernandez, like Garcia – like all of them – had no social media profile of his own: this was virgin territory.) Accordingly, he was sure to include at least one spelling mistake in each post he created. Introducing an ABC News report on the Deportation Force, he wrote:

You cant deport a whole comunity.

Garcia scrolled through what he had so far. He had not yet pressed the button that would make the page go live. That too could wait. Jorge Hernandez was not yet ready to be launched into the world. Garcia imagined the context in which this would be read, and by whom. How they would search for clues, how they would need a stand-out line or two, one that would appear to make sense of the madness they had just witnessed. Judged like that, he could tell something was still missing.

He took a unilateral decision, beyond the scope of anything

he and the Secretary of Defense had discussed. A quick search offered up multiple options, but he settled on a line he found in Psalms 146:9. *The Lord watches over the strangers.*

Garcia read it over and it pleased him. Proud of his heritage, he liked to think that, thanks to this addition, when people came to explain what Hernandez had done, they wouldn't only talk about his ethnicity. They would not talk of his action solely as the work of a 'crazed Latino man'.

He read the line again and proceeded to add more like it. Next to a photograph of a weeping six-year-old child in Laredo, Texas, torn away from his parents by a squad of uniformed officers of the USDF, one read:

In the name of Jesus stop the deportacions!

Attached to a picture of the President at the White House podium, the eyes blotted out by Satanic bursts of red, he wrote:

He will punish those who do not know God and do not obey the gospel of our Lord Jesus!

And introducing a Spanish-language news story from three months earlier, alleging that the administration was planning to construct internment camps for undocumented migrants, he cut and pasted another Biblical quote, this one from the Book of Deuteronomy. He read it once, then read it again. He tried to picture it as a screengrab on the TV news, hours after what would be the biggest news story since 1963. He nodded to himself. It read as he wanted it to read – as an unheeded warning from the grave.

It is mine to avenge. I will repay. Their day of disaster is near.

21

The White House, Wednesday, 3.10pm

Maggie was in her office, glancing at intervals at the door, guarding against the possibility of a McNamara visit. She'd closed it and, were it not the sort of action that might have been interpreted by her colleagues as paranoia or even madness, she'd have locked and bolted it too. She had considered jamming a chair against it, but decided that too might look . . . eccentric.

She had chewed her way through two pen tops and was now on a third. Fuck, if she didn't feel like a cigarette. A memory floated into her head of those nights in Africa, or Jerusalem, when, no matter what stress she was under – talks deadlocked, the parties accusing each other, or her, of some unforgivable act of betrayal – she would take a moment and stand outside, under the stars, having a fag. Best was when she was not alone, but sharing a smoke. One of the greatest pleasures life had to offer, the pre-coital cigarette.

And not a pleasure she had yet shared with Richard – or was ever likely to. Like most people in Washington under the age of thirty-five, Richard regarded his body the way federal law regarded the Arctic wilderness, as a pristine, sacred domain that was not to be violated at any cost. (Or rather, Maggie corrected herself, the way federal law *used* to regard the wilderness. In his first week in office the President had drastically shrunk the list of nationally protected areas, mainly so that his pals could do what they'd been itching to do for decades: start drilling for oil.) Minimal consumption of alcohol, zero consumption of nicotine or any other artificial substances, frequent and intense exercise.

Of course, that had its upsides – and instantly Maggie found herself thinking, once again, of the taut strength of Richard's body. Strange to admit it at this point in her life, but she'd never known sexual attraction like it. Attraction wasn't even the word. Too mild. Richard had a sexual *hold* on her.

She went back to the screen, forcing herself to concentrate. She understood her own distraction. She was in shock, still reeling from what she'd been told by Lieutenant Rajak, every word of which had rung true.

In normal times, the graphic and brutal account of sexual assault at the hands of the President would, on its own, have been enough to shake her. But the appalling truth was that these days it no longer registered as a surprise. Given everything that had come out about this man, such revelations had lost their sting. Maggie feared that what was happening to her was happening to the American public. They were becoming inured to it. Not that she would ever admit such a thing to Mary Rajak's face.

No, what had rocked Maggie was her description of a President on the verge of ordering a nuclear strike against North Korea and China, a move that would, at a minimum, have left hundreds of millions dead. Even if North Korea's threats had proved to be empty, and their new missiles had failed to reach the US West Coast, China's would have had no such trouble. Large stretches of the three countries involved would have been incinerated. And, surely, the madness would have spread. There'd have been nothing left.

And what had provoked it? A few incendiary – and stupid – words from Pyongyang. Nothing that a ferocious statement from a spokesman couldn't have dealt with. She half-wondered if it was a tactic, a ploy the President had worked out – perhaps with that lunatic he'd installed at State – to scare the bejesus out of every foreign capital, in Asia and beyond. The old Nixon trick. But when Nixon did it, it was all about sending a signal. He'd once ordered his Defense Secretary to put US nuclear forces on high alert. No one could miss that: eighteen B-52s packed with nukes flying towards the Soviet Union, for Christ's sake. The message: Nixon means business.

But from what Rajak had said, nothing like that had happened here. The President wasn't merely trying to send a message or rattle America's enemies. As far as Maggie could tell, there was no way they'd even know about it. (Though what was it Rajak had said? *Maybe there was a recording or something.* What on earth was she talking about?) Besides, Nixon had only ordered an alert. By contrast, according to Rajak, the President had steamed in and ordered an actual *attack*. That was not about sending a bloody signal. By the time the other side had got it, everyone would be dead.

Displayed in front of her was the record of all calls routed through the White House switchboard connecting all White House personnel. It backed up Rajak's account perfectly. It showed calls from the Situation Room to Kassian's personal cell at 3.20am and to Bruton's a minute earlier. It then showed a second call to Bruton just after that, surely the one Rajak had hoped to route through to the side conference room. That showed up as lasting just a few seconds and fitted what Rajak had said: in grabbing her wrist, the President had cut off the call before it could be properly connected.

What she needed most, though, were the logs of Bruton's phone and Kassian's. If she were determined, she could get them too. But that would require a formal and elaborate process of authorization that would immediately announce to both men that they were under investigation. It might well require the permission of the President himself. Not an option.

Still, there was plenty she could look at directly, given the authority of the Counsel's office. She quickly consulted the White House entry and exit record. She could see that Kassian's pass was scanned at 3.41am on Monday morning, Bruton's two minutes earlier. Enough to know that Rajak was telling the truth.

Now she pulled up the electronic appointments diary of the Chief of Staff. Tellingly, she could see that most of his Monday morning appointments had been cancelled. That confirmed Rajak's account too: after an incident like that, of course Kassian would have cleared the decks. He'd have needed to meet with a whole range of people, to limit the damage.

But this was curious. None of those new meetings had been logged. She'd have expected a record of a session with the Chairman of the Joint Chiefs, perhaps a debrief with the overnight team on duty in the Situation Room, certainly a sit-down with Bruton. Instead, it seemed like the morning had been cleared and nothing put in its place. The only thing she could see entered between the hours of 7.45am and 11.40am was a number: #018779411.

160

It didn't look like a phone number, though she tried it just to be sure, adding a variety of area codes in different permutations. None worked.

Then she entered it as a search term into the White House database. Still nothing.

She chewed the pen top harder, cursing the day she gave up smoking. She opened her desk drawer for some nicotine gum. Where had she seen a number like that?

Now she opened her own electronic diary and did a search for a similar number. She typed in 01877 to see what happened. Nothing.

Then she tried 018. It brought up one result. A meeting with the National Security Council, from a while back, which had been titled: 'New strategies for Israel/Palestine, Preparing for 2018'. Useless.

This time she included the hashtag in her search. Nothing for #018. But when she tried #01, several entries appeared. Attached to a date in early January of last year, #014555621. In the previous October, #014234998. Now she understood. These were booking reference numbers, assigned by the White House travel office whenever you were on official business. With a few keystrokes, she could see that the number in Kassian's diary referred to a flight to New York. She could also see that the booking had been made that morning. Whatever he'd been doing there, it must have been a response to the near-catastrophe that had played out during the night.

Now she sought to do the same for Jim Bruton. Much harder, because the Pentagon had its own protocols. She couldn't simply rummage around in the electronic files there as easily as she could in the White House.

Fortunately, she still had a good contact at the Pentagon, someone who, like her, had stayed on. He was a classic Washington type, the kind she used to mock as insufferably dull: straight arrow, humourless and earnest. But, Jesus, how times had changed. Now she positively cherished men like Nick, non-partisan career officials who were faithful to boring things like facts, evidence and the law. The country would be finished without them.

'Nick, it's Maggie Costello.' Her voice sober, one serious public servant to another.

'Hi there, Maggie. What's on your mind?'

She explained there was something she was trying to chase down at her end, an issue that she could not detail at this stage. Someone had claimed a meeting with the Secretary of Defense as a kind of alibi and the only way of checking it out was by knowing if the Secretary had indeed met this person at any stage in the last three days. Before Nick had a chance to say no, she said, 'Basically between, say, six am on Monday and now.'

This was not the kind of information officials liked to divulge. Maggie suspected that, had the request come from almost anyone else, Nick would have refused it. But he understood that she worked for that part of the White House charged with ensuring the law was observed and ethical standards maintained. That gave her the scope to ask questions about any government employee and to expect answers. Nick would see it as his professional duty to help.

'All right, I can see the diary,' he said. 'What's the name you're looking for?'

'That's just it, Nick. I can't disclose that at this stage.' She scrunched her eyes closed, hoping she would get away with it. 'Could you bear to go through what you can see? I know the Secretary began the day early at the White House. Very early.'

Nick began to read out from the appointments diary, Maggie scribbling as fast as she could. What came was an alphabet soup of initials and abbreviations, as he rattled through each fifteen-minute encounter the Secretary of Defense had had with the head of CENTCOM, DARCOM or COSCOM. It seemed endless.

She thanked him and then explained that she had a further, perhaps more sensitive request. On hearing it, he gave away no reaction, merely saying he would contact her if and when he had any information. Which she took as a polite, but understandable, rebuff.

She hung up and contemplated the long, yellow sheet with its series of times alongside multiple strings of letters. With a bit of help from Google, she had soon decoded them all – until she had two items circled.

One was *Private social engagement, private address, Chevy Chase, MD* on Monday evening. That, she decided, was the visit with Kassian to Dr Frankel.

The other was more intriguing. It was the only appointment in the diary that broke the format applied to all the others. At eleven am today, Jim Bruton had had a meeting with an individual associated with SOCOM, special operations. Except this person was not identified. All it said of him or her was, *no name supplied.*

Maggie got to her feet. A thought was forming. She needed to walk.

She went down one corridor, then another, until she was by the suite of offices officially held by the First Lady, though these days they were used more by the President's daughter. Indeed, Maggie could see her now, from the back – that impeccable sweep of hair falling down an expensively cut, tightly fitted dress. She appeared to be in animated conversation with someone leaving her office. Now her shoulders were rising and falling. She was laughing.

And as Maggie turned the corner, changing the angle,

she could see who it was who held the First Daughter in such rapt attention, though in truth her instinct had already provided the answer.

There, his eyes locked on the woman's gaze, giving her the full, twenty-thousand-watt smile, was Richard, looking more handsome than ever.

22

Delhi, India, 7.30pm, two weeks earlier
The evening barely brought respite. Looking over his driver's shoulder, Aamir Kapoor could see that the outside temperature was forty-five degrees, at least according to the gauge on the dashboard which, given what this car cost, he had no reason to doubt. A sane man would stay inside this air-conditioned cocoon and have his driver turn around and take him back towards Lutyens' Delhi and the equally refrigerated comfort of home.

But some things were beyond the reach of reason, or even sanity. Once he felt the need to pay his respects, to bow his head in tribute, then he could not refuse that urge. Was it superstition? Partly. But he preferred to think of it as an act of love. Not for the long-dead Sufi holy man whose shrine sat inside the seething, crammed narrow streets of Nizamuddin West, but for a man more recently departed.

What would his international business partners, those who only ever saw him in his office inside the gleaming tower of steel-and-glass or at a celebratory, contract-signing sushi dinner in one of the city's five-star hotels, make of this ritual of his? Some would doubtless think it charming, an exotic custom that was *fascinating*.

But most, he suspected, would find it barbaric, primitive. They would be embarrassed by the sight of him out of his dark suit, one of a dozen he'd had made for him on Jermyn Street in London, wearing instead the worn, nearly thread-bare kurta he had taken from his father's cupboard in the days after the old man's death – a garment he would still hold to his nostrils, hoping for a hint of memory. If, say, his American business partners were to follow him through these side streets, if they were to experience this heat, this dust, this dirt, it would remind them that they were dealing with a country that might do a good job of *appearing* first world, but where half the population, 600 million people, owned no toilet. Like his good friend, Swapan, always said, 'This country is floating on shit and no one talks about it.'

He told his driver to pull up and let him out. 'Keep circling around,' he said. 'I'll text you when I'm ready to go.' A visit to the shrine, a quick bowl of mutton *nihari*, and he would be done. That would give him his monthly dose, enough of a fix to get him through the next few weeks.

And Aamir felt that, given what was coming, he would need the strength. He would need all his resolve to stand in the way of this plan and the men backing it. Not so long ago, he had had plenty of allies: in the city council, in the national government, on his own board. But ever since the key investor had become – what was the word in English – *elevated* to a new role, Aamir's one-time friends had suddenly undergone a dramatic change of heart.

Now they saw the merit in the American's scheme: to build a California-style 'Indian heritage' theme park, right in the heart of one of Delhi's most historic neighbourhoods, sweeping away centuries of history and leaving perhaps twenty-two thousand people homeless. 'We can lose that many people in an hour's flooding in Uttar Pradesh, what's the big deal?' Those were the actual words spoken by a man he had once regarded as a friend. The acquisition of enormous political power could be very persuasive, Aamir had discovered.

So he would need all his steel to hold back this tide. Coming here on a Thursday night, the way his father had done every week, would help, he was sure of it.

He waved the Porsche away and began to walk west, instantly grateful for the teeming crowd, the noise, even the stink. His European friends told him they needed to get away to the Scottish Highlands, or the Alps, to relax, to clear their heads. For Aamir, it was the opposite. Being here, in this packed square kilometre of narrow lanes and tiny stalls, allowed him to think. The buckets of boiling oil at every turn, fizzing as they turned folded pastry and diced vegetables into samosas, the heat emerging from the gaping mouth of the tandoor ovens, the sweat on the bodies he passed, the great leveller of body odour, unavoidable even among the most fastidious – it did not disturb him. On the contrary, it allowed him to relax, to disengage from the office and the phone calls and the emails, and to enter some other state.

He was closer to the shrine now, this place that had meant so much to his father. If Aamir had his way, they'd build a statue to the old man right here. Who else better embodied the greatness of India than his father, a man who had begun his life pushing a rickshaw in these streets and who had hassled and hustled and scratched together enough rupees to pay for Aamir, his favoured son, to attend an elite school, with a little help from a scholarship for the exceptionally gifted? Who?

He brushed past a couple of white women in their thirties – they never looked whiter than when they came here – and passed the open butcher's shop, with its great slabs of red buffalo meat luridly lit by the neon overhead, bright enough to turn the blood coagulating on the floor to scarlet. He took in the smell of the meat, simultaneously sweet and rotting. A goat navigated around his ankles and moved on.

He nodded to the shopkeeper, standing watch over his collection of plastic replicas of the Taj Mahal – each one with a cheap clock embedded in it, primed to chime when it was time to pray – green flags and poster prints of Mecca. And he waved aside the first bidders for the right to take custody of his shoes: all in good time.

First he handed over a couple of rupees to a girl selling offerings for the saint: as always, he bought some sweets and a handful of red petals. The same combination favoured by his father.

Next he took off his shoes, placing them in the rack to the right. He had dressed down to fit in, as he always did. But not enough. Apart from a couple of pairs of stout walking boots – backpackers' – the rest of the footwear kept here barely passed for shoes at all. Most were little more than bound rags.

Then to the shrine itself, with its fluted marble columns, its arches decorated in patterns of green, pink and gold, and then, inside the chamber, the walls of marble perforated in complex, latticed patterns, filigrees of intricate geometry. The surface of the marble was worn now, rubbed over the centuries by fingers like his. He looked up at the ceiling, painted in red, blue and more gold, just as he had done as a child. The chandeliers seemed nearer to him now than they did then, when they had seemed to be suspended from heaven itself.

He took a second to assess his fellow pilgrims, pressing their hands or foreheads on the (relatively) cool stone. Some had tied glittering ribbons or shiny charms to the latticework, to bolster their prayer for recovery from illness, for success in exams, for a pregnancy, especially one that might bring a boy.

Aamir did not feel the need to stay at the shrine long. His homage was less to the saint than to this place, and to those to whom it meant so much. Maybe it was no more than ancestor worship. The thought, even with its faint accusation of primitivism, didn't bother him.

In the marble courtyard, he paused to take in the sounds. With his friends, even with his wife, he affected to dislike Qawwali music, with its repetitive, percussive rhythms. But here in this place, he never failed to be moved by the music these men, seated cross-legged on thin carpets for hours on end, could make. They were said to be members of the same family that had played here for centuries. Ancestor worship, again.

He headed off to find something to eat. And even then, when he had already been followed and watched for nearly thirty minutes, he had no inkling of the men whose eyes had never left him.

He walked past the first food-sellers he came to ('restaurants' would be overstating it). He had a destination – his usual – in mind. With its tin plates and stained Formica tables, it was on no tourist map. But the spice of the bone marrow stew it brewed, the sweetness of the red onions, the texture of the na'an – to go anywhere else would be a betrayal.

With the first bite, he was transported back to his childhood, the flavours working their instant magic. And yet, at the edges, there was a sensation of uneasiness. He looked up and saw a familiar face, smiling at him warmly: an old friend of his father's. The man walked over to him, he stood and they embraced. The man said little, but he nodded with satisfaction at how the boy had turned out. As if his success was a collective triumph for the people of these streets.

But that did not dispel the unease. Once the old man had gone, Aamir still felt himself watched. He scanned the tiny room, each table packed with people and with two dozen more standing, spilling out onto the street. Nothing he could see, except for one rapid movement: he had the feeling someone had turned his back to hide his face as soon as Aamir had looked up.

His plate was only half-cleared, but he decided it was nevertheless time to pay up. He pressed several notes into the hands of the proprietor, paying his bill at least twice over, and darted out, slipping into the current of humanity that, he knew, would all but carry him away from here.

Still the sensation did not leave him. He looked over his shoulder. The man who had moved so swiftly to avoid being spotted at the restaurant – lithe, his cheekbones pronounced – now held his gaze in a way that was cold, detached.

Unnerved, Aamir turned to face forward and at that moment felt a hard shove into his left shoulder. The teenager who had bumped into him did not apologize or hesitate but marched on, disappearing into the throng. Aamir put an instinctive hand onto his shoulder. He had been hit hard; it ached.

The road ahead was about to fork. He would take the left path, heading west, towards the crematorium, towards the car. He would phone ahead, then get out of here.

He was about to dig into his pocket to pull out the phone, to feel its reassurance, when he felt another shove, from behind this time. He turned, to find another youth looking at him, smiling in a way that struck Aamir as . . . gloating. There could be no doubt about it: that push had been deliberate.

Aamir swivelled again. The staring man from the restaurant was still staring, but now he was much closer. He was gaining on him.

The sweat and the heat were becoming unbearable. Aamir could feel the cotton on his back getting stickier. A goat got in his way, so that he nearly fell. The smell of incense, sickly and cloying, from one of the scores of tiny shrines that dotted this area filled his nostrils. He wanted desperately to get away.

He tried to move toward the left fork but the street was too full, the tide of humanity too strong. When he tried to move leftward, he was jostled and, unless he was now becoming paranoid, pushed back. He felt hands at his back, nudging, even steering him. He glanced around again, but couldn't see the staring man.

And now that he'd taken it, maybe the right fork hadn't been such a bad move. He was heading towards the police station. He felt for his wallet. Still there. It meant he could prove who he was and demand some assistance, despite the state of his clothes.

Now a new, much more pleasant scent reached him. There were stalls selling guava, melons and some early mangos brought into the city from the south. The street opened out into a small square, one that was coming up in the world. He saw the perfume shops and a few four-storey apartment buildings, with their hopelessly impractical, wannabe New York-style picture windows, and he breathed out.

He looked for a street address; he would phone his driver and tell him to meet him here. He dug into one pocket, then another, then patted himself before he understood.

Shit. So that's what that little performance back there had been. A basic hustle. The man with the staring eyes and the teenage shove-artists were in cahoots, a tag-team intent on depriving him of his phone. To think he'd grown up on these streets; he was as naïve as those women. He would walk to the police station.

These streets were far emptier than the ones he'd left behind; darker too. He came to a crossroads. It was so dark, it was hard to make out. Taking a right would bring him into a more residential area. He needed to go left.

And there he was, as if he'd been waiting for him. The same staring man, alone. Aamir turned to take the other road, but found four men standing in his path. Among them, Aamir felt sure, was the one who had shoved him the second time. The expression on his face had graduated from a gloat to a smirk.

Deciding to take the initiative, he pulled out his wallet, removed a thick wad of notes and said, 'Here. That's nearly forty thousand rupees. Take it. It's yours. And leave me alone.'

The men did not move. They just stood and stared, like their leader.

Aamir glanced back towards the road from which he'd emerged. That too was now blocked, by another knot of young men. They had the same look of hungry menace.

He would not be beaten by them. He might be in his forties, but he was no sap. He was not a tourist. He was a native of this godforsaken place; he'd outrun tougher bastards than these punks. And so he ran.

He headed left. With only one man to beat, it was the obvious choice. Though he told himself the real reason was that that's where he had wanted to go in the first place – and he was feeling bloody-minded.

He dodged past the staring man, who put up next to no resistance – indeed, he all but stepped out of the way. Aamir credited his own genius and the element of surprise for that. See, these hoodlums liked to pose tough, but when it came to it, they weren't man enough for a fight. *Dumb kids*, Aamir thought to himself: *they should have taken the money*.

He looked over his shoulder. Now they had started their pursuit, though languidly. Aamir was sure he saw a glint of metal. He ran harder.

He took a little dogleg that guided him past the petrol station. The men behind were gaining on him: he could not only hear their footsteps, but feel the heat of them, or was that his imagination? He remembered the blade and forced himself to run harder.

It had been too many years since Aamir had lived on these streets. Otherwise he'd have remembered that once you were past the petrol station you needed to stop running. If you didn't, you'd run straight out onto the Mathura Road, a four-lane highway where the traffic was constant and unruly.

And where a man could be knocked down by a Mercedes moving at speed, killed so fast and amid such heat and noise that it'd barely be noticed – and where no one would think it was anything but an innocent, if tragic, accident.

23

Washington, DC, Thursday, 3.43am

How did Richard manage to sleep like that, she wondered. Still, almost soundless, deeply unconscious, turned away from her. Perhaps it was a fitness thing.

An ex had once wanted to film her sleeping, but she had refused him outright. Cameras in the bedroom were banned, as far as she was concerned: they were just one click and one break-up away from spelling 'revenge porn' in capital letters. So she had no proof of what she looked like when asleep. But her strong guess was that she was a restless sleeper, shifting, turning and resettling and, probably, muttering throughout. Perhaps it was a nicotine and booze thing.

Whatever the explanation, she was awake now. Her mind was flipping like a TV remote. Sometimes she was rerunning the tape of her conversation with Mary Rajak, the comms officer who had looked as traumatized as any victim of sexual assault and as terrified as anyone who had stared into the abyss of nuclear apocalypse had every right to be – but something else too. Her eyes, in their sunken hollows,

174

had struck Maggie as the eyes of a woman whose heart had been broken.

She stared at the ceiling. Now she was picturing Richard and the beautiful, glossy, long-limbed First Daughter. They were suited to each other. They both could have walked straight out of a perfume ad in a magazine, with their perfectly sculpted features and treadmill bodies.

Stop, she told herself. *Enough*. If you're not going to sleep, then think about what matters. She reached for the floor by the side of the bed, and the stack of not-yet-read editions of the *New Yorker*. Somewhere in there was a pad. There. She had a pen on the nightstand, next to the radio. Finally she fumbled for her phone, turned on the little torch, then arranged herself so that it lit up the long yellow pages.

Start with Kassian and Bruton. What did she know? They had both rushed to the White House in the dead of night, averting what would have been a catastrophe. Kassian had then cancelled everything to go to New York. Why New York? Straight after a near-war with North Korea: it could only be the UN. Nothing else made sense. But he hadn't gone to the UN itself; Maggie had checked. So where? And to see whom? Surely not . . .

She rearranged herself, and looked at what she'd written so far. It looked like gibberish. Next to her, Richard was lying with the sheet draped across his waist. She wondered what would happen if she lifted it, ever so lightly. She didn't want to wake him, but she loved looking at him there, the length of his back, the curve of his buttocks and jut of hip masked by the Egyptian cotton. They had had sex just a couple of hours ago, but she was hungry again . . . She pushed the thought away.

And then, that evening they had gone to Dr Frankel's house. Why would you go to see the President's physician?

There were only two possible explanations: either you had something to tell the doctor or there was something you wanted him to tell you. But what? Did they believe the President was hiding something? Or was there a medical secret that Kassian or Bruton knew and which they needed to convey to Frankel? But that made no sense. The doctor would know all there was to know . . .

Richard seemed to shudder. She held still. She didn't want him to stir. She needed to think, to keep writing. If he woke, he would be bound to ask what she was working on. The pair of them had become good at policing the Chinese wall they had constructed between them, even if Richard was always climbing up, trying to sneak a peek over the top at her side. They joked about it, how his work in Commerce must be boring, given that Maggie rarely probed him about anything, while hers was obviously riveting, judging by the way he questioned her about it all the time. 'You get to hear all the office gossip and call it your job, Mags. Go on, just throw me a tiny little morsel.'

He had a point. The Counsel's office dealt with staff issues: ethics, conflicts of interest, disciplinary matters. It was her job to know where the bodies were buried. If the roles had been reversed she'd have been just as inquisitive. Curiosity was natural. Still, you couldn't last a day in a role like hers unless you had the ability to be discreet. You had to hold onto your secrets, keeping them back even from those you loved. Even from those who lay so close you could inhale the smell of their skin . . .

She forced herself to concentrate. The late-night visit to the home of Dr Frankel. It was obvious. It had to be connected to what had happened the previous night. She circled the names of Kassian and Bruton. They had clearly been petrified. They believed their boss had come within a whisker of blowing up the planet. They thought he was out of his mind. They went to see the doctor to ask if it was true. Was he mentally unstable? And if he was . . .

It was a hot night. She imagined the President's daughter. Was she in bed now, wearing next to nothing? Was her husband there with her? If he was, was she actually thinking about Richard? And what had Richard been doing on his phone earlier, when Maggie came out of the shower? Was he texting that woman? Was he?

For fuck's sake, get a grip, Maggie told herself. She couldn't remember the last time she'd been jealous like this. As a teenager perhaps, in Dublin, with Liam Mangan, her first love. Uri always had a string of beautiful women trailing after him, but he had never seemed interested in anyone but her. Edward had been possessive and jealous and Maggie had hated it. She wondered now if this was what it had been like for him: the runaway imagination, the pictures in your head, visualizing your lover with someone else . . .

Maggie shifted her position again, as if that might force her to shift thoughts. She wondered about using her phone to turn on the air-con. If there was one thing about new technology that she loved, it was that. The app on her phone, with its little icon of a house with a chimney, that allowed her to warm up the place, or cool it down, even when she wasn't there – or when she was, but couldn't be bothered, as Liz put it, to move her 'lazy Irish arse out of bed'. Liz had called her 'an old slattern' for installing it – and then promptly installed one of her own. 'Not that I ever use it,' she insisted in a string of texts that struck Maggie as ever so slightly defensive. 'Last time I turned the central heating on, whole place filled with bloody smoke. Besides, it's *roasting* in Atlanta . . .'

Focus, Maggie. Focus. What if the President was, you

know, mentally unstable? What would that mean? Was that what the Chief of Staff and the Defense Secretary wanted the doctor to tell them? *Course not.* They knew that already. They knew it would mean Frankel would have to declare the President was unable to exercise his duties . . . Oh my God, that was it.

Now it all came at once, with the clarity of the sleepless. She started scribbling furiously. They'd gone there to demand the White House physician certify the President as mentally incompetent and the doctor had refused. And then a few hours later he was dead. Of course they had killed him. Of course they had. Of course, of course, of course. Once he knew what they were thinking, that they planned to overthrow the President, he knew too much. Just a word from him and the two of them would be destroyed – jailed for sedition or treason or whatever the fuck it was. So they went round the next morning, or called him out maybe – yes that was it, they called him out on a house call or they got someone to do it, someone else, a hit man, or a contract killer or maybe a soldier. Which was why Bruton had seen someone from SOCOM! He got special ops to do it!

No, no, scratch that. Think. That didn't make sense. Frankel was already dead by the time Bruton had the meeting – just yesterday morning – with the 'no name supplied' guy. Whoever that was, Bruton must have been seeing him about something else.

And now, at last, another thought broke the surface. Something her subconscious mind had known for a while, perhaps as soon as she had spotted that reference to SOCOM in Bruton's diary, maybe even before. People can know something without knowing they know it, or being able to admit they know it, even to themselves. She had to overcome her reluctance to write it down – or even to think it.

Yet it was so obvious. She sat upright, eyes wide. Thwarted in their attempt to have the President removed from office on medical grounds, they had decided they had no alternative. First they had to kill Jeffrey Frankel. And then they would kill the President.

The night was quiet. Richard was still, the street was silent. But inside her head, it was throbbing. She had a crush of thoughts, falling over each other, roaring like the sound of the sea in a shell when you put it to your ear. Blood, rushing through her veins.

Part of her was appalled at what she thought she had uncovered. She imagined the consequences for America, already so divided against itself. The country would be plunged into civil war. Look at how the Kennedy assassination had haunted America for decades. No matter how much you hated this man – and, my God, there was every reason to hate him – this, surely, was not the way to get rid of him. If the reason to oppose him was because he was trashing democracy, then how could you justify removing him by the most undemocratic means of all: assassination? You'd be destroying democracy in order to save it. It was madness.

She imagined how it would play out, not in theory but in practice. She had read enough to know how the killing of JFK had traumatized America when the country had seemed so full of hope, turning the sixties into a decade scarred by horrible political violence, and more assassinations. But surely it was worse now? Even in the years she had lived here, America had become more starkly polarized. People were vicious to each other on social media, spraying abuse at anyone who held a different opinion. Could you imagine what the President's supporters would be like if their hero was murdered? Their fury would be total. He'd be a martyr,

179

and they'd turn on anyone they deemed to be an enemy. Maggie doubted that rage would be confined to foul tweets and vile Facebook posts. She could imagine the atmosphere of hate spilling out onto the streets. Things could get ugly, very fast. Unbidden, a picture of Liz and her young boys formed in her head, the children running away from a stone-throwing mob. And suddenly she was visited by the familiar feeling of nausea. This whole mess: if only she hadn't . . .

She pushed that thought away, made herself concentrate instead on how she had figured out the puzzle, allowing herself a moment of professional satisfaction at her own ingeniousness.

She wondered what it would be like to tell McNamara, striding into his office to let him know she had exceeded his expectations, that she had cracked the mystery. She only had to picture it for a moment to feel the revulsion. Why give that man anything? Whatever nugget of intel he had, he would only exploit it for his own twisted purposes. Surely she had learned that lesson: if you had information, you didn't let it out of your grasp till you had thought through all the implications, starting with how it would be used. She thought of McNamara and his circle of devotees – 'Mac's boys', the papers called them, or 'the servants of the Big Mac', according to a Twitter meme doing the rounds – and couldn't bear the idea that, even for a moment, she might be deemed part of it.

But then she looked at her notepad once more, contemplating the conclusion she had come to, and she felt her pulse quickening. A small, secret voice inside whispered, *Thank God someone is doing something to stop this horror show.* Liz had been right when she said *I cannot believe you work for that evil man.* Well, now there were two good men who were going to stop him.

Reason intervened, tugging at the leash to pull her back. How 'good' could these men be if they were prepared to kill an innocent man, a doctor who loved his family and had devoted his life to healing the sick? How good could they be to consider killing – murdering – anyone? Maybe they were just a different shade of evil. She had seen that before too.

It was nearly five am. Maggie went to the bathroom to splash cold water on her face. She needed to calm herself, to cool down.

On her way back temptation beckoned her. It was there on the nightstand, on Richard's side of the bed. His phone.

Look, she said to herself. *If he wasn't texting that woman, perhaps it's better for him if I know that. Why should he, an attentive, faithful lover, have to be under this cloud of suspicion?* She couldn't just ask him outright. Once you asked a question like that, you could never unask it. It was out there, a shadow over the relationship thereafter. A destruction of trust.

How much better to do this now, quietly and discreetly.

Noiselessly she picked up his phone, pressed the home button and the screen lit up. *Slide to Unlock*. She slid and then it offered her a choice:

Touch ID or Enter Passcode

There he was, sound asleep. His fingers, long and slim, the same fingers which had stroked her, entered her, just hours ago, were resting on top of the sheet, available. She slid the phone close to his right hand and, with the gentlest guidance, placed the pad of his index finger on the home button. The screen brightened and she slid the phone away and along the sheet. As she climbed back into bed, he took in a larger breath, but did not stir.

Maggie went straight to his text messages. The first name, at the top, was her own, inviting him over. Below that, a colleague telling him that the documents he'd needed would be ready on Monday. Below that, a text from his brother about seeing the Orioles. Nothing from the presidential daughter.

Now she glanced at the email. Nothing there of any significance. That was hardly surprising. Given the last few years, no one did anything that mattered on email. She checked WhatsApp: nothing. And Signal: nothing.

But the next icon along said simply Notes. The first couple seemed innocuous enough but then she opened the third. She felt her brow crinkle. Her heart began to plunge. This file consisted of a string of Signal messages copied and pasted into a single document, dozens of them, going back months, all written in a tone of easy familiarity, even intimacy. Except they were not between Richard and the President's daughter.

They were between Richard and Crawford McNamara.

Comrade! Put on Fox now. She's hitting it out of the park.

No clue what that referred to, but the brevity, the lack of formalities, suggested frequent if not constant contact. This was how friends talked to each other.

Here was Richard's reply:

Totally agree. She nailed it. She looks hot as fuck too

Maggie felt herself pale. All drowsiness had gone. She was sitting upright. She scrolled through the messages, most of them written in the same register of locker-room, towel-snapping guy talk.

Another one from McNamara.

Good job in the Oval today. The big man likes you. And as for the princess, she's dripping wet for you, comrade . . .

Maggie glanced down at Richard, still sleeping. *The princess*. It could only be one person. And the way McNamara referred to her, like he was some kind of voyeur, jerking himself off at the thought of the two young lovers getting it on. He was pimping the President's daughter.

The next message had her confused. This time from Richard to McNamara.

Mid-Atlantic package has been dispatched. Presume we have delivery address for the next one. Let me know and I'll prepare.

More in that vein and then one that made Maggie go cold. From Richard again:

Is there anything more hilarious than these libtards wetting the bed over the Muslim registry? I fucking love it. I almost want to do the whole yellow star thing - yellow crescents, anyone? - just to see them pee their pants. Didn't you say the boss was up for it?

McNamara's reply: Moment not right just yet. Need to get the ban fully in place. Shutdown on all foreign ragheads, from everywhere (Europe especially). Then once we have register for "American" ragheads, we're good to go. Yellow: too blatant? Or worth it for the lulz?

Richard: Lulz, man, lulz! If your balls are big and hairy enough - and I know they are - then what are you frightened of? Some pushback from (((you know who)))?

McNamara: You're showing your youth and inexperience. First rule of DC: you never, ever cross the (((mighty, globalist powers that be)))

Maggie closed her eyes as a wave of disgust, physical and visceral, crashed over her. The coldness she had felt before now spread throughout her body: it was as if she was shuddering, inside and out. The triple brackets were just too much. For a while, it had been like a secret handshake in the alt-right universe, putting three sets of brackets around the name of anyone they suspected of being a Jew. When social media got wind of it, plenty of Jews – and others – had done it to themselves. The way the King of Denmark wore the yellow star during the Nazi occupation: an 'I am Spartacus' gesture of solidarity. Maggie had assumed that that had killed the whole thing off. But here they were, using it casually to signal their shared suspicion of Jews. She looked at Richard's reply.

Richard: Yoda, I have been naive. Please guide me in the ways of the Joooooooz.
McNamara: Money like they.
Richard: Money of lots have they.

Maggie's revulsion was complete. The man lying next to her, the man she had allowed inside her, was a racist bigot – smart, sophisticated and well-dressed, but a hardcore neo-Nazi. She felt an urge to retch.

Yet there was an equal urge of masochistic cruelty that made her keep scrolling through these messages, a terrible compulsion to expose herself to it all until she had hit rock bottom. But there were just so many. It seemed Richard and McNamara were in the habit of communicating with each other twelve or fifteen times a day. There was another one about the daughter.

Was in the Residence today. Not even sure the husband is that interested. He works hard! So there might be an opening – if you get my meaning ;)

Richard's reply: I want to make my way into that opening
McNamara: Get in line. Hey maybe I can get Rosemary
on it, see what the deal with those two is

Another one she could not decipher. From McNamara:

Our friends will need instructions on the next package.
Shipment in Delhi, dispatch details as discussed.

What could that even mean? Something to do with
Richard's work in Commerce perhaps. She gave it barely a
second's thought, for at that moment Richard stirred, his
hand instinctively reaching for her bare leg, resting on her
skin. A reflex of desire pulsed through her, fleeting but
enough to make her disgusted with herself and the
unthinking, animal ways of the body. She inched herself
away from his touch.

The sun was beginning to rise. She lay there, rigid and
tense, conscious she should put the phone back soon, before
he woke. But she needed to read it all.

Now an unusually long one from Richard.

Remember that lecture at the Utah conference? By the
French guy, the one who worked with the Front National? We
need to find a way to adapt that message for a US audience.
Bottom line: no reason why every ethnic group in America
gets to celebrate its heritage except the white race. White
folks, white men especially, should be allowed their pride.
'We are children of the sun!' Loved that line. Want me to
draft some paragraphs for POTUS?

Maggie's hands trembled as she thumbed her way down
the screen, scanning the messages as fast as she could. She

was now back to February, when she and Richard had only been involved a few weeks.

From McNamara: So how's it going with Firebush?

Richard: I keep telling you: she may be Irish, but she's not a redhead. Not on top and not down there.

McNamara: A guy can dream, can't he? Love the idea of a fish dish with a side of ginger.

Richard: You are disgusting.

McNamara: Vag in red sauce

Richard: Stop

McNamara: But seriously, anything you've picked up yet? Apart from Fenian crabs.

Richard: Actually, she's very clean in that department. Nothing yet. But she's in touch with all the old crowd. Think she might even be in contact with the former P.

McNamara: Really?

Richard: It's a maybe at this stage. But one thing I can tell you. She fucking hates our man. Fucking *hates* him. I have to console her sometimes, reassure her that "we're doing the right thing." Boo hoo.

McNamara: Hilarious.

Richard: I know.

McNamara: Listen, you're not banging her for fun you know. Intel, my boy. Intel.

Richard: I know.

McNamara: And she has no idea?

Richard: About what?

McNamara: That she's, you know, sleeping with the enemy.

Richard: Not a clue.

24

Garcia had made several decisions about 'Jorge Hernandez'. The first was that he would hew as closely as possible to the real Jorge Hernandez. He was a Latino man who had served in the military. He kept himself to himself. He was passionate about the state of his country.

The second decision was that, when 'Jorge Hernandez' had to enter the real world, he would be very much like Julian Garcia. That was not too difficult. They were roughly the same age and of similar height and, until the wasting illness that had hollowed his friend out, similar build. Basic racism would take care of the rest: if – when – people saw a photo of Hernandez, few would swear it was not the man of that name they had briefly glimpsed a day or two earlier. Thick-set Hispanic man, late forties: they all looked the same, didn't they?

For now the real Hernandez was in a reclining chair in his living room, watching his former comrade get to work. Garcia was focused on the walls. The next canvas in his series.

He opened the bag and took out his collection of papers. He had fewer original, hard copies than he would have liked and rather too many printouts. But he had taken care. The newspaper clippings, some going back nearly two years, which he had neatly excised with a scalpel from the stacks kept in the library – not the one at Anacostia, but the much grander Martin Luther King building in northwest DC – were varying shades of yellow. He had worked out a sliding scale. Articles that were a year old, he had left out in yesterday's afternoon sun for an hour. Six months old, half an hour. And so on. Such was the intensity of a Washington sun in May, even a few minutes left a fragment of newsprint looking suitably aged.

He began gumming a selection on the wall, interspersing them with a few of the printouts from web pages. Some of the online articles were spread over seven or eight sheets of A4 paper, including the roll of comments. No reasonable person would pin up the whole thing – so Garcia decided that Hernandez would pin up the whole thing.

He had brought a couple of Sharpies, so that he could circle certain headlines in red or black. He also had string and pins, so he could tie one report to another. But now that it came to it, that struck him as a Hollywood cliché. Hernandez was not laying out a PowerPoint presentation; he was not trying to persuade anyone else. He was simply emptying out the contents of his own, troubled mind. So Garcia underlined a few key words: *deportation, internment, snatch squads, families.*

After an hour or so, he stepped back to inspect his handiwork. He had covered much more of the wall than he intended. It worked. Had he confined himself, as he had planned, to just the area above the table, it would have looked too ordered, too controlled – like one of those collages of calendars and school notices you see in a suburban kitchen. Papering over the entire wall was more extreme. It had the requisite intensity.

Now Garcia walked alongside it, his eyes a TV news camera panning at slow speed. What would it see?

A screaming front page from the *New York Post*: 'No Papers, No Home'. A photograph of the President, his face apparently contorted with hate, his lips appearing to spit out the f-word from behind a lectern. Next to it, a mock-up picture of the President appearing to dance with three hooded Klansmen. It was a fake, assembled by some artist. But Garcia had decided that his Hernandez, such was the fevered state of his mind, believed it was real.

The newspaper stories would be a blur of accounts of both forced round-ups of illegals by the new US Deportation Force and protests against them: the human chain that formed in Miami, the burning tyres during the riot/pogrom in Phoenix; the 'This Is Our Home' march on Washington. The detail was less important than the overall impression.

But Garcia was not done. He pulled out the item which would be the emotional centrepiece of the story he was telling, one he and Hernandez had worked on together. The core facts were borrowed from Julian Garcia's life, but rendered in such a way that they would be compatible with Hernandez's, should anyone check (which they would). And so now, with what he hoped was the right degree of solemnity, he pinned up a portrait photograph of Alicia Hernandez, Jorge's dead mother. He placed it in the middle of the display.

He stepped back one more time, surveyed it all and decided it was good. He looked over at Jorge, who nodded. It worked.

There was one last task. He pulled out a map of Washington, DC, and pinned it on a patch of wall he'd already covered. Using the red Sharpie, he circled the area just north of the National Cemetery in Arlington, Virginia, where tomorrow there would be a formal, televised ceremony – and where the guest of honour would, of course, be the President of the United States.

25

Dupont Circle, Washington, DC, Thursday, 7.16am
'Morning, darling.' Richard's voice was bright, rested.

'Morning.'

'Sleep well?'

Maggie braced herself for her first lie of the day. She knew there would be many, many more. 'Yes, actually. I slept well. What about you?'

'Good.' He leaned over for a kiss. She allowed him to come towards her, but she did not meet him halfway. He pulled away, with a perplexed expression.

'Haven't brushed my teeth yet,' she offered by way of explanation.

In truth, she had spent the last hours wide awake, lying next to him as rigid as a board, staring at the ceiling. Her body had been frozen, recoiling from the proximity to this man. Her mind had been racing, horrified by what she had discovered, disgusted by him, but most of all, and inevitably, appalled at herself for being such a fool. How had she not seen it? How had she allowed her judgement to be so clouded? How, how, how?

She got out of bed first, another break from the usual pattern. She was not handling this well. 'Are you running this morning?' She could hear the strain in her voice, the pitch too high. And if she could hear it, so could he.

'No,' he said, stretching languorously, his abs becoming taut. Once again, she felt the instinctive stirring of desire and resented her body for allowing itself to be lured so easily, for being so ready to betray her. 'I thought we could have a shower together – and then a slow breakfast. What do you think?'

'Actually, I really need to get in early. Lot on.' Her second 'actually'. Such an obvious tell. She turned around and headed for the bathroom, where she could do less damage.

She caught a glimpse of herself in the mirror. The red rims around her eyes were offset by grey shadows underneath. Her hair was lank. She entered the shower, hoping Richard wouldn't follow her.

But he did, opening the door, walking in and beginning to soap himself. His semi-erect penis brushed her thigh, as if by accident. On any other day she would not have been able to resist him: she'd have turned and started to kiss and touch him. This time, too, her skin and her nervous system automatically responded in the usual way. But in the same moment a deep loathing was churning, partly in her brain and largely in the pit of her stomach. The things Richard had said to that awful man. The repugnant racism: *I almost want to do the whole yellow star thing.* Referring to white people as 'children of the sun', quoting with approval that neo-Nazi maniac. And the misogyny that ran all the way through their nauseating little bromance: *She looks hot as fuck too . . . I want to make my way into that opening.* Line after line came back to her, as they had for the last couple of agonizing hours.

192

But what sat in her gut like a stone was what he had said about her. She winced as she recalled the words on that glowing screen: *Actually, she's very clean in that department.* All that talk about the colour of her pubic hair.

And then, more shaming, more wounding, was that reminder from McNamara of Richard's purpose, his mission. *Listen, you're not banging her for fun you know. Intel, my boy. Intel.* She had been such an idiot, no better than a teenage convent girl duped by a sleazeball smoothie who swears he only wants to put his hand in her knickers because he loves her. Why did she keep making the same mistake?

She hurried out of the shower, doing her best to cover her nakedness, hating her own body for the fact that he'd touched it.

She wanted to throw him out, telling him what a lying, cheating, worthless scumbag he was; to scream until she went hoarse, spitting her venom at him until he felt himself shrivel, wounding him so deeply he'd never recover, forcing his toxicity back down his throat until it choked him.

Of course, he would then tell McNamara that she now knew: the piece of Irish ass had got wise. She would be out, or at least sidelined – assigned to the Inspectorate at the US Department of Agriculture would be her guess. The thought of it was tempting. She could go to the White House right now and quit, jump before she was pushed. She could tell McNamara what she really thought of both him and that puffed-up, corrupt, lying ignoramus he called Mr President.

And then she could run a thousand miles away from these cruel, bigoted, *disgusting* men and their project to wreak havoc on America and the world. She could phone Liz and tell her she had had enough, she had done the right thing, she had quit and would fight them from the outside – and Liz would tell her how proud she was, that she always knew

Maggie was principled and courageous and a fighter, and maybe she'd get a flight to Atlanta and see those gorgeous nephews of hers and maybe she could leave Washington altogether and start again.

Tempting though all of that was, she knew she could do none of it. In the dead of night, before she had unlocked that bastard's phone, she had come close to figuring out what was happening here. In her fevered, sleepless state she had begun to see the outline of an attempt by the White House Chief of Staff and the Secretary of Defense to have the President of the United States removed from office, first by means of the Twenty-fifth Amendment of the Constitution and, when that route was blocked, or so she supposed, by his assassination.

She was not sure she was right. More disturbing, she was not sure they were wrong. She found herself going back and forth. If you'd asked her at this particular moment, she would have been ready to barge into Kassian's office, give him a salute and ask where she could sign up.

That was partly her rage at Richard talking, she knew that. But not only. She deplored this President and everything he stood for. She lamented what he was doing to this country that she had grown to love. She resented the impact he was already having on the lives of people she cared about. She thought of Liz's student, hanging from that rope. She thought of Mary Rajak, grabbed, abused and in pieces. She thought of all those families who had been broken up, of the deportations and detentions, of the ban on people deemed to have the wrong faith. She thought of all the pain this President was inflicting – and the fact that he'd only just got started.

But then she remembered Jeffrey Frankel, an innocent man, loved by his family, who had been murdered simply for getting in the way. Whatever sympathy she might have for Kassian and Bruton, it did not extend to shooting a good man in cold blood. What kind of people would do such a thing? And if they were prepared to do that, then what kind of fate awaited an America governed by such men?

And these, she knew, were minor considerations compared to the big, unavoidable one – too large to ignore, even if she had sought to shove it to the margins of her own mind. Of course, she didn't like this President. Nor did half the population (actually more than half, if you counted the number of votes he had received). But he had been elected under the rules. To kill the President was not only to kill one bad man. It was to kill the idea that politics is settled by argument and debate and elections. If Kassian and Bruton were to be allowed to succeed, and if she did not do all she could to stop them, then she would be declaring – to use the language she grew up with in Ireland – that the bullet was stronger than the ballot, that the latter had to give way to the former. And she did not want to live in that kind of world.

Oddly, she suspected the same was true of the Chief of Staff and the Defense Secretary. They didn't strike her as the fascist coup types; they didn't want to be part of some ruling junta. But they, along with Mary Rajak, and a handful of others, had seen what this man was capable of. They had seen him give the order that would have killed hundreds of millions of innocent human beings, that might – and this was not hyperbole – have ended civilized life on this planet. Set against that, maybe the life of Dr Frankel did seem worth sacrificing: surrendering one life to save all humanity. Compared to the catastrophe that would otherwise be inflicted on the earth, all the talk of democracy must have sounded so abstract. Just hot, vaporous air.

195

Still, there had to be another way. This couldn't be the choice. Either you let democracy prevail, and left the world vulnerable to a man who could blow it all up the instant he felt his pride had been insulted, or you saved the world but destroyed the world's most important democracy, possibly triggering a civil war, in the process. There had to be another path. If Maggie had a natural calling, it was as a peace negotiator; that was how she had come to be in Washington in the first place. And if mediators had a professional creed, this was it: whenever you see a fork in the road, look for the third path. The two sides will tell you it's either/or, our way or their way. Your job is to find a way through that neither side loves, but both can live with.

That was what she would have to do now. She couldn't knowingly allow an assassination to go ahead, not if she didn't want to see America plunge into a second civil war, not if she truly believed in democracy rather than violence. Others might be able to do that, but not her. With the familiar stab of guilt, she remembered that she had done enough damage already. That secret she carried on her back, a sack packed with lead weight, never felt heavier than it did just now. All this mess, all of it: it was her fault.

So she would have to dig deep, to mine her innermost resources, and stick this out. She would have to conceal what she knew from Richard – and, harder, conceal that she knew at all.

She changed hurriedly, and in the bedroom, to avoid seeing him. She threw on whatever clothes she could find, rescuing a skirt from the laundry basket. It had just the one stain: she dabbed at it with a licked finger and tried to persuade herself the mark was less visible. Armoured by her clothing, she rush-dried her hair and rubbed make-up on haphazardly, trying and failing to mask the shadows under her eyes with concealer. She looked awful, but it would have to do. The important thing was to be ready to go, pre-empting the prospect of the 'slow breakfast' Richard had had in mind. She would claim pressure of work.

She was rounding up things in the living room, shoving them into her bag, when Richard emerged, his hair still wet, a couple of small damp spots on his shirt. He had dressed quickly. He had his phone in his right hand.

'You hurrying off, darling?'

'Yes, I'm afraid I am. Horrendous day today.'

'Oh really? Have you got an early meeting?'

Maggie was searching for her keys, glad of the excuse to avoid eye contact. 'Just a lot on.'

'Yeah, you look kinda rough. You sure I'm not wearing you out, honey?' He smiled. And when she said nothing, he added, 'Or is it this whole investigation thing?'

She looked up from turning cushions over on the couch. All she could see was the phone in his hand. Had she done something stupid in the night, something that had given her away? She had been careful not to open any unread emails: that was always a giveaway that somebody had been poking around. But something else? Could the Notes app have left some trace, telling Richard when it had last been opened?

'Yes,' she said. The keys were in the fruit bowl (which hadn't contained any fruit since Christmas). She had everything she needed. She was desperate to get out. Then, as if apologetic that she couldn't say more, and with a comic shrug, she added, 'That damned Chinese wall. Sorry.'

'No worries,' Richard said, the phone still large and glaring in his hand. 'I just thought we might chat, you know, over breakfast.'

'That would have been lovely,' she gave him her sweet

smile, but she suspected it looked wonky. She turned towards the front door. 'Anyway—'

'Maggie.'

She turned around. 'Yes?'

'Look, it's probably nothing. But I was thinking about, you know, what happened.'

Maggie crinkled her forehead.

'With you, I mean.' He could see the penny had not dropped. 'Under the last President.'

'Oh.' The bile of guilt began to rise inside her. He was almost the only person she had ever discussed that with. The thought that he held that over her made her want to close her eyes, in exhaustion and despair. But she knew she had to show him nothing. 'What about it?'

'Nothing specific. Just that these are pretty intense times. Lots happening.'

'That's certainly true.'

'And so you might need to be careful. That's all I wanted to say.'

'Okayyyy,' Maggie said, as if indulging an eccentric aunt whose heart was in the right place.

'Tread carefully, Maggie. Tread carefully.'

Only now did she meet his gaze. For a fleeting moment, much less than a second, he held his expression: it was unsmiling, cold. But then, perhaps aware that his face was under scrutiny, he let his features take the shape of those of a kind, tender lover. 'Have a great day, my darling!'

26

New York, Thursday, 7.53am

'We're back with more Morning Joe here on MSNBC. I gotta tell
you, I thought we'd seen it all from this President—'

'Oh yeah.'

'But last night, actually in the wee small hours of the morning—'

'Three eleven am, Eastern.'

'Thank you, three eleven am Eastern time, here's what the
President of the United States said on Twitter. Let's get that up on
the screen there. OK. Mika, you going to read that for us?'

'I won't do the voice!'

'No, just the words are gonna do it. You go ahead.'

'OK, here goes. "Black caucus attacking me over Forty Acres.
Too much white guilt over 'slavery'! Nobody really knows what
happened."'

'Let's just keep that up there on the screen. OK, take a good
look. You wanna read that again?'

'No, thank you kindly!'

[Laughter]

'Eugene, why don't you kick us off with your reaction to this?'

[Silence, then more laughter]

'I gotta tell you, Joe . . . I mean, where do you even begin with this? Let me back up a little bit, OK? Can I do that?'

'Sure.'

'This is not wholly new, OK? I mean this is new, this subject. But the President questioning basic facts? That is not new. He's done it on climate change. He's done—'

'He's done it on the size of his vote, he's done it on the crime figures.'

'Absolutely. He has, that's right. And let's not forget when he said millions of people are getting six-figure salaries from the federal government for jobs they don't do and that don't exist. Remember that one?'

'I do.'

'And we kind of got used to it. You know, "it's the post-truth presidency" and all that. But this is something else now. This is a historic event he's talking about. Perhaps the most important historic event in terms of the destiny of this country.'

'We fought a civil war over it.'

'Right. And now you have the President in the middle of the night, denying that event? Saying it never happened? I mean, I am sitting here, as the descendent of slaves who were brought to this country—'

'But is he saying it didn't happen? He said, "Nobody really knows what—"

[Crosstalk]

'Come on, one at a time. Come on, you guys. Eugene, I'm sticking with you: now make your point.'

'That's what he always says! "Nobody really knows." That's denial, right there. He did the same with climate change. "Nobody really knows." Well, I've got news for you, Mr President. We do really know. We do. The record is there. The documents are there. The ships' manifests are there, with the list of their "cargo". And you know what that cargo was? That cargo was the

200

great-grandparents of my great-grandparents, who were brought here – I'm sorry, this makes me very emotional.'

'That's OK, this—'

'Nothing to apologize for.'

'—is emotional. The President has hit a very raw nerve here.'

'You see, though – and you I know I love you, Joe. But even that, what you said, "He's hit a raw nerve", that makes it sound like he's just said something controversial, like he's offered a controversial opinion on something. But this isn't an opinion. He's not said, "Hey, I think slavery was a good thing." He's said "Slavery. Did. Not. Happen." That is very different.'

'Mark, why don't you come in here?'

'Well, look, I was just going to say that the response to the tweet shows—'

'Retweeted twenty-two thousand times already.'

'—that this – really, twenty-two thousand? Wow. What I was going to say, and I hate to say it, but that response shows that there's a lot of people who are going to rally to this kind of message. The liberal elites will hate it, of course. But the base will love it. And what they will love is the very fact that the liberal elite hate it, you know, including people on this show and on this network especially.'

'Gene?'

'All I'm trying to say to you – and I'm not singling you out here, Mark, I really am not – but these are my ancestors. Actually, that makes it sound like it was ancient history. It really is not that long ago. When I was a child, there were people around whose grandparents had been slaves. All right? So this is like . . . Imagine he said, "Nobody really knows about the Holocaust. You know, all this stuff about Auschwitz: nobody really knows." Imagine what we'd be saying. We—'

'We need to take a short break soon—'

'We'd be calling him a Holocaust denier, Mika. We wouldn't

say, "He's standing up to political correctness" or "He's ruffling the feathers of the mainstream media." We'd say he's a Holocaust denier.'

'Slavery denier.'

'So why should this be any different?'

'All right, but I just want to get the reaction of all of you to this tweet from the President which he sent a little after the first one. OK, let's get that up on the screen. There we go. You gonna read that one for us, Mika?'

'So this is like a subtweet. He does this a lot actually. He's kind of quoting a tweet that's been sent to him, applauding what he said about slavery. So the reply to him had said, "Kudos to you for saying it, Mr President." And his response to that was, "Americans want to have this debate. The lying press want to shut it down. Too late!"'

'But here's the thing. That tweet, the one saying "Kudos", that came from an account that is, in fact, a leading white supremacist organization. And the President got in trouble before for retweeting some of their tweets—'

'That meme with the Jewish star, the Star of David—'

'That's right. So that's gonna be a point of controversy as well, giving a kind of shout-out to this group—'

'Even when he knows who they are.'

'But look, there's one more. This was kind of a Twitterstorm by the President during the night when, you know, you might have thought he would be focusing on the situation with North Korea—'

'I mean, that's what makes this even more incredible—'

'Mark, we're going to come back to that – I promise! – but let Mika just get to this last tweet from the President. It came at—'

'Three eighteen am.'

'That's right. Three eighteen. So, you gonna read this last one for us?'

'All right. Last one. No more!'

[Laughter]

'Again, he's quoting a reply he's had. And this one is from someone whose handle is @ProudAmerican1776 and what they said was, "They always whine about 'slavery'" – you see the little quotes he's put around that – "but where's the evidence?"'

'Eugene, I can see your face.'

'I'm just stunned, you know. Stunned and so disappointed. That this is the leader of . . . I'm . . . I'm . . .'

'Lost for words.'

'We understand that. I understand that. I was born in Georgia. I represented Florida in the United States Congress. I'm a son of the South. But help out our viewers here, help out our young viewers especially. If someone's watching this, maybe they don't know all the history. The President has kind of thrown down the gauntlet, the question is out there now. So when we come back, Gene, after we take some ads here, I want you to answer this as if we were in a court of law, because you know people can make things up, documents can get forged, so what is the actual evidence that there was slavery in America? Gene?'

'He's taking his mic off.'

'Gene, please. Gene, don't – please come back. Eugene. I'm sorry, folks, we seem to have lost him. He's left the studio. We'll be right back.'

27

The White House, Washington, DC, Thursday, 8.04am
It wasn't easy to get facetime with the White House Chief of Staff, not this one, nor any of his predecessors. He was the conductor of the orchestra, the station master, the top traffic cop as well as the CEO and team leader of the White House. He made the trains run on time, he was everyone's line manager, but he was also and often the lead strategist, most trusted counsellor and right hand to the President. He was the President's representative on earth, but also his guiding star.

Perhaps the worst kept secret in Washington was that Bob Kassian fulfilled only half of those duties for this President. He was certainly the Chief Operations Officer, the man who made the machine work. For that he was admired, regarded as that rare creature in DC: a highly capable administrator. But no one could pretend that he was a presidential confidant. Everyone knew that he had only been hired as a sop to the party establishment, someone who could bridge the divide between the President – so wholly alien to the ways and means of Washington – and everyone else in the capital. He had been appointed as security, a way for the new occupant of the White House to reassure a nervous governing class that he would not go wild. Bob Kassian was a comfort blanket in human form.

Still, even if everyone knew he sat outside the President's inner circle – at whose centre lay Crawford McNamara – his diary was nevertheless packed. Maggie would have to deploy every ounce of charm and skill to get five minutes alone with him not next week or next month but today. Right now.

And she didn't feel either charming or skilful. She felt dirty, not only used by McNamara and his – what was the right word for Richard: rent-boy, whore? – but also comprehensively outplayed. She had been led into a honeytrap, lured there by her own lust for a stupidly attractive, apparently empathetic man. She was no better than those dumb men who were again and again seduced into revealing secret or sensitive information by some clever, pretty spy. She remembered mocking that general who lost his job – and paid a hefty court fine – for handing over classified info to his mistress. 'He should learn to keep it zipped,' she had said, along with every other woman in Washington. Well, she was no better.

She picked up coffee on the way. After a night like that, she needed a double espresso just to stay conscious. While she was there, she saw a missed call from Nick, her contact at the Pentagon.

She had rounded off their call yesterday by pushing her luck, asking for some detail on the résumé of a former veteran. Specifically, the military service record of one Robert Kassian.

If he felt discomfort at that, Nick's voice did not reveal it. But she had assumed that he would resort to the bureaucratic stonewall, not refusing her request exactly but simply delaying it into the Washington eternity.

'Hi there, Maggie.' The voice as reliable as a speaking clock. She braced herself to hear that, 'We are not able to share that information at this time' or, if he was feeling expansive, 'I suggest you ask Mr Kassian about those two missing years yourself.'

'How you doing?'

'Listen, are you at work? At Sixteen Hundred?'

'Not yet, but I will be in about five minutes.'

'OK. Call me when you get there. Use Signal.'

Maggie did as she was told, using Signal – the app that promised maximum encryption – from her cellphone. Her door was closed.

'OK, obviously you didn't get this information from me personally. Protocol is that the Department never speaks about this category of veteran, for reasons that will become obvious. Also, I need to be sure that this information is for your use only.'

'It is.'

'And that you will not be putting it in writing or any form of documentation for circulation, distribution or duplication.'

'Absolutely.'

'Sorry, Maggie. Them's the rules!'

'I understand.'

'Probably best not to write this down at all. Anywhere. Even in a note for yourself.'

'OK. The suspense is killing me!'

'All right. So Robert G Kassian served in the Army Rangers between 1989 and 1990, as you know. From 1992 to 1995, he was attached to DIA.'

'Defense Intelligence Agency.'

'Exactly. Now, the period you asked about spans March 1990 to August 1992. In that time, Sergeant Kassian served with the 1st Special Forces Operational Detachment-Delta.'

'Delta Force.'

'Yes.'

'And that would have been during the first Gulf War.'

'Yes, between August 1990 and June 1991, Sergeant Kassian was stationed in and around the Persian Gulf.'

'I see. So that means he would have been in Delta Force at the same time as—'

'Correct. This is highly classified information, Maggie.'

'Of course.' Maggie could feel the debt between them growing.

'In the Persian Gulf Sergeant Kassian's commanding officer in special operations was Major James Bruton. They were members of an elite unit, the cream of the cream.'

'What did they do?'

'Maggie, I must stress again: this is for your use only.'

'Absolutely.'

'The unit was small. Functioned like a cell. Initially, undertaking search and destroy operations – looking for and taking out Saddam's Scud launchers.'

'And then?'

'After the first phase of hostilities, the unit moved on to different work. Its prime area of specialism was targeted assassinations.'

28

Falls Church, Thursday, 8.44am

Dear Mr President

I keep trying to think of reasons why you deserve to live. Maybe your going to change. Maybe your going to allow people to keep living the way we were living before. Maybe your going to stop saying people like me are not reel Americans even when I fought in a war and nearly had my leg blown off and you were so chicken shit you got out of fighting and even boasted about it like it showed you were smart.

But why would you change, why. Youv made so much money, your like one of the richest people in the world and now youv got power too. So why would you change. What you do, all this shit you do its made you rich and powerfull.

My mom loved America do you know that. She really loved this country she told us when we were kids that we had to be greatfull that we were in the best country in the world and we all believed her. Thats why i became a soldier because I believed all that shit.

And now you come along and at first everyone says dont worry hes just making up all that shit he's saying it to get votes he's never gonna actually do any of that shit theyd never let him do it there are laws and courts and he cant. Like this is America you cant just round people up and kick them out, like thats not how it works.

I reely believed it and now I see that i just WANTED to believe it which is different. Not the same thing. Deep inside I think I knew that you were serious, you were actually serious. You were going to take people like my mom and you were gonna put them on a bus - like a fucking bus man - and drive them to the border and dump them on the other side. Even when that woman had a son in the army who was ready to die for America even then you would dump her like she was some bag of shit that you didnt want like you were taking out the garbage.

This is not right and if you gave any sign that one day you woud change I woud maybe feel different. But your making it worse every day saying all these things about Latino people and also making Muslims be on a list like there an enemy and saying black people live shit lives and we should be greatfull that so many of them dont vote its all wrong man its wrong.

And i sometimes think you want everyone in america to hate each other and then they wont hate you or maybe its like you feel so bad about yourself you want everyone to feel bad about thereselves but some people are good like my mom was good but now shes dead and you killed her because she couldnt cope being on her own without me and so far away and she needed me to look after her and just because shes Latina doesnt means she from Mexico she was from El Salvador but you dumped her in Mexico but she know no one there and thats why she got sick and died and i hate you and the only way to stop you is if I could find another way to stop you that would be better but i cant and i know that theyll kill me when i do it but im doing it for my mom and all the other moms and children who cant fight back and i still love this country but you wouldnt under—stand that god bless America.

Sitting in a café on West Broad Street, Julian Garcia read it over one more time and wondered whether it was too much. Less is more, that was always the best policy. He wondered if this had crossed that all-important line. No use if it seemed over the top. And yet, it had to fit the deed that it would apparently explain. Not much room for nuance there.

Besides, the key audience was the one after the event. It had to make sense to them. It needed to feel plausible. He submitted it to the same test he had applied to the art installation he had mounted on the wall of Hernandez's living room. Imagine a screengrab or a quote on the news or on Facebook. Would it do the job?

He checked the grammar and spelling. Too much? Too little? Garcia had stuck to the rule he'd learned in those secondments at the Defense Intelligence Agency: make your cover as close to reality as possible. Based on the samples of Hernandez's writing that he'd seen, this was about right. His friend was an outstanding soldier, but the two of them had taken different routes within special ops. The written word had become a crucial tool for Garcia; not so for Jorge.

But if this document rang true, Garcia knew it was not because of the spelling or punctuation. It was because it was telling a story, conveying a fury, that was real. And that fury, that story, belonged to Garcia himself.

When they met, Jim Bruton had only made the most glancing nod to it. Garcia had mentioned that he had been visiting his sister, dealing with family stuff, and Bruton had said, 'Yes. I know about that. And I'm sorry.'

At the time, Garcia had thought nothing of it: his commander was being polite. But not long afterwards, and especially as he began to work with Hernandez, he became convinced that the particular circumstances of his mother's death had played a part in Bruton's selection of him. The general was not just relying on the blood loyalty they shared as soldiers – though, as it happens, he could have. He was trusting that Garcia felt a rage of his own for the man he was being asked to . . . remove.

Not that that was relevant. Indeed, it was completely irrelevant. This was a mission, to be carried out with calm, neutral professionalism. It was vital to remember that. Ask any military assassin and they'll tell you the same thing. You must never hate your target. Begin to hate and you will fail.

So, he decided, the content was OK. The look worried him more. Ideally, he would have had Jorge write this out himself. But the early start this morning, when Hernandez had opened up his home and let Garcia construct the collage on the wall, had left him tired. Besides, Julian wanted to get out early, rather than linger at the house too long and risk getting spotted. So he had asked his friend to write out a few lines, watched him do it and left it that.

Afterwards, away from the house, Garcia had practised the handwriting again and again, until he was happy it was a match for Jorge's. He had seen that, even apart from the illness, handwriting had been an effort for Jorge, each word laboured over. Punctuation seemed to be a luxury beyond reach, as it was for many of the men they had both served with all those years ago. So, as Garcia wrote, he visualized the men in his unit and their very occasional cards or letters home. And then he had filled pages with handwriting until it looked right.

He would post the letter later today. Not from this neighbourhood. Jorge was angry but he was not stupid. Besides, Garcia thought, his Jorge was a determined man. He did not want the Secret Service knocking on his door too early, before his mission had been accomplished. Jorge would do nothing that could be traced too easily. He would send his emails to the White House from the Anacostia public library: they would be backdated, but no one would know that had been done artificially. (And they would appear to come from a regular computer: clearly the Tails system was beyond a man like Jorge.) There could be no recklessness.

He was, Garcia understood, walking a very thin line here. He needed to do just enough that, afterwards, the police and the press would agree that the warning signs had been there all along, but not so much that they would stop Jorge too soon.

Garcia had a job to do. He had to create a presidential assassin. Not a potential one, not a suspected one. But a real one. And that meant there was one more task ahead.

29

'Good to see you, Maggie. You thriving?'

Kassian had moved out from behind his desk, so that the two of them were seated at the round table where, Maggie suspected, most of the work here was done.

She had not had to barge in physically, though she had been ready for that. She simply told Kassian's PA-cum-gatekeeper that she had urgent questions to ask regarding the Frankel death and that she would need only a few minutes. The PA asked her to wait and Maggie did as she was told, watching as the woman typed a one-line email that she suspected was a distilled version of her request. A moment later, the PA suggested Maggie should go back to her office and the PA would let her know the instant Bob was free.

'In that case,' Maggie said, 'could you rephrase my request? Could you tell Mr Kassian – Bob – that I want to discuss not the Frankel death but the Frankel *killing* and that I'm keen we talk about this before I have to give a scheduled briefing to Mr McNamara later today?' The woman said nothing, though Maggie swore she saw her pale at the word 'killing'. Thirty seconds later, Maggie was ushered in.

Maggie had only ever had brief dealings with Kassian. Just because they were both outside the inner circle did not mean they coincided often: there were rather too many residents of White House Siberia for that. But she had always found him courteous and polite, capable if a little unexciting. She was struggling to square that, and indeed the man in front of her now, with what she had learned less than an hour earlier from Nick at the Pentagon.

That Jim 'the Brute' Bruton had killed with his bare hands would surprise nobody. But Kassian seemed meeker, more cerebral. She would have had him down as one of those 'defense analyst' types, perhaps an aide to the general staff, the military equivalent of a clerk to a Supreme Court justice. She'd have assumed that Kassian had been on a graduate fast track into the military, catapulted to the upper echelons from the start, rather than a hands-on, boots-on-the-ground soldier.

But if that had upended her expectations, what Nick had revealed reinforced her working hypothesis in one key particular. He had told her that Bruton and Kassian had served together in a tiny elite unite. Maggie had seen enough of warfare to know that few bonds tied any two men closer together. These two shared a bond of blood. The trust between them would be total and unbreakable.

What was more, and so rare in Washington, was that their connection was secret. It appeared in no press profiles and had never once been mentioned on television – which meant it was all but certain the President himself had no idea of it.

'I'm well, thank you.' As it had several times already

today, a thought of last night, and this morning – the messages on the phone, the look on Richard's face as he warned her to be careful – pulsed through her cerebral cortex. It occurred to her that she almost certainly looked like shit.

With an act of will that verged on the physical, she shoved that thought aside. She would focus – *like a laserbeam*, as her old boss Stuart Goldstein always put it – on the matter at hand. 'I need to talk to you about Dr Frankel.'

He nodded, unfazed. If he felt a smidgeon of guilt, he did not show it. So maybe that's what they taught in special ops: guiltless murder.

She explained what she had found so far: a personal history and family life wholly at odds with suicide, unexplained forensic discrepancies at the scene – the mud-free shoes and the wrongly positioned driver's seat – and, earlier today, phone records including an unexplained call apparently summoning Dr Frankel to leave home at a time out of sync with his usual routine. 'Above all,' she concluded, 'Dr Frankel's widow said that something highly out of the ordinary took place the evening before his death.'

'And what's that?' Kassian asked. Pro move: see what your interlocutor knows, because she might know nothing.

'I thought you might tell me, Bob.'

'I'd rather hear it from you, Maggie.'

They paused for a while, a professionals' stalemate. Eventually Maggie smiled and said, 'You and the Secretary of Defense made an unscheduled social call. At the home of Dr Frankel.'

'That's right. We did.'

'It would help my inquiries if you were able to tell me what that meeting was about.'

'I don't think "meeting" is quite the right word.'

'What would be the right word, Bob?'

'I'd say it was a conversation.'

'OK. It would help my inquiries if you were able to tell me what that *conversation* was about.' She smiled, a smile that had once worked miracles for her, disarming warlords in Darfur and settler leaders on the West Bank alike. Now, after what she had read on Richard's phone, she wondered if that power was beginning to fade. Involuntarily, she pictured the President's daughter.

Kassian got up and walked back to his desk. Was he about to produce a key document that would explain everything? Was he going to call his PA and ask for Maggie to be removed? Was he about to open a top drawer and reach for a revolver . . .

Instead, he did a few keystrokes on his computer, which then proceeded to broadcast classical music, at a high volume.

'Rosemary doesn't like it,' he said, gesturing towards the music. 'But it helps me relax. As do these.' He held up a set of worry beads, the kind you might pick up in any *souk* in Baghdad or Damascus. 'I think we have that part of the world in common.'

Maggie nodded, but she was not going to be diverted. The music was unsettling; she had to talk over it. 'What was so urgent that you needed to see Dr Frankel at home on Monday night? Why couldn't it wait till the next morning?' She chose to hold back, for now, what she knew of the incident in the Situation Room.

'Maggie, do you mind if I ask you a question?'

She said nothing.

'Why are you still working here?'

'What?'

'I mean, you were a loyalist to the previous incumbent.

216

Everyone knows that. One of his most trusted counsellors. Everyone assumed you'd leave. But you're still here.'

'Look, if you want to give me my annual appraisal, then today might not be—'

'Don't get me wrong. I'm *glad* you stayed. Real glad. We need people of your calibre on this team. There are so many people who are . . .' The sentence drifted away.

'Why did you both go together, you and Mr Bruton?'

'I mean, this President. You don't believe in him, do you? You can't. I've read your résumé. You're the last person who'd want to serve him.'

'You arrived, unannounced, at nine thirty pm. Why no advance phone call? What was so urgent that it had to be done then, that night, and in person?'

'I think you're a patriot for your adopted country. But I don't see you as a natural supporter of the—'

Maggie cut him off. 'Let's just say, I believe in the office of the presidency. I serve that. For as long as I believe I can do some good. Now, to my question. Did you get what you wanted, Mr Kassian? Did you get what you came for?'

'I don't—'

'Or did Dr Frankel say no? To your scheme, to you and Bruton? Did he refuse to go along with it?'

'You don't understand at all.'

'Help me understand then. Tell me what happened.' She wondered if she could be heard over the music. It was getting louder.

'I can't tell you anything, Maggie. Except that I was as surprised – and as alarmed – by Dr Frankel's death as you were. Perhaps more so. The same goes for Jim.'

'So you—'

'Had nothing to do with it. Of course we didn't.' He was

217

examining his fingers. He looked glum, weighed down by whatever it was he was not saying.

Maggie fell silent. She had a sense that he was about to say more, that he *wanted* to say more, maybe even to unburden himself.

He looked up and met her gaze. 'There are things at work here that are far bigger than even you realize. The smartest play might be to walk away. Stand back, see what happens. You can always investigate afterwards.' He smiled. 'Washington is a town built on a swamp, I'm sure you know that. Maybe it's best to walk around this one, rather than wading right in. Do you know what I mean, Maggie?'

He stood up, as if to signal that the meeting was over and it was time for her to leave. But he had one last thing to say. 'Love of country takes many forms, Maggie. Like I said, I think you love your country. But your country might not always love you back.'

30

Holkham Beach, Norfolk, England, 9.10am, eleven days earlier
Was there a more perfect spot in all the world? He had travelled through much of it and had yet to find somewhere that moved him the way this place did. The beach, so wide and, when the tide was out, so deep you could barely glimpse the water's edge on the far horizon. The dunes, ever changing, remoulding themselves into new shapes for each day. And, above, a vast sky, a canvas of pure blues and glowing oranges. Through some trick, when the rest of the country, including villages just a few miles away from here, was suffocating under dishwater skies, this beach was favoured with a clarity of light. It was as if England wanted to give a good account of itself just before it yielded to the North Sea, like a sailor's girl wearing her Sunday best before waving farewell at the shore.

Only here did Anthony Vale ever think such thoughts. The rest of the week, his head was full of cases and meetings and clients and precedents and billing hours. On the train down on Friday night, it was no better: he was still reviewing papers, typing emails on his laptop or, on those occasions when he couldn't get a seat – no first class on the London train to King's Lynn – thumbing them out on his phone. Saturday was lovely, of course. A lie-in, time spent cooking lunch, while Matthew played the piano. Perfect. But truth be told, it was only by the time Sunday came around that he had properly unwound. Specifically the Sunday morning walk with the dog: this moment was, for him, the summit. At last, he could notice the sky, smell the sea and, if he closed his eyes, he could see something other than his caseload.

Buddy was tugging at his trouser leg, making that little pleading sound Anthony could hardly resist. Funny how things worked out. He would have been the last person anyone in their circle – himself included – would have expected to become a dog lover. Buddy had been Matthew's idea. One weekend he put Anthony in the car, and started driving without revealing the destination. He had assumed they were going to the Union Chapel or perhaps the Wigmore Hall for a recital. Instead they pitched up at Battersea Dogs Home. One look at that little West Highland white terrier and Anthony was molten; Matthew didn't even have to make a case. Anthony was sold.

He put the ball in the thrower, pulled his arm back and watched it fly far into the distance. Buddy hared off, his eagerness to please as delightful and heartbreaking as ever. These little moments would re-charge him for the week ahead.

And it would be quite a week. In court, starting tomorrow, he would do battle with the most high-powered legal team he had ever faced. Certainly the most expensive. All representing surely the most formidable client he or any other British lawyer had taken on. Oh, of course, everyone insisted that the High Court would treat this like any other case, without fear or favour. But no one seriously believed that.

Officially, the point of law at stake was clear: had the government followed its own processes and acted lawfully in barring the complainant from taking full ownership of a business in which it already owned the lion's share? Was the government right to say it was not in the public interest for this US-based company, for this man, to control so much of the UK market that it would – *he* would – in effect enjoy a monopoly?

And when he said 'the government', that too was hardly straightforward. True, the Competition and Markets Authority had issued its recommendation that the takeover be blocked and that advice had been accepted by the relevant government department. But that was before the complainant had ascended to his, ahem, position of influence. Now that he was there, different parts of government took different views. The law was a delicate thing and no one wanted to be seen to be meddling in the judicial process – heaven forfend – but several well-informed columnists had already reported that the Foreign Office and, most likely, Downing Street itself would not be too unhappy if their colleagues in the Department for Business were to suffer a reverse in the courts. A few red faces in Whitehall were a price worth paying to keep things sweet with the Americans. By which they meant one American – and his family – in particular.

Buddy was back with the ball and hungry for his reward. Anthony bent down and stroked him all over, rubbing his ears especially, just as he liked. 'Such a good boy,' he said, hoping that with every word, and every stroke, he was compensating for the hurt and neglect this wonderful, blameless creature had endured at the start of his life. He tossed the ball once more.

So tomorrow's case was daunting, on any measure. And yet Anthony refused to feel overwhelmed. He had prepared thoroughly. He knew what arguments to make, what weaknesses in his opponent to exploit. He had only failed in one area and it was the usual one. Matthew always said it, 'You've got to learn to delegate!' It was a bad defect, he was willing to admit it. The entire case was located in his head. His colleagues knew bits of it, but only he could see the whole. In a thousand-piece jigsaw, each member of the team held maybe a hundred or so pieces. Only he held the box with the picture.

Whatever had happened to that dog? Buddy would normally have raced back by now. Doubtless, he had got distracted by another ball, or another dog, sniffing around with his usual unrestrained curiosity. Sweet, silly old thing.

He scanned the horizon. A group of walkers; a father and son trying to launch a kite. Ah, there he . . . no, different breed.

'Buddy! Come on, buddy.' He always felt ridiculous doing this, too aware of his own voice, of the absurdity of the endearments he, Matthew and Buddy shared. Fine indoors, but not for public consumption.

'Buddy, come on, fella. Where are you?'

He heard a yap, which made him turn sharply to his left. There, by the dunes, was a man struggling to hold a white terrier by the collar. Surely that couldn't . . .

Anthony walked faster, his gaze fixed on the animal at the man's hand. The colouring was the same, but it didn't make sense. Who was this man?

Now, just as he came within a hundred yards or so, he got a clearer view. The man stepped back, so that Anthony assumed Buddy was about to come bounding towards him. And the dog did separate from the man, creating daylight between them. But only for a second. Because it was clear that though, yes, that was indeed Buddy – he was now on a leash.

'Excuse me, that's my dog,' Anthony heard himself say.

Perhaps the man was not near enough to hear, because he ignored Anthony, turning his back to the sea and walking briskly in the direction of the woods.

'Excuse me!' Anthony shouted. The man in front did not turn back and started jogging towards the trees, with Buddy in tow. Anthony could see the dog was reluctant, and Buddy was a strong animal, yet he was getting dragged along, which meant this man must be pulling on that leash with serious force.

Now Anthony broke into a run. 'Hey, you there. That's my dog. Give me back my dog!'

Was this man deaf? He didn't so much as turn around. Now anger mixed with concern turned into adrenalin, injecting itself straight into Anthony's bloodstream. How dare this man – dressed in black and with a beanie hat low on his head, even on this spring morning – steal his beloved Buddy?

Anthony scrambled across the sand, through the long grasses and finally felt the ground harden as he went among the trees and bushes. He looked around, worried he'd lost them. But then he heard that sound, a low, anguished keening he recognized. Buddy.

He ran towards the noise, but there was a dip which made him stumble. He put out his hand, which landed on a clump of thistles. *Shit.*

He got to his feet, disoriented. Buddy was in pain, he was sure of it. He wasn't sure which way to turn. He listened for the dog again, almost wanting to hear that awful whine, but there was only an empty quiet.

'Buddy!' And then, unbothered by who could hear and what they would think of the way he and Matthew spoke to their dog, and what that said about them, he called out, 'Don't worry, Buddy. Daddy's here.'

And then, thank God, he felt a tug on the bottom of his trouser leg and he looked down and there, God bless his little face, was Buddy and as Anthony instinctively reached down to touch the dog's ears, searching for the source of his pain, noticing that one of his legs was hanging limply, he felt something he didn't understand – more like a sound than a feeling, a thick thud at the back of his head, where the skull meets the neck.

He fell forward, almost landing on top of Buddy, so that the last scent in his nostrils, as the second, confirming blow came and Anthony Vale slipped into unconsciousness and death, was the warm, wet aroma of the animal he loved.

31

Washington, DC, Thursday, 10.40am

Maggie's head was throbbing: from the coffee, from the exhaustion, from her meeting with Kassian, from what she'd seen on Richard's phone, from what he'd said, from what Kassian had said, from the fact that an assassination plot seemed to be unfolding before her eyes, in real time, and that she had no idea how to stop it.

Kassian had threatened her, albeit in the nicest possible way: *your country might not always love you back.* And so had Richard: *Tread carefully, Maggie.* One White House employee was already dead, and Kassian had done nothing to convince her that Dr Jeffrey Frankel had not paid the price for standing in the way of the Chief of Staff and his commanding officer, Jim Bruton.

She got into her car, wishing she could see the one man she reckoned might be able to untangle this mess. Stuart Goldstein had played the central role in pulling her off the diplomatic track after the Jerusalem episode and recruiting her to work as a foreign policy adviser for his client, then a little-known state governor who, within eighteen months, would become President. They had been such an unlikely duo, she and Stuart: he a wheezing, morbidly obese, middle-aged Jew from Brooklyn, wise to the cynical complexities of politics and therefore all human affairs, she an Irish Catholic girl barely out of her twenties brimming with beauty pageant platitudes about making the world a better place (or so her earlier self seemed to her now). And yet they had clicked, bonded chiefly by their loyalty to the president they served. She heard herself sigh at the memory of that feeling.

She had barely got onto the E Street Expressway when the phone rang. The name of the caller was displayed on the dashboard: *Liz*. Nightmare timing, when she needed so desperately to think, but when else would she have half an hour to speak to her sister? She felt for the phone symbol on the steering wheel and pressed it.

'Hi Liz. How're you going?'

'I got fired, Maggie.'

'You? Fired? But you're the best fucking teacher in the world. Why would they fire you?'

'You know that court case, in Oklahoma?'

'What court case?' Maggie had the strong sense of her brain as a computer that was overloaded, unable to process any more information. If she could have displayed a spinning wheel, she would have.

'The one with the school board. The Supreme Court.'

'Oh, that. Sure, the creationism thing. What about it?'

'So there's a new school board here. And because of the Court ruling, they've decided: all schools have to teach creationism as science. We can teach evolution, but only as an "alternative theory" – that's the actual term they use, can you believe it? And so the head – or the principal or whatever these people fucking call it – he comes to all of us today, the whole science department, and says, "This is how it's going to be" and – this is what kills me, Maggie – they only go and fucking agree. Can you believe that? All these science teachers sit there nodding, like this is OK. But it's not OK. No way. This is *science*. It's reason. It's not faith. That's what I've been telling the kids, this is not just—'

'Whoa, Liz. Take a breath. Are you saying you *resigned*?'

'It's not like some creed. Like, "I believe the earth is round and you believe the earth is flat and that's cool, because we're all entitled to our own beliefs and our own traditions." Fuck that.'

'You weren't fired. You resigned on principle.'

'I'm not going to pretend to these children that Adam and Eve is fucking science. It's not. OK? It might be a sweet story, but it's no more science than Father bloody Christmas.'

'So you refused. You took a stand.'

'If I wanted to be a Sunday school teacher, I'd have stayed in Ireland at that bloody convent. I thought: what would Maggie do? She'd tell them to fuck right off. So that's what I did.'

'You told the school principal to fuck off?'

'Well, I told him I was hired to teach science. If he wanted someone to teach fairytales, then he needed to look elsewhere.'

'Oh right.'

'And then I told him to fuck off.'

'Wow.' Maggie turned off the I-66 and onto the George Washington Memorial Parkway. 'You're amazing.'

'Not really. You'd have done the same in my position.'

The words hung in the air just a second too long. 'So what are you going to do now?'

Liz began to answer, but Maggie could barely hear her. The air-conditioning had somehow come on and the fan was blowing full blast. Maggie stabbed at the buttons but nothing seemed to work.

'Maggie? Are you there?'

'Liz, I can't hear you! Let me just . . . I'll call you back.'

But before Liz had a chance to reply, the call dropped out. Maggie would have assumed it was no more than a loss of signal but, a second later, the car radio came on. It was pumping out an ear-splitting noise at full volume: the dashboard display told her the radio was tuned into Sirius XM's metal station and that the 'song' was 'Hammer Smashed Face' by Cannibal Corpses.

She reached for the knob and turned it, but it made no difference. The sound, so violent it made the car shake, would not be dimmed. Maggie twisted the knob again and pushed the power button, but it made no difference. She now hit every button she could. Nothing helped. Randomly, and aware of the gesture's uselessness, she screamed.

Only one thing seemed to have worked. She had managed to lower the rear window on the passenger side. But still the cold air was blasting directly into her on its maximum setting, chilling the sweat on her back.

Through all this, Maggie drove at seventy miles per hour. Other cars sped past her, utterly unaware of what was happening. She pushed the hazard lights button at the centre of the dashboard, but that too did nothing. Only now did she have an inkling of what was happening – and the realization terrified her.

She signalled to change lanes, but of course the signalling did not work. And, just as she was about to make her move, a thick spray of soapy fluid covered the windscreen, clouding her view. The music – wild, discordant, screeching – seemed now to be inside her head as well as the car. She could hear no other sounds, not her car nor any others. She felt as if she had been deprived of at least two of her senses, suddenly rendered temporarily blind and functionally deaf.

Desperate to move across to the shoulder, she lightly touched the brake and felt the dread inside her rise. She pressed down harder, just to be sure. There could be no doubting it. The brakes did not work. She tried the accelerator, giving it a small tap, to see if that made any difference. It did not. There could be no denying it: she was on a highway, at speed, in a car over which she had next to no control.

She gripped the steering wheel tighter, devoting all her mental strength to screening out the grinding, sawing metal noise coming from the radio that was splitting her brain in successive blows, an axe chopping through a tree stump. Her skin was cold and clammy at the same time. Every sinew in her body was straining to get out of this vehicle. It was, she knew, carrying her to her death.

Maggie understood what was happening. She had read about it not so long ago: the hackers who had staged a stunt designed to expose a flaw in the software favoured by all the big car companies, demonstrating that they could take wireless control, over the internet, of almost any vehicle, via the car's onboard entertainment system. From a laptop anywhere on the planet, they could send electronic commands to the dashboard – operating the radio or air-con – but also to the engine, steering or brakes. Someone sitting at a keyboard or screen miles away from here was driving this car. But whoever they were, she knew they had no mechanism for seeing the road ahead, for seeing what obstacles or dangers lay in her path. There were no traffic-facing cameras on this car. She was being driven by someone else far away – and that person was wearing a blindfold.

Now she saw an opening to change lanes, to inch closer

to the shoulder. She moved the steering wheel and, to her relief, that at least responded. They had left her that much. She touched the brake, in the hope that perhaps that too had been restored to her. But no. It remained dumb and useless. If a car stopped suddenly in front of her, she would plough into it, bringing death to her and to God knows how many others.

That gave her an idea, one fraught with risk. She glanced at the dashboard. The display told her that the metal station was now playing Morbid Angel; the noise level was undiminished. But she also saw, just below the hazard lights button, the illuminated green circle she was looking for.

She held her position in the middle lane and then, looking over her shoulder, changed lanes once again. Now she was where traffic was slowest. The shoulder was at her right side.

One touch on the accelerator confirmed that that function was still lost to her. Her only option was to wait. Signs for the exits to Rockville were approaching. She half-wondered if her unseen masters might soon take the wheel and drive her somewhere of their choosing, down this side road or that, into a disused layby or area of wasteground. Was that what this was, a kidnapping as well as an electronic car-jacking? But the exits passed, the car still forging ahead at a steady seventy: a metal box hurtling towards a disaster she could not stop. Were her captors offering her a choice: to jump out and die instantly on the roadside, or to wait for the inevitable crash? Which death would be worse, which more painful? And which would inflict most calamity on others?

She watched the tail of the car in front coming closer, an SUV with a reassuringly substantial rear bumper. She checked the rearview mirror once and then twice. No one too near. The speedometer told her she was still going at seventy, the same speed that she had held in the fast lane. Simple maths meant that soon she would catch up with the car in front.

Who would be driving in an SUV in the slow lane of a highway in Maryland on a weekday morning? She pictured it: a young mother, her baby strapped into a seat at the back. Maggie imagined Liz in Atlanta, fussing over her own two baby boys in the car. She felt her face twist into a grimace at the thought of what she was about to attempt.

The SUV was closer now, its speed probably closer to sixty than Maggie's menacing seventy. Was that a 'Baby On Board' sticker? Her dread was rising.

There was now the distance of two cars between them, no more. She glanced at the dashboard. It was saying nothing yet, though if there had been any kind of alarm she knew she wouldn't hear it. The radio drowned out all else. Not for nothing was blasting hardcore music into the ears of prisoners deemed a method of torture: the noise was unbearable.

Now she could see the ridge of the baby seat in the car in front and, though she could not be sure, the outline of a child's head. Surely she should pull off now, swerve into the shoulder and hope for the best. She had to face facts: her gamble had not paid off. She was doomed. The only task now was to prevent her own death killing others.

She put her hands on the wheel, readying herself to give up and make the turn when she saw the green circle on the dashboard turn red. Was it working?

And then she felt it: the descent of the engine as the car itself changed gear and then the brakes, applied sharply and automatically, bringing the car to a sudden, lurching halt. She felt her neck snap forward and then back.

But her hunch had been right. The car's forward collision warning system had overridden whatever control the hackers had.

Heart hammering, she put on the hazard lights and turned the steering wheel rightward to get herself onto the hard shoulder. But it was no good. The car was stalled, the engine killed. It wouldn't move. She looked over her shoulder: cars were coming towards her right now, in her lane.

Maggie threw open the car door on her side and leapt out into the shoulder – hoping the sight of the open door would act as some kind of warning to the oncoming traffic. A split-second later a car came towards her now-immobile vehicle, swerving just before impact. Then another and then a third, honking angrily as it sheared off the wing mirror on the driver's side.

She ran away from her car, in the direction of the traffic, so that she could give the oncoming vehicles sufficient warning and time to brake or change lane. She stood there, her hands waving in a desperate semaphore, the buffet of wind as each car passed a terrifying, physical force. She did not have time to register that her hands and knees were trembling.

And yet even in that state, her mind did not stop whirring. On the contrary, it was throbbing with two sets of questions. Had Robert Kassian had sufficient time following their meeting this morning to have ordered this lethal hacking of her car? Were the resources at the disposal of the White House Chief of Staff and his ally, the US Secretary of Defense, so great that they could make such a thing happen so fast?

At the same time, she wondered: had the man she regarded as her lover until a few hours ago realized that she had broken into his phone and read his most confidential messages? If he had, had he shared that information with Crawford McNamara? And did McNamara have sufficient resources at his disposal to order an act of hacking against Maggie that could very easily have ended her life and the lives of several wholly innocent others, including at least one child?

The awful thing about these questions, as she put each one to herself in quick succession, and as she saw the flashing lights of a police car approach, was that she knew the answer to all of them.

32

Olney, Maryland, Thursday, 12.23pm
'So what you got?'

Classic Goldstein. No time for pleasantries.

'It's a mess. That's what I've got.'

'Why not start by telling me who you trust? Warning: the correct answer in Washington DC is always and forever—'

'Nobody with two legs.'

'Good girl. Somebody taught you well.'

'That would be you, Stuart.'

She looked around. This place was gorgeous in springtime. Leafy, beautifully maintained, quiet. Completely ridiculous that Stuart Goldstein, of all people, should be here. He was loud, unkempt and a creature of the city. He'd always looked out of place in Washington, let alone Olney, bloody Maryland. For a New Yorker like him, all pastrami sandwiches and pickles straight from the barrel, DC was the sticks. This place was the sticks of the sticks.

But after what had happened on the highway, she could think of no place she'd rather be. It had been her original destination, but even if it hadn't she'd have come straight here anyway.

The police had appeared quickly. She'd explained how her vehicle had suffered a complete system failure and how she believed she was the victim of external hacking. She produced her White House pass, said that she suspected this touched on questions of national security and added that her colleagues were likely to be investigating this episode themselves. She gave the officer the name and contact details for Eleanor as the person to liaise with, hoping that she'd done just enough for them to leave it at that.

She did not tell them about the final display on the dashboard screen, which stayed on for a full minute, even after the engine had cut out. WARNING, it said. Except the word filled the entire screen and was not in the standard, corporate typeface for the car. That came direct from the hackers, she was sure of it. As if she hadn't already got the message.

'So put it this way, Maggie. Who do you distrust least?'

'No one. Now that the president has gone.'

'You mean the old president?'

'Yes.'

'Isn't it about time you were getting over him? Isn't it time to moveon dot org?'

Maggie smiled. 'It's past time.'

'So come on. Who among your colleagues don't you hate, besides Eleanor and the others?'

Maggie paused, looking towards the trees.

'That's pretty telling, isn't it?'

Maggie nodded.

'All right. Different approach. What do you know for certain?'

'That Frankel is dead and someone killed him.'

'Who would do that? Come on, Maggie. *Cui bono?*'

'Well, that depends on what the doctor told Kassian and Bruton, doesn't it?'

'All right, walk me through it.'

'If Frankel refused to declare the President mentally unfit, then Kassian and Bruton had every reason to kill him.'

'He held their secret. OK. What if the doctor agreed?'

'Then they needed him alive.'

'Which means, Maggie, that someone else would have needed him dead.'

'Yes. Anyone whose loyalty was to the President.'

'OK, who do we have in mind?'

'McNamara, obviously. Backed by Richard.'

Stuart's tone became sympathetic – and weary. 'People say politics is brutal, but I tell ya, it ain't got nothing on love.'

Maggie paused before answering. She was worried her voice was going to wobble and that if that started, she wouldn't know how to stop it. 'I just feel so stupid, Stuart. So completely stupid.'

'Not you, Maggie. Plenty of people I could name. Long list of them, in fact. But not you.'

'I mean to be so *used* like that. And not even to see it. I mean, why, for Christ's sake? Was I flattered, because he was younger than me and, you know, so good-looking? Was that it? Because that would be pathetic. And, Stuart, the things he said. The things he *believes*. I mean, how could I not see that this man – this man in my bed, touching me . . . Christ, it makes my flesh crawl just thinking about it. He's a proper racist bastard, Stuart. A racist, misogynist, antisemitic bastard.'

'Oh, I'm glad they didn't leave us out of it. They usually keep a spot for us, these guys.'

'I mean, I do have to ask myself, Stuart. At this stage of my life, why do I keep making this mistake? This same stupid, idiotic, naïve mistake.'

'*Keep* making? I think this is the first Gestapo agent you've dated, unless there's something you're not telling me.'

'I mean, you know . . . getting it wrong. With men.'

'Like I say, love makes politics look like a stroll in the park.'

'I'm not sure it was ever love, Stuart. More like lust.' As she said the words, she wasn't sure they were right. Sex had drawn her to Richard and kept her there, that was true. But those evenings together, those nights on the couch, watching cable news, lamenting the state of the world and their part in it – all that was true too. She might try to deny it now, but they had become close. She had let him in.

'Well, lust is one of Goldstein's big three, as you know.'

'"Sex, money and power. The only three things that truly motivate people to act."'

'With an honourable mention for religion, in all its forms. Faith, idealism. Don't forget that one.' He was steering her back to the topic in hand.

'With McNamara, he's hungry for power, no doubt about it', Maggie said. 'And money.'

'Kind of a package deal for those guys.'

'And for Richard, sex seems to be a factor.' She thought of the daughter. She thought of herself. 'That's not all. They're true believers. Those messages from Richard. Like I said, they're hardcore racists, Stuart. Hardcore. I kind of wish it was just about money and sex or whatever. They're much more frightening than that.'

'Are you scared, Maggie? Not a crime to be scared.'

She laughed. 'Someone just tried to crash my car with me in it.' She paused and then said, 'I'm scared for myself,

Stu. Always got to be, at least a little bit. Otherwise you start taking stupid risks. But this feels different.' She looked up. 'I don't think he was bluffing. The President, I mean. The other night. I think he did want to launch a nuclear strike. He *ordered* it. So yes, I'm scared. Not for me. Not only for me.'

'Who for, Maggie?'

She could feel her eyes pricking. 'The first people I think of when you say that . . . I think of Callum and Ryan.'

'Liz's boys.'

'Yes. I worry we're going to mess everything up. For them.'

'So let's see if we can't get to the bottom of this crater full of shit. You got your shit-shovelling clothes on?'

Maggie smiled. 'Always.'

'Right now, you need to focus on the key question.'

'Which is?'

'Remember I told you about JFK's desk? Two in-trays?'

'Urgent and Important.'

'Right. And?'

'They're not the same thing.'

'Right again. So what's the *important* question?'

'Who is behind all this? Who killed Frankel? Who tried to kill me?'

'That's three questions, but OK. Now what's the *urgent* question?'

Maggie bit her lower lip, looking into the distance at a tree that, somehow, still had a last whisper of blossom on its branches. The sky was a perfect blue.

'Come on, Maggie. I haven't got all day.'

'Oh, am I keeping you, Stu?'

'Places to meet, people to go.'

'All right. The urgent question is . . .'

'Come on, Mags. What do you need to know now? What is it you must know *now*?'

'I need to know when.'

'Precisely.'

'And where.'

'Even better.'

'I need to know when and where they're going to kill the President.'

'That's right. You do. And I have an idea for how you can find out.'

33

Chantilly, Virginia, Thursday, 12.27pm

There were hundreds of them, an embarrassment of riches. Wherever Julian Garcia looked, there were men – there may have been one woman – walking around with rifles slung over their shoulders, each one with a tell-tale little flag popping out of the barrel, to indicate these weapons were for private sale. It was ideal.

He'd not been along to many of these things. He spent too much time around the real thing for a gun show to hold much appeal. As he parked up outside the hangar-sized venue, assessing the vehicles – with their 'Don't Tread on Me' plates and occasional Confederacy-themed bumper stickers – he let his prejudices fill in the blanks. He imagined this place would be filled with weekend wannabes and armchair commandos, overweight white guys desperate to fondle the butt of a rifle they wouldn't know how to hold, let alone use in anger.

But once he'd paid his $10 admission fee and started wandering around, he saw that, yes, there were plenty of those types but also large numbers of vets, most of them from the first Gulf war rather than the second. Some, Garcia supposed, were reliving the glory days: everyone knew of men who never again found the happiness they had felt in uniform. Others, he guessed, just liked all the gear, over-grown boys who could never quite get enough of all the toys. For others it was politics. The government, the Feds, the liberal elite were always on the brink of imposing a dictatorship: the only thing that stood in their way was good patriots keeping themselves armed and protected.

Garcia had expected that feeling to have diminished now that they had a President who talked like them. What would they have to fear from this guy, who believed all the same conspiracy theories as they did? But, he discovered, most had simply adapted to the new situation. 'He's just one man', had become the new mantra. 'He's taking on a whole *system*.'

What was more, Garcia thought to himself with a smile, they weren't completely wrong, all these wingnuts, were they? There *was* a conspiracy, behind the scenes, hidden from view, at the highest levels of power. Hell, he should know. He was part of it.

How would 'Jorge Hernandez' explain why he was here? He would do his best to avoid being asked the question, for a start. He would talk to nobody. But if he stopped one of these men looking for a private sale, as he would soon have to, he would make clear he too was a man comfortable around guns. He had grown up in Texas; his dad, Garcia had decided, was a keen duck hunter. And, of course, he was a veteran.

Jorge's budget was finite. As he threaded through the stalls in this indoor marketplace, each trader setting out his wares – vintage muskets, knives, T-shirts emblazoned with the slogan 'The Second Amendment . . . It Ain't About Duck Hunting' – on tables arranged into long, long rows, he was on the look-out for a solid, unflashy rifle. He wouldn't buy it from any of these official sellers: that would mean showing ID, same as at a regular gun store. Better to find an individual, pay in cash. No paperwork required.

He knew precisely the weapon he wanted too. Which made this an odd exercise. He thought he should make a show of browsing, but he was more focused than that. He would pace the aisles until he had found what he was looking for.

Forty-five minutes had passed when he finally spotted it. A man – white, mid-fifties, big gut – was looking at a range of Tasers, with a rifle over his shoulder. Even from a distance, Garcia could see it was the Savage III Long Range Hunter: long, slim, powerful. This one had its own bipod rest already attached. And from the barrel, there popped out a Post-it note, wrapped around a Popsicle stick.

'Excuse me, sir? Is your gun for sale?'

'Yep.'

'Can I take a look?'

The man took it off his shoulder and let Garcia get a hold of it, testing the weight. Like all the weapons here, the trigger was secured by a plastic cable-tie.

'Can I ask how old it is?'

The man was eyeing Garcia slowly. 'Three years.'

'Trigger pressure OK? No strain on the suppresser?'

'It's all good, buddy. If you want it, it's yours for nine hundred dollars.'

'I'll give you eight hundred for it.'

'Not a cent less than eight hundred and fifty.'

Garcia made a face, as if wading deeper than he wanted to go. 'All right, eight fifty it is.'

He dug into his pocket and produced the cash, a thick wad of worn twenties. The seller's expression had not changed. Garcia was not perturbed. As he handed him the money, he decided that the prickliness of the encounter only helped him. Racist white guy would remember that he had sold his cherished gun to a swarthy Hispanic man in a baseball cap. And that was all he'd remember. *To be honest, officer, they all look pretty much the same to me.*

After that, it was straightforward. After two attempts, he found an ammunition dealer selling the rounds he needed. Busy stall too: too many customers for anyone to remember who bought what. (And, unlike in a gun store, no CCTV at all. These guys would rip out a camera if they saw one; no way they'd let the jackbooted Feds spy on them.) He picked up three boxes of .338 Lapua bullets, twenty per box. Not cheap at $300 but worth it for the dead-eye accuracy.

Next was the sight. Here, Garcia had decided, was where Jorge would spend the money. The gun was a machine: as long as it worked, it worked. The sight, along with the rounds, was what mattered. Given what he knew of the job, he had decided that what he needed was an infra-red night sight and it didn't take long to find the one he wanted: the X35 FLIR Thermal Rifle Scope. He gladly handed over the $3000 the dealer was asking; steep, but nearly $500 less than Jorge would have paid online. That, Garcia knew, was a big sum to pay in cash: memorable. He kept his cap down low.

Last came the sound suppressor. He had wondered about this. Would Jorge use one? On one level, the answer was clearly no. But what if he needed to fire more than one shot? Silence might buy him a vital extra second or two. It would be the prudent option. Expensive, true, but still compatible with what, according to Julian at any rate, Jorge had been doing since last November: spending next to nothing, saving every cent of his veteran's benefits for this one project. He found the AAC Titan-Ti, opened the box to check it was new, and handed over the thousand in twenties.

As he went back to his car, the sound of survivalist rock playing over the PA system, he wondered if he had made a mark on anyone present. He had said next to nothing; he had kept negotiations to a minimum. If anyone remembered anything it would have been his use of cash and that he had been one of the very few non-white faces present. But, he hoped, those were memories that, when the time came, could be of use. Otherwise, as he passed a knot of paunchy bikers, their ponytails turned grey, and loaded his backpack – now heavy with hardware – along with his rifle into the trunk of his car, he believed he had slipped through the Chantilly Gun & Knife Show the way he slipped through the wider world: silent and unnoticed.

34

Washington, DC, Thursday, 4.14pm

Perhaps it was a delayed reaction, but once she had taken a cab back into town from seeing Stuart, and found a café with a corner table, Maggie all but collapsed into the chair. Luckily, Stu had been in listening mode, sparing her his usual lecture about men and her uncanny knack in that department, though she had heard it so often she could have delivered it herself. *What is it with you, Miss Costello? Seems to me that, if they're good, they either live a million miles away or they're involved in a war you're meant to be ending or some other* meshugge *situation or, if they* are *available, then they're rotten to the core. Why can't you be as smart about all this stuff as you are about everything else?*

To which she'd have offered the standard reply. *Says the guy who thinks the most important thing about Valentine's Day is that it falls halfway between the New Hampshire and South Carolina primaries – your exact words, Stuart.*

The truth was, it was painful to admit what she had seen during the night – the way Richard had spoken about her, the clear implication that they had only got together because

McNamara had asked him to, as part of an intelligence gathering operation focused on the rump of loyalists to the previous regime that had, like Maggie, clung on. It was humiliating to have to ask out loud, in front of another person, the obvious question: was that all it had ever been to him? All that intimacy, all that sex – was it just a performance? What was going through his mind when they were in bed together? Was he like those porn stars, skilled enough in acting that they could seem consumed by desire on the outside, while in the privacy of their own heads they were composing that week's shopping list? Was that what sleeping with Maggie was for him, a job?

Or did he arouse himself with thoughts of another woman? Did he imagine himself with 'the princess'? Was that what turned him on, the proximity to power?

It was all useless, she knew that. So she shoved those thoughts behind the wall she was constructing in her mind, where, she knew, they were building up like floodwaters behind a dam. When this was all over, who knew what havoc they would wreak?

Compartmentalization: she had a doctorate in the subject. Men were supposedly the more naturally gifted in that area, but she reckoned she could take on all challengers. Her head was made up of little compartments. Today alone, she had walled off the small room where the shock, maybe even the post-traumatic shock, of the near-death experience in the car was stored. There was an adjoining room where she had neatly deposited the anguish – and inadequacy – she felt at Liz's principled resignation. Next a cupboard – she pictured the bin room at the convent – where she hoped to dump all the toxic waste, sludge and slime still oozing from Richard. As always, there was a section for Stuart Goldstein and the state he was in these days. To say nothing of the area reserved for her angst over the man she still worked for – and her belief that the President of the United States was quite happy to bring the world to the edge of destruction; indeed, that he was happy to go right over that edge. And finally, the largest and darkest room of all, where she locked away the guilty, queasy conviction that this perilous, lethal situation was all her fault.

Each of these rooms would have to stay locked and sealed off from each other. As any compartmentalizer could tell you, the one thing you had to avoid at all costs was a breakdown in those walls and partitions. If all the various woes were allowed to burst out of their individual silos and, worse, combine with each other, they would overwhelm you. Keep them separated, the doors bolted.

She pulled out her phone. The first task, though the very idea of it appalled her, was to send some kind of holding message to Richard. She couldn't be sure if he knew what she had seen during the night. He had acted strangely this morning, but that might have been a reaction to her behaving just as oddly. It was possible that he suspected nothing, and the longer it stayed that way, the better. Which meant acting normally. On a normal day, she'd text him at least a couple of times. So now she thumbed out a few words, aimed at both maintaining the illusion and buying herself some time.

She laboured over them, deleting and rewriting, worried that this formulation sounded hysterically hyper-normal, while that one was too flat and distant. Eventually she settled on:

Hi there. Sorry I was so rushed this am. This whole work thing: it's too much! Let's make sure we have a real weekend together xx

She read it, reread it, pressed Send and sighed deeply.

Next, she opened Twitter, an enterprise in which she was a silent partner. The job meant she could listen, but not speak. She was a pseudonymous egg on there with zero tweets to her (false) name, but she could see what everyone else – from Liz to McNamara, from Jake Haynes at the *Times* to the President himself – was saying.

As it happened, Haynes had just linked to a story written out of London, saying that the President and his business interests had received an unexpected, if tragic, boost: the lead lawyer in an upcoming case opposing the President's company's proposed expansion in Europe had been found dead, so weakening the legal challenge to those plans. But the rest of her timeline was consumed by a story that would once have appalled the Washington political class but which now just induced eye-rolling and a torrent of ironic, detached one-liners from the Twitterati. She clicked on the first link that promised to supply not a witty take but the basic facts.

Senior staff at the White House are in discussion with the Department of Defense as they seek to implement an unusual request from the President: his demand for a military uniform to reflect his role as Commander in Chief of US armed forces.

The officials, who requested anonymity in order to speak freely on a topic that they have been barred from discussing in public, said the President has taken a close interest in every aspect of the project. He met last month with a team of fashion designers, including several stars from the long-running Project Runway *TV show, as well as former and serving heads of the military to determine the right look.*

'He knows the risk is that it could look a bit "Third World dictator" and he's adamant that the team avoid that,' one senior aide said in a telephone interview. The President is said to have

studied photographs of general-turned-president, Dwight D Eisenhower and sent pictures of the World War Two commander to the design team as a potential source of inspiration.

He has also examined Hollywood depictions of former military leaders, including Douglas MacArthur and George S Patton, with particular interest in Gregory Peck's 1977 portrayal of MacArthur. One scribbled note from the President included a photograph of Peck in costume and said, 'Why can't I have a hat like him?'

Designers face one specific problem. The uniforms of the men the President admires most left space for the many medals and ribbons they had been awarded for valor and participation in past campaigns. Since the President has no record of military service, it's not clear what would go in their place, though one aide said, 'One option would be to put a few ribbons there that would be kind of symbolic. I'm not sure anybody besides the Times and MSNBC would object. Veterans groups are very supportive of this Commander in Chief.'

However, presidential and military historians contacted by the New York Times poured scorn on the notion of fake medals and indeed of creating a uniform for the President. 'It was very important to our founders that military and civilian power be kept separate and distinct,' said Norman J Evans, Emeritus Professor of War Studies at Emory University in Atlanta. 'The role of Commander in Chief is a civilian post.'

A White House spokesperson, while refusing to confirm or deny that such a uniform was under discussion, dismissed the historians' concerns. 'The universities are as out of touch as the lamestream media. None of these liberals wanted the President elected in the first place and I think the American people have had enough of these so-called experts.'

Asked whether the President would consider wearing a military uniform, she said, 'It's no secret that the President is keen that Americans have a leader they can look up to and salute.'

Naturally, Twitter had gone to town. First out of the blocks was one that said simply, Want a uniform Mr President? Here's a selection, before offering a rogues' gallery of Gaddafi, Noriega and Pinochet, each man wearing increasingly outsized peaked caps. Another, inevitably, showed a picture of Adolf Hitler, though it slightly misfired, in that the Führer was in civilian clothes. The rest had got busy with Photoshop, grafting the President's face onto assorted historical monsters.

Maggie put the phone away. This repeated response from the President's critics – the wry, world-weary, humorous take – was beginning to grate. Like that woman had said on the radio the other day, *We're laughing all the way to a totalitarian state*. And if all the meme-makers and cast of *Saturday Night Live* and the rest only knew what she knew, they'd understand that this was no joke. The man was prepared to blow up the planet, for Christ's sake. Go ahead, make a GIF of that.

She looked at her watch. The day was slipping away. She needed to answer the questions Stuart had put to her: the when and the where, especially. And for that, she needed to get to work.

She approached the White House via the northwest entrance, as always, nodded to the guard, as always, and held her pass up to be scanned, as always. Except this time, instead of a satisfying green tick, the screen on the machine registered a red cross and a sound of electronic displeasure.

'Try it again,' the guard said, looking at his monitor rather than at Maggie.

She tried it again. Same cross, same sound.

'I'm sorry, ma'am. I can't allow you to proceed.'

'But this is—' Maggie began. 'This card worked fine this morning. There must be something wrong with your machine.'

'The machine works fine, ma'am. Your card is the problem.'

'But I've worked here for—'

'Any issues – go to the visitors' entrance, Southeast Gate.' His eyes remained fixed on the screen.

She sighed. Her hand reached for her neck, to soothe the whiplash she had sustained a few hours earlier. Liz's voice floated into her head. 'You ought to get that looked at.'

Liz. She hadn't spoken to her since their call was cut off, drowned out by the air conditioning and that infernal noise in the car. Liz would be thinking, not for the first time, that Maggie was too absorbed in her own work to care, that she had just heard about her own sister losing her job and still hadn't bothered to pick up the phone. She would call just as soon as she got to her desk.

Maggie was now at the Southeast Gate, next to Hamilton Place. She could see a group of tourists waiting to be let in and behind them a silent protest: a dozen or so people with tape over their mouths, demonstrating against the President's latest attempt to restrict those bits of the media that weren't his.

She held up the pass to the scanner and once again it was rejected. She headed straight for the glass box where several staff were on duty.

'I'm Maggie Costello, Special Assistant to the President in the Counsel's Office. My pass seems to be faulty. Can you let me in, please?'

The guard took the pass, typed a few instructions into his computer, then called over a supervisor. They both conferred, inaudibly, while pointing at the screen. Maggie watched as colleagues swept in and out, talking on their phones, oblivious to the civilians forced to queue up to be granted access. 'Muggles', Richard called them.

The more senior official came to speak to her.

'The access rights on this pass have been changed, Miss Costello.'

'Changed? What do you mean "changed"? Do I have to use a different entrance?'

'No. Your terms of access to the facility have been changed.'

'Changed to what?'

'This is now a non-access pass.'

'You mean, I can't get in at all?' Maggie was aware of two people behind her, sighing noisily.

'That is correct.'

'But . . . I work here. I don't understand. What the hell is a "non-access pass"? This worked this morning. Did someone change it?'

'It has been changed, yes.'

'But when? It worked only a few—'

'I cannot disclose that information at this time.'

Amazing. She had been waved through here for so long; now they talked to her as if she were a woman who had just wandered in off the street.

'All right, then. Does your little screen there' – stupid to take it out on this guy, but she couldn't help herself – 'tell you *who* decided to change my pass and block me from coming into my place of work?'

'I cannot disclose that information at this time.'

She turned around, looking towards the street in frustration. She was aware of the people filing in and out, only a trickle given the time of day, but enough to add to her humiliation. What was worse, though, was what the visitors and Secret Service guards could not see, which was her realization that there was next to nobody inside that building she could call to come out here, have a word with security and let her in. There was a time, not that long ago, when she could have thrown out two dozen names, from the President downwards, who would have insisted she be allowed through. But who could she call now? Most of her allies and friends no longer worked here. Eleanor? She'd probably have gone home by now and would, brutally, be of too low a rank to start issuing demands. McNamara? He could well have been behind this order. Kassian? Same was true of him. Her own official boss, the White House Counsel, was never around anyway. Who did that leave, with enough juice to get her through the door? Richard? That joke wasn't even funny.

She was about to head home, to regroup and work from there, when two men, neither one in uniform, came towards her. One in his forties, short; the other in his twenties with longer hair – so that Maggie instantly decided he must be the geek sent to resolve the technical problem with her pass – they approached her with brisk purpose.

The older man spoke first. 'Miss Costello?'

'Yes.'

'Some problem down here with your pass?'

'That's right, yes.'

'OK. Please, come with us.'

Maggie smiled with relief. 'Thank you. Thanks so much.'

'Sure. We'll see if we can't get this straightened out.'

Maybe it was the tiredness or the headache from the whiplash or just everything that had been building up, but Maggie began to babble. As the three of them headed west in the direction of the Eisenhower Executive Office Building, past another knot of protesters waving placards – all of them wearing masks of the President's face – Maggie straining to keep up, she began telling these men how she was sure this was some kind of mistake, that her pass had always worked before, that no one had indicated to her that there was any kind of problem, and that she was sure if her access terms had needed to change, someone would have informed her and it'd been quite a day, in fact she'd been in a car crash, actually, not really a crash, more of a near-miss but still it felt . . .

Only now, as they found themselves in a delivery bay behind the EEOB, walking down a ramp into some kind of underground storage area, did she pay attention to her surroundings. Scolding herself for dropping her guard, she sought to regain her poise. 'All right, I see what's happening,' she said. 'Now, why don't you tell me what's going—'

In that instant, and with astonishing speed, the younger of the two men put his hand on her mouth and, at the same time, shoved her backwards and into a pillar. 'Now, why don't you shut the fuck up?'

She stayed like that, pinned against the column. His hand was not only gagging her mouth; the ridge made by his fingers was also blocking her nostrils. She couldn't breathe.

She could hear the older man speaking. His mouth was close to her ear. 'Listen closely. No more games now. We know what you're doing and we want you to stop. So why don't you be a good little girl and stop poking your Irish bitch face where it doesn't belong? Do you understand me?'

Maggie was wriggling, but the man who was gagging her mouth was also using his left foot to stand on her feet while his right knee was pressed against her legs, keeping her jammed in place. She was desperate to breathe.

Now the older man was shouting. 'DO YOU UNDERSTAND ME?'

Maggie's focus was elsewhere, on the hand covering her mouth. With a small instinctive movement of her jaw, she managed to open her lips just enough to bare her teeth and catch part of one finger between them. She bit down hard, gratified to realize that she was reaching not just skin and flesh but bone too.

The young man sprung away, yelping in pain. Maggie gasped for air as she ran up the ramp, heading for the outside. She had covered two, maybe three, yards when she felt a hand around her ankle, pulling her down to the ground. She landed hard, on her knees. Now she felt the weight of a man's body – the older one, she felt sure – on top of her. In an instant, his hands had encircled her wrists, ensuring she stayed pinned to the ground, face down.

Now his mouth was by her ear. 'You're making this a bit too much like fun, Maggie. There's no one here. Just the two of us – and my friend.'

'Get the fuck off me.'

'Why would I do that? This party's only just getting started.'

Maggie closed her eyes. The pain in her neck was so intense. The grip around her wrists was getting tighter.

She sensed the man adjusting his weight. It gave her the opening she needed.

In that instant, she used her now-unguarded right arm to press hard into the ground, levering herself up just enough to turn over. She had only half-completed the move, but it generated enough momentum to break his grip on her left wrist. Now she could move her knee upward, doing it with sufficient force that it landed squarely in his balls.

Both his hands went to clasp his groin and now she was back on her feet. The younger man, still nursing a finger spurting blood, was coming towards her when she heard three loud beeps, followed by the sound of an engine. All three of them looked round to see the red brake lights of a truck reversing down the ramp. Maggie staggered towards it, aiming to get in sight of its wing mirrors.

The two men looked at each other, made an instant calculation and ran in the opposite direction, into the darkness of the storage area. Maggie drew level with the cab of the truck, lifted her hand in acknowledgement of the driver and staggered onto the street. The driver began to open his door, as if about to come to her aid, but she waved him away, semaphoring her insistence that she was OK. She hoped he didn't see that her tights were in tatters, her knees bruised and bleeding. Finding a doorway, she peeled them off and dumped them in a garbage can.

Bruised, shaken and stone-cold furious at the attack – how dared they do that to her? – there was also room for thinking. First, she raised with herself, and then dismissed, the notion of going to the police. What would be the point, when she already knew more about this case than they ever would? Given who and what was involved, they could hardly protect her. Besides, the amount of time it would take, the explanations she would have to give, the information she would have to reveal: she would end up removing herself from the battlefield. She didn't know who had done this to her, but the last thing she was going to do was reward them with her surrender.

The second thought that struck Maggie now, as she walked unsteadily towards home, was that her tormentors had made a mistake. They might not have realized it, but she had. In the process of pursuing her, they had revealed themselves. They had pointed a sign at their lair – and she had seen it.

35

The Bull Run Shooting Center was just off the I-66, surrounded by parkland. There was a waterpark for kids nearby, though it was all but deserted on this school day. There was an archery area and some corporates doing an afternoon of clay pigeons, but none of that was of any interest to Julian Garcia. He wanted to be outside, in the green and facing the trees.

To someone from New York, say, this would probably look like a golfers' driving range. A mixed crowd, as many women as men, each in their own lane, facing a big stretch of grass that eventually yielded to forest. But instead of a set of clubs, each paying customer was set up with a gun.

Some had several, held in a rack: trying them out, seeing which one they liked best. Garcia clocked a bossy husband, demonstrating different weapons for his wife. He overheard the man talking to the rangemaster: 'All these protests going off now – riots and all – I reckoned it was about time the lady got saddled up to protect herself. Just in case.'

Garcia was here on different business. He had paid his

$30 to the men at the counter – all of them armed – and taken his own ammunition and weapon, the Lapua .338s and the Savage, to the end lane. The lane next to him was empty too, which was how he liked it.

He set himself up on the table, extending the bipod legs on the rifle so that it rested evenly. He opened his backpack and pulled out the rest of the kit: ear defenders, shooting glasses, spotting scope. This hour would be the most critical in his preparations so far.

He watched the amateurs having their fun, as he waited for the signal from the rangemaster. To his irritation, they were using zombie targets: instead of a generic human figure, each target was decorated with some skeletal, undead creature, most with a red dot at the centre of the skull or chest inviting a bullet. It made the exercise more fun, Garcia supposed, more like a coconut shy at the fair. But on some level he had never needed to articulate, it offended him. If he'd had to spell it out, he'd have said that war was not a game, shooting was not a sport and all the people he'd had to aim at had been human rather than zombie. But those thoughts remained unformed.

Now came the klaxon and the voice over the loudspeaker announcing that it was time for 'All shooters to change their targets.'

Garcia had already aimed his rangefinder at the target, letting its laser tell him that it had been placed one hundred and seventy yards from the barrel of the weapon. Now he lifted the target and, without asking permission, carried it much further back. At intervals, he stopped, put down the target and pointed the rangefinder, as if it were a TV remote, back towards the table where his weapon, unloaded, remained in place. Three hundred yards. Still not far enough. He kept walking until he had reached the distance he required. Exactly three hundred and forty-five yards. He noticed the other shooters noticing him. No problem with that at all.

Then he reached into his pocket and pulled out a hand-warming pouch he'd picked up at a camping store on the way over here. Filled with a clear gel, with a metal disc suspended inside, you simply had to break the disc for the pouch to become warm. Given what he'd been told about the location for this job and how his subject would be defended – the distance involved and, above all, the degree of visibility he would have to work with – a headshot, which required a clean line of sight, was out of the question. And so he broke the metal disc and pinned the pouch to the middle of his target, over the red dot covering the zombie's heart.

Now he paced the way back to his station, feeling the rounds in his jacket pocket. Once returned, he sat himself at the table, loaded the rifle, and then looked through the thermal scope. There it was, the pouch's warmth registering in the sight as a small circle of white, enough to guide the first shot or two until it was obliterated. He checked through the iron sights on the rifle and, once he was sure all was in line, he fired.

He sat back, then consulted the spotting scope to discover that he had gone nearly three inches awry at eleven o'clock. The handwarmer was still in place. He adjusted the sight and took aim again. Then back to the spotting scope. The pouch was gone now, but there was still more work to do.

On he went, firing dozens of rounds, each one followed by a series of ever more tiny micro-adjustments. This weapon was new to him; he had allowed for spending this amount of time. And if he looked purposeful, deliberate – like a man engaged in a very specific job of work – then that was all to the good.

The rangemaster's klaxon went three times, each one announcing a change of targets, before he was satisfied. In the session that followed, he made only one small tweak, right at the start. After that, the spotting scope revealed that he had hit the red dot – located in the chest of a drooling, rotting zombie, its hands dripping blood and outstretched as if seeking fresh flesh – every single time. Each red dot, like the handwarmer, had been pummelled and perforated into oblivion.

Given the bullets he was using, he reflected as he packed up and walked back out through the shop, with its holsters and its gun cleaning kits, his target would have been dead the very first time. But on this day at least, he had the satisfaction of knowing he had gone one better. He had killed the President many times over.

36

Washington, DC, Thursday, 8.22pm
Maggie had made it back to the apartment. It felt like reaching safe harbour. But it seemed emptier than usual. It was back, she understood, to being a place for one.

She glanced over at the couch, which still bore the indentations of two people. To think that had only been last night. She had sent Richard a holding text, which he had answered several hours later with an equally holding reply – Jammed just now. Talk later? R x – but that was all that had passed for contact between them.

Maggie wanted to shower, to rid herself of everything that had happened in the last, hellish few hours. She caught a glimpse of herself in the mirror. The concealer had worn off, leaving the shadows under her eyes dark and grooved. She looked like a hunted animal. The thought of giving her pursuers that satisfaction appalled her. Squaring her shoulders, Maggie ran a hand through her hair and stalked into the kitchen.

Listlessly, she tried having something to eat. But she could not relax. It was clear she was being tracked, if not 'eyes on' then virtually. Doubtless they were watching her here too. But this was her terrain; there were steps she could take to protect herself.

For the dozenth time, she assessed her situation. They had known when she was in her car; someone had sat at a computer, following her movements and then controlling them, attempting either to kill her or to send a mortal warning.

And they had known when she had tried to enter the White House, alerted no doubt by her failed attempt to use her security pass: that must have been the signal which summoned the two thugs to come and find her. Were their orders to kill her – or simply to leave her so scared she'd back off? She suspected the latter.

Still, that was only a calculated guess on her part. That they had planned to kill her, and would have done so had they not been interrupted by that delivery truck, remained at least a possibility.

The fact that her White House pass had been mysteriously voided was a body blow in itself. To be shut out of her place of work, where she had felt so privileged to serve these last few years, to have the door slammed in her face: it was a humiliation. Had Kassian fired her, was that it? If he had, what possible reason could he give that would not constitute blatant obstruction of justice?

It was irrational, she knew, but she also felt plain hurt. A matter of months ago, she was deemed indispensable by the White House and by the previous president. Now she was so unwanted, they wouldn't even let her in the building.

Focus, she told herself. Put your emotions to one side. The important thing was that her failed attempt to use her pass had brought out her assailants, and that confirmed that this was an inside job. Her enemy, whoever it was, lay within that building.

Did that mean, perhaps, that Richard had realized that Maggie was now aware of his secret dialogue with McNamara, and the two of them had decided to put the squeeze on her to ensure she kept this knowledge to herself? Something about that didn't quite add up. Sure, it would be devastating for Richard to be exposed as a liar, a cheat and a closet racist and bad for McNamara to be caught talking like a drooling, sexist predator (though, Lord knows, you could say the same of the President and that hadn't stopped him getting elected). But surely there was nothing in that correspondence so radioactive that it warranted the murder of Maggie Costello just to keep it hidden, was there?

If anything it was Bob Kassian, backed by Jim Bruton, who had the clearer motive. In her meeting with the Chief of Staff that morning, Maggie had all but accused him of involvement in the killing of Dr Frankel. Hushing that up alone was sufficient reason to get her out of the way. But if her calculation was right – and the two men were planning the assassination of the President – then that was all the more reason to ensure her silence.

There was a chime from her phone. A text. Was that Richard, at last? What if he invited himself over? That was the trouble with messages: there was no way to ignore them, without it being obvious that you were ignoring them. At least with a call, you could screen it and claim you were tied up . . .

It wasn't from Richard, but her sister.

Hope you're OK, Mags. Didn't like the way you rang off so suddenly before – and you were in your car too. Stay safe. I'm off to bed now – early, I know, but I've got a horrible headache coming on. Don't worry about ringing tonight. And don't worry about me. I'll get a job soon enough. If not, there's always the convent ;) L x

She reached for the iPad, a hand-me-down from Liz, as it happened, who had, as always, upgraded to the latest thing. Maggie used this machine only rarely, for personal things; it was the only device she had that was completely disconnected from the White House system. Of course, Liz being Liz, it was loaded with state-of-the-art encryption software. Maggie had teased her about it: 'And what exactly is it you have to hide, Liz, that would so interest the world's spy agencies?'

'You see, that's the exact mentality they rely on. "If you have nothing to hide, you have nothing to fear." I'd expect better from you, Margaret.'

'Ooh, it's Margaret now, is it?' Maggie had said, making a face towards the children, who began to laugh. '*Margaret*. Boys, you'll always know I'm in trouble – that Auntie Maggie has been very naughty – when your mother starts calling me *Margaret*.' She wagged her finger. 'Naughty, naughty Margaret.' The older boy, Callum, not yet four, had loved that. Maggie and he had spent the rest of the afternoon deciding what *his* naughty name should be.

She switched on the machine, and opened up the browser. She had no idea what she was looking for. She went to whitehouse.gov, clicked on the 'Briefing Room', then on 'Latest News' and then 'The Schedule'. She opened it up but, as she feared, it only listed events for 'Today'. No detail on what the President's diary held.

She thought about contacting Eleanor, but hesitated. If they had electronic tabs on Maggie's car, they were certainly monitoring her phone. They would know the instant she called a White House number. Mind you, she could call from Skype using this iPad. They wouldn't see where that—

Hold on, something was happening. The cursor was moving across the screen of its own accord, without any direction from her.

Maybe this was what happened when you left a machine unused for too long. She would follow the one bit of technical advice she'd absorbed from Liz. She was about to turn the machine off and on again, when she realized that the cursor had opened up an app which now filled the screen. It was, of all things, the one that controlled the thermostat in the room, operating the central heating.

This was odd. The big dial in the centre showed the temperature set for thirty degrees Celsius. The dial was glowing orange, which was its way of telling you the system was fired up, the boiler fully on.

But there was no way she would have the heating on now, in the warmth of a Washington spring that was already turning into early summer. Had someone been in the apartment since this morning?

She went to look at the thermostat on the wall. It was set at twenty-one and the dial was in black, a sign that the heating was not on. She felt the radiators: cold. But the iPad was adamant: it was still lit in orange, the boiler striving to reach thirty degrees.

Of course. This was not Maggie's heating app that she was looking at. It was Liz's, still left on what had been Liz's iPad. (Maggie had been meaning to 'wipe the machine', as her sister put it, but naturally she had never got around to it.) Maggie went back to the sofa, fleetingly lamenting a climate now so out of whack you needed to put the heating on in Georgia in May.

Right, she needed to get a sense of the President's movements over the next few days. In the last week or so, he had barely appeared in public. She suspected all events had been cancelled, making way for the rolling crisis meetings that were happening in the Oval on North Korea. She imagined Kassian and Bruton sitting there, shooting the occasional glance at each other, wondering if they were making a terrible mistake. Or alternatively, did the President say things at those meetings that only confirmed them in their resolve, convincing them afresh that he posed a danger?

She tried to open the browser on the machine to start some new lines of inquiry. Once again it refused her. Only the heating app was open. For some reason it refused to disappear. Maggie pressed at the temperature controls, touching the down arrow. It had no effect. She touched it again. Still nothing. She stabbed at other, random buttons on the display. None had any effect. The dial remained on orange, the central heating on and impossible to turn off.

And then, in an instant, it came to her. A second later she felt such nauseating dread she thought she might be sick there and then.

Please God, no.

Liz had done the job herself, hooking up her boiler to this app. But it hadn't worked. *Last time I turned the central heating on, whole place filled with bloody smoke. Besides, it's *roasting* in Atlanta . . .*

It came back to Maggie now with full force. Liz never used her central heating. She had been warned that while her old boiler could cope with hot water, it was dangerous for heating: it could cause fire or generate clouds of carbon monoxide.

Yet now it was switched on.

Maggie checked the time. Jesus Christ, the kids would be fast asleep. And what was it Liz had said? *I'm off to bed now – early, I know, but I've got a horrible headache coming on.*

Maggie knew enough about carbon monoxide poisoning to know that was how it worked. It didn't fill the room with billowing clouds of grey, foul smoke. It was odourless, slipping under the doorway and filling the corridors before you even knew it. The headache came first, then the dizziness and vomiting and, if you didn't get out, death.

She reached for the phone and dialled her sister's home number. It was ringing.

Come on, come on. Please Liz, pick up. Pick up.

'You've reached Liz, Paul, Callum and Ryan. Sorry we can't get to the phone right now. But leave a message after the tone.'

'Liz, it's Maggie. Please, listen to me – I think there's a gas leak or something in your apartment. Get the children out right now! Please, Liz – I'll explain later. Please, please, pick up if you can hear me.'

But something about the sound made Maggie sure that this was one of those electronic voicemail systems: her message was being stored digitally, but it was not being broadcast around the house. No one could hear her, she was sure of it.

Maggie tried the cellphone number for her sister.

Call failed. Retry?

She did it again, with the same result. Then she tried the cellphone for Paul. Again: *Call failed. Retry?*

She thought of Callum, lying there breathing in those noxious fumes. She pictured Ryan, crying out for his mother. And Liz, unconscious and unable to help.

Jesus, what the hell was she to do?

She would have to call 911 and explain. Her fingers were quaking but there were the words again.

Call failed. Retry?

Someone had blocked her phone.

She picked up her landline, so rarely used. No dial tone. Good Christ, they had blocked off every phone in the place.

Please, please God. Let them live. Please don't let those boys die.

She ran out of the apartment and into the corridor,

knocking on doors of neighbours she had never met. But it was getting late. This was Washington, some would be asleep – or at least preferring to be selectively deaf rather than get involved with a stranger. She was pounding on the doors now, one after another. 'Please, please – this is an emergency.'

Finally, a door at the far end of the corridor opened and an Indian-American woman stood there, in a T-shirt and not much else. Maggie felt sure she recognized her, though she couldn't tell where from.

Maggie looked straight at her and said, 'I need to call 911. Right now. My phones are not working.'

Without asking for a word more explanation, the woman opened the door wider and ushered Maggie in. Standing in a doorway on the other side of the living room was a man in boxer shorts who also looked oddly familiar.

She took the phone and jabbed out the three digits. A dispatcher came on and Maggie babbled a description of the situation that would have made no sense to anyone.

'Slow down, sweetheart.'

Maggie closed her eyes. The truth was, she wanted to break down into fast, hot tears. She wanted to curl up into a ball. She wanted to cry out to Jesus, Mary and Joseph. She could handle all the shit they kept throwing at her – when it was just her – but not this. Not this.

Instead, she made herself dig deep and focus. As calmly as she could, she explained that the lives of two children were in immediate danger. They needed to contact their colleagues in Atlanta, Georgia, and send urgent help to the following address because a carbon monoxide leak was underway, poisoning a sleeping family at this very moment. Inevitably she had to repeat each point at least twice. The address, three times.

Eventually she put the phone down and looked up to see a glass of whisky, stretched out to her. 'Or a cup of sweet tea?' said the woman whose apartment this was. 'Whichever you prefer.'

Maggie downed the Scotch, said thank you and began to head towards the door. But the woman placed a hand lightly on her shoulder. 'Why don't you stay here, just until you know what's going on?' The kindness in her voice made Maggie's eyes prick.

It was perhaps seven minutes later that her phone, now apparently unblocked, rang.

Maggie picked it up. Then she heard the words she had feared:

'Is that Maggie Costello? This is the Atlanta Fire Department.'

'Yes.' Her voice was quiet, meek.

'Your family members are currently being ferried by ambulance to Grady Memorial Hospital in Atlanta.'

'Are they alive?'

'Yes, they are.'

Maggie closed her eyes and breathed out.

'The children are unconscious, but I think they're going to be OK.'

'Thank God.'

'Him and the people on this street you contacted. They're the ones you want to thank.'

'I'm sorry?'

'They got here before we did. They had the presence of mind to break the door down. I think they might well have saved your family's life.'

'I don't unders—'

'I need to attend to things here. Thanks for your vigilance.' And he hung up.

Maggie looked up at the couple, now in dressing gowns, who had taken her in. She pointed at the phone. 'I think they're going to be OK. Thanks so much.'

'Are you sure you don't want to stay here? Or have another drink?'

'No, that's OK. But thank you so much for what you did. I can't thank you enough.' Maggie rose slowly out of the chair and walked down the corridor back to her apartment.

Once inside, she collapsed into a chair and, for the first time, allowed herself to sob long, desperate tears.

What terrible thing had she done that had caused those two little boys to be exposed to such grave danger? Why hadn't she just stayed out of this mess? OK, so Frankel had not killed himself: why couldn't she have just looked the other way like every other fucker in Washington? What did any of this have to do with her? More importantly, what did any of this have to do with Liz and her family? Nothing, was the answer. Nothing.

She should get in a car and drive down to Atlanta right now – drive all night and hug her sister and apologize for drawing her and her family into this nightmare. They had targeted Liz and her children as a way to get at Maggie: to hurt her, to threaten her, to scare her off whatever it was she was onto. She would have driven to Georgia this very moment, were it not for the fear that even proximity to Maggie Costello right now meant mortal peril. She had done enough damage.

But thank God they were OK. The fire department had got there in time. Although it sounded like someone else had got there first and it was they who had made all the difference. *The people on this street you contacted.*

Maggie had a shower and was about to let herself fall into a deep sleep when she picked up her phone again, hoping there might be a message from Liz. There wasn't. Instead she saw a string of tweets under the hashtag #TwitterSavedALifeTonight.

It turned out that at 9.36pm, a leading anchor on CNN, Anushka Saddiqui, had tweeted an appeal to her four hundred thousand followers asking anyone in the Cabbagetown neighbourhood of central Atlanta to head to a specific address and rescue a young family in danger. That had been retweeted by thousands of others in seconds – until it was seen by someone on Liz's street. That man had rushed to Liz's house and knocked the door down. The fire department came later, turning off the boiler which had somehow been set to thirty degrees Celsius.

So that was why Maggie had recognized that woman. Come to think of it, the man she had seen in boxer shorts was a familiar TV face too, with an even greater number of Twitter followers – though a quick peek at Wikipedia told Maggie he was married to a woman who was not Anushka Saddiqui.

Exhausted as she was, Maggie could not sleep. She was resolved: this had to end, before more innocent lives were put at risk. She had to find out who was behind all this mayhem.

She glanced down at her phone and what she saw there told her, at last, what she had to do.

37

Omaheke province, Namibia, 2.21pm, four days earlier
Ron Cain had a Hemingway in his pocket, a gesture he thought the old man would have appreciated. He felt for the book now, as they rattled along a dirt track close to the Botswana border, the Land Rover bouncing their heads close to the roof with each rut in the road.

Ron looked again at his travelling companions. The 'professional hunter', or PH as he styled himself, in his shorts, thighs as big as hams, and with a defiantly pre-hipster beard. He had a map on his lap. Next to him, staring out of the window, the younger of the two guides. In the driving seat, the older man. Not for the first time, Ron wondered what these two black men – master and apprentice – made of him.

He was black, like them. But he was American and he was rich. Did they think of him as a distant cousin? (He wouldn't presume to be a brother.) Or was he as alien a figure to them as their usual clientele: pampered, privileged and fundamentally soft?

The race thing was, Ron reflected, the least of the doubts

he'd had to overcome to make the journey here. He hated the dynamic that existed in these situations, regardless of race. You instantly became the weakling westerner, less natural, less masculine, less worthy than your earthy, son-of-the-soil hosts. They were real men, you were an effete creature of the indoors. You became – or at least Ron became – repeatedly apologetic: sorry for not knowing how to carry a hunting tripod, sorry for whispering too loudly by the watering hole, sorry for not knowing that that constellation up there was Orion.

He dealt with it by being deferential to the local men's expertise, playing the character he had played since adolescence, if not childhood: the dutiful, attentive, curious pupil.

But it was fraught, because the deference was not one-way. They might have been more macho, but they were also paid servants. The PH would have fought that designation, it was true, but the guides' default stance was supine. Money made Ron the boss. Black, white, who cared? The colour that mattered was green.

But still. Serving a black man was complicated for all of them, he could see that. The PH spoke with a strong Afrikaaner accent. Ron could tell that this man had not been raised for this situation.

The vehicle bounced on, lolling from side to side. Outside, the grasses were so thick and so tall, the car seemed to be enveloped in cloud. From the way the PH was looking at the map, occasionally glancing out of the window, and from the briefly exchanged words between the driver and his assistant, Ron suspected they were close. The black rhino had eluded them for the best part of two days. But perhaps now they were on his trail.

The driver brought the vehicle to a juddering stop, allowing the quiet to rush in. 'On foot now,' the PH said.

Ron stood up and jumped to the ground, no longer even bothering to look for the foothold he had used yesterday to get in and out of the car. *You see*, he wanted to say, *I'm getting better at this.*

The lack of conversation as they walked suited him. His job in Texas, as the founder and chairman of what had grown into a large electronics company, the maker of specialist TV satellite and broadcast equipment – the dishes, the transmitters, the set-top boxes – involved so much talking. Meetings, meetings, meetings, all day. The chance to be on the other side of the world, in the bush – away from spreadsheets, swivel chairs and annual reports – was why he had come here.

Not that he had planned it. He had bid for this ridiculous, morally questionable prize on a whim. 'Lot Number Seventeen is a licence to kill – literally!' That's what the compere had said at the fundraising dinner, announcing the offer of a rare permit to hunt and kill a member of the world's most endangered species: a black rhino. The idea was that selling a permit for astronomical sums would bring in money for conservation but also incentivize the Namibians to keep the rhinos alive and to fend off poachers: now these animals would have a value measurable in hard cash. As trophies for rich, bored Americans whose heads were filled with Hemingway fantasies, these animals certainly commanded a steep price. The bidding had reached $350,000.

Ron's wife had looked on aghast. Her husband had never even hunted for ducks, let alone rhino. He was about to tell her how he planned to use this licence, but her attitude annoyed him: 'Are you serious? Hunting in Africa: *you*?' *Yes, me. Why the hell not me?* For a reason he could not quite fathom, his wife had never seemed so white to him as she did that night.

They were walking now in single file, the older guide marching at the head of the column, followed by the PH, then Ron, with the youngest man at the rear. Ron carried a rifle on a strap over his shoulder, but he couldn't escape the feeling it was a glorified prop. Sure, he knew it was loaded. But he would only fire it when he'd been told to. He would not be relying on his own, predator's instincts. He was not sure he had any.

At least not here, in the bush. Back home, different story. Those instincts had made his fortune. In business he could be rapacious – and strong. That's why he had not given up the lawsuit, despite all the advice. He couldn't care less how high a position that man had won for himself: he was guilty of theft, plain and simple. Five years ago, long before any talk of politics, he and Ron had signed a contract for services running into the hundreds of millions of dollars. Ron had fulfilled his side of the bargain, providing equipment and personnel over a period of eighteen months. It had cost him a fortune in salaries alone. But his company's bill had never been paid.

He had played nice and patient, but it became clear that he was being stiffed. This man, now on TV every minute of every day, had in effect stolen from him. He had got what he wanted – setting up an infrastructure in several cities, as he had demanded – but he had not paid for it. He'd been confronted over it, but refused to apologize or seem even vaguely embarrassed by what he had done. To have 'got so much stuff for free', as he put it, made him 'smart'. What he had done for himself, he would now do for America. The crowds loved it, imagining their new President stiffing the Chinese or the Europeans or whoever. But Ron had been appalled.

Which was why he was taking this to the courts. Not

that he was confident of winning. The judges seemed as scared as everyone else of this man's power. His supporters called him 'the King' and had taken to talking of him being in power for the next eight years *at least*. Ron had noticed that 'at least' and it had chilled him. What exactly did this man have in mind?

The PH stopped, wheeled around – twisting his torso, while keeping his feet rooted to the spot – and placed a finger over his lips. They all halted and hushed.

After a moment, the older guide nodded, as if agreeing. Only then did Ron hear what the other man had heard, the faintest crunch of a twig underfoot. Could he hear a whisper through the grass, as if it was being thrashed aside? He listened as closely as he could. The sound seemed to be coming from behind them. He felt his pulse quicken. Could the rhino be pursuing them? He liked the irony of it; he imagined it as a Hemingway short story, with a neat little twist: the predator becoming the prey.

The men paused a while, read each other's expressions – ignoring Ron, he noticed – and eventually decided to move on. More than thirty minutes passed, the heat beginning to bear down, when the guide held up his hand to signal another stop. Once they had, he pointed at the ground. At a pile of shit.

'Rhino faeces,' the PH said quietly. He bent down and sunk his hands into the soft, brown mess. 'Still warm,' he said. 'Still moist. Look.' He pointed at the dung beetles, already at work. 'He was here an hour ago, tops.'

They kept walking, but now with new vigour. The PH was excited, Ron could see that. They were getting close. They would surely see the beast today, maybe even this afternoon.

He thought back to yesterday when they had come to a

small clearing, marked by a lone tree and no grass, where a set of bleached-white bones were scattered against blood-red sand. The PH had beckoned Ron to come forward and pick up one of these giant bones, to imagine the body it had once supported. Ron felt its weight in his hands.

'Just think. This is an animal that would have weighed over a ton,' the PH said solemnly. 'And do you know what happened here, my friend?' Ron shook his head. 'A rhino bull – a younger bull – clashed here with our rhino. But he lost. Our rhino gored him. Left him here to die.' The PH, his skin sandy and weathered, paused, hoping Ron was getting the message.

Then, in case he hadn't, the PH said, 'These dominant bulls are very aggressive, do you get me? Very aggressive. This is what they do to preserve their turf. They don't care about any conservation programme. They don't know rhinos are endangered. They just do what nature tells them to do. Which means killing off any rhino they see as a threat. So now you see: when you finally get to kill this beast, you're actually doing the others a favour. You're conserving the rhino population. Do you get me?'

The image of an animal so powerful that it could gore another one to death, leaving a pile of bones, had almost weakened Ron's resolve. But not quite. And now here they were, closing in on their prey.

When it happened, it happened very quickly. They'd been walking for perhaps two hours since they saw the rhino shit. The grass was so thick, they could only see about thirty feet ahead of them. There was a noise, the sound of bush trodden underfoot at speed, and then there it was: an animal running, with what seemed to be a sword emerging from its head.

'Ron! Now!' the PH whispered. But Ron was still looking,

struck by the prehistoric strangeness of this animal, so heavy, yet moving so fast on its tiny legs, in a kind of rapid, comic, glorious shuffle.

Ron was about to explain the secret he had held back since the auction, from the moment he had raised his hand and made that bid. He was about to explain that he did not want to shoot this majestic animal after all. That he had paid the $350,000 because he had wanted the Namibian conservation agencies to have the cash to spend on game parks, wardens and rangers and the like, and because he wanted to see what it felt like to stalk and pursue a rare beast with a gun in his hand and, above all, because he wanted to prevent some other fucker having the licence and using it to kill. He was about to explain all that when he heard a shot, loud like a firecracker.

Oh no, Ron thought. The PH has done it for me. He's shot that beautiful animal, even though he had no right to. The licence was mine, but he couldn't wait. It's my fault, Ron thought. I should have told him before. You stupid, stupid man.

It took him a while – it seemed like minutes, but it could only have been a second or two – to see that there was blood spreading across his shirt like a stain. He touched it and was astonished by how wet it was. He looked up at the PH, as if to ask: how on earth did the rhino do that?

But now he was thrown to the ground, shoved there by the young guide. The PH had his rifle raised and was shooting. Not in the direction of the rhino, which had fled, but in the direction of the shot that had hit Ron. Spread on the ground, his hand still feeling the hot wetness of the blood across his chest, Ron understood that there was now an exchange of gunfire, bullets coming both ways. The guides were crouching, but they too were firing. Until one of them seemed to buckle at the knee and collapse, as elegantly as a gazelle.

How long did it last? Minutes? Seconds? Ron could not even guess. But eventually he heard the PH's voice and then the weeping of the older guide.

The last thing he heard was the PH talking into his radio, announcing that his party had come under fire, possibly from poachers, and that one man was dead. As Ron Cain slipped into unconsciousness, he earnestly wondered if that man was him.

38

Washington, DC, Friday, 2.56pm

Maggie Costello had learned one trick above all others from the years she spent as a mediator in peace talks. In fact, 'trick' underplayed its significance. It was the whole pastrami sandwich, as Stuart would say. If you didn't understand this one thing, then you didn't even have a chance of success. You might as well tell the parties to go back home, tool up and get ready to start fighting again in the morning.

But *understanding* it was not enough, not on its own. You had to be able to *do* it, to make the mental and emotional leap.

Put simply, you had to think like the enemy – or, in the case of peace talks, both enemies. You had to put yourself in their shoes and into their skin. You had to think of what you would want, what you would have to get, if you were them. In fact, even that was not good enough. She remembered Stuart on the subject. *I don't give a fuck what you would do if you were them. I want to know what they will do, given that they are them.* He had been talking about campaign strategy, outwitting the opposition. But the same logic held.

So this was the task now. If she was to thwart this attempt on the President's life, she had to put herself in the mind of Kassian and Bruton and, above all, of Mr 'no name supplied' who, she guessed, had been tasked with the assassination itself. She needed to think of the when and the where.

The starting point was the sort of information that, for her, would once have been a click away. She needed to pick up where she had left off when the hackers had started meddling with Liz's heating system: she needed to know the President's upcoming movements.

Maggie read again the text from Liz, confirming that she and the boys were all fine, and that they were now staying safely . . . somewhere else. Smart girl, Liz: smart enough to know that she needed to stay off-radar till this was over.

When they had finally spoken, Liz had breathlessly thanked her sister. 'You saved our lives,' she said. But that could not last. Eventually Liz would learn the truth and she would amend that sentiment: *You saved our lives, Maggie – but only after you'd endangered them.*

Was it a coincidence? Had her tormentors simply detected that Maggie was using an iPad, assumed it was her own and taken control of it? Were they merely trying to freak her out, by making her apartment unbearably hot? Was it just another little 'warning', designed to intimidate rather than kill?

Or was this an act of terrible escalation? Did they know that they were controlling Liz's heating, which was faulty and dangerous? All they'd have had to do was read through the texts and emails Maggie and Liz had sent each other and they'd have known. The two of them had talked about it, it was there in black and white. It seemed ridiculous, and yet she knew what these agencies were capable of: it would have been the work of an hour or two at most. If they had an algorithm capable of searching her online life for what might terrify Maggie most, they would surely have found this pretty rapidly.

And if they knew that, did they also know that Liz was the mother of two small boys? What kind of people were they, ready to turn on a machine they knew was likely to kill two small children? Was Robert Kassian capable of that? Was Jim Bruton? Or was this the handiwork of their recruit? Was he embarking on this mission without a moral compass?

The only way she would find out, the only way she would be able to hold to account those who had endangered her nephews' lives and nearly driven her off the road, the only way she would ever bring Dr Frankel's killers to justice, would be to discover the truth behind this plot.

She walked downtown and called Eleanor from a payphone. She told her to meet her at the usual place and advised her to do everything on hard copy. She hoped to God that that might minimize the risk. Maggie felt she had brought so much harm to so many innocents already, she couldn't bear the idea of dragging Eleanor down too.

Eleanor kept her waiting, unable to make a discreet escape from the White House till the mid-afternoon. But within a few minutes they were at a corner table, poring together over the document she had managed to get from a colleague – a similarly aged woman in the office of the White House Social Secretary. It was an inspired move on Eleanor's part. Traditionally the domain of women, and dismissed as the department for tea and china dishes, the Social Secretary's office was bound to be overlooked by McNamara or Kassian or whoever else was standing in Maggie's way.

But the one document to which it had permanent and updated access was, of course, the presidential schedule.

Maggie cast her eye over every event. Closed-door meeting with the Congressional Leadership. Photo-op with the Prime Minister of Greece. Roundtable with Senior Leadership of the US tech industries.

She had to rule out all of those, though she did wonder about each of them. What if the conspirators could kill the President at close quarters? Surely that would be ideal. The Secret Service presence would be minimal. How might they do it? They could poison his food. But there was an official who supervised, and tasted, the President's food to guard against precisely this possibility. How likely was it that that person had been won over to Kassian and Bruton's cause?

Or maybe the plotters planned simply to catch the President at a quiet moment and lunge at him with a knife. Impossible to get into the building with one that could cause sufficient damage. A syringe, filled with a lethal drug? Was this what the Chief of Staff and Defense Secretary had asked of Frankel, not just to write a sick note but to administer a fatal dose? Impossible to imagine, if only because to do such a thing would have required an act of suicide on Frankel's part – sentencing himself to spend the rest of his natural life in jail – and she had concluded long ago that the doctor was not the suicidal sort.

And nor were Kassian and Bruton. They were clearly bent on ensuring their own fingerprints were found nowhere near this crime. The safest way to do that was to stage what would look like a public assassination.

So what public events were coming up? Four days from now the President was due to address a large rally in Cleveland, as part of his interminable 'thank you' tour. But the venue was an indoor arena: security would be intense. No one could get in with a weapon of any kind.

What if the assassin were ready to sacrifice his or her own life? Could someone strap an explosive vest to their chest and charge at the President? In theory, that could work. But, again, how would you ever get through the Secret Service cordon wearing one of those things?

No. The only way was the old way. If someone wanted to kill the President and not be immediately identified as the culprit, then it had to be a shooting from distance. And that meant the President would have to be outdoors and in a place known in advance, to allow for preparation.

She looked again at the schedule. Monday looked obvious. It was Memorial Day, with a ceremony long arranged at Arlington National Cemetery. It would be out in the open too. And surely any soldier could get in carrying a weapon. Surely that was it. *No name supplied* was a military man: he'd be able to breeze in with a gun.

But the Secret Service would certainly have a procedure to prevent that scenario. They were used to securing that site, they did it every year. They would be checking everyone coming in and out. Indeed, she had heard years ago that, even at military events, the only people allowed to carry real, usable weapons were the agents of the Secret Service themselves. They couldn't risk a member of the public rushing a soldier, grabbing his gun and taking a shot.

Besides, she had been at Arlington twice with the last President and she remembered what some of the team had told her back then. The place was naturally protected, enfolded in trees and offering no real vantage point.

Nothing was leaping out at her. Finally she looked at one line on the schedule she had skimmed over, not least because she hadn't understood it.

Eve of MD weekend, restricted event, USMCWM.

'What's that?'

Eleanor lifted her glasses to take a better look. 'USMCWM. Hmm. Not sure I've heard of that one.'

Maggie was already keying the letters into Eleanor's phone. The answer came a second later. 'United States Marine Corps War Memorial. Where is that?'

She hit a couple more buttons and now looked at a map. It showed that this was a separate memorial, in a clearing of its own, just north of the cemetery at Arlington. But far enough away that it enjoyed none of the cemetery's natural protection. It was close to a road, Arlington Boulevard, and within a clear line of sight of several tall buildings.

'Eleanor,' Maggie said, pointing at the words on the schedule. 'What is this?'

The older woman was leafing through the rest of the sheaf she had brought from the office. 'Here,' she said, pointing at a document laid out like a grid. 'It says it's a private ceremony, press pool only, two cameras. Seems the President is going to be laying a wreath, taking a salute, maybe handing out a medal. No remarks.'

A distant bell rang in Maggie's mind. Her boss had once done something similar, early in his term: a visit on the eve of Memorial Day, a moment of quiet prayer as he weighed his responsibilities as Commander in Chief. He had gone to the Vietnam Memorial, on his own, long after dark, with no cameras. Typical McNamara: he had ripped off the idea, borrowing the veneer of solemnity, but taking care to ensure he got a TV hit out of it all the same. She could almost hear his voice: *Love the whole sincerity vibe; it's gonna really work for us.*

'What does this say?' Maggie was pointing at a line of small print, underneath each item on the schedule. It indicated when that part of the document had last been modified, or when that entry had been added.

It took Maggie a moment to understand the combination of digits in front of her. This event had only been added to the schedule on Wednesday, the day after Frankel was murdered and less than three days after the President had his nuclear meltdown in the Situation Room.

It was hard to make last-minute changes to the presidential schedule. Very few people could do it. But one of those few was the White House Chief of Staff. It was similarly hard to organize ceremonies at a place like the US Marine Corps War Memorial. Very few people would have the authority. But one of them was the Secretary of Defense.

'So when is this?'

'You're giving me one of your intense looks, Maggie, the kind that freak me out.'

'Eleanor, please.'

She lifted her glasses again and peered at the document. 'It's today. It says 16.00.' She looked at her watch. 'Jesus, Maggie. That's *now*.'

She looked up, but Maggie was already halfway out of the door.

39

Was it wrong to admit to pleasure at this part of the job? Of course he drew satisfaction in the preparatory stages – in ensuring everything was just so – but this was something else. This was no longer a job that a meticulous IT engineer or an able civilian could do. This required the skill and the eye of a marksman.

Set back from the window, so that there would be no tell-tale barrel visible to the probing eyes of the Secret Service, Julian Garcia had arranged the hotel desk and chair into a shooting station. Getting the desk to the right height had required some improvisation involving the base of the second bed, but he was satisfied with it.

He peered into the night scope. The hessian canopy and screenings had gone up several hours ago, as he had been told they would. It was standard Secret Service procedure for a location of this kind, an attempt to enclose the event – and deny a clear line of sight to any of the surrounding buildings. Looking through the infra-red sight now, Garcia could see a series of white shapes: the White House advance team, making sure everything was in place.

He had been down there earlier today, happy to be taken for a tourist. With his cap down low, and avoiding being caught in any photographs, he had been among the small, polite crowd shuffling reverentially around the US Marine Corps War Memorial just north of Arlington National Cemetery. It was impressive, no doubt about it. The sculpture of those six Marines, forever planting the flag at Iwo Jima, mounted on a deep base of polished black granite: it had required no acting on Garcia's part to bow his head in respect to those who had fallen in all the battles commemorated on this spot. He looked at the words, etched in gold, and he believed them. *Uncommon valor was a common virtue.*

He had stepped back, identifying the spot just in front of the memorial where he had been told the target would stand. As promised, there was a tiny square of black tape on the ground, invisible if you weren't looking for it, to mark the place where the subject would shake hands and receive a handful of representative honourees of the Marine Corps, current and former. Nothing unusual in that: the President knew he had to hit his mark if he was to give the cameras their best angles. But it helped Garcia enormously.

The other elements of the day's work had gone smoothly. Hernandez had marshalled all his strength and taken a cab, alone, to the Virginian Suites hotel, where he'd checked in that morning. He had secured the third-floor room that Garcia had earlier identified as the ideal choice and which Hernandez had requested in advance by phone. He had been carrying a bag that looked appropriately heavy.

Garcia had made his way there using the rear entrance and service elevator. He wore workman's overalls and carried two big bags and was confident that, even if he had been seen, he had not been noticed. When he arrived, he found

Hernandez stretched out on the bed, dozing lightly. Garcia had noticed that, on the nightstand, were several packets of tablets. The sight of that futile medicine made him grieve for his friend.

Now Garcia looked through his scope again. The distance was three hundred and forty-four yards, just as he had planned.

He checked his watch. Not long to go now.

'Please, there's a very big tip for you if you can drive as fast as you can.'

It was 3.53pm. The driver was speeding down the E Street Expressway, not as fast as Maggie would like, but as fast as he would go short of Maggie producing a gun and holding it to his temple.

She was on the edge of the back seat, leaning in towards him, so that her head hovered by his shoulder, filling the space between the driver's and passenger seats, her mouth close by his ear. She wanted her instructions to be heard the first time, without repetition. The driver, who had the flag of Ethiopia dangling as a pennant from the rearview mirror, was rattled, she could see that. He thought his passenger might be crazy. She didn't blame him.

Her hand was gripping her phone, and she could feel it growing clammy. She had tried calling the head of the Secret Service but she had not been put through. She had tried both the numbers of an agent she knew well. The first had gone straight to voicemail. Now she dialled the second.

It was ringing. One ring, then a second. *Please, pick up. Pick up, pick up, pick up.*

Four rings. And then a voice.

'Bailey.'

'Jeff? It's Maggie. Listen, I have reason to believe that an attempt on the President's life is imminent. Right now. You've got to—'

'Maggie? Is that you?'

'Yes, listen to me. Someone is going to try to kill the President. It's about to happen.' Maggie could see the driver's eyes widen into a stare of cold panic. He was gripping the steering wheel. As a pre-emptive move, she said to him in a quiet, but firm voice: 'Keep driving.'

'Maggie, this is a really bad line. What are you saying?'

Now she shouted. 'You need to get the President away. He's at the Marines memorial. In Arlington. Just—'

'Where are you calling from?'

'For fuck's sake, Jeff. This is urgent. I can explain later. For now you need to contact the team on the ground and tell them that a White House official has clear evidence that an attack on the President is imminent. They need to pull out now!'

The line was silent. She hoped to God he had hung up and was doing as she had said. But now she heard those three beeps that told her the call had dropped out. The phone was asking if she wanted to retry and she did. She hit the green button but a second later got the message. *User busy. Retry?* One more time, same result.

They were now crossing the Theodore Roosevelt Bridge. It was 4.02pm. She looked over her shoulder to see if they were being followed. She glanced at the dashboard of the car: it struck her that this taxi was sufficiently old and lacking in computer technology that it'd be impossible to hack. The only person steering this vehicle would be her petrified driver.

She reckoned they were five minutes away. She didn't have five minutes.

She tried the White House again, this time asking to be

put through to McNamara. *Voicemail*. She left a frantic, incoherent message. 'Mac, this is Maggie. I know this sounds crazy but I believe an attack is imminent. On the President. Any minute now. An assassination attempt. You've got to get him to pull out. Please.'

She tried again, this time asking for McNamara's office. The secretary picked up and, without waiting, Maggie said, 'This is a matter of life and death. This is Maggie Costello. I need to speak to Mac now.'

'Please hold.'

Maggie waited, but McNamara never came on the line. Nor did his secretary. She tried the Secret Service again, but was directed to the information line where a recorded voice assured her that, 'Your call is important to us. We check this line frequently and will take note of any information you have. You don't have to give us your name and number, but if you do it will help us . . .'

What the hell was she meant to do? No one would speak to her, every door was being slammed in her face. Six months ago, she could have dialled any number in the White House and she would have known who would be on the receiving end and they would have taken her call in an instant. Now she was like some crazy woman off the street, banging on the doors of the White House, utterly ignored.

She thought about calling the police but she knew that they too would dismiss her as a crank. By the time it would take her to explain who she was, it would be too late.

There was only one person left to call. She would not have done it in any other circumstances but these. But too much was at stake. She found the number and dialled it.

The audience was small: twelve rows of twelve outdoor chairs, filled by uniformed Marines and their wives or husbands, just enough to look like a modest outdoor quorum. The wreath was already there, positioned on an easel, to the left of the base of the statue. But otherwise, the scene was as simple and pared down as it could be for a presidential visit. There was no military band striking up a memorial tune, no pastor clearing his throat to intone a prayer. There were just two pool cameras, a handful of reporters and of course the Secret Service detail. On McNamara's orders, the optics were meant to convey sombre modesty: a man engaged in a private moment, contemplating the loss and sacrifice of America's heroes.

From his third-floor hotel window, Julian Garcia could see very little. The screens and canopy had made sure of that. But with CNN showing a live shot of the memorial, the camera fixed on the sculpture of the men of Iwo Jima, planting their flag, he had a good idea of what was going on. While the flagpole they gripped was made of bronze, the flag itself was real: it formed the centre of the image on the TV screen, fluttering in the May sunshine.

Minutes away now from the arrival of the President. No word yet on whether he will be making any formal remarks, White House sources telling CNN they expect him to have a moment of silent contemplation as he lays the wreath in memory of those Marines who have given their lives to the United States in battle since 1775. This is an almost impromptu addition to the President's schedule, very little preparation. CNN understands it was very much the initiative of the President himself. Formal ceremonies on Monday of course, but for now, on the eve of this Memorial Day weekend, he wanted his own moment of prayer and reflection. We'll keep watching that for you, and when the President arrives of course we'll be right there. In the meantime, let's hear from CNN Senior Political Analyst . . .

On the bed, Jorge was now sitting up but saying nothing. He knew better than to disturb a fellow soldier.

Julian glanced at the TV and then back to the image through the infra-red sight. They corresponded perfectly, barring a small delay. When someone moved into the frame on TV, Garcia could see a white shape move into his shot.

The audience were seated, expectant. Any minute now.

'Richard, is that you?'

'Yes, Maggie. It's me.' The voice was flat, but Maggie didn't care.

'Thank God. Listen, I can't explain why, but I believe there's about to be an attempt on the President's life. Any second now someone is going to try to kill him.'

'What?'

'I know it sounds crazy, but you need to get a message to whoever's with him. Body man or Secret Service or McNamara. They have to pull him out.'

'Pull him out? From where?'

Maggie felt a small pulse of relief. At last, someone was listening to her. 'He's at the Marines War Memorial. Please, Richard. Do it. Do it now.'

'Maggie, this sounds a bit crazy. Are you sure about this? This is not one of—'

'Richard. If you do this, you'll be a national hero. If I'm wrong, you can just blame the crazy Irish woman you've been fucking. OK? Just do it.' She hung up. The dashboard clock said it was 4.11pm.

The taxi was now turning off Arlington Boulevard. She could see a cluster of vehicles parked ahead, blocking off the road. Several of them had their roof lights flashing silently: state troopers. The rest were black SUVs. No guarantee that the President was already here; this could be the advance party. She might still have time. She threw a twenty down on the passenger seat and got out of the car while it was still moving.

Maggie began running towards the impromptu roadblock. She knew it was a mistake. She knew that it would announce her as someone unhinged, a member of the public who had to be kept at bay. So much better to stroll towards them with confidence, purposeful in her Washington pantsuit, flash her White House pass and then say she had information that needed to be passed to their commanding officer right away.

Instead, she reached them breathless, holding up her pass and saying, 'I'm from the White House. Someone's going to shoot the President!'

'Excuse me, ma'am. This is now a secured area. You cannot proceed.'

She tried to push past this first man, a Virginia state trooper, but that only raised the alarm.

'Ma'am!' he said, turning around to catch up with her. That alerted two other troopers who now stepped forward to block her. Noticing the disturbance, a fourth man – in plain suit and with a curly wire emerging from his ear – approached too.

'My name is Maggie Costello and I am a Special Assistant to the President in the General Counsel's Office.' She tried to lift up her pass, so that all four of these men might see it, but the sudden movement jolted the first trooper. He now grabbed her forearm, gripping it tight.

'Ma'am, I must ask you to stop right there and—'

'Listen to me!' Maggie said, shouting so loud her own voice shook her. 'Just fucking listen to me. Someone is about to kill the President. I'm here to warn you of a credible threat on the President's life. Now. One of you needs to tell the team with him right now or it will be your fault. Do you understand?'

His eye was still in the sight when he heard the voice on the TV.

And here now is the President, come to pay his respects ahead of Memorial Day. He shakes hands first with the curator of the US Marines War Memorial, as you can see there, and now greeting several of the veterans and their families who have gathered here in this sacred place. He's pointing towards a couple of faces in the crowd, smiling almost as if this were a campaign event. And now an aide seems to be whispering in his ear and the President's expression becomes more sombre, more in tune, some might say, with an occasion of this solemnity.

Garcia stretched his hands out twice, loosening up his fingers. He glanced at the TV. Now the curator was guiding the President, leading him as they circled around the monument. CNN showed the two men pausing at some of the battles whose names were engraved on the base: the Philippine Insurrection, the Boxer Rebellion, Grenada.

The assassin trained his eye through the scope once more. Once the President had completed his circuit, that would be the natural moment to pick up the wreath, move to the planned mark, pause and then step forward onto the dais. It would be in a few seconds.

'For God's sake, don't waste any more time. Just get on your fucking radios and tell them what I'm telling you!'

She saw the Secret Service agent glance over at the most senior of the state troopers, a moment of silent consultation. *Is this woman nuts? Or are we gonna end up blamed for not passing on this information?*

Finally, and with studied reluctance, the agent stepped forward, signalling for the state troopers to let go. 'All right,' he said, taking his time. 'What is the nature of the information you wish me to pass on?'

There was no time for Maggie even to exhale her exasperation. 'Tell them you have credible information about a threat to the President's life. He needs to get out of here. If he's exposed to the public, you need to get him somewhere—'

But she never finished her sentence.

Garcia had waited for this moment. It was, he believed, what set him apart from his peers. In this instant of maximum stress, he felt his pulse not quicken but slow down. It was a physical sensation, his body dropping to a steadier, almost meditative state. He was sure he could feel it: the pressure of the blood in his veins falling, as he readied himself. Put a hand on his forehead and it would be cooler; he was sure of it.

He was in the eye of the hurricane now. There would be noise and clamour soon, but for this second it was serenely quiet. At no other time did he know tranquillity like this. The sense of purpose, of complete and total focus. The dedication of mind, body and spirit to a single goal. He loved this moment. If he could extend it, he would. But, he knew, its nature was fleeting, transient. It could not last.

He waited a half-second more and there he was, the white shape of the President's thermal image standing exactly where it was meant to stand, corresponding perfectly to the picture on TV. The white silhouette filled the lens of the sight, the neat lines of the glass bisecting just across his chest. He was a big barn-door of a man, there was plenty of target to aim at. And so all those intense hours of preparation and planning, all the years of experience and training, now flowed through him and into the index finger of his right hand. With not even a microscopic tremor, he felt the trigger yield to him and he watched and listened as the bullet exploded out of the chamber and into the air, rushing across those three hundred and forty yards of parking lot and trees and parkland, ripping through the hessian canopy and over the heads of those hundred odd people and finally into the expanse of dark blue suit that covered the chest of the President of the United States.

She heard a single scream first, loud enough to silence her. Maggie froze, as did the men around her. The interval between that and the subsequent screams would, when she heard it again – in the TV clips that played endlessly – last less than half of a second. But then, that first time, it seemed to endure, a long, echoing hiatus in which the air itself vibrated with fear, disbelief and shock.

And when it ended, the noise was a concentrated explosion of sound, a raucous rumpus of shouting and hoarse-voiced panic.

The agent who had been speaking to her turned around and instantly ran towards the commotion. Only then did Maggie realize how near she was. She had been held on the road that separated Arlington Cemetery from the Marines memorial. The ceremony was little more than a hundred yards away.

Still, for the first few seconds she could not see it. As she followed the agent towards the source of the noise, she could only hear the screams of the people who were running past her, families getting away from the memorial as fast as they could. Did that mean the assassin was there? Had he been in the crowd? Had he been sitting in the audience and suddenly stood up and opened fire? Maggie had considered that.

Or had it been the other scenario she had imagined? She wondered about the assassinations of Anwar Sadat and Indira Gandhi, killed by their own bodyguards. Is that what Kassian and Bruton had done? Had they recruited a member of the Secret Service for this mission?

But now, as she got past the trees and closer to the sculpture, she could see a thick knot of agents surrounding a man on the ground, that group itself circled by an outer ring of agents whose guns were cocked and aimed at anyone who dared come close.

She didn't need confirmation but it came over a radio used by a cop or a paramedic, in the melee she couldn't tell which. Even with all the noise and the crackle, its message was clear. 'The President is down. Repeat, the President is down.'

Jorge was on his feet now, standing alongside Garcia. He didn't look at the TV or out of the window. He focused only on Garcia. 'Wipe your prints,' he said, nodding towards the rifle.

Garcia did as he was told. And then they faced each other. 'It's not too late, you know,' Julian said. 'You can change your mind.'

Jorge smiled. 'It is too late. Now get the hell out of here.' They hugged, only for a second but long enough for nearly thirty years of comradeship, trust and gratitude to flow between them.

Julian looked around one last time, checking that he had left nothing behind that was his. Then he ripped off the plastic trousers and apron he'd been wearing, scrunched them up and put them into his backpack. He noticed that

Jorge already had his Glock 17 in his right hand. He was ready.

'Go,' Jorge said.

'Thank you, brother,' Julian replied.

He closed the door behind him quietly and headed for the fire escape directly opposite, just as he had planned. He had taken a couple of steps when he heard the shot, single and clean. Jorge Hernandez, the faithful soldier, had followed the plan to the last letter.

As Garcia took the stairs, he could hear voices from the third-floor corridor. But he wasn't alarmed. As far as he could tell, his mission had been accomplished.

40

Washington, DC, Friday, 5.41pm
This is CBS News with an urgent update. Here's what we know so far.

The President was shot this afternoon during a ceremony at the United States Marines War Memorial, just north of the National Cemetery at Arlington. He is believed to have been struck by a single bullet. He was rushed urgently, in the presidential limousine, to George Washington University Hospital, where he was treated immediately. No word at this hour on his condition.

Law enforcement officials believe the gunman was this man, forty-eight-year-old Jorge Hernandez, whose body was found in a room on the third floor of this hotel, the Virginian Suites, which is just a few hundred yards away from, and which overlooks, the memorial. Police sources telling CBS this hour that they found a sniper rifle aimed precisely at the spot where the President had been standing when he was hit. They say Hernandez had appeared to take his own life. Witnesses at the Virginian Suites hotel report hearing a gunshot seconds after TV pictures showed the President shot.

Live now to correspondent Clare Romine who's outside the George Washington University Hospital for us. Clare, what's the latest?

John, we're waiting for an official news conference at the top of the hour from the Medical Director here, but let me pass on one important piece of information, which I ought to stress is still unconfirmed at this stage: White House sources telling CBS that the President was wearing some kind of protective body armour, a bulletproof vest if you will, and that might have an important bearing on the President's condition going forward. Again, that's unconfirmed at this stage. John?

Clare, is that usual? For a President to be wearing protective armour like that?

John, I've been covering the White House for several years and, as you know, the Secret Service never discuss operational matters – they never talk publicly about how they protect the President—

OK—

But, just on the basis of what I know, I would say the answer is no – it is not usual for a President to be protected in that way. That seems unusual to me. Which will of course raise questions in the coming days about what knowledge or information or warnings this White House had about any threats to the President.

And, Clare, obviously what is going to be on the minds of most Americans right now, and indeed people around the world – and of course we appreciate information is very sketchy at this stage – but what more can you tell us about the state the President was in when he arrived at the hospital there?

Well, John, as you say, official information in very short supply just now, but I've spoken to some healthcare professionals here and what they have told me – and, again, this is not confirmed – is that the President was conscious when he arrived here. Different accounts of whether he was able to leave the limousine unassisted – one eyewitness says she saw a wheelchair used, another says he was supported by two aides – but the key point is that the President was, according to these unofficial reports, conscious on arrival. John?

Thanks, Clare. Reporting live from the George Washington University Hospital, Clare Romine. And we'll be going straight back there when we have that briefing from the Medical Director, which of course we'll bring you live.

Let's just see what we can tell you about the alleged shooter. As you can imagine, just fragments of information at this time – lot of people in a state of grave shock and confusion. But social media moves very fast, as you know. For more on that, CBS News National Correspondent Kyle Chapman. Kyle, what can you tell us?

John, obviously we are in the first few hours of this investigation and there's lots we don't know but if it is confirmed that the shooter was Jorge Hernandez, as has been reported, then what we can say is that this was not a man who hid his hostility to the President. His Facebook profile—

And there, we can see that on the screen now.

There we go, and you can see he identifies himself as a 'patriot, militant and fighter'. And then goes on to say, and this was posted just a matter of weeks ago, 'In the name of Jesus, stop the deportations!' And then you can see, a very disturbing image of the President—

And obviously some viewers will find this material distressing.

That's right, John, a very disturbing, doctored image of the President, the eyes kind of gouged out—

Sort of Devil Eyes—

That's right and then there's this quote: 'He will punish those who do not know God and do not obey the gospel of our Lord Jesus!'

Gosh.

But I think the one that is kind of chilling in the light of what happened today, this is from soon after the President's inauguration back in January. Hernandez is posting an article about the President's plan to build detention facilities for illegal migrants, but he introduces it with another quote from scripture. And as I say, this does look like some kind of warning, in the light of today's event.

Have we got that on the screen?

Here it is. 'It is mine to avenge. I will repay. Their day of disaster is near.'

And, I suppose, there will be questions to the Secret Service about how they could have missed these very stark warnings. Kyle Chapman, for now, thank you.

If you're just joining this special CBS News update, let me say again that the President of the United States has been the victim of what appears to have been a failed assassination attempt. He was shot at 4.13pm today, at the United States Marines War Memorial. He is believed to have survived and is currently undergoing emergency medical treatment. Stay with CBS as we bring you all of the detail on this as it comes in.

And there's been a new development in the last few moments. Let's go to that right now . . .

41

She had failed. That was the only way Maggie could see it. She had been determined to stop this attempt on the President's life, to find out who was behind it and stand in their way, but she had done no such thing. Today a man had shot the President – and she had been a matter of yards away when it happened.

That he had survived brought little compensation, only confusion. In some ways, she thought, it meant the worst of both worlds. Now there would be all the division, fear and paranoia unleashed by an assassination attempt – including the risk of civil war, as one half of this divided nation believed the other had tried to murder its leader – but without the purging, curative effect of removing what her sister had called this 'evil man'. He would still be there, more livid and bellicose than ever. Put more crudely than she would ever say out loud, America was about to get all the pain of a presidential assassination but none of the gain.

And she had let it happen. If only she had got there quicker. If only she had made that taxi drive even a bit faster. If only she had been able to reach her contacts in the Secret Service. If only she had had better contacts. If only she had not made so many enemies. If only, if only, if only. This had been an evening of if onlys.

Despite the chaos at the memorial, one of the Secret Service agents who had stopped her when she jumped out of the cab had had the presence of mind to apprehend her afterwards and demand she face an immediate interview. They had done it there and then, in one of the security tents.

To the repeated question – how did Maggie know an assassination attempt was imminent? – Maggie offered the same, bland answer: that in her capacity as part of the office of the White House Counsel she had been proceeding with an investigation that related to the President's security, the details of which could not yet be disclosed. She insisted that there would clearly be a full inquiry in due course and that she would, of course, co-operate with that. But for the moment, the information she had was classified at a grade that could not be shared with those who were interviewing her. Essentially she was engaged in a double-play, simultaneously pulling rank and blinding them with White House legal science.

It worked. Once the Secret Service had confirmed her identity with the Counsel's office – and, interestingly, there was no hint that she was off the payroll – they told her she was free to go, but that they would be in contact for a further interview in the coming days.

As she finally headed away from the memorial, hitching a ride with a TV journalist she knew, she saw that Twitter was as confused and ambivalent as she was. The first wave of reaction felt obliged to observe the appropriate solemnity. There was a hashtag, of course: #PrayforUSA. A rush of celebrities issued the predictable pieties:

Lord knows, I have my differences with the President. But I am praying for him tonight.

And:

Whether you're red or blue, always remember this: we have more in common than divides us.

A comedian who had been vicious about the President from day one bowed to the respectful mood.

The guy's a jerk – but even jerks have a right to life. #MyPresident

But slowly, as the hours went by, and especially as reports filtered out of the hospital suggesting he was awake and had suffered no more than a superficial flesh-wound between his chest and shoulder, along with a broken rib, the forced decorum eased a little.

JFK, MLK, RFK: all on target. The one time the shooter misses, it has to be this guy. #TooSoon?

A leading foreign affairs analyst, strongly critical of the White House, tweeted:

Sigh of relief for the First Family, of course. Rest of America and the world? Not so much

That opened the door to a few more in that spirit.

Of course this is not the way we do things, but this could have been a perfect way out of the N Korea crisis #justsayin

And:

Memo to God: so a guy who lies, cheats, steals and race-baits is somehow blessed with the best luck on the planet. How's that work?

Maggie switched off the screen and flung the phone onto the couch. None of it was helping. She'd had a missed call from Liz, but sensed that wouldn't help much either. She suspected her sister would be cursing the missed opportunity. Whichever line Liz took, Maggie would somehow be on the wrong side of it.

But her confusion was not just of the emotional or moral variety. Maggie was also puzzled by the facts of the situation. The same question had been going round her head as soon as she heard the first news reports, even from the moment she saw that cluster of agents surrounding the President at the war memorial and sensed that he was down but not dead.

How on earth had he come to be wearing protective armour? It meant that the Secret Service had had advance warning of the threat, but how?

Maggie had said nothing of her inquiries to anyone. Actually, that was not quite true. Stupidly, she had told Richard about Kassian and Bruton's late-night chat with Dr Frankel, which he was bound to have passed on to McNamara, but that was all.

Unless that had been enough. Handed that one fact, had McNamara followed the same train of thought she had and reached the same destination? The sudden addition of a new event to the schedule would certainly have caught McNamara's eye, especially if he was already suspicious. He was a vile, sexist, racist boor but he was not stupid. Far from it.

But that only left a much harder question. If McNamara knew the President was at mortal risk, then the rational response was not to dress him in a bulletproof vest, but to withdraw him from all public events until the threat had been neutralized. What on earth was McNamara playing at, knowingly exposing the President to that kind of danger?

She wanted to talk to Stuart. She needed to think this through with him, to hear his voice as they worked it out together. But then, from across the sofa, her phone lit up with a news alert. She grabbed it: a fresh tweet from the President himself. Once she read it, and then read it again, she had an inkling of an answer to her question.

42

The White House, Friday, 7.31pm
'What the fucking fuck happened?'

'I really don't think we can have this conversation here, Jim.'

Robert Kassian and Jim Bruton were standing in their regular spot in the colonnade, the open-columned walkway between the West Wing and the Residence. They had been summoned to see Crawford McNamara and Kassian hoped this looked like nothing more than a chance encounter of two officials arriving early for the same meeting. But Bruton looked far too agitated for anyone to be fooled by that.

'I mean, somebody has to explain to me what in hellfire's name went on here, because I sure as fuck don't know.'

'Jim,' Kassian said, speaking steadily and quietly. 'If anything, that's a question for you. You were handling the operational side of this.'

Bruton's neck turned puce. 'Nothing went wrong at my end. Nothing! Our guy was ordered to hit the target and he did. Bullseye.'

'Is it possible he or,' his voice dipped, 'the other one mentioned something to someone?'

'What?'

'Just a heads-up? Maybe to a friend in the Service?'

'Come on, Bob. You know these men. You know who they are.'

'I know.' He shook his head, a combination of both resignation and disbelief. 'It's just. I mean, the President doesn't wear body armour. Except this one time. Which just so happens to be—'

'Look, we did this right. Circle of trust was tight. Neither of those men would have breathed a word. Not ever.'

'OK.'

'And there is no record of any links between us and them. Total omerta on the men of that unit. No, something else happened here, Bob. I don't know what, but something else. And in terms of us, no one knows anything. Don't lose sight of that.'

Kassian took a deep breath, drawing in the oxygen through his nostrils. 'You're right. And that's our advantage now. No one knows. So long as we stay strong and stick to our story—'

'Which is?'

'That we know nothing and did nothing.'

'And if he asks how come Hernandez knew about the memorial thing?'

'He was a veteran. Grapevine.'

'OK. And what about Frankel?' Bruton was sweating.

'We had nothing to do with that.'

'I know. But the meeting? Costello knew we'd seen him. Why? Why were we there?'

'Let's tell the truth. We were alarmed at the President's mental state.'

'North Korea.'

'Exactly. It was completely legitimate that we went to his home to discuss it.'

'Not to seek a declaration of incapacity.'

'Absolutely not. Just to get his assessment of the President's stability and fitness. We were concerned.'

'He was behaving like a nut.'

'By his *erratic behaviour*, Jim.'

'OK.'

They paused, looked at each other and then looked outward, facing toward the Rose Garden, its glories hidden by the twilight. Kassian felt something he had not known in many, many years, not perhaps since that skirmish outside Tikrit: genuine, physical fear. He had been aware from the start that he was taking the most enormous risk, of course he had. But, strange as it was to confess this now, even to himself, he had never really contemplated failure. He had not forced himself to stare hard into the abyss, to imagine this moment: the President alive and he, along with Bruton, accused of ordering his murder. He had not pictured how it would play out: the initial accusation, the arrest, the subsequent trial, the conviction, the prison sentence, the disgrace. He felt himself descending into the pit.

'Gentlemen?'

It was McNamara's assistant, a new one. Like her predecessor, she was young, slim and absurdly good-looking. The previous woman had left in a hurry. Kassian had been too swamped with other things to look into what had happened, though he suspected that if he had, he'd have found something ugly. The chances were high that McNamara, like his master, was a class action sexual harassment lawsuit waiting to happen.

It struck him that that was how it was with this

presidency. A single one of the episodes that happened here daily – hourly – would have been enough to destroy previous administrations. But under this President, they came in such a torrent – the tweets, the lies, the grotesque misconduct, the conflicts of interest, the acts of unwarranted aggression, the self-harming threats to American national security – that the media, the Congress, the country itself could not keep up. Just when outrage was building at what he'd done on Tuesday, he'd done something even more appalling on Wednesday. It was like Stalin's old line about a million deaths being a statistic. A single scandal could destroy a good president, but a thousand scandals gave a bad president immunity. The worse he behaved, the more he could act with impunity.

They were ushered into McNamara's office. Predictably, he did not get up but kept his shoeless, bare feet up and on the desk, showing them his calloused soles. He was not in shorts but jeans today, perhaps in honour of the solemnity of the occasion. He was watching TV, remote in one hand, supersized paper cup of Diet Coke in the other.

'Hi guys,' he said, as relaxed as if he were welcoming them to a Saturday barbecue, gesturing for them to take a seat in front of his desk. The optics, as he would have put it, were the principal's study.

'Hello, Mac. Terrible news.' It was Bruton, determined not to be passive.

'Terrible,' Kassian agreed.

'Sure, sure,' said McNamara. 'But somehow I think we'll pull through.' He smiled. 'I would offer you something to drink, but I don't feel like it, d'you know what I mean?'

His eyes remained fixed on the screen. It was Fox, with a live shot of their reporter outside the hospital, intercut with footage of a lightly bandaged and smiling President flashing the thumbs-up from his bedroom window an hour or so earlier. McNamara had the sound down, but the subtitles included the words 'remarkable recovery' and 'superficial wound'.

For a while, all three stayed looking at the screen. In silence. Eventually Bruton and Kassian caught each other's eye and Kassian furrowed his brow. *What's going on?*

Finally, McNamara spoke, still paying attention to Fox News rather than to the two men in his office. 'Either of you guys a lawyer?'

'No,' Bruton said. 'My mamma thought I should aim higher. Had me clean out the sewers underneath the local whorehouse instead.' It was a practised line; Kassian had heard it before. Usually it got a laugh, but not today.

'Pity. Thought one of you boys might be able to advise me on a legal problem.' *Boys.*

'Oh yes, Mac,' said Kassian, willing to play ball if that meant avoiding a return to the silence. 'What's that?'

'"Mac"? Did you say "Mac"?' Finally he had shifted his gaze away from the TV screen. 'Isn't that what all the kikes round here would call supreme *chutzpah*?'

Kassian made the mistake of looking puzzled.

'*Mister McNamara* to you, don't you think? Nothing "Mac" about this situation. Nothing "Mac" at all.'

'I don't—'

'I mean *he* can call me Mac.' McNamara was pointing directly at Bruton. 'He is, for the moment, the Secretary of Defense. But you? I don't think so.'

'Look, Mac—' It was Bruton, seeking to take control. It was the only way he knew how to be.

McNamara raised a palm in objection, which stopped him. 'Shall I get to my legal query? I would ask the Counsel's office, but you'll soon see why that's *complicated*. So, shall I?'

313

Kassian and Bruton both nodded, a gesture whose implied deference seemed to increase by more than a factor of two for being doubled.

'I want to know what the maximum sentence is for conspiracy to assassinate a sitting President of the United States. Either of you boys know that, perchance? I'll take a ballpark figure.' He started making the sound of a TV gameshow clock, loudly counting down to zero. He did a little jingle to mark the last second: *de-der, de-der, de-de-de-der.*

'Let's stop playing these chickenshit games, Mac,' Bruton said. 'I'm not in the mood. I suspect I speak for Bob on that too.'

'Oh, I suspect you *do* speak for Bob on that. In fact, I suspect a whole lot of things when it comes to you two.' McNamara was now on his feet, walking around to get closer to the two men, eventually placing himself directly in front of them, his rear end perching on the ledge of his desk.

'Why don't you tell us what's on your mind, Mac?' Bruton, still trying to regain the initiative.

'You're right. I ought to get this off my chest.' He was back on the move again, pacing around his office. 'You vant I tell you about mein childhood, ya? Maybe a little bit of psychoanalysis will feel therapeutic, ya?'

'Mac. Please.'

'Well, put it this way. I have what you might call Loyalty to the President Syndrome. Do you know what that is? No, I didn't think so. But I got a real bad case. So I'm kind of *obsessed* with looking out for his best interests. And right now, he's in a hospital bed in Virginia having endured an attempt on his life.'

'We know that,' Kassian said quietly.

'And we know who did it.' Bruton again, jumping into

the gap. 'Jorge Hernandez. He shot the President and killed himself straight afterwards.'

McNamara nodded. 'Yep. That's right. Everyone's seen the Facebook posts. And the threatening letters to the President. The crazy guy house. We've got the full Nutcracker Suite on this guy.'

'And presumably the Secret Service had been on high alert because of all that,' said Kassian. 'Which is how the President came to be wearing body armour.'

'That sounds about right,' McNamara said, back at his desk. Except now he paid no attention to the TV screen. He was looking only at them. 'And that's what the public is definitely going to believe. But I'm not talking about the public. I'm talking about me. And I'm talking about the President. What should *we* believe?'

Kassian replied, 'I don't know what you mean.'

'I mean that I have good reason to believe that poor Mr Hernandez – a terminally ill, lonely man with few friends and no family – was not such a lone wolf after all.'

'What are you saying, Mac?'

'What I'm saying, Jim, is that I think you and Bob here made Curious Jorge the fall guy for your own little plan.' He raised his hand again. 'Don't play all innocent with me, gentlemen. You'll only embarrass yourselves.'

He shot a glance over at the TV, now showing – once again – a sequence of still photographs taken by police from the inside of Hernandez's home. Inset was a mugshot. The caption read: *Inside the Mind of an Assassin.*

'I gotta tell ya,' McNamara smiled. 'The news guys are killing themselves right now. This was meant to be their first day off since Christmas. One of them texted me: "We literally cannot get a break with you guys in the White House."'

Kassian did not smile. He was seeing the pit open up.

'Anyway, here's what we know. We know that you went to see the presidential physician on Monday night. And the next morning, that man was found dead.'

Bruton was indignant. 'Those two events are completely unrelated!'

'If you say so, Mr Secretary. I'm just setting out what I know. Remember, I'm not a lawyer either.' He smiled again. 'We also know that an event was added late to the presidential schedule. You, Bob,' pointing at him, 'are one of the very few people with the power to do that. This event just so happened to be added on Wednesday morning, barely twenty-four hours after Dr Frankel "killed himself".' He made quote marks in the air. 'Almost like Plan A didn't work out, so you turned to Plan B.'

'What on earth—'

'Let me finish. And guess where this event is? It's at a location essentially controlled by your department, Mr Secretary. Not difficult for you – for the two of you – to work out the guest list, the format, the staging, for that one. And, once you have, also not difficult for you to share the key details with your man with the gun, whoever that is. Am I right?'

'I gotta tell you, my friend: you are sounding a little, you know, nutty.' Bruton, still trying to keep it informal, light. 'I mean, I know you made a lot of money out of these wacky conspiracy theories, but this is getting a little crazy. Like you're drinking your own Kool-Aid. You don't want to be doing that, not in this town. 'Cause people are pissing in the Kool-Aid all the time.'

'OK. Maybe this is sounding like a bit of a stretch. And let's not even think about the fact that a guy like that – desperate, broke, terminally ill – would be *very* easy to pay

316

off for a job like this. You'd just have to promise to look after what little family he had once he was gone. Nice big veteran's pension, that wouldn't be too hard for – I don't know – the Secretary of Defense to arrange, now would it? But let's not even go there. No *need* to go there.

'You wanna know why? OK, here goes. Minutes before the shot rings out, guess who's dialling every number in this place – including mine – and leaving frantic messages? One Maggie Costello. Trusted, shit-hot, smart-as-a-whip servant of this White House and these United States. And guess what she says? You know what, you don't have to guess. Here we go.'

He made a few keystrokes on his computer and then the room filled with Maggie's voice, panting and desperate: *Mac, this is Maggie. I know this sounds crazy but I believe an attack is imminent. On the President. Any minute now. An assassination attempt. You've got to get him to pull out. Please.*

McNamara was smiling. 'That message was left at 4.06pm today. That's five minutes before a crazed vet – a maverick, rogue, lone individual crackpot – fires into the chest of the President. I mean, that's something else, isn't it?'

Kassian could feel himself paling. He didn't want to look at Bruton, worried that even a sideways glance would look like the gesture of a guilty man. But he sensed, somewhere in his peripheral vision, that the older man, his commanding officer, had swallowed hard.

'And this is the thing, guys. We know that Costello was pursuing only one line of inquiry after Frankel's death.' McNamara paused, shifting his gaze from Kassian to Bruton and back again. He was enjoying this. 'That's right. The only people she was looking at were . . . you.'

There was silence in the room. A hundred different sentences went through Kassian's head – *You've got no proof*

317

of anything; It's all circumstantial; No one would believe a word of what you've said – but all of them sounded like an admission of guilt. So he said nothing.

Now Bruton spoke, with the quiet calm that Kassian remembered from those days in the field, under desert skies, facing their own deaths. 'Mac, you need to take a breath. Neither Bob nor I were anywhere near the Marines memorial yesterday. Law enforcement have the weapon. They have the prints. They have the ballistics. They have the full life history of this man Hernandez. If you try to suggest that we were guilty of this crime, people will think you've lost your mind. You won't destroy us. You will destroy yourself.'

McNamara was grinning now. 'You finished? You have? Pity. I was enjoying that. You're good at it. No wonder every liberal in this town wants to suck your dick. *The acceptable face of an unacceptable administration.* Who was that, *Time*?'

'*Newsweek.*'

'*Newsweek.* My mistake. But I can see the appeal. You're smooth. Silky smooth. Smooth as the ass on those whores they say the boss likes to bang, you know, the young ones? Bob knows what I'm talking about. "Barely legal." How old's your daughter, Bob? The one at Sidwell Friends?'

Kassian winced. 'You're being disgusting.'

'Anyway. You're real smooth, both of you. But bear in mind. I haven't even spoken to Costello yet. I haven't heard what it was she'd uncovered about you two that convinced her – correctly – that the President was about to get whacked. But whatever it was, if it was good enough to allow her to make a one hundred per cent accurate prediction about the future, then I'm damn sure it'll be good enough to serve as the basis of an indictment.'

'This isn't the campaign, Mac.' It was Kassian. 'You can't just lie through your teeth, and when the press call you on

318

it, say, "They're the liberal media, you can't trust them." This is the law. This is about the courts. They're not into your post-truth bullshit.'

'Don't you worry about that, Bob. Once I've drained all that info out of Maggie Costello – once I have suckled on the breast of the Irish milkmaid – I'll have plenty for the courts. You just watch.' Now he was tapping away at his computer keyboard again. 'And oh look. Here's the answer to my legal quiz. So according to the United States Code, assassination of the President of the United States, when charged as murder in the first degree, brings with it a sentence of life imprisonment or death. But, it's true, your little plan didn't work out, so we're talking about attempted murder, which would only mean twenty years in a federal prison.' McNamara turned away from the screen and pretended to wipe the imaginary sweat from his brow. 'Phew, right?

'Ah, but hold on.' He was back at the keyboard. 'What's this? Plotting to remove a president by force, especially when you've taken the oath, counts as an act of treason against the United States. Jeez. I mean, I bet that's how public opinion would see it, don't you think, once we got 'em all riled up? And the judges wouldn't want to stand in the way of that, would they? Not when Fox and Breitbart and, you know, *us* are calling them "enemies of the people". They won't like that. So let's see how treason works.'

A few more keystrokes and then a look of mock concern. 'Oh dear, guys. This doesn't look so good. It seems that under Title Eighteen of the United States Code, section one hundred and fifteen, "Whoever, owing allegiance to the United States, levies war against them or adheres to their enemies, giving them aid and comfort within the United States or elsewhere, is guilty of *treason* and shall suffer *death*."

I mean that is not good. *Death.*' He extended his lips in an expression of distaste. 'Nasty. And look, even if they don't actually put you in the chair, or give you a lethal injection, or however it is they do it these days, it seems they can ruin your life anyway. You "shall be imprisoned not less than five years and fined . . . and shall be incapable of holding any office under the United States".'

He turned his chair to face them, the eyes in his bald head shining with intelligence and satisfaction. 'And before you say the obvious – that you were acting out of "patriotism" and never consorted with any enemies of the United States or some other horseshit – just think for a moment about how this will *look*. That's what matters here. Trust me, plotting to assassinate the President of the United States will look like treason to most Americans.'

'You're getting way ahead of yourself here, Mac. Way ahead of yourself.'

'Am I, Jim? Am I? Because I disrespectfully disagree. I think it only looks that way to you because you are so far *behind*. I mean isn't it painful to you, that feeling? To be so out of step with everyone else – not just here, in the White House, but in the country, in the *world*? Everything's changing so fast and there's you two – holdouts from the old era, the *ancien regime*, as they'd say in your Ivy League schools—'

'You went to Yale *and* Harvard, Mac,' Kassian said, but McNamara was too excited to listen.

'—still insisting on the old ways of doing things, watching from the window in your white powdered wigs, looking aghast at the mob below through your opera glasses. You stand there from on high, whining about "norms" and "ethics" and "standards" and you might as well be talking about sundials and carrier pigeons. The world has moved on, my friends. It's moved on and left you for dust. And the painful thing – the *tragic* thing – is that you don't even realize it.

'You still think it's all about rules and facts and data and reason and science and all those things you built your lives and your careers on. But none of that matters any more. That world is gone.

'And you know who gets it, don't you? You know who got it before any of us, even though he's older than both of you? Hell, he's older than me. But he understands it. Not in here.' He tapped the side of his head. 'He doesn't understand anything in there. Not really. He gets it *here*, in his guts. And he gets it *here*.' McNamara pointed towards his groin. 'In his balls. In his dick, that's where he feels it. Just like all of them, out there.' He gestured at the window, at the great America beyond. 'That's why it's so crazy you ever worked for him in the first place. You've never understood him the way the folks out there understand him and the way he understands them. You never felt the thrill of it.

'You never understood that this man says what you'd say if your mouth didn't check with your brain first. He's the bit of you that would say to your friend – "I really want to fuck your wife in the ass" – but doesn't because it's "not done", it's not right, it's not politically correct. But guess what: he says it anyway. Black men: they're scary, they commit crime and you'd rather not live next door to one. Hispanics: they're lazy and they cheat. Jews: rich, cunning and you can't trust them. Gays: what they do to each other is sick and unnatural and the idea of them "marrying" each other is a complete joke. Women between the ages of sixteen and seventy: you'd fuck most of 'em, in the right light, and the ones you wouldn't, you'd rather not hear another word out of their fat, ugly mouths, thank you very much. Scratch that: women between the ages of thirteen and seventy-five. Gotta make room for Jane Fonda and those cute little twins from *America's Got Talent*. Wouldn't want to miss them out.

'Are you hearing me yet? Are you beginning to understand? The President is every white man in America with the filter taken off. Maybe not you guys, but the rest of us. And that's why they voted for him. Because he's who they would be, if they could get away with it. He makes billions, pays no tax, never pays his bills, dumps his wives as soon as they sag even a *teeny* bit and marries a younger model – literally! – he insults everyone who gets in his way, says whatever he damn well likes and he only gets richer and stronger.

'Gentlemen, don't you see? He's our national id, unbound and unleashed. He's the toddler within every one of us, allowed to run free. "I want to eat that, I want to hit that, I want to fuck that, I want to own that. I want, I want, I want." And you know what? Everything he wants, wants, wants he gets, gets, gets. It's beautiful.

'So of course, they voted for him. He's like a fantasy. He's a dream come true. He's like America when it started, when white dudes could ride around this country on horseback, shooting Indians and screwing the squaws, taking whatever land they liked and dragging along some negro on the end of a rope to do the dirty work. I mean, who wouldn't want that, if they could get away with it? It's what we were raised on, boys like me, when we went to the movies on Saturday mornings. Cowboys weren't gay or "Latino" or female or gender-fucking-fluid. They were white and they were male and they were on top. That was their destiny. And now, after all these years, along comes this guy and he says, "Damn right. That's how it should be. And that's how it will be again. I'm gonna give you your job back and give you your self-respect back and I'm gonna put you back where you belong – back on top."' McNamara began crooning: '*A-number-one, top of the heap, king of the hill.*

'Top of the heap, guys. Where you can look down on everyone who was always meant to be below you. Starting with the women and the blacks and the gays and "the Latino community" and "the disabled community" and all the others who've been whining so long they've made you apologize simply for getting up in the morning and being a straight white guy. Well, fuck that. No more apologizing. We're back where we belong."' McNamara's eyes were burning and the veins in his neck were throbbing.

'That's his message. And I don't think you guys even *heard* it. You've listened to all the nannies and the mommies telling you to behave, to listen to all sides, to remember to be "inclusive", to respect "diversity" and all that other crap, for so long that you couldn't even pick up the signal. It was like you were there in the field, twiddling the dial and you weren't even on the right wavelength. Imagine that. A pair of military men too. So filled with Geneva Conventions and human rights and UN Declarations and all the rest that your dicks have shrunk into little acorns. What once were mighty oaks! God help us.

'But the folks, out there. They heard it. Loud and clear. They understood what he was saying. And they loved it so much, they made him President. And it was them, Mr Secretary and Mr Chief of Staff, you betrayed with your conspiracy to murder the man they voted for. Sure, treason is defined as an act against the United States, rather than the President, but those people decided to make this man – this man you despise – the embodiment of the United States for four years. He's the head of government and the head of state. And you wanted to *kill* him. You are guilty as charged. You are traitors – and you should pay with your lives.'

The silence that followed seemed to vibrate and hum, the way your ears ring after a loud concert. Bruton felt as if he'd been punched in the solar plexus; the wind seemed to have escaped him. He had kept up his guard for most of the time McNamara had been speaking, a sceptical smile playing at the edges of his mouth, as if he was amused and bewildered by McNamara's performance rather than alarmed by it. But in the closing stretch something closer to fear seemed to have infected him, spreading through his bloodstream.

Kassian understood. He felt it too. He had begun to glimpse the outline of the mountain that stood before them, a silhouette in the darkness and a daunting one. He tried to regroup, to strip away the rhetoric, the compelling persuasive power of what McNamara was saying and to focus. But he was struggling. Because he feared that on one point, if on no other, this wild-eyed man might well be right.

43

The White House, Friday, 8.24pm
The Chief of Staff could see how it might play out. The facts and the evidence were surely with him and Bruton; there was not enough concrete proof to make a legal case against them. The pair of them had been careful, meticulously so, to ensure that there would not be. Garcia would take his secrets to the grave. He was trained in discretion. And his loyalty was total.

Besides, he had no conceivable incentive to come forward. Sure, they could promise him immunity if he became a government witness. But why would that even arise? Why emerge from the shadows to volunteer a confession that you had pulled the trigger, when not a shred of evidence pointed in your direction? Even McNamara accepted that Hernandez had fired the fateful shot. No one was looking for anyone else.

But McNamara was onto something all the same. He was right that the usual things – facts, proof – might not be decisive. Not any more. Kassian and Bruton could comfort themselves that there was not sufficient proof of a conspiracy to meet the legal standard, but the world had changed. This was the world after truth. Now it would be about perception and emotion and a hated elite defying the people and their sacred will – embodied by this man they had installed in the White House – and in that battle, the Chief of Staff and the Defense Secretary would be on the wrong side.

If this ever came to trial, it would be a PT Barnum production complete with blood-hungry mob sitting ringside, and in that fight there was no guarantee that truth would prevail. And here Kassian caught himself. Because, of course, the truth was on McNamara's side. He would be the master sorcerer of the press and the cable TV channels and social media, naturally he would, but he would have another advantage too. The fact was, he was right. Kassian and Bruton had indeed plotted to kill the President of the United States. And, as McNamara had so acidly pointed out, he, like Bruton, was old-fashioned. He believed that, in the end, the truth would always out.

The pit was opening up.

'Hey, Bob, you don't look so good. You all right, hun?' McNamara tilted his head to one side, a parody of therapeutic concern.

Bruton answered for both of them. He decided to take a leaf out of the President's book, to go on the offensive. 'With respect, Mac, you are an employee here. I am the head of the Department of Defense, confirmed for that role by the United States Senate in a near-unanimous vote. I am the head of an organization which employs more than two million Americans. I am also a man who has led troops into battle and has killed with my bare hands. As has Mr Kassian here. I can vouch for that, because I've seen him do it. You—' and then, without a word of warning, Bruton slammed his fist on the desk, making McNamara jump with fright. 'You, on the other hand, have never been anywhere near combat. You ducked out of it, so you could keep smoking weed and jerking yourself off at Yale. So don't you *dare* sit there in your jeans and your Hawaiian shirt and lecture me about America. You don't know the first thing about this country. You don't know about sacrifice. You don't know about duty. Talking about cowboys and Indians: hell, the closest you got to the Wild West was when you took your wife on date night to see *Brokeback Mountain*. So don't think you can take me down so easily.' He raised a crooked index finger on his right hand, and let it hover in front of McNamara's face. 'I won't let you get anywhere near me.'

McNamara sat back, as if recoiling from Bruton's threat. Kassian felt something like an intimation of hope. Not for the first time, his commanding officer had stood by his side in a situation of utter despair and somehow found the words to inspire him, to make him believe that there might just be a way out.

McNamara tilted his office chair as far back as it could go and then a bit further. He began nodding, a small smile spreading from the edges of his mouth. He picked up a pen, flicked it so that it rotated in the air several times before landing between his lips.

'Good speech,' he said. 'Impressive speech, Mr Secretary. But guess what? You can save it. No one's ever going to hear it.'

He got up and paced around behind his desk, past his version of the Washington ego wall. Studiedly, it included no photographs of himself with senators or ambassadors or foreign leaders. Instead, it was a gallery of Crawford McNamara with assorted blue-collar heroes: NASCAR drivers, football players, country singers. Anywhere else it would have marked McNamara out as a ridiculous poseur. But in Washington, it added to his mysterious aura of authenticity.

'Nope, no one will hear that case for the defence, Jim.'

'Don't tell me you're going to deny us—'

'Because no one is ever going to hear the case for the prosecution.'

'What?' It was Kassian.

'There'll be no trial.'

'What, is this Soviet Russia now? You're just going to throw us—'

'Hold your horses, gentlemen. There'll be no trial because there'll be no accusation. I'm going to keep this little piece of knowledge to myself.'

'I don't follow. Why on—'

'Me and you. We'll be the only three people who will ever know of the evil intent you carried in your heart towards the elected President of this great nation. And Costello, I suppose. But don't you worry about her; I'll take care of her.'

'What is this, Mac? What are you talking about?'

'You guys are so impatient! Jeez. All right. Think for a second. Put yourself in my shoes. I go to the Feds and the press and tell them the truth about you two. What happens? The next three years of this presidency are consumed by the juiciest bone the Washington press corps has had to chew on since you-know-who jizzed all over that girl's dress. "Valkyrie in the White House: the failed plot to kill the President". Can you imagine how they'd cream themselves over that one? The trial, the pre-trial, the hearings on the Hill. They'd set up a special cable channel: all assassination, all the time.

'And you two? Christ! You'd be the Redford and Newman

double handjob to every liberal in America. NPR would get a hard-on just thinking about it.' He lowered his voice, into the stentorian baritone of a broadcast anchor: '"The war heroes who couldn't take it any more." *Vanity Fair* would be rubbing themselves raw. "The inside story of two decorated veterans – and their struggle for the soul of America." No thank you!'

'So—'

'Wait, would you! Like I said, put yourselves in my shoes. Or try this exercise. Think of the question that the President asks himself every hour of every day.'

'What works for *me*?'

'There you go! You see, Kassian, you're smart. Useless. And too weak for this game. But smart. That's exactly the question. So what's the answer? If you're me, I mean.' McNamara was enjoying himself. 'What works for *me*?'

Bruton was clenching his jaw. It looked like he was exerting an enormous amount of strength just to stop himself punching McNamara's lights out.

'Give up? OK, I'll tell you. What works for me is the sudden discovery that Jorge Hernandez was the latest example of – and let's say these three words together – radical Islamic terrorism to strike at the very heart of the United States.'

Kassian leaned forward. 'But that makes no sense. You've seen the Facebook stuff. The crazy letters. He was a Latino veteran, angry about the deportations. They'd deported his mom, for Christ's sake. And he was quoting the gospels every third sentence. He wasn't a Muslim at all.'

'Maybe not, according to what's been disclosed so far. But you know how the news works. This is just the first wave. More new information will come to light overnight.' He grinned. 'And before you say anything else, Bob, reflect on this: you're not the only ones who can invent a convenient backstory for Mr Hernandez. This happens to be my skill set. Remember?' And he pointed at the only framed newspaper article on the wall. It was a mini-profile of McNamara from the *New York Daily News*, published the day he was recruited to the President's campaign. There was a picture of him looking rumpled, carrying a wad of newspapers under one arm, a cardboard cup of coffee in his hand. The headline read: *Behold the King of Fake News*.

'It won't take long. Give it a few hours. We'll soon have "I saw Mad Jorge in Mosque". I'm sure there'll be some anonymous fellow veterans who witnessed Hernandez roll out the prayer mat five times a day, bending his knee to Allah. All those Bible quotes? Why, he included those to mock us and our faith. And didn't I hear something about him demanding his comrades call him by his new name, Muhammed Raheem?'

'But why would anyone believe that?'

McNamara laughed. 'Seriously? After the stunt you just tried to pull off, you're asking *me* that? Oh, you guys. Haven't you realized yet? People will believe *anything*. Just so long as two conditions are met. First, they have to *want* to believe it. Second, it's got to be on Facebook.'

Bruton now spoke, more quietly than before. 'And why would you do this, Mac? What are you planning?'

McNamara smiled widely, extending one arm at full-stretch, pointing at the Defense Secretary, while touching the tip of his own nose – as if Bruton had just guessed correctly in a game of charades. 'Smart guy! Smart, *smart* guy. Such a good question. Can you guess?'

'I don't want to guess.'

'Oh, go on. It'll be fun. Do it for the *lulz*.'

'Mac, this is not a game.'

'The boss is right: you two are a total buzzkill. All right, I'll tell you.' He resumed his seat at the desk, then placed his forearm across it, in the manner of a 1960s news anchor. The voice dropped an octave and he started performing. 'Good evening. Tonight the United States is under attack from radical Islam. The President continues to receive treatment as it becomes clear that the men behind his attempted assassination were the forces of "international jihad". The White House is in discussion with Capitol Hill, as Congress considers a request for emergency powers and the temporary suspension of the Constitution. The Senate Majority Leader told reporters, "This is an unprecedented move. But these are unprecedented times."' McNamara sat back and folded his arms, proud of his work.

'You'd never dare.'

'Don't keep making the same mistake, Bob. Don't keep doing it again and again and *again*. You did it with him and you're doing it with me. Don't underestimate us. It's a bad move, Bob. Very bad move.'

'The Supreme Court would stop you. They'd never let—'

'You sure about that, Jim? This Supreme Court? He's got a six-to-three majority on there now. And those two headbangers he just put on there? They owe him everything. You saw what he wrote, the young one, Justice Whatshisname?' He reached for a piece of paper, then for a pair of reading glasses, in amongst the debris on his desk. 'Here we go. "The Constitution was never intended by the Framers to be an impediment to public safety, but rather its protector. If the Bill of Rights somehow limits the nation's ability to protect itself, then it is not the nation that must give way. The Constitution itself must yield to those whom that document is meant to serve: We the People." You think that guy is gonna object when the President says he needs

331

to shield the country from the jihadist enemy? We couldn't believe we got that wingnut through the Senate. Really. Very pleasant surprise.'

'And what will the President do with this blank cheque you think everyone's going to write for him, impose martial law?'

McNamara smiled and shook his head, as if dealing with a pair of especially stubborn pupils. 'Whatever we do, we're not going to call it *that*, are we? I mean . . . Jeez.'

'I don't care what you call it. What are you going to do?'

'Which do you think sounds better? The America First Act? Or the Saving American Lives Act? I like the simplicity of America First. But the daughter loves the whole "saving lives" thing. Thinks it sounds humanitarian. We're going back and forth. But the big guy listens to her.'

'I said, what are you going to do?'

'That's the whole point, Jim. We don't have to decide now. We don't have to limit ourselves. We get this through, which on the back of the attempted murder of an elected president by a deadly terror organization we will, we can do whatever the fuck we like. We can step up the deportations. We can get on with the ragheads ban. But we wouldn't have to be so prissy about who gets kicked out. We could start including US citizens, which, let's face it, is the whole point. And they don't just have to be Muslim. It can be anyone "whose presence is not conducive to the public good".'

'Jesus.'

'No, he can stay. For now!' He laughed with delight at his own joke. 'But seriously, our scope for executive action will be hugely increased. We can finally move on the press. You know, that whole licence scheme thing? We can expedite that. No official licence, no publish. Simple. And the internet. I mean, that needs some serious housecleaning. And once all that is out the way, we can really start changing things in this country.'

'I've heard enough.' It was Bruton, rising to his feet.

'Oh, not yet. I've not thanked you yet.'

'What?'

'I need to *thank* you. You've done your country a great service. By dreaming up this crazy – and I mean, *crazy* – assassination idea, you've given us this amazing opening. The chance to seize real, serious power. And can you imagine what this is going to do to our poll numbers? Oof. We're indebted. Really.'

Bruton was at the door. 'Send me a bouquet. Goodbye, Mac.'

'I'm afraid that won't be possible. You really do need to sit down.'

Kassian turned in his seat and without saying anything implored his commanding officer not to abandon the battle-field just yet. Bruton remained by the door, but he was no longer gripping the handle. 'I'm listening,' he said.

'All right. Thank you. To sum up. You're not going to be arrested. You're not going to be executed. No one will know of your treason. That's the good news. But I can't just let you go. You need to stay in your posts. If we're going to have martial law – oops, I said it – then we're going to need the military headed by someone the American people trust. And I'm afraid that's you, general. Your poll numbers are so high, they make me dizzy. And genuinely nauseous. But it means we need you.

'Same goes for you, Kassian. Except the bit about the ratings. No one's heard of you, obviously. But folks in Washington trust you. And it'll look like continuity if you guys hang around. "Nothing to see here folks. Same old, same old." Put in new faces – at Defense especially – and everyone starts saying the c-word.' He paused for effect. 'You know,' he whispered. 'Coup.'

'So you're going to trust me to run the Pentagon? Even after everything you've just said?'

'Fuck no! Whatever gave you that impression? Absolutely not, Jim. I wouldn't trust you to pick up my dry cleaning. I'll have Bob for that. Just kidding! No, no, no. No trust necessary. You will sit in the Secretary's chair at Defense, but you won't be running anything. Your deputies – our people – will be in control. You will be there as a figurehead. Same goes for you, Bob. No power at all.

'And I will be watching and listening to you all the time. Twenty-four seven. Cameras, microphones, special agents: constant surveillance, at home, in the office, whether you're texting your mistress or rubbing your haemorrhoids when you take a dump. The instant you so much as nod to each other, I'll have a seven-bell alert. You order pizza, I'll know about it. You sniff your daughter's underwear, I'll know about it.' He broke into song again, an eighties hit which dated him precisely. *They're watching you, watching you, watching you!'*

'You're putting two members of this administration under virtual house arrest.'

'You've got it in one, Kassian. You're sharp, I'll give you that. Not as smart as me, or you wouldn't be in this mess. But smart.' He squared the papers on his desk and exhaled sharply, a man tired at the end of a long, but rewarding day's work. 'All right,' he said finally. 'Get out. Go. Go!'

As Kassian rose to his feet to join Bruton by the door, McNamara remarked – more to himself than to them – that there was only one more person left to deal with. As Robert Kassian left the office of Crawford McNamara, and as he contemplated the abyss into which he and his mentor and friend had fallen, he was sure he could hear the senior adviser to the President humming a familiar song. He was not mistaken. Crawford McNamara was amusing himself to the tune of 'When Irish Eyes Are Smiling'.

44

Getting many congrats on being first President to take a bullet and live. Many say we can do nothing about terror. They are WRONG!!!!

Maggie read it once, then again and then once more. As always, reading one of his tweets was a multi-layered experience. First came the disbelief. Was this for real? Was he really saying this? Surely he couldn't . . .

That sensation was doubled on this occasion. Maggie had to absorb the fact that this meant the President had clearly survived the attempt on his life and had done so sufficiently comfortably that he was now able not only to pose mutely for the cameras, as he had last night, but to take up his phone and resume tweeting to tens of millions of adoring followers. She knew he had lived, but she had wondered if perhaps he would require surgery or if he had suffered at least a few internal injuries, in defiance of the upbeat briefings his team had been giving all evening. Taken at face value this tweet suggested the spin was, for once, true and that he was all but unharmed. Her instinct was to believe it.

Next came the fact-checking reflex. She knew she was not the only one to suffer from it. It had become a habit – a bad one, she had recently concluded – among many of those who opposed the President during the campaign, and the habit had endured. The President would say or tweet something outrageous and immediately all the hyper-educated media savants would be online, pointing out his error or outright lie. In this case, the mistake – or lie – was so obvious, it was almost comically ignorant. A previous president had of course survived an assassination attempt, taking a bullet, just a few decades ago. The episode was famous and within the current incumbent's adult lifetime, as several hundred on Twitter could not resist pointing out.

Maggie felt the same urge, but it was lunacy. Because it distracted you from whatever new horror he was actually proposing. He could tweet, 'Listen up, Latinos. Your all going to be deported on trains to labour camps in the Alaskan wilderness. Round-ups begin at 6am' – and the liberal chorus of reply would be instant: 'It's *you're*'.

So Maggie hurried herself past that instinct and forced herself instead to examine the content, to pay attention to what this man was actually saying and to take it seriously.

Many say we can do nothing about terror. They are WRONG!!!!

Terror. That was the key word. They were going to spin this as a terrorist attack. Not as the deranged act of a single, damaged man but as the work of a sinister enemy. Oh and here was a follow-up, tweeted a minute later.

An attack on the President is an attack on the United States! THIS WILL NOT STAND!!

And then another:

We will be holding a major news conference to discuss the ACTION we will take against America's enemies, at home and abroad!

Now she saw it, and it was as if the sky had instantly darkened. McNamara always said it: never let a good crisis go to waste. And he wasn't going to waste this one. Instead, he was going to jujitsu it, turning this attack to his advantage. God only knew what he had in mind. Would he try to pretend that Hernandez was secretly working for the North Koreans? The very idea was absurd, laughable and lacking all evidence – which meant, yes, he might very well try that.

Or would the President use it to ramp up his war on migrants? He and McNamara would like nothing more than some bogus security pretext to accelerate the deportations. Naturally, it would make no sense: Hernandez was not an illegal immigrant but a US citizen, born in the US. But that wouldn't stop them. They would twist the logic to show that the attempt on the President's life demonstrated exactly why they had to widen the net to include native-born Americans like Hernandez. She could imagine the words McNamara would draft for his boss. *Somehow foreign enemies have exploited our generosity – and our welcome – by breeding a new generation of terrorists right here, in our neighbourhoods, in our towns and in our communities. This new generation may look and sound like Americans on the outside, but they carry evil intent in their hearts . . .*

Or Muslims. The ban could always be contracted or expanded in scope. She remembered the text exchange between McNamara and Richard. *I almost want to do the whole yellow star thing – yellow crescents, anyone? – just to see them pee their pants. Didn't you say the boss was up for it?*

The thought made her heart sink. How many Muslims were there in America? A little over three million? No more than one per cent of the population, give or take. Yet McNamara had managed to terrify his party's base into believing that Muslims posed an existential threat to the country, every last one of them concealing a suicide vest beneath their clothes, if not an ancient scimitar, ready to be pulled out at any moment to slice the head off an unsuspecting infidel.

Maggie was not naïve: she knew that jihadist terror was real. She had been at the last president's side as he dealt with it. But that threat had consisted of a few thousand hardcore fanatics at the very most, not an entire community of millions. To turn on all of them, to make every Muslim child, every Muslim grandmother, an enemy – this was madness. And dangerous madness. Surely the world had seen where that kind of hate led. Surely Americans didn't need to learn that lesson all over again?

Now she wondered: did the President even believe all this anti-Muslim hate himself? Did McNamara? Or was it just convenient for them to make Muslims a whipping boy whose beating could serve as a handy distraction while the White House got on with stealing people's most basic freedoms? It could be conviction or it could be cynicism. What was unnerving was that she couldn't tell which was worse.

She thought again of the message she had seen on that glowing screen in the dead of night: *yellow crescents, anyone?*

To think those words had been written by her own lover of the last few months. It felt as if everything around her, everything she touched, was mysterious and confusing and Richard was no different. She had called him in that moment of desperation, just minutes before the President was shot, and the truth was, she had been glad to hear his voice. But that exchange of messages between him and McNamara. Beside the insult to her, what on earth did it say about him? How deep was he in with these people?

She looked around the apartment which they had never formally shared but which had been their . . . safe harbour. Or at least that was how it had felt. She'd been wrong, of course, but at the time it seemed this was their place of retreat from the lunacies of the new administration. After another insane day at the office, they'd flee to these rooms to vent, to trade atrocities (as they called them), to laugh at the maniacs they now worked for. And to console each other through touch, through smell, through their skin and their fingertips and their tongues. Here they came to hold each other and to make urgent, necessary love.

Though love was the wrong word. For him, even lust might be stretching it. He might not have felt even that. It might only have ever been a task for him, an instruction from Crawford McNamara that had to be followed. His prime purpose had doubtless been the acquisition of information – and Maggie had provided it. She had told him about Kassian and Bruton's late-night conversation with Frankel and he had surely passed on that vital nugget to his handler, his pimp: McNamara.

She felt angry at both of them, of course. But it was nothing next to the fury she directed at herself. She was not a child any more. How could she have been so pitifully naïve? She who, in her professional life, was meant to be a good judge of character, a shrewd reader of situations. She thought back to the moments she and Richard had shared together – the long January walk down the Mall in the snow, the visit to Mount Vernon at the first breath of spring, the long Saturday night that had turned into Sunday morning, both of them too full of desire to sleep.

Or maybe he had been faking the whole thing, even the sex. Maybe it had only ever been an acting job for him: every touch, every endearment no more than a stage direction. Those moments when his eyes had been on fire with what she thought was appetite for her, perhaps he had merely been excited at some new confidence she had accidentally let slip. Maybe his biggest thrill of the night came when she looked the other way and he could finally pull out his phone and report back to McNamara.

And to think of the disdain he must have felt when she confessed her fears about this presidency. She thought she was sharing her deepest anxiety with a kindred spirit; but he saw her as nothing more than a whining 'libtard', a bleeding-heart lover of blacks and Jews and Muslims and all the people he hated. She shuddered again.

Now, she looked at her own phone. The voice she wanted to hear belonged to Stuart Goldstein, an adult who would calm her nerves and force her to weigh the evidence and think things through. She thought about it, about making contact, and kept the phone in her hand, staring at the screen for a few seconds, barely noticing that, after a broken, restless night, her eyelids were sinking lower and that she was drifting into an exhausted, shell-shocked sleep.

Maggie woke with a start some twenty minutes later. It took her a while to understand that the buzzing noise that had inserted itself into her dream was, in fact, coming from downstairs. She got herself up and to the intercom, but there was silence. No one there.

A second later, three firm knocks on the door. She looked through the spyhole: Richard. Maybe it was the sleepiness, but for a moment she genuinely wondered if he or

McNamara or both of them had somehow hacked into her head, if it was her earlier thought of Richard that had summoned him here. She opened the door.

'Well, it's all kicking off at Sixteen Hundred Pennsylvania Avenue,' he said, speaking as he walked in. The words were the same he might have used on any visit over the last few months. But the voice was different. As cold and flat as steel.

'I can imagine,' Maggie said, holding back.

'No, Maggie. I'm not sure you can imagine. I'm not sure you have the faintest idea.'

'Of what?'

'Of what you've unleashed.'

'Me?'

'Yes, you. You, my love.'

Richard threw off his jacket – linen, cobalt blue, one that would have been very fashionable five years earlier and therefore counted as achingly on-trend in Washington – and took his regular place on the sofa. He rolled up the sleeves of his white, cotton shirt. The sight of his forearms sent a familiar erotic pulse through Maggie's nervous system, dispatched before her conscious brain had a chance to send it back. She wondered if he'd run here.

Still standing, still near the front door, she watched him and then said quietly, 'What's happened, Richard?'

'Well – with thanks to you,' a phrase he punctuated with a nod of his head, 'Mac's made his move on Kassian and Bruton. You should have heard him describe it. He was magnificent. Turned them over like a pair of Texas steaks.'

Christ, Maggie thought. Now he was even talking like McNamara. 'Turned them over? For what?'

'For plotting to kill the President, of course.'

'But, I don't—'

342

'We don't even need to think about them any more. Put a fork in them: they're done.'

'What are you talking about?'

'Treason. High crimes and misdemeanours. Attempted assassination. One of them. All of them.' He was grinning. 'I don't know. I'm not a lawyer.'

'But this makes no sense. What possible evidence is there against them?'

'You.' Richard smiled. 'You, Maggie. You're the evidence.'

'What's that supposed to mean?'

'You were looking into those two, investigating them, convinced that they were planning to kill the President. And guess what? Someone tried to kill the President. QED.'

'That's not proof! That's—'

'What? A coincidence? Come on, Maggie. You called me, and God knows who else, saying "It's about to happen! Any minute now!" And you were *right*, Maggie. It did happen, right on cue.'

'But that doesn't mean—'

'Enjoy it, Maggie. For once in your life, just enjoy it. In this town, that's the greatest success anybody can ever have. "Correctly forecasted the future." People kill to have that on their résumé.'

'But I didn't say it was Kassian and Bruton who were behind it.'

'If I were you, I'd go in and see McNamara and demand a promotion. You could go back on the NSC. Do foreign policy, maybe the Middle—'

'I *didn't* say it was Kassian and Bruton. I never mentioned them.'

'Who cares? You said an assassination attempt was imminent. That's what—'

'No, Richard. You said, specifically, that I was the evidence

343

against Kassian and Bruton. But I never mentioned them to anybody.'

A look of calculation, like a thousand tiny wheels turning, passed across his face. 'Well, you told me that's who you were looking at. Right here, in this apartment.'

'No, I told you I was looking at them in connection with *Jeffrey Frankel*. Because of the meeting they'd had with him the night before his death.'

She stared at Richard. She heard his lips make a tiny clicking sound; his mouth was drying. 'So that must have been it,' he said. 'You were suspicious of them and then you were talking about an assassination, so McNamara must have put two and two together.'

'No, Richard.' Her voice was rising, getting louder as she began to see the outline of what had happened. 'No, no, no, no. That doesn't add up. Not at all. I mentioned the Frankel thing to you, but not to McNamara. And the first time I so much as breathed a word about assassination to a living soul was when I made those phone calls – including to you – *minutes* before the President was shot. And yet, by some kind of fucking miracle, everyone was prepared for it. He was wearing a bulletproof vest, for Christ's sake. They *knew* it was coming.'

'Now you're getting hysterical. It's not—'

She stepped forward, so that she was close enough to point a finger in his face. 'Don't you *dare* call me hysterical, you misogynist bastard.' Her Irish accent was gaining strength. 'I am thinking perfectly clearly, thank you very much. And here's what I'm thinking right now. That the only way they could possibly have known of my suspicions regarding Bob Kassian and Jim Bruton would be if *you* had told them. You're the only one I told.'

'Maggie, please. Listen, the whole—'

'No, *you* listen. You didn't just give them that little morsel, did you? No, no, that wouldn't have been enough. Because someone had to have been listening to my phone calls, or hacking my messages or something for McNamara to know what I was onto. That's the only way they could have—'

'I don't know what you mean.'

'You know exactly what I mean, you two-faced fucking snake.'

'Maggie! What the hell is—'

'I think you hacked into my computer or my phone or something – and handed over every last piece of information to your pathetic little locker-room buddy, Crawford McNamara.' A thought struck her. 'Jesus, that's how they knew about Liz's boiler. You told them, didn't you? You told them. They were *children*, you evil bastard. They could have been killed.'

'I had nothing to do with that.'

'Don't lie to me. They hacked into my sister's heating system and nearly—'

'Hacked? Did you say, hacked? First, I didn't even have to hack you, Maggie. You left it all on a fucking *notepad*. You wrote it down in black and white: Kassian, Bruton, assassination, the whole deal.'

Now she remembered it. Those jottings in the middle of the night, left by her bedside. She'd been so shaken by what followed, she'd forgotten they were ever there.

Richard was not letting up. 'And *you* talking to *me* about hacking phones? That's rich. I mean you're the world authority on hacking, aren't you, Maggie?'

Maggie hesitated. Now Richard was facing her, pushing his chest forward, intruding into her space.

'Eh? I can't hear you, Mags. Cat got that silver Irish tongue of yours? Or you lost for words because you don't want to admit that, while I slept in your bed, you broke into my phone? Had a good rummage in my Notes file, didn't you? So that when I checked it the next morning, that document was suddenly top of the pile. "Last opened: 5.33am". Which was when I was sound asleep. Bit fucking obvious, Maggie.'

'Don't even think about claiming the moral high ground, Richard Parris. The things you said to that man. About me. About *us*.'

'Oh, save me the convent school bullshit, Maggie. You've been around this place long enough to know how it works. And if you don't, you damn well should by now.'

'Go on, Richard. Tell me how it works. Enlighten me.'

'You don't want me to do that, Maggie.'

'No, Richard. I really do.' She folded her arms and stood across from him, waiting.

'All right, Maggie.' He took a step back. 'The only thing people want around here is power. That's right. Not love. Not friendship. Not "making the world a better place". Power. That's what I want, that's what Mac wants and that – though you're never big enough to admit it – is what *you* want.'

'Oh, don't—'

'Your sister's right, Maggie. You're always standing there on your pedestal, with your halo, your résumé packed with good works in Africa and the fucking Middle East, but look at you. You're still here. In Washington, DC. Clinging onto your precious job in the White House because even the smell of it gets you hot: power. You can't let go of it.'

'Thank you, Dr Freud. I really—'

'And the way you get power is the same as everyone else. *Information*. That's the currency. So sure, I took a picture of your notepad while you were in the shower, just like I kept an eye on your texts and emails when I could. I was

346

keeping McNamara in the loop. I've been doing it since we started sleeping together. But, newsflash: you did exactly the fucking same. You're no better than me. You're no better than any of us.'

Maggie spoke quietly. 'Actually, Richard, I think there's a very big difference. I was investigating the killing of an innocent man. Dr Jeffrey Frankel was killed because he got in someone's way.'

'The someone being Bob Kassian and Jim Bruton.'

'Maybe. When you read my messages and emails, that's all you saw. Me doing my job. But what I saw you say to McNamara: I mean, Jesus, Richard. The way you talked about women. About Muslims. I couldn't believe—'

'Welcome to the twenty-first century, Maggie. You need to keep up.'

'You say that because he talks like that. The President. But he's the only one who can get away with it. The big charismatic TV star. God knows how it's happened, but it has: different rules apply to him. But McNamara? You? If that stuff ever got out, can you imagine? McNamara would be finished. He'd be too toxic, even for this place. And as for a little Nazi lowlife like you, you'd be done. Like a Texas steak.'

Richard's handsome features curled into an expression she hadn't seen before, a snarl of pure loathing. 'You bitch,' he said. 'You wouldn't dare.'

'Are you sure about that?'

'Yes. I am.' He took a half pace back and pulled himself up to his full height. 'Because I know, Maggie my love, that we will always protect each other.'

'What?'

'Don't pretend you don't know.' Richard sighed. 'Do you want me to spell it out to you? *Maggie's dirty little secret.*'

347

She felt herself pale.

'Oh, don't look so alarmed, darling. Your secret's safe with me.'

'Richard.'

'I mean it. You will never tell anyone what you saw on my phone the other night because you know that, if you did, I would only have to pick up the phone to . . . who should it be? The *Times*? The *Post*? Who would hate you most? NPR? MSNBC? Maybe the *Guardian*. Or Mother Jones. They'd all run it very big. "Revealed: The Woman who—"'

'You'd have no proof.'

'But I know you, Maggie. You wouldn't deny it. Because it's the truth. And St Margaret of Costello is the last person left in Washington who still believes in telling the truth.' He raised his fingers in the three-fingered salute of the devoted girl Scout. 'Bless.'

'It's so long ago,' Maggie said quietly.

'Not long enough.'

'I can't believe I told you. I'm such a fool.'

'Oh, but I'm so glad you did, Maggie. My secret is safe with you, because if it's not, then your secret is no longer safe with me.'

45

Two years earlier

She got up from her desk and did a wide stretch. Maggie had been staring at the screen too long. Her eyes creaked when she rubbed them.

She glanced down at her phone. An invitation to dinner with a group of girlfriends sent nearly two hours ago. She had stalled them, promising to join them soon, then suggesting they order without her, then offering to skip the starter and finally vowing to make it in time for dessert. The replies had dried up around then. It was too late now.

It's not even as if this work was especially interesting. But it was important. The President himself had asked her to take it on. He had been told that a mid-ranking official in his administration faced possible corruption charges. The suspicion was that he had been receiving direct, cash bribes from large foreign companies keen to gain preferential trading access to the US. The case was already under investigation by the relevant department but the President worried that the inquiry might not be fair, that the official might be being set up to take the fall for a wider corruption problem.

He wanted Maggie to be his 'eyes and ears', to look over the shoulder of the investigators and make sure they were doing a proper job.

Which had led to her being in the White House on a Saturday night, going over pages and pages of phone records, checking who the official had called and when. So many numbers, they had begun to swim before her eyes.

It was while she was stretching, looking down at the sheets in front of her, with row after row highlighted in a rainbow of shades, that she spotted something she had not seen until that moment. One number that recurred but which had not, it seemed, been identified by the investigators.

She checked it, then cross-checked it and saw that it appeared several times, at odd hours of the day and night, apparently from several countries around the world. She turned to her screen and, using the database established by the inquiry, typed in the phone number, hoping to put a name to it.

Not identified.

It was a US number and, these records confirmed, no attempt had been made to disguise it. According to the database, it was not even a secure or encrypted line. It was a regular US, domestic cellphone.

She looked at the clock. Nine twenty pm. Saturday night. There really was no one around who she could ask. And yet she needed to get this report to the President by Monday morning, at the same time or even before the official inquiry reported.

Maggie dialled what the older hands still called Signal, the department that handled all White House communications traffic.

'Hi there. Can you help me with a number?'

'Who are you looking for, ma'am?'

350

'That's just it. I have the number but I don't have the person. Can you work backwards from that?'

'Is this a White House number, ma'am?'

'I'm not sure. It might be. Can you help?'

Perhaps ninety seconds passed, as Maggie read over the number and was placed on hold. Eventually the operator came back on and said, 'Please hold for the duty commander.' A reminder that even the switchboard in this building was run by the military.

More clicks and then a male voice. 'Can I ask what this is in connection with?'

Maggie explained who she was, on what authority she was making her inquiry and added that her system showed this to be a non-classified, regular phone that should, therefore, be subject to none of the usual restrictions.

The commander then said that, according to his information, the number Maggie had supplied matched the private cellphone of – and his voice dipped as he said the name.

Maggie might have gasped, but if she did, she moved swiftly to disguise it. She thanked the commander and put the phone down. She sat back in her chair and let the implications sink in. She had discovered that the Secretary of State had been using an unsecured, private phone line routinely and regularly, from all points of the globe, even to conduct what looked like the official business of the United States government. Any intelligence agency anywhere, including those of hostile powers, would be guilty of professional malpractice if they had *not* tapped that line.

Now she had to decide what to do with this information, whether she was duty bound to report it to the relevant authorities. Ordinarily, that question would be straightforward. Of course she should.

But there was a complicating factor. The Secretary of State, who stood to be hugely undermined by this discovery, was not just a senior figure in the current administration. The Secretary was widely – universally – expected to run for, and very probably win, the Presidency of the United States,

If Maggie kept this finding quiet, a candidate she respected and admired would have a smoother path to the White House. But it would also mean that Maggie would, by her inaction, be saying that the law was only to be applied when it was convenient. Maggie would be declaring that no one was above the law – unless you happened to be a politician Maggie liked.

It was tempting. She could put these phone records to one side, declare her investigation complete and no one would be any the wiser. The Secretary of State would be on course to the White House, an outcome Maggie very much wanted.

But she knew it wouldn't be right. If she hushed this up, it would make her no better than the hordes of partisan hacks and hustlers who filled this town. It was quaint, she rarely said it out loud – except when she was with the President she served – but she believed in something better than that: in old-fashioned things like the rule of law and doing what was right, even when it was inconvenient.

No, she would have to pass what she had found on the Secretary of State to the relevant officials. What they did with it would be up to them. She had enough faith in the American people to believe that, even if they learned of this mistake by a soon-to-be candidate, they would not let it cloud their judgement. They would still, surely, pick the most qualified person to be their next President. As Maggie collected up her papers after a long night, she drew great comfort in that thought.

46

He had hit her in her most vulnerable spot. It was her fault: she had revealed it to him, a matter of weeks after they had become lovers.

They were in bed, having the perennial conversation, she in earnest, he – she now understood – with complete fraudulence. What on earth were they doing here, working as servants of this appalling monster of a President?

She had offered her reasons only partially at first. A job in the White House was a privilege; if you had the chance to do even a little bit of good, you were obliged to take it; maybe she could, in her own small way, mitigate the impact of the new regime – all that bullshit. But eventually, and under Richard's sustained questioning, the two of them facing each other, warm under the covers on a bitterly cold February morning, she had begun to tell him.

Maggie first explained that she felt a terrible responsibility, which meant she felt obliged to serve. 'You mean duty?' he had asked. No, she explained. She felt a sense of responsibility in the sense of being responsible for what had happened.

'Is this a Catholic guilt thing?' he said.

'No,' she said. 'It's an actual guilt thing. I did something terrible.'

He had furrowed his brow into a question mark, encouraging her to say more.

'You know the whole "unsecured line" scandal?'

'You mean the issue which destroyed the candidacy of our President's main opponent—'

'Yes, thank you very much. That was me.'

'What do you mean, it was you?'

'I discovered it. I was the one who saw that the Secretary of State had been using a private phone line. Which turned into an "unauthorized" phone line, a "secret" phone line, a "compromised" phone line. That was me. I discovered it – and I reported it.'

'You went to the FBI?'

'Department of Justice, actually. But yes.'

'Jesus.'

'I know.'

'That was you. Christ, Maggie, you changed the course of history.'

'Thanks a lot.'

'I mean, there's no way he'd be President now if it wasn't for—'

'Yes, thank you, I'm quite aware of all that.'

He smiled and said, 'I'm sorry, Maggie. I take it back. Seriously, that whole campaign was so badly flawed. Even without the phone line saga, there's a good chance it just wasn't going to happen. And it was a change election. You can't beat yourself up over—'

'Are you kidding? Beating myself up is the least I can do.

Can you imagine what this feels like? This complete sociopath is in the Oval Office, this nightmare for the entire world is unfolding, and all because I had to open my big mouth.'

'Maggie, really—'

'I mean it, Richard. This is on my conscience every hour of every day. I can't stop thinking about it. Every time he insults someone, every time he trashes something good or makes one of his wild threats – all the time – I'm thinking, "This is my fault. We wouldn't be here if I hadn't destroyed the one person who could have beaten him."'

'I'm not so sure.'

'Every day during the campaign, I was checking every poll, gobbling up every tiny point of data I could, just to reassure myself. "Don't worry. He won't win. And then it will all be over. What you did won't have mattered. You can get this millstone off your neck."'

'Oh, Maggie.'

'And then all those scandals and revelations came and I thought, "Thank God. There's no way he can win now." But somehow he kept in there, soldiering on. And these voters would be interviewed on TV and they'd say, "Yeah, sure, he's done some bad stuff. But, you know, what about that secret phone line?" And I wanted to shout at the top of my voice, "Who gives a fuck about one fucking phone line?" But I couldn't say a word. Because it was my fault.'

'And then he won.'

'And then he won.' Maggie let out a long sigh. 'My first instinct was to run away. I wanted to go back home, to Ireland. Start again. Be a teacher or something. Do something useful.'

'But?'

'But I talked about it with the boss and he was adamant. "You owe this to the country, Maggie. If you leave, there's one less good person in the White House. And we need all the good people we can get."'

'Sounds like him. And McNamara kept you on?'

'To my amazement, yes. Or at least he didn't block me. Kassian was the main backer though.'

'"Professionals".'

'Exactly. He wanted as many as he could get past McNamara. But, seriously, God knows what I'm doing it for. The old boss said, "Some day – I don't know when, don't know how – there'll be a way for you to make a difference." Well, I can't see that day ever coming, I really can't.'

That had been more than three months ago. She had stuck to it, clinging to those words of the former president. In the last few days, she had seen a way to make amends: if she could halt an assassination and the mayhem that would follow, perhaps then she would have made her contribution. But even in the best-case scenario, it would have been a strange kind of atonement: she'd have saved the life of a President she despised and preserved a presidency she believed was truly malevolent.

But this was not the best case. The President had survived and now McNamara and his henchmen had pulled off a putsch in which – according to Richard and backed up by the early rumblings on Twitter – McNamara had crushed the last remnant of internal resistance, sweeping aside Bob Kassian and Jim Bruton. Now he and his circle would be able to do their worst. And if the latest news was any guide, they were moving swiftly.

She glanced down at a news alert on her phone.

The President has accepted the resignation of the head of the Federal Communications Commission, CNN has learned. White House sources tell CNN the new FCC head is likely to be a close presidential ally, with speculation focusing on the President's eldest daughter. According to a senior administration official, 'Her job will be implementing a new licensing system for the broadcasters: only those networks she deems "fair and balanced" will have their license to broadcast renewed.' The official adds that plans are well-advanced and that from his bed at the George Washington University Hospital the President has signed an executive order instructing that this be done "not in months or weeks, but days – for the sake of public safety".'

The country was on the verge of a coup that would trample all over the Constitution and the only two men who might have stopped it were now powerless. And she had let it happen. She had given the President's henchmen what they needed to make a move they'd never have risked otherwise. She had handed them the shock event of a genuine assassination attempt, but with enough advance warning that they could guarantee its failure. She had let herself be betrayed by a lover and, in the process, she had betrayed the country she had come to love. Her despair was total.

It was raining heavily outside; the apartment was dark, but she couldn't find the strength to turn on the lights. She sat there in the gloom and prepared to go deep, to plunge into the abyss, to aim for the bottom of the pit, a place whose contours and rough edges would at least have the comfort of familiarity. She deserved no better.

But a voice nagged at her. She knew she could not resist it. In moments like this, the one person who might speak sense, who might somehow help her make amends, was her old mentor Stuart Goldstein.

'Whaddya got, Costello?'

'I'm not in the mood, Stuart.'

'Bupkis. That's what you got. Bupkis.'

'Please.'

'A big fat nothing.'

'Stuart, seriously. I know that.'

'So Mr Crawford McNamara knew what you knew: that somebody was about to whack our so-called President.'

'Because Richard told him.'

'Yes. Silly girl. I told you that one was trouble. Not for you. Too pretty.'

'Too pretty?'

'You can't trust a man who dresses better than you do. We need to find you a big, balding schlub.'

'Like you, you mean.'

'You could do worse, Costello, believe me.'

Maggie found herself laughing, and it felt good. It'd been a long time. 'Stuart, can we go back to what—'

'Sure, sure. Don't distract me with the personal stuff. Not my strongest suit, as Mrs Goldstein will testify.'

'You're not helping, Stuart. I need something.'

'All right. We're looking for a way to make this right. So: what do you know about Eisenhower?'

'Stuart, please. Now is not the time.'

'Now is *exactly* the time.'

'Not for a history lesson. I've got to—'

'Do you want my help or not?'

'Yes.'

'All right. Eisenhower. Three things. Go.'

'Jesus, Stuart. I don't know: Supreme Allied Commander during World War Two. Called Ike. Won two terms.'

'What else?'

'Warned of the power of the "military-industrial complex".'

'What else? Something he said.'

'I think I'm all out of Eisenhower trivia, Stuart. Can we move on to the Film and TV round?'

'"Whenever I run into a problem I can't solve, I always make it bigger." That's what he said. "I can never solve it by trying to make it smaller, but if I make it big enough, I can begin to see the outlines of a solution." That was Eisenhower.'

'And that helps me how exactly?'

'Stand back, Maggie. See the big picture.'

'I *am* seeing the big picture, Stu. A President using a national emergency to impose martial fucking law, shutting down the press and rounding up minorities seems pretty fucking big picture to me.'

'What else is going on here? While you've been so obsessed with Kassian, Bruton and Friedman—'

'Frankel.'

'Whatever, what else has been happening?'

'The nuclear thing? The President nearly losing his mind and blowing up the planet?'

'OK. That's more like it.'

'But Kassian and Bruton knew all about that. They were so worried about it, they thought their only option was to kill the President. They didn't think they had any other options.'

'OK. So let's think of something else. Something else that's been going on, kind of offstage. To the margins. Remember what I always say?'

'"Check your peripheral vision."'

'Exactly. Still my star pupil, Costello. So look off to the sides. Think about what you've only half-heard or what you've fully heard but only half-remembered.'

'That's hard, Stuart.'

'I know it is. That's why so few people do it. But there's

something there, Maggie, I'm sure of it. With bona fide assholes like McNamara and his boss, there always is.'

'Thanks, Stuart.'

'Don't thank me. Get digging.'

Maggie stared into the gloom of her apartment for a moment or two longer and then reached for a light switch. It was time to begin looking – and she knew exactly where to start.

47

Washington, DC, Saturday, 10.23am

Three nights ago, when she had opened up Richard's phone, she had been shaken, distressed and disgusted – but she had not completely lost her mind. She had maintained just enough equilibrium to do a quick copy and paste of her then-boyfriend's Signal exchange with Crawford McNamara, dump the text into an email to herself – from Richard's account – before deleting the message from his Sent folder.

She had sent it to an email account so private, she was the only person who knew of its existence, let alone its address. When setting it up, she followed the advice of Eleanor's son, who'd just been hired into the White House IT department, during a particularly fraught back-channel negotiation she had conducted for the last president. As he had suggested, she made up a pseudonym for the address and installed what he called 'three-factor authentication', meaning she had placed three different security hurdles at the entrance to the inbox. She was also careful to access it only from a computer or IP address that was not her own. If she couldn't make it to an internet café, then she was to get online using a VPN that would hide her IP address. Once on, she would use the super-encrypted browser favoured by security purists as well as assorted criminals, terrorists and consumers of forbidden pornography. To a truly determined hacker, it was probably not impregnable. But since no one knew the email account was hers or would have any idea of its importance, she felt it was as secure a hiding place as she could find.

She logged in now and there it was in full, that sickening exchange between McNamara and the man who had shared her bed through most of this bitter winter: the references to the President's daughter – her 'opening' and its 'dripping' wetness – and to Maggie's own private parts and personal hygiene.

Maggie felt the weight fall on her heart again but, almost physically, tried to push it out of the way. She needed to heed Stuart's advice, not to look at the obvious but to look left and right, to check her peripheral vision.

There was the overt talk of white supremacism. It was unconscionable, of course. It could terminate the careers of both Richard and McNamara. Reading it again now, she could see that the latter was not nearly as exposed as the former: the very worst things had been said by Richard. Besides, McNamara would simply insist that the entire exchange had been faked. Without video or audio, there was always that risk, especially with the team around this President. They thought nothing of cheerfully, brazenly, denying the obvious truth even when it was staring them in the face. It drove the press corps mad, but the lead came from the top. The President would happily say that black was white and night was day, if it suited him. And there was a chunk of the country that was so devoted, they would cheer him when he said it.

So the trick was to look in the margins. She attempted that now, scrolling through the pages of messages, trying to ignore the locker-room references to 'the princess' and to herself, as well as the jaw-dropping racism. The Stuart approach demanded she find something else. 'Think like a reporter' was one of his favourite lines. 'No good proving that what everyone already knows to be true is really, really true. Find something new.'

The racism, even the hideous registry for Muslims, was in the first category. So what was in the second? At first she could see nothing, certainly nothing of substance. She wondered who the 'Rosemary' that McNamara referred to might be: it was not a name she recognized. Then again, that was true of most White House staff these days. She would have to read the document again, more slowly this time.

Even now she could only see two lines that might pass Stuart's peripheral vision test, both of which seemed prosaic and wholly unpromising. First, was that odd reference to Delhi.

Our friends will need instructions on the next package. Shipment in Delhi, dispatch details as discussed.

It was no more intelligible to her now than it had been in the middle of the night. What could it refer to? And who were 'our friends'?

The second was in a similar vein. The same word – 'package' – appeared in this equally opaque message from Richard:

Mid-Atlantic package has been dispatched. Presume we have delivery address for the next one. Let me know and I'll prepare.

Clearly he wasn't bothering the President's most senior counsellor with the mundane business of the mailroom. 'Package' was obviously code for something else. Could it be drugs? Or – yes, surely this was it – bribes? Was that what Maggie had uncovered in the dead of night? Was part of Richard's role at Commerce the dispatch of envelopes stuffed with cash to various parties around the world? Given the President's global business interests, it was plausible. That would represent a serious abuse of power, given that Richard – and McNamara for that matter – were both employees of the federal government. They were paid by the US taxpayer, yet here they were, apparently doing the business – the corrupt business – of a private corporation. (Already Maggie could hear the talking heads on cable TV, swearing that none of this was a problem. *Helping an important American business is exactly what the White House should be doing. I'm sure they'd do the same for any good American business. In fact, I bet they didn't even realize this company was owned by the President. And as for those 'enhanced cash payments', that's just the way of the world. Business is not for boy Scouts and if that shocks you, you need to grow up a little. All I can say is, how lucky is America to have someone at the helm who understands that. His predecessor didn't lift a finger for American jobs . . .*)

Now she looked more closely at messages she'd skimmed past when she'd first seen them. There was a reference to a 'complicated drop' in Africa. Richard had written: *Delivery location remote, inaccessible. Close to the land of the Bushmen! Large team of postmen and equipment required. Some ours, some picked up in Nam.*

Maggie read the sentence over at least three times, but her bafflement only increased. Her chief confusion was the location. This bribe was to be paid in Africa – again plausible given the reach of the President's commercial activities (which, despite a few feeble legal ploys to conceal the fact, were active and ongoing). But why then did Richard speak of hiring local people in Vietnam, using the cringe-worthy, movie-style abbreviation? Who did he think he was? 'Nam' indeed . . .

It was only when she got up to stretch her legs and splash some cold water on her face that it came to her. *Nam.*

Of course. 'Nam' wasn't Vietnam. It was Namibia.

The word alone set off a small chime in Maggie's head. The longer it rang, the louder it became. She reached for the keyboard and could sense her hands trembling as she typed in those first few letters.

48

Washington, DC, Saturday, 10.55am

She put 'Namibia' into the search engine. Wikipedia, Tourism Board, Lonely Planet. Then the news stories. Top of the list was a Reuters report posted nine hours earlier which, given what had been happening in Washington, had surely received no attention anywhere. That in turn linked to a report from three or four days earlier. She read the older one first:

From our National Security Correspondent
Windhoek, Namibia

Four US citizens are being held in custody in this southern African city, following a shootout in the bush which left one American tourist wounded and a local ranger dead.

Ron Cain, CEO of a leading broadcast technology firm based in Dallas, was shot in the shoulder during the firefight, as he stalked a black rhino under a permit scheme operated by the Namibian government. Cain, 44, bid $350,000 for the controversial license at a charity auction earlier this year.

US consular authorities said Cain's party had spotted the rhino moments earlier, and were about to open fire, when they came under attack from a group of armed men. Initial reports suggested the gunmen were local poachers, anxious to bag the rhino – and its lucrative horn – for themselves. The Namibian authorities, however, have now established that all four men were Americans. None has yet been named.

Cain's guides, including a professional hunter recently discharged from the South African military, returned fire. One of the local rangers was shot dead, but the hunting party succeeded in subduing their assailants, two of whom sustained serious injuries. One is said to be in 'critical condition'.

Mystery surrounds both the identity and motives of the US gunmen, though more details are expected at a court hearing later this week. Both poachers and anti-poaching units in southern Africa have been known to employ veterans of the US military as advisers and security consultants.

The black rhino earmarked for death by Cain's license is thought to have escaped unharmed.

It didn't look like much. Now Maggie read the latest story.

Windhoek, Namibia – One of the four US citizens held in custody following a fatal jungle shootout died from his wounds in hospital earlier today. Both Namibian and US consular sources refused to name the man, saying that they first wished to notify the next of kin.

The Americans were detained after a clash in Omaheke province, formerly known as northern Hereroland, a remote area in the north of the country, left an American tourist injured and a local ranger dead. The tourist was taking part in a licensed hunt for a rare black rhino, amid speculation that the gunmen belonged to a well-organized group of poachers. US officials in Windhoek have refused to confirm or deny that the gunmen were veterans of the US military.

The injured American, named as Ron Cain, is now back in the US.

Maggie's mind began to turn over. She opened up another tab on the browser and, on no more than an instinct, typed in 'Hereroland, Namibia'. Slim pickings at first and Google Maps drew a blank, but eventually she came across an image of a 1960s surveyors' map, dividing up the country into regions. She could see Damaraland, Tswanaland and there, in the east, Hereroland. Now she peered closer and when she saw it, she felt a surge of adrenalin enter her veins as surely as if it had been injected. The neighbouring area, bordering Hereroland to the north, was marked on the map by a single word: *Bushmanland*.

Now she looked back at Richard's message to McNamara. *Delivery location remote, inaccessible. Close to the land of the Bushmen! Large team of postmen and equipment required . . .*

The land of the Bushmen. *Bushmanland.* It could not be a coincidence.

She reached for her phone, then thought better of it. They were bound to be monitoring her calls. Come to think of it, there was a good chance they were eavesdropping on the man she was about to call too.

Maggie went into her bedroom, and headed straight to the tall, wooden cupboard she'd picked up at an antiques market soon after she first moved here. She didn't open the doors, but gathered her strength to shift it a couple of inches away from the wall. Then she reached behind the cupboard and felt along the back. A few seconds of groping and there, she'd got it. Closing her eyes to aid her concentration, she grasped the object and gave it a strong tug. It was taped in place, but it came away without too much resistance.

It was a burner, a back-up, unregistered phone she'd used to communicate with her opposite number at State during those peace talks (though in those days it was Russian intelligence, rather than her own government, who she feared might be listening in).

She turned it on, opened Signal and sent a short, fully encrypted message to her contact.

Hi Jake. It's Maggie C at the White House. Can you call me when you get this? Use Signal.

As she expected, he called back no more than twenty seconds later.

'Maggie. How'ya doing?'

It always amused her, that Washington-style of greeting. Enough warmth to count as human, maintaining the pretence that you might be friends rather than simply parties to a transaction. But not so warm that it might invite actual conversation and delay the business at hand. The tone, a brisk impatience kept sufficiently in check to stay on the right side of rude, said: *Great, we know each other: what do you want?*

To be fair, you could hardly blame Jake Haynes for having little time for small talk. He was the *New York Times'* lead writer on the intelligence community: it was doubtful he had slept in the last twenty-four hours.

'I'm OK,' Maggie said. 'Something I wanted to ask you about.'

'Jeez, Maggie, not you too.'

'Not me too what?'

'Spinning this jihadist thing. They've got everyone on it.

Full court. But you know what I keep noticing? It's only White House folks who are doing it. No offence. And if it's Agency, it's only political appointees who are picking up the phone. Professionals don't want to know. Which, forgive me, doesn't smell so good.'

'It's not about that.'

'I've spoken to people in Tanzania, Kenya, Lebanon, Libya and they're not feeling it, Maggie. Basic message seems to be, presidential assassination is kind of beyond them. Too hard—'

'Jake?'

'Yes?'

'It's not about that. Something else.'

'Something else? There *is* nothing else. Not this week.'

'Just hear me out. What do you know about that Namibia thing?'

'Namibia? This is a joke, right? Maggie, I don't know if you noticed but somebody tried to *kill the President of the United States* last night. That's kind of a big story. Do you want me to transfer you to Foreign?'

Maggie made an instant decision. She'd have to take a risk. 'Jake, listen. I could have something very big for you. It relates to the President.'

'Bigger than an assassination attempt?'

'Maybe.'

'I'm listening.'

'When it's ready, I'll give you what I have. Remember Jerusalem?' Thanks to Maggie, then part of the mediation team shuttling between Israelis and Palestinians, Jake had been the first journalist to know of a development that had changed everything.

'That's the story that made my career. How could I forget?'

'All right then. So you know: I keep my word.'

'OK.'

'So. Namibia. Four US citizens were held in custody there. Except now it's three. One died this morning.'

She could hear some keystrokes at the other end. Either he was ignoring her and going back to the assassination story – or he was already on the case.

'Hold on, I did hear something on this.' She could tell he was reading something off his screen as he was talking. 'Yesterday. Before the shooting.'

'What did you hear?'

'It's one source, Maggie. It's not—'

'Jake, we have a deal, remember? We'll share what we have. You'll end up the winner, I promise.'

'Careful, you're beginning to sound like the President.' He did the voice, the way everyone did these days. *'Big winner. BIG!'*

'Jake?'

'All right, all right. We didn't have enough to run with this. Our correspondent in Johannesburg was following it up – I got a note from him – and we were ready to throw some bodies at it, and then, you-know-who gets you-know-what. So we—'

'Abandoned it?'

'For now. Give us a break, Maggie: only so much bandwidth. Anyway, what are you talking to me for? You must have CIA guys you can talk to. You know, that big building in Virginia. It's area code seven-o-three—'

'There's been quite a lot of change in that agency recently, in case you haven't noticed.'

'Victims of the purge? Tell me about it. It's like year zero over there. Burnt, like, half my contacts book. More in fact.'

'Anyway,' said Maggie. 'What did your Jo'burg guy say?'

'Woman actually,' he replied, not too busy to be smug.

'What did she say?'

'Like I say, not confirmed—'

'But?'

'But she had it from the Station Chief there that the four Americans were veterans of the US military—'

'We know that already.'

'Jesus, Maggie, if you'd let me get to the end of a sentence! They were veterans of the military.' He paused for effect. 'Who are currently employed by Langley.'

'Seriously?'

'Seriously. Agency operatives. Undercover. Christ knows what they were doing there. We wondered if it was maybe some rendition thing. You know, picking up some African jihadist, take him to a black site. It's an oldie but goldie.'

'And was it?'

'I told you. Thanks to the little incident at the Marines War Memorial, we dropped it.'

'But they were nowhere near any jihadists. They shot some random tourist out looking for rhino. Why would the CIA care about that?'

'Maggie, last time I checked you were the highly placed, senior White House official and I was the underpaid reporter with his ear by the air-conditioning vent. You're meant to be the one who knows stuff, and I'm meant to be the one asking the questions. The federal government's pretty big, you know. If Langley's a brick wall, what about State?'

'Relations are a little strained right now,' she said, choosing not to reveal that she had no idea who she could trust any more, not after Richard. 'But you're right. About questions, I mean. Go on. Ask a question. Anything you like.'

'All right. Here goes.' He cleared his throat. 'Rosemary.'

Maggie waited. Eventually she said, 'Rosemary who?'

'Exactly. "Rosemary, who?" That's my question. Everyone keeps mentioning this name to me. Rosemary this, Rosemary that. But I've checked the White House staff directory and there's only one Rosemary and she's, like, some old lady in the protocol office. Doesn't make sense.'

'And who keeps mentioning her?'

'I'm obviously going to tell you that, aren't I?'

'No, I mean what kind of people? What level?'

'Senior. So is Rosemary a new appointment? Is she going to be the new liaison with the agencies? That would make sense, given what's just—'

'Jake, I'm going to get back to you on this.'

'Oh, for Christ's sake, Maggie. You can't do that. Not after what I gave you! Come on, Maggie, there's—'

'Because I want to give you the real deal. Believe me, it will be worth it. Just a little patience.'

Maggie hung up and made a mental note to herself, which she filed away. She then went back to the news stories she had called up. Jake had initially suspected that what had happened in the Namibian jungle was a case of extraordinary rendition, though one that had been botched. That would outrage a few liberal bloggers, and would bring some loud tutting from the *Times* editorial page, but would barely make a ripple anywhere else. If that's all this was, Maggie could forget it.

But her instinct said otherwise. If this was a straightforward counter-terrorism operation, then why on earth were McNamara and Richard involved? This was something different, Maggie could feel it.

The key was the target of the operation. She doubted those CIA agents were after the local ranger, the man unlucky enough to have been killed in the crossfire and so far not even named. The brutal truth was that they would not have devoted that much hardware and manpower – *Large team of postmen and equipment required* – to taking out an African tour guide. Even if he was a secret jihadist fanatic, there would have been easier ways to get him.

No, the place to start was that American 'tourist'. She knew the basic facts but no more. Who, really, was he?

49

The news stories had revealed one critical fact. Ron Cain was in Namibia stalking a black rhino, one of the rarest creatures in the world. And he had done it with a licence.

Fortunately, those licences were themselves rare – so precious, in fact, that when they were auctioned off at a charity fundraiser in Texas, it made the newspapers. A quick search, using the key words 'rhino', 'licence' and 'hunt' had yielded the story.

Dallas technology entrepreneur Ron Cain sparked controversy with animal welfare groups last night, when he bid $350,000 for the right to shoot an endangered black rhino in southern Africa later this year.

Cain, who founded the KRG broadcast equipment company, headquartered in Dallas, shocked bidders at the annual fund-raising gala . . .

Maggie skimmed the rest, then typed in Cain's name. A few potted profiles from the business pages of the *Dallas*

Morning News, a smaller item from the *Wall Street Journal*, various stories on annual profits and then a story from the *Washington Post*, dated to the election campaign.

. . . among those suing the candidate is Texas businessman Ron Cain. He claims his broadcast technology firm KRG undertook 'hundreds of millions of dollars worth of work for this man and we never received a dime'. According to Cain, KRG fulfilled a contract to build a satellite and fibre-optic infrastructure that would allow for a huge expansion into the Texas market. 'But the customer never paid up. Our company had to pay wage bills for hundreds of workers, as well as suppliers, and we are still waiting to be paid back.'

The Texas case is one of several investigated by the *Post*, revealing a pattern of 'stiffing' contractors that, according to industry analysts, is so constant it 'all but amounts to a business model'. One of those unpaid contractors, who spoke only on condition of anonymity, said, 'What you've got to understand is that, with this guy, this isn't a bug: it's a feature. His default is not to pay his bills. That's his M.O.'

She now did a more focused search. *Ron Cain, lawsuit, KRG*. It turned out that Cain hadn't dropped it, the case was pending. In fact it was due to be heard . . . next month.

Maggie took a breath, closing her eyes briefly. Her nerves were jangled; she was exhausted; she was getting ahead of herself. She needed to do this methodically.

All right. The next point of reference was Delhi. What had McNamara said? She scrolled through the messages till she found it. *Our friends will need instructions on the next package. Shipment in Delhi, dispatch details as discussed.*

This search was harder. 'Delhi' turned up rather more results than 'Namibia'. She narrowed it with the President's name and that produced hundreds too, many of them dwelling on his business interests in India, which were extensive. She narrowed it again, this time by date. She only wanted to see stories from the last month or two.

She rushed through the headlines. *Plans for early summit with Indian PM* and *Trade is our top priority* sped by. She needed to narrow it more. She added the name of the President's company to the filter.

Now she was looking at dozens rather than hundreds. She had speed-read most of them when she came to one from the *Times of India*. The headline: *Heritage park given green light.* Below it was a sub-headline: *US President joins partners in celebrating 'new dawn for Delhi'.*

She read further and had all but given up when she came to the penultimate paragraph.

The plan was approved by a consortium of landowners in the district after several years of wrangling and legal delay. Opposition had previously been led by property magnate Aamir Kapoor, who died earlier this month. Groundbreaking on the site is scheduled for spring next year, following a programme of compulsory purchases, clearances and 'voluntary relocation' of local people, according to the Delhi municipal authorities.

Now Maggie had a name. A few clicks later she read:

The funeral was held yesterday for Aamir Kapoor, following his tragic death in a road traffic accident on one of Delhi's busiest roads. Tributes were paid to Mr Kapoor, who was 43, including by the co-founder of his real estate company who said: 'Aamir never lost touch with his roots. He wanted to preserve the Delhi he had known from his childhood. He stood firm against those who would destroy the city, even when those people were very powerful. He will be sorely missed.' Mr Kapoor is believed to have been run over by a speeding car on leaving the Nizamuddin neighbourhood. No one has been charged in connection with the incident.

Maggie was feverish now, moving fast between tabs on the screen, always returning to that conversation between Crawford McNamara, perhaps the President's closest confidant, and Richard, her ex-boyfriend. Even now, having read it so many times, she could hardly believe the words were real.

She was about to get to work on the third 'package' they had referred to, the one they gnomically described as 'mid-Atlantic', when she came across a line that she had breezed past at least the first dozen times she had read it, but which now leapt out at her.

Get in line. Hey maybe I can get Rosemary on it, see what the deal with those two is.

It was McNamara, talking about the presidential daughter and her husband. Specifically, whether the two of them were having sex any more. But who the hell was Rosemary?

Jake Haynes at the *Times* thought Rosemary might be the name of an official, possibly the new White House liaison with the intelligence agencies. That had struck Maggie as implausible. She may have seen her entire network of allies, contacts and acquaintances culled in the purge, but even so: there were not so many senior women with backgrounds in national security hanging around the White House that one could exist whom Maggie had never heard of, let alone met. The truth was, such a woman would have been a direct peer – if not rival – of Maggie's. Of course she'd have known of her.

There was something else too. This President and White House had the most appalling record on promoting women. The chances that McNamara was about to break that habit by handing such a senior role to 'Rosemary' were slim.

But now that initial scepticism had a firmer basis. Because here was McNamara, in the transcript, suggesting that Rosemary could be a useful source of gossip on the state of marital relations between the presidential daughter and son-in-law. Which made it more likely that Rosemary was on the social staff or perhaps worked in the Residence. She might be a servant, maybe a cleaner. (Maggie had a sudden, guilty memory of Lieutenant Mary Rajak and of the unnamed cleaner who had been groped and grabbed by the President: she had still done nothing for either of them.)

And yet, if that was right, then why on earth had Jake asked about her? *Everyone keeps mentioning this name to me. Rosemary this, Rosemary that.*

Who the hell was she?

Maggie reached for the burner phone and dialled the number. When she heard that voice – live, not on voicemail – she felt the relief pass through her, as warm and reassuring as a glass of Laphroaig. 'Hi there. It's me. Don't say anything out loud, but can you meet in the usual place? Great. How about now?'

50

The White House, Saturday, 2.45pm
Maggie went to the women's bathroom for one last check. It was empty, which given the gender balance of the West Wing these days was hardly surprising. Maggie looked at herself in the mirror. She had applied a little lipstick and just a hint of eye make-up. It was not that she wanted to make herself more attractive: since she was about to go and see Crawford McNamara, she'd have happily aimed for the very opposite look.

No, her primary objective was to disguise the exhaustion that would otherwise be written all over her face, those grey shadows now etched into the landscape as a permanent feature. She knew enough about McNamara to be sure that you showed him no weakness, and visible fatigue was a definite weakness. Strength and self-confidence: that was what the boss projected and that was what McNamara looked for. If he didn't find it, he'd either ignore you or crush you, depending on his mood. With decent clothes and her best face on, she could pull back her shoulders, hold her head straight – and take him on.

Getting the meeting had been easier than she had expected. She'd emailed McNamara directly:

Have some info that might be useful. Need to brief you. When might suit?

He had replied immediately, from his phone.

Who can refuse an offer like that? Come to my office at 3pm. M.

That suited her well. It gave her enough time to . . . prepare. And to have the two conversations she needed ahead of this one. Before handing in her phone at the visitors' entrance – her pass still didn't work – she had sent one last, confirming text.

About to go in. Wish me luck. M x

Of course he kept her waiting. Five minutes, ten, twelve. Maggie refused to get nervous, even if – especially if – that was the intended purpose. Punctuality and the lack of it were weapons in Washington, rarely deployed by accident. The trick was to be unswayed, to refuse to receive whatever message was being sent. Perhaps McNamara was engaged in a petty power trip – *See, I can keep you waiting* – but Maggie would not let herself be played. She used the delay to go through the key points one last time.

At first, she had refused to believe it. As the pattern emerged, she had started from the assumption that it was obviously false. She had checked each element, waiting for the flaw, the contradiction, the date or place that did not fit and that therefore blew apart the entire theory. But it had not come.

She hankered for a second opinion; she longed to talk it over properly with Stuart. She thought of heading over there, walking him through the details. But even to talk about it out loud seemed too great a risk. So she'd had to be content with staring at the notepad that had sat on her desk at home, the page steadily growing darker as she filled in more and more of the blanks. The picture she was left with was so striking, she had started all over again.

It had gone on like that for hours, even when she tried to get half an hour's rest to compensate for that sleepless night. At intervals she would wake, return to her desk, convinced she had found the loose thread which would unravel it all. Half of her wanted to find it. She could then curl up and hide, hoping that everything about this would disappear – taking her with it.

But the harder she looked, the more she interrogated each angle, the more solid it seemed to become. Now, though – only now – would it be tested. To destruction.

'Ms Costello?' Maggie looked up and nodded at the absurdly glamorous secretary, in a dress so low-cut Maggie's mother would have branded it indecent. What, Maggie wondered, had Richard said about this one to McNamara? What fantasy had the two of them hatched, smartphones clammy in their hands, about this woman? Maggie could guess.

'Mac will see you now.'

Maggie walked in, remembering her memo to herself about posture and eye contact. McNamara was at his desk, cargo pants on, feet up, crunching on a breadstick – one of several, sprouting from a cup like pencils – and using his free hand to scroll pages on his computer.

He raised a hand in greeting, but didn't divert his gaze

from the screen. 'You know what I love?' he said, still not looking at her.

'What's that, Mac?'

'These liberals soiling their Depends undergarments about *truth*. They never stop! Always going on about facts and evidence and all that shit, even when they have the biggest possible dataset showing them – *proving* to them – that the American people do not give a rat's ass about any of it.'

'The dataset being—'

'—the election. Like, they *know* it. They can see the numbers, same as you and me. They know our guy was often, you know—'

'Hazy on the truth?'

'—in a relationship of creative tension with the conventional wisdom. Let's put it like that.' A smirk was budding at both corners of his mouth. 'But it didn't matter. Not one bit. They all had their "fact checkers" and their "truth squads", keeping these little lists of all the President's "falsehoods" – such a polite word, don't you think? So dainty! – and they'd tweet out these lists every night', he did his po-faced, TV anchor impression: '"Tonight he made twenty-three false statements" – and you know what the voters thought?'

Maggie was not about to reply, because she had decided that, in this meeting, she would not allow herself to be goaded. Still, her resolve was not tested because McNamara answered his own question by placing the heels of his hands to his lips and blowing a loud, wet raspberry.

'That's what the folks thought.' He was still looking at his screen. 'And yet, our beloved media and the liberals just won't let it go. They're doing it again now!' He was pointing in disbelief at his Twitter feed. 'And meanwhile the big guy is getting on with making history. Making the weather. Literally in the latter case! I mean it, have you seen the photo-op from this afternoon? Oh, it's so great. First day out of the hospital and he does this. You know, this sends the perfect message: "Straight back to work." Video's all over Twitter. You've got to see it.'

Like a movie director, McNamara held up his hands in the shape of a TV screen. 'OK. So the location is the Rose Garden. There's a bonfire going, like crackling away, with little sparks and everything. And then, emerging through the smoke, is this figure. And you realize as soon as you see the outline of him: it's the President. Kind of wreathed in smoke. Very powerful. And then, in front of all the cameras, he takes out this thick document. And he holds it up, so they can all see it. And do you know what it is?'

Maggie shook her head.

'It says on the cover, in really big letters, *Global Treaty on Climate Change*. We mocked up the cover, especially for this. Anyway, he holds it up, lets them all get a good look. And then he shows the page with the last president's signature on it. Holds that up to the cameras too, gives them time to zoom in on the signature. And then he rips off that page, and tosses it on the fire. And of course there's huge applause.'

'From the press?'

McNamara did a scold face. 'From our people. First three rows, as always. They're cheering and hollering. And he takes out another page and he tosses that on the fire. And then another. And now they're whooping. And he rips out page after page. And the crowd are kind of ecstatic, you know? Until he's burned the whole thing. Nothing left. And then he says, "I want to thank everyone for their good wishes and prayers for my recovery. As you can see, your prayers have been answered. Your leader is back – and the work goes on." Just like that. And he turns around and heads back into the White House, back through the smoke. And the crowd are still applauding. Really, it was great. You should have been there. You'd have loved it.'

Only then, as if remembering himself, did he look at Maggie properly. He leapt to his feet. 'Where are my manners?' He smiled widely, his eyes shining with warmth. 'Talking of applause, I should be giving *you* a standing ovation.' He started clapping. 'Jesus, Maggie Costello, what you only did there. The service you have rendered your country, I can't even . . .' He shook his head, as if overcome by emotion.

'I didn't do anything, Mac.'

'Didn't do anything? Are you kidding me? It was your work that saved the President's life! If it hadn't been for you alerting me to the fact that Dr Frankel had been murdered, we'd have had *no idea* there was a conspiracy against the President. I'm serious, Maggie. It's all down to you.'

'With some help from Richard Parris.'

Maggie saw a flicker in McNamara's eyes, no more. 'You gave us the heads-up we needed to give extra protection to the President of the United States. The republic owes you a great debt, Maggie.' He reached over to shake her hand and then sat down, gesturing for her to do the same. 'I will make sure that act of patriotism does not go unrecognized.'

'I'm grateful, Mac. But that's not why I'm here. I want to talk to you about Gary Turner.'

Not even a flicker this time. 'I don't know that name, Maggie. Can you help me out?'

'Sure. He's the undercover CIA agent who was killed a few days ago while on duty in Africa. He died from his injuries yesterday.'

McNamara kept up the eye contact, but also reached for the speaker button on his phone.

'April, can you ask Stowe to send in one of his female staff please?' McNamara made a gesture towards the phone – as if to say 'Bureaucracy, what can you do?' – and went back to his computer screen.

Maggie was watching McNamara's face closely when a tall, toned and ludicrously glossy young woman – long, bottle-blonde hair falling in thick curls, lustrous red lipstick and a tightly fitted uniform – knocked on the door and walked in, looking to McNamara for instructions.

'Maggie,' McNamara said, 'this is purely routine but I'm going to step out for a minute or two while this nice young lady checks to make sure you're not wearing a wire. Not happy about it, but given what happened to the President we're having to tighten some of our procedures around here. OK?'

Maggie clocked McNamara's obvious excitement at the scene he had created, but understood there was no option of saying no. She stood, ready to be patted down. What followed was, in fact, a much more intrusive, intimate search. This woman, who said nothing, closed the internal blinds in McNamara's office, and then asked Maggie to remove her clothes, item by item. She checked Maggie's underwear, running her fingers under the straps of her bra, peeking into each cup, as well as examining under her armpits. She had Maggie remove her shoes and she looked through Maggie's hair, the way the nuns at the convent used to search for lice.

It was as thorough a search as Maggie had ever endured, and given where she had travelled, the warlords whose lairs she had been led to, blindfolded and in the dead of night, that was saying something. While it was happening, and partly to make conversation, Maggie said, 'So I notice that's not a Secret Service uniform you're wearing.'

'I'm not Secret Service.'

'Oh? Which bit do you work for then?'

The woman was running the palms of her hands across Maggie's back, when she answered: 'Presidential security.' It took Maggie a moment to realize that what she was saying was, in fact, Presidential Security, a new private protection force established to run alongside the Secret Service. It was formed mainly out of the personal body-guard the President had employed as a businessman. Inevitably the press had dubbed it his 'Praetorian guard', with the New York tabloids becoming particularly excited by the regiment of 'glamazons' who were increasingly seen – and photographed – at the President's side. But this was the first time Maggie had encountered the new force in person.

Eventually the woman gave her a curt nod and brought McNamara back into the office. Maggie could not be sure, but she thought she heard her whisper, 'She's clean.'

'Apologies again,' McNamara said, retaking his seat behind his desk. 'Everyone is on edge just now, you understand.'

'Of course.'

'So. Where were we?' Maggie focused on McNamara's Adam's apple as she said the next few sentences. 'I was asking you about Gary Turner, the agent who just died in Namibia. You see, I think he was there to dispatch a package sent by you. A "complicated drop", you called it. In your exchange with Richard.'

McNamara swallowed, but recovered himself swiftly. 'I don't follow.'

'Sorry,' Maggie smiled. 'I should try to make myself clearer. I'm always doing that!' She smiled again, girlishly. 'In your series of encrypted messages with Richard Parris, which Richard kept tucked away in a file, you discuss the delivery and dispatch of various "packages". One of these packages was located in the Namibian jungle. As it happens, exactly coincident with that message, a group of CIA operatives were in the Namibian jungle, where they made a planned, coordinated attempt on the life of an American citizen: Ron Cain of Dallas, Texas.' Maggie paused. 'Tell me if I'm going too fast.'

She did not look down, did not consult her notes, maintained eye contact throughout. 'I've looked into Mr Cain, to see what he could possibly have done to have aroused the interest of the Central Intelligence Agency. It turns out he had never been on the CIA's radar before. No links to terror, never on a watch list, no links to suspected espionage against the United States. No connection with organized crime, no suggestion of sanctions-busting. Nothing.'

McNamara was holding her gaze. Neither wanted to be the first to break off.

'Indeed,' Maggie went on, 'he has only one connection with the US government.' She paused again, waiting for a question. But it didn't come. 'He is owed many millions of dollars by the President.'

'Well, Maggie, you're tireless, I'll give you that. This sounds very interesting and I look forward to you compiling a full, detailed report which we can—'

'I'm not done, Mac.' She smiled again. 'You see, it seems Ron Cain was the lucky one. Other business figures around the world were far less fortunate.'

McNamara sat back in his chair, feigning a smile. A change of tactic.

Maggie chose this moment to glance down at her notes, even though she didn't need to. She turned over one sheet, to look at the next. She knew that in Washington what people like McNamara feared most was not a single accusation but a dossier full of them.

'Your exchange with Richard mentions another "delivery" in Delhi. As it happens on that day, a Mr Aamir Kapoor also met an untimely death. And he too had business dealings with the President. He was the sole obstacle standing in the way of a very lucrative project in that city.'

McNamara's smile had grown wider and less forced. 'You know who you sound like, Maggie? You sound like the losers who made me a very rich man.' He adopted the voice and facial expression of a paranoid nerd: '"Did you know that on 9/11, there was a delivery truck that re-routed off the New Jersey turnpike ten minutes before the first plane struck?" Circumstantial evidence, coincidence, two and two makes ten!

'Maggie, I don't want to be rude, but you're sounding a little nutty. Weaving an elaborate conspiracy theory out of whole cloth. Some curry-eater gets run over in Delhi and you think the CIA did it? D'you think they might be sending secret messages to you through your TV set, Maggie? Perhaps you should check the microwave, too. What if all those beeps are really a *code*? I've got to admit, I expected better of you.'

Maggie had anticipated this. With a studied calm she did not feel, she said, 'You've purged most of the awkward squad from Langley, Mac. Almost all of them. But there's still a few holding on. And when they see something they don't like, they talk. Especially to an old friend they trust. Like me.'

That seemed to slow, if not halt, McNamara. He sat back again, eyes narrowed.

'You see, Mac, what they tell me is that this has become a new area of operations for the CIA. Like that "mid-Atlantic" package, for example.'

'Maggie, this is not—'

'That was how Richard described it to you, in what was clearly – from the context – a term you understood. I have to admit "mid-Atlantic" threw me a bit. I was looking at the Azores, Bermuda, all kinds of places. But then I read about Birkir Arnason.'

She was sure McNamara paled, just a shade.

'You know who he is, right? I didn't. He's not exactly a household name. He's an Icelandic app developer. Big in online gaming. Iceland: who knew?' Another smile. 'Well, a few weeks ago he came to a very nasty end. He's this super-experienced climber and hiker and yet, somehow, on a clear, crisp morning – not windy or stormy, perfect visibility – he falls into a geothermal pool and is not just burned, Mac, he's *dissolved*. Really sweet guy, by the sound of things. Major philanthropist. He'd already endowed three children's hospitals and he wasn't even thirty. But, get this. He too had a connection to the President's business interests. He refused to sell his company, which was meant to be the last link in a global chain that would make the President billions. The President really, really wanted his company. But Birkir kept saying no. Silly Birkir.'

'Maggie, you're embarrassing yourself. Just piling one coincidence onto another.'

Now Maggie leaned forward, the smile gone. In a quiet, but firm voice she said, 'No Mac, I'm afraid you're the one embarrassing yourself. *Shaming* yourself and this office. What I have here,' she tapped the dossier, 'is *prima facie* evidence of your abuse of American service personnel to advance private, commercial interests. You did it in Africa, you did it in India. You sent the CIA to kill some tech entrepreneur in Iceland and – we haven't even got to this yet – to murder a corporate lawyer out walking his dog on the English east coast.' She glanced down at her papers. 'Not one of these people posed a military threat to the United States. Yet you sent armed Americans onto the territory of some of our closest allies to murder innocent people, just to boost the profits of companies belonging to the President. You used the United States military as a private army. And now a young American, who signed up to do his patriotic duty, is dead in an African hospital. What are you going to tell his family, Mac? That he gave his life attempting to rub out a business rival of the President? How do you think Sergeant Turner's parents will take that?'

McNamara stayed rocking back in his chair, using the tilt function to its fullest, twirling a pencil in his hand. He said nothing for a moment and then another. Eventually he spoke, his clear blue eyes now full of a steel that she hadn't seen before.

'Richard was right. You've got balls. It took balls to come here and say all this to me. Big balls. You took a risk, because you must have known that you could leave here now and – well, God knows what could happen to you, Maggie. Your car could skid out of control, say, or something awful could happen to, I don't know, your sister's kids—'

'So that was you.'

'Look, Maggie. You know how this works. Or if you don't, you should. Once Richard kindly let me know that he'd seen your notepad – which showed you had the whole thing worked out – I had to take action, you understand that. I couldn't risk you getting in the way.'

'You mean, you didn't want me stopping an attempt on the life of the President.'

'Let's say I didn't want you stopping nature from taking its course.'

'Nature! You wanted an assassination attempt to go ahead,

391

so that you could mount your coup. Nice and controlled, mind. The way the Secret Service do their job, you knew no one would ever get close enough to do a headshot. As long as you had the President in a vest, he'd be OK. And you were determined to make it happen, removing any obstacles in the assassins' path. Which meant scaring me away. And you were prepared to risk the lives of a couple of children to do it. Jesus.'

He was smiling. 'I have no comment to make at this time.'

'And now you're threatening to do it again.'

'Oh no. I'm just talking hypotheticals here, Maggie. Just hypotheticals. But you know, the world is an unpredictable place. And then suddenly your dossier, pfff' – he made an explosion gesture with his hands – 'it's gone.'

Maggie made a conscious effort to regain her composure, to maintain at least the appearance of calm. 'Oh, don't you worry about my dossier. I've made arrangements for that. An electronic version of this document is stored in a folder that stays locked and encrypted. But if – for any reason – I fail to log in and open that file for three full days, then it's programmed to publish itself online. On multiple platforms and to a string of email addresses. It will also make clear exactly why I've disappeared and who's responsible. So getting rid of me would only make your problem much worse.'

'*My* problem?'

'Yes, Mac. *Your* problem. I have here the evidence that you have been running an illegal covert military operation from the White House. You did not have the authorization of Congress to run this operation, which was directed against civilians, including an American citizen, and which was conducted, in part, on the territory of our allies.' And now she came to the sentence that mattered most. 'You will go

392

to jail for many years for doing that without the explicit permission of the President.'

Now it was his turn to grin. 'Oh you are sweet, Maggie. I can see what Richard saw in you. Besides his sense of duty to me, I mean. You're so *innocent*. Is that a Catholic thing? I thought it was all sin and darkness with you people. Maybe it's because you're a girl. Listened to the nuns more than you should have.'

'Why am I sweet, Mac?'

'Because you understand so little about the world. And so little about *him*. Why do you think we did all this? Two years! Of rallies and speeches and debates and balloons and God Bless America, in nothing towns talking to nothing people, with their stupid hats and all their dumb, *dumb* "hopes and dreams"? Such stupid people, Maggie. I mean, really, you should have been there. These lines of morons and in-breds, with one tooth in their head and a flag in their hands, ready to believe absolutely *anything*. I felt sorry for them, I still do. But the President had their number from the start: "easy marks", he called them. You could tell them you're going to bring their jobs back, re-open the mines, bring back the horse-and-buggy – whatever you like – and they'd lap it up. Even when it was there, written down in *black and white*, that what you were actually planning was a tax break for the top one per cent, paid for by the removal of their healthcare. I mean, really.

'So why do you think he put up with it? Why do you think he went to these shitty places to talk to these shitty little people? You don't think he had better things to do, girls half his daughter's age he wanted to bang? He did it because he wanted *power*. And this is what you don't get: the whole point of power is to use it. That's the whole fucking point.

'Your crowd never understood that, your beloved former

president especially. He was always "exercising restraint" or "engaging in power-sharing" with our allies and all that horseshit. No! If you have power, you *use* it. If you don't, you lose it. That's what your president did: he watched his power, *American* power, get steadily weaker and weaker. It was like Superman and kryptonite: it was painful to watch. Our country was waning before our eyes.

'Well, not now. This man has power and he is using it. And this is the amazing thing. This is the *beautiful* thing. The more he uses it, the more of it he has! He's getting stronger every day.

'And his wealth is part of that power, Maggie. That's why they fear him in India and Russia and the Persian Gulf and all those other dirty, brown shit-holes. They know he's *rich*. And they respect that. He gets what he wants. They respect that too. So, sure, a few retards are dumb enough to stand in his way and they get taken out. But that only helps. It makes the others fear him more. And if they fear him, they fear the United States. That's another thing you and your friends never realize.' His voice was rising. 'It's not the Massachusetts Feminist Collective of Basket Weavers out there, you know. There are no points for being soft and gentle and kind and understanding. You act like that, you'll get eaten alive. You "draw a line in the sand" and then do nothing, well, guess what? Next time you try to draw a line, everyone will walk all over it – and walk all over you.

'It's about power, Maggie. *Personal* power. You're always going on about "the importance of the UN" and the WTO and NATO and all that shit, all the international organizations and "multilateral alliances", when the only thing real people – billions of them – really understand is the *individual*. The mighty individual. A king, an emperor – that's what they understand. That's what they *want*. A world where one ruler gets his way by scaring the shit out of all the others. Now, at long last, we have one of those, a real ruler, in the White House.

'So of course the CIA should be doing whatever it takes to make him stronger. The taller he stands, the taller America stands. That's their mission, isn't it?'

Maggie jumped in. 'So you ordered the CIA to kill those men without the President's explicit permission?'

'Of course I didn't! Are you not listening to me? This is what the President *wants*. I give him what he wants.'

'Well, Mac. You can tell that to the judge when he sends you down for putting an American soldier in harm's way. That that's what you thought the President wanted. I should warn you, lots of people in your position have tried that line over the years. It never works out so well.'

Now McNamara pulled out his phone and started jabbing at the buttons. 'You think I'm stupid, is that it? You think I'm as stupid as those assholes who wound up taking the rap for their bosses? No way. Not going to happen. I told him, "Mr President, these people – Cain, Kapoor, Arnason, that English guy – they have been a pain in your ass for *years*. Well, now you are the most powerful man in the world. You have the world's most powerful military at your disposal. If you want these men taken out, then just say the word."'

'And what did he say?'

McNamara hit a few keys and then held up his phone.

She listened as a voice, loud, clear and unmistakable, filled the room.

OK, sounds good. Get it done.

Then she heard McNamara's voice, even louder. The tone was different, more deferential than she was used to. 'All right, Mr President. We'll have these taken care of. And clearly there will be some legal issues. There might be people at Langley who are worried—'

I thought you got rid of all of them, wasn't—

'We did, we did. But if anyone says, "Look, these are not military targets. They don't pose a threat, it's illegal—"'

We went through all this with the, you know, the torture thing? Just tell them: when the President does it, that means it's not illegal. OK?

Now it was Maggie's turn to pale. She fell back in her seat, as if she'd been winded.

McNamara smiled. 'You see, I'm covered. My own little insurance policy. And before you get any ideas, I've got that recording backed up and stored in several places. No way they're getting Mac McNamara.'

'You're smart.'

'At last. Something we can agree on! You go after me, you're going after the President of the United States. And you really don't want to do that. Not this guy, not now. Not with the so-called evidence you've got. A few deaths in strange places that no one's heard of? Never going to fly. Those messages you say you've got, me and Richard engaging in a bit of locker-room banter? We'll just say they're doctored. Forgeries. *Fake news.* And then we get it out on a few blogs that you're a disgruntled former employee, a partisan for the former president, who, sadly, recently went off the rails.' He adopted his news voice. '"According to White House sources, Miss Costello started making increasingly wild accusations. She even confronted the highly respected Chief of Staff Robert Kassian, accusing him of plotting a presidential assassination. Amid security concerns, her access pass was revoked. 'I'm afraid she was very disturbed,' one source said, citing the recent, acrimonious break-up with senior White House aide Richard Parris, which Miss Costello could not accept."'

McNamara sat back, proud of his instant handiwork. 'It writes itself, Maggie.' He leaned forward again, excited. 'Ooh, I nearly forgot. Just in case there's any liberals and bedwetters who are thinking of rallying around you, you know, hashtag "I stand with Maggie"' – he raised his hand in a clenched fist salute – 'we can tell them exactly who it was who broke their hearts last time around. We can reveal the name of Miss Goody Two-Shoes, the woman who spilled the beans on a certain leading politician's use of an unsecured phone. Yep, your boyfriend shared that little confession with me.' He adopted a high-pitched, strangulated tone, and clasped his hands together in a mocked gesture of female panic. '"It was me, Maggie Costello. It's my fault that that *evil man* is President!"'

Maggie felt her jaw tighten. She was determined not to be knocked off course. 'Richard told you everything, didn't he? Whatever I said, the moment it was out of my mouth, he let you know. So you knew what I was thinking about Kassian and Bruton, after the death of Dr Frankel.'

'Richard is a very loyal colleague, yes. Or he was. I mean, keeping a record of my messages to him: that's not so nice, is it? I suppose he thought that would be his insurance policy, just in case. But he's young. Perhaps he didn't know what you and I know, Maggie: never play a player.

'But sure, it was Richard who first gave me the heads-up. Once he told me that Batman and Robin had made their late-night house call to Dr Frankel, well, I had an inkling what was going on. Just like you did. You see, great minds think alike!'

'Hold on,' Maggie said, as much to herself as to him.

'It was obvious. What else would they want with the doctor, except for him to certify that the President was out of his mind?'

'Hold on, hold on.' She looked up at him, her mind

turning over at double speed. 'I never told Richard they went to see Frankel at home.'

'Wherever, it doesn't matter. The point—'

'All I said was that they'd had a meeting with him, following the incident in the Situation Room. So why did you say they saw him at home?'

'Look, the point is—'

'No, no, no. You *knew* they went there. You always knew. You probably had the goons from your private security force tailing them that night. Of course you did. And the minute they came out of his house, you thought there was a risk Frankel had agreed to certify the President. You had to stop him before he signed that declaration. *You* had him killed. It wasn't Kassian and Bruton. It was *you*.'

'Like I said, Maggie. If you have power, you use it. So endeth today's lesson.' He pressed the speaker button on his phone once more.

'April, Maggie has decided to leave us. Could you ask security to escort her to her office? She has fifteen minutes to pack her boxes – under supervision – and be gone. And please ask Comms to revoke all email and access codes instantly. Thanks, April.'

McNamara stood up. 'Maggie, it's been real. You're a smart girl. You know the drill. You make any of these baseless accusations again and you will feel the full might of the Presidency of the United States come down on you. And remember, you've got nothing that can't be dismissed as speculation, deranged conspiracy theory or a malicious, partisan smear. Maybe all three. Bottom line: we will destroy you. And, as you've seen for yourself, we don't mind taking the ultimate step if we have to.'

He extended his hand. Maggie ignored it. As she left, she could hear him cry out, 'Have a great day!'

51

Silver Spring, Maryland, Saturday, 5.45pm
Maggie was holding a mug of tea in her hands, more for
the warmth than for the drink. It remained stubbornly true
that Americans could not make a cup of tea to save their
lives, even an American as kind and welcoming as Eleanor.

Still, she was glad to be here. She felt as sure as she could
be that this was a safe place, though she had come by a
circuitous route – one cab, two buses – just in case. But she
suspected that even the Praetorian guard would not have
the home of a mid-ranking, middle-aged White House secretary, on a residential street in the Maryland suburbs, under
constant surveillance.

They took precautions, all the same. Eleanor ushered
Maggie into the house quickly, not letting her linger on the
doorstep. She drew the curtains, turned the TV on loud and
only spoke euphemistically about the meeting Maggie had
just come from. The rest of the time, she sought to make
Maggie comfortable, giving her something to eat, letting her
settle into a deep armchair, watching her as she closed her
eyes and drifted into a brief sleep.

While they waited for him to arrive, they chatted, as indirectly as they could, about everything that had led to this moment. Maggie said she now understood why McNamara had worked so hard to get her out of the way: hijacking her car on the road, having her beaten up by those goons, nearly poisoning Liz and the kids. He was worried she might foil the assassination plot, when McNamara had decided it was in his interest to let it go ahead. Once he had seen Maggie's late-night jottings on that pad, McNamara resolved to let Kassian and Bruton's effort play out.

Still, the topic they wanted to discuss most, but which they could only tiptoe around, was 'Rosemary'. When that reporter had asked Maggie what she knew of this woman everyone was talking about, she was not feigning her ignorance. True, she had heard the name a couple of times, but she had not been lying when she said she didn't know who she was.

And so, when Maggie and Eleanor had met at Au Bon Pain soon after she'd come off the phone from Jake Haynes, Maggie had asked her old friend straight: 'Who is she?'

Eleanor had looked down at the table, focusing on her fingernails, then at the door, then back to her fingernails. 'You know I love you, Maggie, but there are some things . . .'

Maggie had reached across the table, placing her hand gently on the older woman's. 'You know me, Eleanor. I'm careful. I'm thorough. And I would never, ever put you in danger.'

'I'm in danger just sitting here with you.'

'Say I've got boyfriend trouble. You're consoling me.' Maggie gave a weak smile, one that conveyed that she understood the risk Eleanor was taking, that she would not downplay it. 'But you can see what's happening. You can see why I have to do something.'

400

The TV on the wall just above them was tuned to CNN. The caption along the bottom read: *Military announce new emergency powers*. The network had even designed a special logo: *Crackdown*.

'So,' Maggie said again. 'Who is she?'

Eleanor let out the sigh of a woman who feels she has no choice. 'Rosemary is a secretary. Kind of.'

Maggie thought of that name on the staff list, the one she had considered too junior to count. She kicked herself for being so dismissive.

'What do you mean, "kind of"?'

'I mean she used to be. She's dead now.'

'Dead? Don't tell me she's been killed too. What the hell—'

'No, listen. I'm not explaining this very well. You know about Watergate, right?'

'Sure.'

'You ever hear the story of Rose Mary Woods?'

The name rang a distant bell, but nothing more. 'Tell me.'

'So Rose Mary Woods was Nixon's secretary. Very, very loyal – even at the end. She became famous because there was a gap – eighteen and a half minutes long – on one of the Watergate tapes, and Rose Mary put her hand up and said it was her fault. She said she was transcribing the tape and must have accidentally hit the erase button, while her foot was on the pedal.'

'The pedal?'

Eleanor smiled. 'You're too young to know about all that. Heck, *I'm* too young. It was a long time ago. Different world; before computers. Anyway, the tape was recorded in the Oval Office: you know there was a secret recording system, right? It's a long story. Nixon didn't put it in there, but he used it.'

401

'And the tapes helped bring him down over Watergate?'

'Right. They got rid of the whole thing after Nixon. Ripped it out. No recording system.'

'OK.' Maggie was beginning to get impatient.

'So "Rosemary" is kind of a codename.'

'For what?'

Eleanor hesitated, then looked up to meet Maggie's gaze. Her eyes said, 'Don't make me spell it out.'

Maggie bit her lip as the thought took shape. 'Oh, my God,' she said eventually. 'They've brought it back. Rose Mary is the name for the recording system?'

Eleanor nodded.

So that, thought Maggie, was what Richard was referring to in those messages to McNamara, even if he'd spelled it wrongly. *Hey maybe I can get Rosemary on it, see what the deal with those two is.*

'And I bet it was McNamara who put it in.'

Eleanor nodded again.

'And it records every meeting in the Oval Office?'

'Not just there. It's all over.'

'What?'

'All over. Audio and video. Any room they want to listen to, any time.'

A memory came back to Maggie, something she had barely registered. It was when she had gone in to see Bob Kassian. As soon as the conversation had turned sensitive, he had put on some classical music. It had been oddly loud. Maggie had not made much of it: she was too focused on questioning him over the death of Dr Frankel. Now, though, she remembered what Kassian had said as the music started playing. *Rosemary doesn't like it, but it helps me relax.*

At the time, she assumed 'Rosemary' was Kassian's wife

or perhaps his assistant. She'd given it no thought. But now she understood. Kassian was having to act like a dissident under an authoritarian regime: working on the assumption that he was bugged and taking suitable steps to make his conversations inaudible. And this was the Chief of Staff of the White House.

'So at any moment,' Maggie said, 'McNamara can listen in to any office, anywhere?'

'And not just at that moment. He can play back recordings going back weeks. It's state of the art.'

'My office too?'

'Everywhere. Including his own office. He wants to have a record of everything people have said, everything they've agreed to, so he can use it against them if he needs to.'

So her office had been bugged. McNamara would have seen and heard every one of her conversations, in person and on the phone. She had been exposed from the beginning. At home, through Richard. And at work, through a hidden, all-seeing eye.

'How do you know all this, Eleanor?'

Now she looked away, even warier than before.

'Eleanor?'

'Listen, Maggie. I've told you what I know because I like you. And I think you're trying to do the right thing. But I've got to put my family first.'

'Your family? What's this got to . . . Oh. Of course. Martin.'

Eleanor's eldest son, the one who worked at the White House. He'd got an apprenticeship there during the last administration, back when they were still hiring African-Americans. He was in IT, one of the geeks who made everything work.

'Maggie, please. Martin can't afford to lose this job. I'm

old now, they can fire me. I'll get by. But Martin. He's got his life ahead of him.'

Maggie said nothing.

'Oh no. Don't give me that look. I know that look, Maggie Costello. That means you've got an idea.'

That had been more than five hours ago, before Maggie's meeting with McNamara. And now here they both were, in Eleanor's home, Maggie with her eyes closed, trying to rest, while Eleanor was picking at her eyebrow, a habit that returned at times of high stress.

Finally, they both heard a key turning in the front door. Eleanor got up and hugged her son without saying a word. Her head barely reached his chest. 'Thank God,' she said quietly.

Maggie noticed that Martin was not smiling.

He nodded in her direction, sat down on the couch and breathed out – a long whistle of air.

Maggie braced herself for disappointment. 'So,' she said. 'Was it impossible?'

Martin met her eyes and said, 'Yes. Impossible. The security protocols on Rosemary are, like, triple tight. And there's the time it takes to transfer HD video files. Completely impossible.'

Then he dug into his right pocket to produce a USB stick, which he held up for Maggie and Eleanor to see. 'But I did it anyway.'

52

They spent the rest of the evening watching the video
recording of Maggie's meeting with Crawford McNamara
and deciding what to do with it.

Eleanor wasn't kidding about 'state of the art'. Both the
sound and pictures were crystal clear. There could be no
mistaking that it was McNamara who was speaking – and
no mistaking what he was saying either.

The three of them – Maggie, Eleanor and Martin – sat
huddled over a laptop watching it together. Maggie winced
when the video showed McNamara revealing that it was
she who had sounded the alarm over the unsecured cellphone used by the President's election opponent. Eleanor
had closed her eyes and rubbed her forehead. 'Oh, Maggie,'
she said quietly.

Soon afterwards, Martin had offered to edit that bit out.
'I can do it easily,' he said.

Maggie considered it. After all, it would complicate
matters unnecessarily; it could confuse the point; better to
keep it simple.

But then she thought of how McNamara and his team would respond. 'You see,' they'd say. 'That tape has been doctored. What else did they edit out?' No, the tape would have to be left intact. It had to show the whole meeting – and the whole truth. The thought filled Maggie with dread. The secret she had held onto so long, the one that would destroy her career and, much worse, would shame her in the eyes of everyone whose opinion she valued, would be secret no more.

Martin did what he had to do, converting the file, turning it into a protected link. 'We need a password,' he said eventually.

'How about "Rosemary@1974"?' Maggie suggested.

With that done, Martin then handed over the keyboard. She would be the one sending it out, and deciding where it went. It was up to her.

Maggie sent it to four addresses – the leadership of both parties in the House and the Senate – and then a fifth: Jake Haynes at the *New York Times*. It was the least she could do.

Early the next day, Jake gave her advance warning for when the story would go online, allowing her time to get out of DC before she, and her apartment, got deluged. It meant that she was in her car when the news broke. She heard it on the radio.

This is NPR News in Washington with a reminder of our top story. Leaders in the House of Representatives have announced that they will bring impeachment proceedings against the President as soon as this week. The move follows the release of a videotape in which the President's senior counsellor, Crawford 'Mac' McNamara, is seen admitting the secret deployment of CIA personnel to kill civilians, including US citizens, solely for the advancement of the President's private business interests.

The tape also includes a recording of the President's own voice, apparently authorizing the killings.

The revelations come after the death of Sergeant Gary Turner, a CIA operative involved in such a mission in Africa earlier this month.

Speaking this morning, the Chairman of the House Judiciary Committee said hearings would begin on Monday, with a view to drawing up articles of impeachment . . .

Maggie carried on driving, parked up and then walked along the paths and through the gardens until she reached Stuart.

'So what's up, my girl?'

'"My girl?" Since when did you call me "my girl"?'

'Since today. That's quite something you pulled off there, Maggie Costello.'

'I hope so.'

'Though, I must confess one small disappointment.'

'Oh, really? What?'

'Rosemary. Or rather "Rose Mary". How could you not have got that? How many times did I tell you about Watergate? Rose Mary Woods. I mean that's Watergate for Dummies, Maggie.'

'Have I let you down, Stuart?'

'No, Maggie. You really have not.'

There was a pause, while Maggie listened to the breeze. Then she heard his voice again. 'So. Are you ready for what's coming? The stuff about you, I mean. The unsecured phone and all that.'

'I think so. I'll just have to say, I believe in upholding the law. Whoever's broken it.'

'That sounds good. Sincere, authentic.'

'And true, Stuart.'

'Which, like I always say is—'

'—always a bonus.'

Maggie smiled. 'In a way, Stuart, it'll be a relief. I've been carrying this around too long. I think it'll be good to have that weight off my shoulders.'

'And what will you do next?'

'Next? Jesus, I haven't even thought about that. But I'll think of something. There's no shortage of work to be done, you know that. I mean, have you seen the state of the Vice President?'

That brought a warm laugh. Even if it was only in her own head. After a minute or so of silence, Maggie bent down and, as she always did on these visits, she found a stone – a smooth, round one – and, following the custom of the cemetery, she placed it on the gravestone.

She read the inscription to herself one last time. *Stuart Goldstein, Wise Counsellor, Loving Husband, Enduring Friend.*

'Goodbye, Stuart,' she said. 'Thanks for everything.'

She got back in her car, checked the map for the route to Liz's house in Atlanta, and readied herself for the long drive. She didn't mind that. In fact, she was looking forward to it. She would be out on the open road, the sun was bright and summer was on its way.

ACKNOWLEDGEMENTS

If this book is about a conspiracy, then I had several co-conspirators along the way. Tom Cordiner and Steven Thurgood were once again generous with their expertise on all matters computer-related, while Nick Hopkins enlightened me on the dark arts of encryption. Steve Coombe remains a fount of knowledge on arms and armaments – and a shrewd and encouraging reader. Jason Burke was an inspired guide to the backstreets of Delhi, Andrew Miller shared his knowledge of Atlanta and I'm grateful to Nizad Salehi for helping me with the arcane science of heating systems gone rogue. Robin Niblett of Chatham House instructed me on the geopolitics of nuclear confrontation in Asia, while the writings of Bruce Blair proved indispensable on the protocols and powers that govern a US president in charge of the world's mightiest nuclear arsenal. I also learned much from Radiolab's documentary, *The Rhino Hunter*.

As always, Jonathan Cummings proved an energetic ally, able to locate any nugget of information with laserbeam accuracy. The team at HarperCollins, including Sarah Hodgson, Liz Dawson, Julia Wisdom and Kate Elton, have backed me for many years now and I could not value their professionalism more highly. Once again, Rhian McKay did an eagle-eyed copy edit. I must, however, single out Jane Johnson – my editor from the very start and still, seven novels later, a true comrade on these journeys. No matter the pressures she faces, her patience, enthusiasm and insight never flag: I appreciate her talent more with each book I write.

Jonny Geller, Kate Cooper and the team at Curtis Brown deserve huge thanks. Jonny shared my belief in this project from the beginning. I hope he knows the debt I feel towards him: he is the greatest friend any author could hope to have.

Finally a word to my sons, Jacob and Sam, and my wife, Sarah. I'm aware that things can seem quite dark these days, thanks to world events that surround us from all sides. But between them, they provide constant warmth, light and love. I love them more with each passing day.